Teradam
Ricard Ribatallada

Teradam
©Ricard Ribatallada Soriano, 2017.
This edition published 2021
First published in Spain, 2017

Contact details:
Website: www.teradam.com
Email: rribatallada@teradam.com
Twitter: @ricard_teradam Facebook: teradamnovela
Instagram: ricard_teradam
Cover design: Artur Montserrat Vàzquez and Roger Vila Crespo

ISBN: 979-84-848-9916-6
Legal deposit: B-2823-16

All rights reserved. No part of this publication may be reproduced or transmitted in any form or by any means, electronic or mechanical, including photocopying, recording, or any information storage or retrieval system, without prior permission in writing from the publishers

For my family, because when I told them I was going to quit my job to finish this novel, they didn't tell me I was crazy (although they could have).

Thank you for always being there.

Index

Prologue: Did we find them…? 7
Chapter 1: The Great Light 9
Chapter 2: Apparition 11
Chapter 3: No one else 14
Chapter 4: Pact of light 21
Chapter 5: Night Serpent 24
Chapter 6: The stories we grow up with 29
Chapter 7: Close your eyes 34
Chapter 8: Choose 39
Chapter 9: Light in the oasis 54
Chapter 10: A Free Child, a Zebra and a Mongoose 59
Chapter 11: Stop when I tell you to 78
Chapter 12: What do you want? 86
Chapter 13: The Beasts 93
Chapter 14: Those who know us 101
Chapter 15: Men like you 114
Chapter 16: Our secret 119
Chapter 17: The lagoon 134
Chapter 18: Listen to the voices 146
Chapter 19: Give me a reason 159
Chapter 20: I've seen them 165
Chapter 21: The tomb of the Forgotten One 178
Chapter 22: For Eliria 186
Chapter 23: Undershell 193
Chapter 24: Two Lights 201
Chapter 25: Walk, don't stop 207
Chapter 26: One More 215
Chapter 27: Whom I really wait 225
Chapter 29: In another life 239
Chapter 30: Make him come back 255
Chapter 31: The Shell 264
Chapter 32: The person you admire 274
Chapter 33: It chases and traps us 283
Chapter 34: Injustice 291
Chapter 35: Those who hate us 301

Chapter 36: Hunters 311
Chapter 37: With the Beasts 316
Chapter 38: When I find him 327
Chapter 39: Straight to the heart 338
Chapter 40: Teradam 348

Prologue: Did we find them…?

'Siro, I can't believe…' Matildet began. 'We found them!'
Siro quickly placed a finger to his lips.
Matildet looked at him, bewildered.
'Don't shush me,' she said.
'Quiet. They might be close'.
Siro surveyed the area. The remnants of a fire still breathed a light smoke by the pond. Charred boar ribs lay in a pile, chewed almost clean and discarded, and above, hanging from a pole suspended between the branches of a tree, the animal's head. Careful not to disturb the leaves beneath his feet, he moved closer.
Beneath the quieted face of the slaughtered pig, a bag hung from a lower branch. Siro took it in both hands and looked inside.
'What is it?' Matildet asked.
The hunter Siro reached into the bag and pulled out a staring bore eye.
The Daughter of the Light gasped and stumbled backward.
'They're not human,' said Siro, paying little mind to the slimy sphere in his palm. 'Let's go.'
'Are you crazy?' Matildet protested. 'Of course, they're people. Monkeys don't hunt like this. Bears don't start fires and stick heads and eyes on ceremonial plinths.'
'They are not people,' repeated Siro, tossing the eye to the ground and wiping away the blood from his hand on the trunk of the tree.
'They are beasts.'
The Daughter of the Light watched the eye, its tail of veins and nerves flailing behind it.
'I've seen the trails,' she said, 'they're people. We can follow them.'
Siro looked into the depths surrounding them. The only sound was from the nearby waterfall.
'They could be watching us,' he said. 'We go now.'

'Are you afraid?' Matildet asked.

Siro nodded slowly.

The young man noticed the perfume of moon flowers that flowed from the Daughter of the light. The girl in turn examined his face hardened by the elements.

After a moment, Matildet spoke softly: 'I must go, Siro. I know you don't want to see them,' she said. 'If there are people… You've been alone for a long time and I understand it, but an opportunity like this may not come along again. I won't ask you to come, but please, wait here. Thank you for everything you've done. I hope you can forgive what happened in the cave. It was not my intention'.

The Daughter of the Light reached for the hunter's hand and held it gently.

'I'll be back,' she said. 'We have a deal.'

Chapter 1: The Great Light

'Come on... Where is it? Why does it take so long?'

Siro waited impatiently to see Teradam illuminated. Sitting on the cold sand, he kept his eyes at the bottom of the Sacred Valley. At the centre of the city stood the tower lit only by the stars, a colossal shadow in the night.

The surface of the sand began to pulsate.

This is it, felt the hunter, wrapping himself tighter in his cape.

A dull siren rose and fell, growing louder until a cacophony of echoes reverberated back from the mountains, then it stopped.

A spark ignited within the core of the tower and surged upward. Siro stared, unblinking, and for a moment the whole world disappeared from his sight. Total darkness yawned over the land and lingered like forgotten dreams.

Then the Great Light appeared.

The night had been transformed. The sky cleared, bright as daylight. The moon and the stars seemed to have fled from the Sacred Valley, turned into a sea of incandescent light.

Below, the Great Light climbed the surrounding mountains. Siro raised his hand and the glow bathed his fingers, followed its outline, and explored its folds. His skin, hard and dark, became white and soft. His dark eyes, full of all the cruelty and loneliness of the desert, were once more those of the naïve and hopeful child.

Siro smiled, satisfied. He had sought the Great Light through the eastern gorges, the Mirror Rocks, the salt desert, and even beyond the stony *hamada*, where the ravines of the north begin. He still remembered the impact he had felt when he had seen that white flame rising toward the sky. His heart had turned over. The Great Light was finally before him. The same Light that Liduvin had spoken of.

The Children of the Light are real. They're there! he thought.

Since that day, Siro had never left it. He had found a cave at the foot of one of the seven mountains that enclosed the Sacred Valley and made it his home. And every night, he climbed the slippery rocks and sat on the top to see the light show unleash on the other side.

How long have I been here? One year? Two?

The nights in the desert were hard. He did not know what would happen to him or who he might meet. How many times had he avoided the Beasts, or even worse, the Nightborns? How many times had he killed to survive? How many days had he gone hungry because there was nothing to hunt?

Siro spent all his days looking for a way to enter the Tear-City, but his efforts were in vain. Teradam had no door, no gap, nothing at all.

Liduvin is waiting for me there, he told himself.

Some nights, he contemplated the Great Light, dumbfounded, absorbed; but others, he was filled with fury because everything he had always wanted was within its walls, so close that it seemed incredible that he couldn't reach it. He didn't know how to enter Teradam and he believed that he would never make it... until he met Matildet.

Chapter 2: Apparition

The sun was rising and the dunes were shining with the first light. Siro crawled over the sand. He moved silently, holding his necklace with the quartz stone between his teeth.

The hunter cut the distance to the Biter. An hour had passed since he saw it jumping over the dunes. The animal had the shape and the thick skin of a lion, but it was big and muscular like a bull. Its vigorous legs erased the drawings the wind had sculpted in the sand, and its long, curved tail swayed from side to side with each step. It was enough to look at his nose to understand its name. The animal had a double row of huge teeth capable of crushing even the bark of a centennial pandanus.

One with the sand under his cloak, the young hunter followed the trail of wide footprints. He waited for the moment when the animal would stop to drink water or entertain himself hunting a viper or a lizard. Then he would pounce on it.
Siro gently fingered the handle of the knife he had found years ago in the Tomb of the Forgotten.

The Biter sniffed the air.

Siro was upwind but the gesture stiffened him. Lying on the orange sand, he felt the heat of the desert against his body as his muscles clung perfectly still.

The animal sniffed again, this time with a loud snort. And this time Siro smelled something, too.

Perfume, thought Siro. Keeping his eyes on the animal, he inhaled slowly into his nose.

A rally of pinpricks struck his cheek and he dropped his head to curse into the sand. A second before it descended, Siro peered out across the dunes and saw the raging cloud of a sandstorm.

Man and Biter were engulfed in grey darkness. Blades of dust stabbed Siro's legs, his back, his arms, and he fought to keep hold of his cloak as the wind threatened to tear it from him. The animal moaned and snorted and seemed to be everywhere as the cloud distorted the sound. Siro held his eyes tightly closed and his face down under the cloak and still mercilessly sand continued to lash.

The Biter's howl rose above the storm and Siro came out from under the cloak. He released the knife from its sheath and lashed out all around him. The blade hit something in the middle of the sand cloud. He felt the animal's body striking his naked torso. The sand burned his side as he fell rolling, but the hunter regained his balance and waited with his weapon ready.

He breathed slowly and listened.

Wind whistled in his ears.

Attack! He thought. *C'mon, do it quickly.*

The wind stopped as quickly as it had started. Siro wiped the sand from his eyes. The landscape had changed. The wind had taken the dunes and now the desert looked smooth until the ravines of the north on one side and the mountains of the Sacred Valley on the other.

Where is it?, thought Siro.

A thick liquid rolled down his forehead. Siro touched it and saw his fingers stained with blood. He touched it again, this time feeling all over his head for the source of the viscus substance. No wound. It was not his own.

The crimson trail continued along his arm and covered his blade, where he found a sticky knot of orange fur. Siro lifted it to smell but was again hit by that most intriguing of aromas.

Perfume.

Siro saw the girl walking towards him like an apparition. She was dressed in white, a tight suit that made her appear naked to Siro's still focussing eyes. The girl approached him with an uncertain step, stopped suddenly, and collapsed.

Siro considered running. He couldn't be sure what the girl was, did not think she was human, but the pure white of the girl's clothing held his focus. So pure, brighter even than the sand of the salt desert. *The white of the Great Light*, he thought.

Long, blond hair shrouded the girl's face. Her eyes were closed. She gave off that strange smell, the same one that he noticed before the storm. Now that it was closer, it reminded him of moon flowers.

Are you a Daughter of the Light?, he wondered.

If she was, she could help him get into Teradam. But what if he were wrong? What if this was a trap of the Nightborn? What if she was a

Beast in disguise?

She wore no slavery or Beast Brand on her skin, as far as he could see, and her hands seemed thin and soft.

She's no desert creature. If I leave her, she'll not make it.

Liduvin was waiting for him inside Teradam, behind that glare.

It's not worth the risk, Siro argued with himself, *leave her*.

And yet he remained still.

The sun burned. Siro brushed his hair, sweaty and bloody, away from his face. The wind was blowing again and began to bury the girl's body. Her legs had already disappeared under the sand.

She will die.

The heat pressed him. He had to move. Soon the sun would be high in the sky and it would be impossible to get back to the cave before he died of thirst.

He stroked the quartz stone that hung from his necklace.

What should I do, Liduvin?

Chapter 3: No one else

'Where do the Children of the Light live, Siro?', Liduvin always asked.

The boy used to get into bed as soon as the woman started one of her stories. He loved the feeling of being only the two of them in the hut, when the gentle trickling of Merco's river was the only sound.

'In Teradam!', he responded, enthusiastically.

'And where is Teradam?'.

'Uh... Oh, yes! At the bottom of the Sacred Valley, behind the Great Light!'.

'And how are the Children of the Light?'.

'They say their hair shines like the of sun over the desert,' he repeated by heart. 'And their clothes are white as the Light'.

'Well done, little one. You could almost tell the whole story, huh?'

'No! Please, you do it!'

Smiling as she knew the request was coming, Liduvin sat back and began to tell the tale of the Children of the Light.

'Long, long ago, or maybe not so much, who knows. Nobody remembers when. No one! Yet everyone - I do not know how to say it - everyone feels deep in their hearts this is how it went, right, little one? Do you feel it?'

And then Liduvin tickled him under his ribs and he laughed unstoppably. How old was he then? Five or six. He'd been a little embarrassed she was telling him tales before going to sleep. The rest of the children in the village would tease him if they knew, but he felt special when Liduvin told him stories, especially ones about the Children of the Light.

'The Creator,' Liduvin continued, 'set his eyes on a black and sad rock that floated in the darkness. Darkness, yes, that was the only thing in the beginning. That rock had never caught anyone's attention. All creatures in the sky ignored it. Who was there to care for a black and sad rock?' Liduvin shrugged and waited for Siro to answer.

'The Creator cared!' Siro shouted, jumping to his feet.

'Yes,' Liduvin confirmed, her pendants and bracelets rattling and jangling as she laughed. 'Yes, very good. The Creator cared indeed. Very good. And what was the name of the Creator?
'Philippe Keerine!'.

'Impressive, Siro! You always listen, huh? Yes, Keerine stared at that stone for a long time and in the end, you know what? He understood that the stone was very special. It was everything he'd looked for all his life. And in that moment, he shed a single tear over the rock.'

Siro remembered the telling of the story so fondly. Ordinarily, Liduvin would hold in her hand a piece of quartz and allow a single drop of water to fall onto the stone from a jar. That night had been different, though. On the Night of Fire, Liduvin had not retrieved water from a jar; on the Night of Fire the drop of water had been a real tear of her own.

'And the rock came to life and became the whole world.'

Liduvin ran her finger over the rock, spreading the tear until a green sprout appeared. A small and shy bud that expanded rapidly to turn the quartz green.

The child always kept his eyes wide open to this prodigy.

'How did you do that?'

Siro had never learnt the trick.

'And from the tear', continued Liduvin. 'Teradam, the Tear-City, was born, and so did the Children of the Light… Do you know remember the words of the Creator? Do you remember, Siro?'.

Years later, the hunter still remembered the words that Liduvin had taught him. He had forgotten many things from his childhood, many stories and most of the faces of the people he had known and loved, but not those words.

'To those who have been born from destruction and hatred, I give you this world. Forgive us and live', he repeated slowly.

Siro was gazing at the white suit of the girl he had picked up in the desert and wondered if he had done well in bringing her.

The Daughter of the Light slept on the hyena and mongoose skins at the back of the cave. Her sleep had been troubled. She'd half awoken at one point and cried out:
'Where are they? Where are the others?'

Siro had remained still, not knowing how to answer. Their eyes had met across the cave, she in the gloom and he in the light. Her blue-marine eyes moved from one place to another with no apparent intent or comprehension. She soon settled back to sleep.

Siro would have wanted to answer her, but the words had not come out, they were stuck in his throat. He needed a few moments to sort the words inside his head. After all, he had not had a conversation in years. But the Daughter of the Light had not given him any time. Before Siro opened his mouth, the girl went back to sleep on the hyena and mongoose skins.

After that, Siro sat next to the Daughter of the Light for a long time. Golden hair cascaded down over her shoulders; her lips were dry and her delicate skin was red from the sun. Her chest rose and fell with her breath... Siro could not take his eyes off her.

How long had it been since he'd seen a woman? Although a Daughter of the Light was not strictly a woman. The women of the Merco village had bathed in the river and although the men were forbidden to go while they were there, the younger children would go with their mothers. Or in Siro's case, with Liduvin. As a child he had been fascinated by the women. He would study them as Liduvin lathered and rinsed his hair by the river, the young and the old, the legs, bellies, buttocks, breasts, the scars, the Brands... None looked like the Daughter of the Light.

Hair golden like the sand, he thought, having never seen blonde hair.

The girl awoke again in the night with the smell of embers filling the cave. Siro had lit a fire next to the entrance of the cave and was engaged in skewering some black vipers on branches.

While the hunter let the snakes brown on the flames, the girl sat up half covered with one of the furs. Siro looked at her for a moment, her blue eyes outlined by the reflection of the fire.

The Daughter of the Light observed the red interior of the cave without saying a word. She scanned the shelves dug into the walls. Cages, ropes and his collection of wise stones, a string of utensils mixed with ripped snake skins, shells of small turtles that had long since been eaten, cactus, gnawed bones and valuable but cracked glass jars were piled high on them. She glanced the cherry tree trunk beside the entrance. The bag and the hunter's cloak hung from its branches, and a double spear, with a crude metal blade at each end, laid against it.

She looked confused.

The hunter unlocked the stick from the coals and offered it to her. She leaned away in shock.

'What? She doesn't like it?', thought Siro.

He took a bite to prove it was safe and pulled the viper's skin with his teeth. It stretched until it broke with a viscous snap and spat on to the flames. Then he savoured the tasty and crunchy flesh of the viper. He chewed with his mouth open for her to see.

The Daughter of the Light took the stick and hesitantly moved it to her mouth. She took a bite and swallowed harshly. She closed her eyes. For a moment, Siro feared she would lose consciousness again, but she held on.

Siro wanted to be able to talk to her at least once before she fell asleep again. He placed a hand on his chest and carefully pronounced his name.

'Siro,' he said.

The Daughter of the Light copied the gesture and replied with a sore voice.

'Matildet. You can call me Matildet.'

Soon after, the Daughter of the Light asked for some water and fell into a deep sleep.

The following day, Siro returned to the cave at the break of dawn. He found the girl rooting through his things, moving around objects on shelves, peering into crevices in the cave wall. She did not notice him.

Again, Siro found himself admiring the girl's movements. She seemed hurried but she went about her search with respectful delicacy. The white suit was as much a part of her as the curious look in her eyes, like she'd worn it all her life, and she flowed with ease in and out of the morning light.

Matildet stopped in front of the water tank and her curiosity peaked. She traced a finger along the drawings on the tank, an expression of familiarity ebbing across her face.

'Where did this come from?', she muttered to herself.

'North ravine,' Siro said slowly.

Matildet screamed and jumped down behind the water tank.

'Oh, my... Why are you so sneaky?! Shit, I almost had a heart attack!', she complained. 'Let... Let me... Siro, right? Yeah, listen, you... You have something of mine, and I want it back, ok? Come on, I do not want to... I don't want any troubles, huh?'

Siro did not answer.

'Do you understand my language? Do you know what I'm saying...?'

Siro nodded.

'It's a pack. It's white,' she gestured to the white of her suit and, drawing out the shape in the air. The cave was full of small hiding places that served Siro to hide his most treasured possessions. The hunter considered the request for several moments and looked up and down the cave walls, imagining each of crack and crevice, trying to remember. Then, with a nod of certainty, he stepped past Matildet and pulled aside a mongoose hide, revealing little more than a ridge.

The Daughter of the Light watched with fascination as the hunter disappeared into the wall.

Siro searched while Matildet waited. When he finally re-emerged, he had with him the white pack. It was dusty and torn.
The Daughter of the Light snatched the pack, opened it, and began checking its contents. Her forehead wrinkled; her eyes trembled. She did not say anything, but Siro realised that she had found what she was looking for. Soon her shoulders dropped, and she sighed.
'Thank you,' she said.

There was a moment of silence. Siro noticed how the girl examined his face. She looked at his right cheek, where he had a scar that rose from his jaw.

'Hyena', said Siro. The animal had challenged him for a dead mongoose and scratched at his face before running away. He had cried, scared he'd die without Liduvin's care. By then, he was already alone. The pain lingered and the wound became infected, but after a week of struggling to eat and sleep, he began to heal.

The Daughter of the Light then pointed to his eyebrow.

Siro's eye dropped. It was too much to explain, and a story too difficult to recall, though the images flashed in his mind. The day he left Undershell. The Exile. The heat. The sullen hum of thousands of people in front of the wooden palisade. Hundreds of families expelled from the city. His mother's brown eyes. His father's strong hands. Then the chaos as the Beasts tore through the crowd.

Matildet had no scars, no freckles, no Brands of any kind.

'Listen to me, Siro', said the Daughter of the Light, her tone firm. 'Does anyone else live here?'.

Siro shook his head.

'Where are the others?'

He raised an eyebrow. *Who is she talking about?*

Matildet stared blankly waiting for Siro to say something.

'It's okay. I see that you do not trust me, but please… Are you trying to protect them? Is that it? I promise, I… Please, tell me. Please.'

Her breath quivered and her jaw tightened and in a flash of rage, Matildet roared and stamped out to the entrance of the cave.

Siro followed and the growing heat of the day struck them.

'Where are the others?' Matildet repeated. 'Here or there?' she pointed out across the desert. 'Tell me! All I've done to get here… I can't be wrong.'

She stood out there for a while, until the heat became unbearable.

After that, the Daughter of the Light was silent for a long time. She looked at the floor of the cave, at the bowl of water Siro had given her, but it was likeshe didn't see anything.

'Why you look for them?' Siro asked.

'I must help them. And you? Why are you here?'

'Also looking for someone'.

Siro climbed the mountain when the sky turned dark. Like every night, he would sit on the top and wait for the Great Light to appear and think of Liduvin, just as he did every time he had to make a decision.

The wind carried the sand in swirls down the valley, as the Tear-City began to shine with the Great Light of Teradam.

'I'll see you very soon, Liduvin. If she really is a Daughter of the Light, she will help me.'

'Liduvin…', he said aloud.

But just as he pronounced her name, he felt embarrassed. Matildet appeared beside him and her white suit reflected the Great Light like a mirror, and Siro thought that both things had to be parts of a whole.

Siro reached out and pointed a finger toward the valley. Matildet nodded.

'We called it Teradam,' she said. 'The city of miracles.'

'Your home?'

'I thought so at the beginning.' Her eyes shone sadly.

Matildet turned around and descended the mountain heading to the cave.

He stared again at the Great Light and felt the ethereal energy on his face. All of his worries evaporated when he looked at the Light. He saw Liduvin's face; Eliria's freckled cheeks; his friend Nazeh jumping around, challenging him to race through the jungle; Grinat's grim face. He saw the people of the village of Merco, the giant palms, the low and hidden houses, the empty trunks of the trees that were used to make canoes; smelled the sweet and pungent spices crushed in the mortars of the market; heard the laughter of the children.

When he looked at the Great Light, Siro saw it all.

Chapter 4: Pact of light

The night gave way to the day and so the show ended. Siro ⟶ the dunes, huddled cold in his cloak. The City-Tear had an impress. appearance. The high tower reflected the first lights trembling like a huge and slowly melting mass of ice. Siro brought himself to his knees, placed one hand on his heart and raised the other to the sky, and prayed.
'To those who have been born from destruction and hatred, I give you this world. Forgive us and live.'
He rose slowly and moved his aching body back to the cave.
Matildet was still asleep at the back of the cave so he moved on to the reservoir to fill a bowl of water. He thirstily finished the first bowl and filled another.
When he returned, Matildet was sat by the cave entrance.
'I have to go to the oasis for water,' said Siro. 'And collect food for the trip. Are you hungry?'
The wind blew over the crests of the dunes and dragged sheets of sand across the valley.
Siro led Matildet down a path into the mountain.
'The nest of cages is protected from the sun by the trees,' said Siro. 'The birds come here to rest. Down there, I spread seed I harvest from the branches, the birds come, then,' he slapped his hands.
Below, dozens of wooden traps lay in a wide hole under a bed of twigs and moss. Siro edged himself carefully down into the hole and began stealthily checking the cages. Matildet followed his example.
'Nothing,' Siro lamented. *The desert spirits are playing with me again.*
All the cages were empty and two of them had been trampled and chewed. In one of them there was blood and feathers. Some animal had beaten him to it.
I should have come back earlier.
'Here!' Matildet waved. 'Look, they move.'
The girl pointed to one of the cages. Inside, two red-headed

…ed their wings and squawked and fought.

'How beautiful,' said Matildet wondrously. 'Look at them. …ontrast of colours. The giant beaks!'

Siro reached fearlessly into the cage. The birds flapped and …uirmed but were neatly cornered. The hunter grabbed one by the …eck.

Matildet looked away expectantly, though she heard the snap of the creature's neck and the sound of its limp body falling back on the path. Siro reached back down and pulled out the cage, the remaining bird still trapped and panicked, and handed it to Matildet to carry.

'Do others live near the oasis?' Asked the Daughter of the Light once they were back at the cave.

Siro was distracted in his preparations and did not answer. He retrieved a drawstring bag from a secret hole in the cave wall and then unfurled a round piece of animal skin on the floor.

'The wise stones tell all,' said Siro. 'Three ambers, quartz, dark onyx and bright scarlet are thrown together over the hide. How they fall will tell us what we need to know.' Siro held the stones in his hands over the skin and threw them together. They immediately scattered. Only an amber landed on the skin.

Siro frowned. 'We leave tomorrow,' he said.

'What do they tell you?' Asked Matildet. 'You believe this?'

Siro, not sensing her scepticism, said, 'the position of the onyx. Danger is nearby.'

The Daughter of the Light sat with the caged bird until nightfall. She gave it drops of water and small pieces of the meal Siro prepared. Dry yuccas and wild tapirs.

She whispered to it and laughed whenever it chirped.

'It wants to know why you kept it alive,' she asked Siro.

'Female,' he answered.

Matildet turned and her hair caught the breeze.

Moon flowers.

'Why did you rescue me?' The Daughter of the Light asked. 'What do you expect from me?'

The hunter hesitated.

'Teradam,' he said.

'Oh.' Understanding flashed in Matildet's eyes. 'You want to go inside?'

'Someone waits for me.'

'I can take you to Teradam. But first I need you to help me find the others.'

When the Daughter of the Light fell asleep that evening, Siro extinguished the last embers in the fire and headed out.

Night had already swallowed the desert. Moonlight illuminated crowns around the peaks of the tallest dunes and down in the valley the light show had begun. Siro climbed the slope and, as he did, he thought of Matildet's face, so full of joy, when he agreed to help her. He worried, though. His entry into Teradam was now dependent on this fragile bargain – how could he explain to Matildet that he did not think there any more survivors in the desert?

He hoped to find an answer in the light that spilled like a waterfall over the arid peaks of the Sacred Valley. This night felt special. He was saying goodbye to Teradam for a while, but perhaps in preparation for a real return, a return that would see him finally enter inside its walls.

Siro tried to hold the light in his hands as he often did and was calmly dreaming of the wondrous possibilities when a crash from down below startled him. The ground began to shake and sway. A deep ache rose up from his stomach. He slipped and stumbled as he raced back down the mountain, and when he reached the cave, he knew he was too late. Shelves by the entrance were in disarray, items strewn and broken across the ground.

And Matildet was gone.

Chapter 5: Night Serpent

The first time that Siro heard of the Nightborn was soon after the Exile.

Those had been hard times for everyone. Just as they reached the oasis, the exiles had put all their effort into building a village in the jungle of tall palms. Men cut logs and loaded rocks and clay from the river. Women drew on the mud the layout of the buildings and raised the first barracks with their own hands. In the mornings, the children were told to pick fruit in the jungle, and in the afternoon, they ran and played among the half-built houses or down by the river.

One evening, while Liduvin and Siro prepared dinner, she told him about the Nightborn.

'Come closer, little one. I want to tell you a story. I think you're old enough to hear it. Do you know of the Nightborn?'

Siro shook his head.

'Well, on one hand there are the Children of the Light. On the other, the Nightborn.'

'Are they bad?' Siro asked.

'Bad? Yes, little one, they're bad. They take people to their kingdom and they never return. The Children of the Light have tried to stop them many times but even they have never succeeded.'

'I've never seen one,' said Siro.

'Good! You would not be here, trust my words.'

'Tell me more about the Nightborn, Liduvin,' Siro pleaded.

'There are many stories to tell,' Liduvin considered. 'The legend of Mother Serpent, the story of the man with two shadows, the Day of the Split. Some of them you may have heard parts of. But tonight, Siro, I'm not going to tell you a tale.'

Siro frowned.

'What I have to tell you is much more important,' Liduvin reassured. 'Maybe you're not big enough just yet.'

'No, I am! Please tell me.'

'You must be brave, Siro. Can you be brave?'

Siro nodded strongly.

'There is no escaping the Nightborn, Siro. But, and I want you to remember this always, they are predictable. When they're coming, there will be three signs. If ever you hear the first, beware. If you hear the second, you must run. Pack up quickly and get away.'

'And what if,' Siro gulped, 'what if I hear all three signs?'

'If you hear all three, little one, pray.'

Liduvin's tone was so severe, Siro knew she was serious. He never doubted the truth of her stories but this one felt particularly important.

The boy nodded his understanding and asked, 'what are the signs?'

'The first sign is silence,' said Liduvin. 'Pay attention. Do you hear every sound that you should? If the wind was blowing, is it blowing now? If there were crickets chirping in the grass, are they chirping still? Can you hear the river flowing as you could moments ago? The crackling of your fire? When the Nightborn are near, these sounds will fall still.'

Siro listened out into the village and tried to imagine the silence.

'The second sign?' He asked, ready.

'The second sign,' said Liduvin, looking deep into young Siro's eyes, 'is the quartz.' She removed an amulet necklace from around her neck and asked, 'what colour is the stone?'

'Black,' Siro answered simply.

'The blackest black,' confirmed Liduvin. 'But when the Nightborn are close, quartz falls sickly pale. It begins at the edges. The colour drains away and blushes white.' Liduvin placed the stone in Siro's hand and closed his fingers around it. 'You take care of this and it'll take care of you, you understand?'

Siro nodded.

'So if silence comes,' the boy considered gravely, 'and the quartz turns deathly white, I have to run, run as fast as I can and run all night if I have to. But then, if the Nightborn catch up to me, if they get really close, just before they take me away forever, there's one more sign? That's when I have to pray and pray hard and hope for a miracle.'

'That's about right,' Liduvin nodded.

'So, what's the third sign?'

'Drums, little one. Drums. My mother's the only one to see the Nightborn and come back to tell of it. She said you hear drums, a growing thunder of drums, the type of beat that feels slow in the ground but looms quicker and quicker, comes closer and closer. Drums of death, she called them.

The hunter ran away from the cave. The ground was still vibrating, and until it subsided he couldn't be sure the roof wouldn't collapse on top of him. He looked around desperately and spotted Matildet's footprints in the dirt, immediately set off following them.

If she's gone too far, I'll never find her, Siro feared, *and she could be lost. She might have gone down to the cages, fearing for the damn birds. But what if she's gone east? I don't think she climbed the hills – wouldn't I have crossed her path? Maybe she's gone towards the ravine – what if she can't see and falls into the abyss? Why did she run?*

Siro came to a sudden stop and looked down around his feet. His footsteps crunching in the sand had faded away. He tapped his foot on the ground and pressed fingers to his ears.

Silence.

The ground pulsed and vibrated with a constant aftershock from the earthquake, but now it made no sound. Siro spoke into the darkness, his lips moved and he felt his words in his throat, but no sound was made.

The hunter reached for the quartz amulet.

I left it in the cave.

He stared around into the darkness, desperately trying to replace his hearing with something visual, anything that would tell him the safest way to go. But the shadows deceived him. Subtle shapes moved in the distance and disappeared; loose stones slid beneath his feet like insects and escaped into nothingness.

Follow Matildet's trail, he told himself, *as far as it goes. Just run. Run all night if you must.*

Siro pushed himself on, straining to make out the faint footprints. His movements were slow and clumsy through the thick sand and it shocked him when he landed hard then on solid rock. But he was filled with relief for just a moment, because as his foot met the rock it had made a sound. The hunter continued cautiously, slower now, seeking out any sign of the footprints, lessening and lessening on the dry ground, and each step made a sound.

An unusual sound, he thought. It was somehow distant, disconnected. Had he chosen the right path away from the Nightborns? Was he moving away from them? Was it that making the sound gradually ebb back to him in this confusing way? No.

Siro took another step, and the sound came before his foot hit the ground. This time louder. This time closer. He froze.

Drums.

He gave up on the trail and ran as hard as he could, across the rocky plateau, back into thick sand and up over more hills and through tufts of grasses he couldn't see. Siro ran up now, up an increasingly steep incline, and his legs burned but he couldn't stop, couldn't slow. And all was silent but for the crash of the drums.

The hunter slumped to the ground. The icy night air of the desert clung to his chest.

It is time.

'To those who have been born from destruction and hatred,' he whispered.

A gust of wind interrupted his prayer, stole his breath. He looked up as if the wind had spoken to him.

Moon flowers, he thought. *The Daughter of the Light.*

In the near distance, at the top of a rise, Siro saw the moon cresting barely above the land. He was near the northern ravine. Maybe they could escape from here, if he could find a path down from the cliffs – but the drums were deafening now.

'Matildet,' Siro shouted. Still no sound came to his ears but maybe she was beyond the reach of the Nightborn, maybe she'd hear him.

He dragged himself to his feet and continued to run up the hill.

'Siro?' The Daughter of the Light's voice seemed to sing from above.

'I can hear you. Matildet?'

Ahead a silhouette formed before the moon, the source of the moon flower perfume. Siro ran to Matildet and held her by her shoulders.

'We have to run,' Siro pleaded, his voice loud and clear.

'Why?' Matildet looked more confused than fearful. 'The earthquake's over. I'm sorry if I scared you but I had to move away from the cave. It was dangerous.'

Siro stared back down the dark path and listened hard into the silence. A gentle breeze caressed his face; Matildet's breath was soft and calm, while his own was hoarse and laboured.

'Look,' said Matildet, and she pointed out across the desert.

Beyond the ravine, sand lifted and fell in great waves and undulated under the pressure of something moving below.

'She caused the earthquake,' Matildet informed, smiling.

Plumes of sand erupted into the sky, blued by the subtle moon. A giant reptile emerged on to the surface, its scales shimmering silver. She moaned deeply and the ground trembled.

'Mother Snake,' said Siro, and he bowed low in respect.

Chapter 6: The stories we grow up with

'It finally sets,' Matildet said, looking back, to the west.

The sun had started to sink a few moments before. The Daughter of the Light had closed the cane-made umbrella and handed it to Siro, who put it inside the tank, now empty of water, but full of all the provisions and tools they needed.

The hunter had spent the whole day pulling the ropes tied to the tank. Step by step, he got the metal cylinder up the dunes.

'How are you doing? Need help?' offered Matildet. She only carried the white backpack and one of the cages made with branches, the one with the bird.

Siro shook his head. Dunes were getting flatter as they went on.

'It is a pity that everything is so plain.' Said Matildet, almost jumping around. 'Do you remember when we slid down the dune? It was fun'.

Siro said nothing. He was too busy pulling the tank. The best moment of that little game had been when the Daughter of the Light had jumped on top of the tank and hurried Siro to do the same. He had smelled her perfume as her hair caressed his face. That part he had enjoyed, not the sliding downhill. Of course, he could not say it.

Matildet had jumped off the tank clapping and wanting more. He, on the other hand, barely dared to drop the ropes after the quick descent.

'If we see another one, we do it again, yeah?' She said.

'No', he replied.

Hours later, Matildet pointed toward the reddish sky.

'Hey, Siro, watch that!'

The twilight sky had filled with red-headed and black-winged birds that flew over their heads shrieking.

Inside the cage, the red-head female cackled with a strange and sharp rhythm. Matildet looked at the bird, which had been silent since they had started the journey, and then turned to Siro with a smile on his lips.

'Oh, now I get it. A female. That's why you left her alive, right?'

Siro let go of the reins of the tank and asked her to give him the cage. He used a thin string to tie the female bird's leg to the cage and another one to keep the trap open and then placed the cage on the sand. He'd better hurry. The sun had begun to disappear over the horizon it wouldn't be long before the birds flew back to their nests.

Only a pair of red-headed ones perched on the sand and bounded towards the female.

The hunter held the string in his fingers. Matildet sat next to him, hugging her legs.

The two males hopped around, undecisive.

'I say the one on the left makes it first,' said Matildet

'I hope so. It fat.'

One of the two birds took off. Matildet stifled a cry of joy, seeing the thin one lifting to the sky. The red-head bird swelled the feathers on his chest and cackled in a strange ritual of courtship. The female cringed in the cage, unsure whether she wanted out. A few more hops and the bird got to the threshold of the trap. Next to him, Matildet was rubbing her legs. Slowly, the head of the bird broke through the bars and, when the tail was inside, Siro pulled the string. The door fell and Matildet got up with a shout. She clapped and praised Siro with words he could not understand. He assumed they were something good.

'How did you find me, in the middle of the night?' Asked Matildet, as he cleared the roasted bird's wings.

Siro touched his nose and pretended to smell the air as a dog would. The Daughter of the Light laughed loudly and the food almost fell off of her mouth. The bones of the male bird melted into the bonfire. It was already night, and the two were sitting, side by side, under the tent Siro had improvised with his cloak and some canes.

'Am I so stinky that you can find me in the dark?' She asked.

'No. Perfume,' Siro explained.

'Does it still smell?' Matildet touched his neck and smelled his hand. 'I see... A perfect blend of sweat and perfume. I'm dying to have a bath'.

'In oasis, you take bath.'

'Do you think we'll find people there?'

'Don't think so.'

'I do not get it. They live *so* far away. How come you don't live with them?'

'I'm alone. It's okay.'

Matildet moved closer to the fire and stood at the height of the young man. Her eyes reminded him of the sky of the last hours of the day, a navy blue mixed with the orange of the fading sunlight. She was gorgeous, perhaps the most attractive woman he had ever seen. For a brief moment, he thought of Eliria, their first kiss and the pretty and starry night they have shared back in Merco.

Forget it. She's a Daughter of the Light.

Siro focused on the crackling of the flames, on its *sound*.

It´s all good.

The Great Light was too far behind them to see it. As soon as the embers cooled, darkness would cover it all.

'I have to confess that I had no idea how to get back to the cave.' Matildet was using her backpack as a pillow. 'If it hadn't been for you, I'd still be there, staring at that thing.'

'Mother Snake?' Said the hunter, eyes still set on the fire.

'Yes, you called her that. What was it?'

'You don't know?'

'Should I?'

Really? Siro raised an eyebrow. Liduvin had told him the story many times.

'Mother Snake was woman before, long time ago. Now creature that wanders in the desert. She looks for her daughter.'

'Daughter Snake?' Matildet did not seem to take the story seriously.

'Ember was her name. She born Day of Tau. Nightborns took her.'

'Why?'

'They do that. Long ago, humans lived in oasis in desert. In one of those oasis, there was a village. In village, a mother, and a daughter,' when he spoke, he realised he mimicked Liduvin's speech.

'I see,' said Matildet. She was distracted, searching for something in her backpack. 'Sorry, keep going'.

'Ember went out to play one night. Mother had told her not to. The daughter was chasing fireflies among the pandanus and strelitzias when they took her'.

She heard the drums, he thought and got goosebumps. Beyond the bonfire, it was pitch black.

'Mother imagined what had happened. Others too. Nobody wanted to know anything about Nightborn. And mother be alone. She decided only Children of the Light can help and walked and walked the desert to find Teradam. Many days she needed, but found Sacred Valley, saw Great Light.'

Matildet was speechless. She listened to everything he had to say. He loved that feeling.

Now I understand Liduvin, he thought.

'After walking inside the Light, mother heard voices and suddenly, she inside the Great Light, in Teradam. In front of her, a man as bright as the sun. A Son of the Light. Mother throw to the feet and explain everything. But not good response. Son of the Light said forget. Too late. Once Nightborn take someone, no hope. He told her to go home and mother got angry... She resented the Children of the Light. She cursed them. Your light will be extinguished, she said. She left but the Nightborn were waiting and...'

Siro remembered how Liduvin used to tell that part and halted for a second. He rescued a piece of coal from the fire, buried it under the sand with a stick and after a while he dug it up again and rubbed the coal over his hand and his right cheek.

'Looking for your daughter, human?' Siro continued narrating in a guttural voice. He turned his head and showed his soot-covered cheek to Matildet so that she understood that it was the Nightborn.

The girl burst in laughter seeing the hunter's performance.

'Please, give her to me,' Siro turned his head to the other side and mimicked the mother's plea. 'I'll do what you want...' He showed again his blackened Nightborn face. 'No promises, no. We no Children of the Light... If you want girl, look, down there!' And he took two handfuls of sand making a circular hole in the ground.

'A pit!' Matildet guessed.

'Yes, a pit,' Siro was doing an impression on the Nightborn. 'Your daughter waits at the bottom...' He turned his head and played the mother's role. 'Liar, my daughter is not there. In pit, only snakes!

But then, mother heard a voice. It was daughter's, coming from under a heap of snakes.'

'And what did she do?'

'She jumped in. And dug through snakes to find her.'

'It does not seem like a good idea,' Matildet pointed out.

'No. No good. Snakes bit mother many times before she found daughter. But daughter turned out to be a tiny blue snake. It spoke with daughter's voice, but not her. Nightborns laughed and looked at mother...'

Siro wiped his face with his arm. Now he did not need to impersonate the creatures of the night.

'And that's it?' Complained Matildet, after a brief silence. 'What happened with the mother?'

'Survived,' Siro reassured her. 'Son of the Light showed up at that moment and Nightborn fled. He helped the mother out of the pit, and she asked for daughter to be human again. But Son of the Light said no. Talking viper was just a Nightborn trick, not her daughter. Mother cried and begged. Too late. She cursed.'

Siro painted scales on his arm with the coal to represent what happened to the poor mother. He performed the transformation with gestures. The skin had begun to turn hard and bright. The arms disappeared, joined the trunk, becoming one; and so did the legs, glued with each other. The eyes changed colour as she squealed, her head reshaped as a reptile's. Her body bloated and grew.

'Mother maddened,' Siro concluded. 'She no longer human, but still remembers. Mother Snake travels the desert and seeks daughter and will do until the end of time.'

Matildet remained pensive for a few seconds. Siro was secretly satisfied. Although he did not intend to scare the Daughter of the Light, he hoped that at least he would get some emotion out of that story.

'Who told you this story?'

The question caught him off guard. He didn't answer.

Matildet laid down beside the hunter and yawned. Siro moved away. Moments ago, he'd have loved that proximity.

'Is it the same person waiting for you in Teradam?' Murmured Matildet.

Chapter 7: Close your eyes

The sand was covered with a thin layer of ice when Siro opened his eyes. It had been such a cold night that they had had to sleep wrapped in blankets. Mother Snake had appeared in his dreams. It was chasing after him and Nazeh. Yes, it had seemed to Siro that it was his childhood friend who was running beside him. The two fled through the jungle so the creature would not catch them. They were about to make it, but then he looked up and saw Matildet on the edge of the northern ravines. At that moment, Mother Snake opened her mouth and swallowed him just to fall again in Liduvin's arms.

A stupid dream, he thought as he stepped on the frost with his bare feet. It was nice to feel that coolness underfoot.

The frost layer stretched to the horizon varnishing the dunes. As the day grew hotter, the frost crackled, broke, and became a fine, pleasant mist. When Matildet woke up, there were only a few small, whitish puddles, not more than tiny oases that would soon be nothing more than steam.

Siro put on his necklace. The quartz was still black.

He tied the ropes back to the water tank as soon as they had cleared the tent. Matildet held the umbrella. During the first hours they did not exchange more than some phrases and indications of where they had to go. The Daughter of the Light did not ask any questions, as if last night's conversation never happened. He was thankful for that.

The sand was boiling hot under the midday sun, so they stopped to rest for a while. Siro's feet had swollen and turned red. He had a tingling sensation when he touched the wounds, but not the pain he used to feel years ago. He kept the memories of the hours he had walked among the cars that formed the exiles caravan. His child's feet weren't used to that. He had to follow the cars, barefoot, and without anyone letting him hop on for a break. Only when Liduvin talked to the drivers did they become more receptive. Nobody wanted to take care of an orphan.

The red-headed bird had passed because of the heat. The chirping of the bird had died out little by little without either of them noticing. Matildet looked distressed and Siro did not dare to ask if he could cook it. But it was not necessary.

'There's nothing we can do now,' she said.

Siro lit the fire with a flame stone, though he thought it would have been enough for him to leave the bird on top of the metal tank to roast it. When he gave Matildet her share, her chin trembled.

After lunch, the girl drank the last sips from the skinful until it was empty. She reached out to grab the next one, but Siro pushed it away in time.

'Hold on,' he said.

'It's like I have a fire in my mouth,' the Daughter of the Light protested. 'Just one last sip, I beg you.'

Siro shook his head. Matildet stared at him for a moment, until she finally gave in. There were only two waterskins left.

They resumed the journey as soon as the sun began to sink among the dunes. The sky had turned orange and it seemed like the desert spilled through the air. The wind started blowing with gentle breeze that pushed them to the east, just where they were going.

The next morning, Matildet, who no longer even carried the umbrella, was behind Siro. Her eyes were watery and there were red marks on her cheeks. The girl was looking at the horizon, trying to see a destination that was still out of sight. Her golden hair stirred in the wind, more and more fervently. Siro looked behind her and saw a sandy cloud that stretched across the horizon: a mass that grew stronger.

'Siro, what you're doing?' Matildet asked, confused, when she saw that the hunter leaving the tank and taking the sticks out of it. The hunter moved with frenzy. One by one, he shoved the sticks in the sand. He buried them with all his strength. He jumped from place to place despite the confused words of the Daughter of the Light. *'It's about to fall on us!'*

He anchored the tank with yet another stick and spread the cloak over them to form tiny shelter. Siro pointed behind Matildet. She turned and understood the urgency of the situation. The hunter put a last stick in the middle, the one that held the whole structure of the awning, and the two travellers threw themselves under the cloak. The sky had turned brown.

The sand rose. The sun had vanished and the dunes darkened under the cloud of dust. Siro had buried the sticks as deeply as he could, but he knew that would not be enough to withstand the onslaught. Matildet's gaze told him she did not believe it either. The tiny sand granules were hitting the cloak with growing intensity. In the middle of the storm, the sand could travel so fast that it could tear the skin. The hits multiplied until they became a continuous buzz.

Matildet was facing the floor, with her hands over her head and the blond hair falling on her face. Siro watched as the tears slid down her cheeks leaving dark spots on the sand.

'It's all my fault,' the Daughter of the Light lamented among tears. 'Why did I have to listen to her? Cas, you're stupid!'

The hunter grabbed Matildet's hand. She raised her eyes for a moment, and Siro put her hand around one of the sticks, the only hope they had left.

An unexpected jolt was about to tear off the shelter. Matildet gave a shrill scream and her crying intensified.

'Fear not,' Siro whispered in her ear. 'Close your eyes. Still long way.'

Their faces were an inch away. Matildet's blue eyes looked at him. The girl's warm breath caressed him. The storm run over them and Matildet's congested face disappeared from Siro's sight like the rest of the world.

The wind and the sand buried him. The earth, the sky, everything trembled. The sticks creaked and the awning sank. In less than a second everything vanished. There was no light, there was nothing, only sand and wind.

I'm trapped! Siro thought in the darkness.

He tried to calm down, but he could not, nor could he move. The air was scarce. The sand pressed on his head and neck. He drowned. He thought for a moment of Matildet. He couldn't feel the touch of her hand.

The sand entered his nose, his ears, his mouth. A bitter taste ran through his tongue. The desert was eating him alive.

He thought of Liduvin.

I'm not dying here, he told himself.

He tried to move his arms. Impossible. He tried a second time and then a third. Nothing. He scratched the sand with his fingers, gritted his teeth and despaired.

He wanted to scream, but he could not.

And just when he was about to give up, he felt something smooth under the tips of his fingers: his cloak.

He pulled it hard and the sand slid over it. Suddenly, Siro could move his arm. He twisted it inside the cloak until it wrapped around his fist and then started digging. The improvised glove helped him rip the sand without skinning his hand. He did it as fast as he could, but the air was scarce. Snorting, he noticed that he was moving, although very slowly. He couldn't go up. He knew he would die before he'd made a couple of inches, but he there was nothing else to do. He shook his body as fast as he could until the sand gave way and he was able to turn face down. The sand slid down the back of his neck and through his hair. It came out through his nose and mouth. It was good to breathe for a change.

Now he needed a good idea to get out of that mess.

The hunter had often seen animals coming out from underneath the sand as if it were no big deal. The white moles were specialists in pulling their heads out where they wanted. He had to do as they did, of course, they had claws and he only weak nails and a cloak to protect them.

He tried to calm down. He did not know how many meters of sand he still had above his head. The sand fell too fast to stand still. Should he start digging and stop halfway up, the sand tunnel would sink and he would be buried again. If he wanted to leave, he had to do it in the first try.

He took another breath hidden under the cloak.

Very well... I can do it. Come on, I can do it

His chest was trembling and so were his hands.

He hit the sand again and again.

I'm getting out! He told himself yet again and kept hitting and hitting.

The cloak made a strange noise against the sand, like a sack of potatoes trying to get out from under the ground. He moved his arms with a frenzy and felt his legs free.

Yes! Yes!

The hunter tore off the sand as if he were disembowelling an animal. A beam of light passed in front of his eyes. It was an instant and then it disappeared, but every time he put aside the sand he saw it, it was so bright that it went through the cloak fabric.

Every time he saw the light, he laughed hysterically.

And just when he put his hand on the surface and felt the coolness of the wind, the sand under his feet sank. The hunter saw himself making his climb up in the opposite direction. He fell without being able to hold on to anything. The light disappeared, like a distant point in the sky. He noticed how his body floated through the air, mixed with the sand... Until he touched the ground.

Chapter 8: Choose

He had fallen on his back on soft ground after floating through the air for a terrifying instant. The blow had not been as strong as expected —in fact, the fall was not expected at all—. Even so, it took him a while to get on his feet. The sand kept coming down from the roof, even though the hole it had fallen through had already closed.

Where am I? Siro asked himself. He reached out and touched something soft in the darkness. *What is this?* It wasn't stone, nor wood or metal. He couldn't understand what he was stepping on.

He decided he did not want to remain still in that place, whatever it was. He put on his cloak, which had been lying on the floor, put his hand against the soft wall to get his bearings and started walking.

His sweaty feet made a sticky noise every time he stepped on that floor. The passage stank of stagnant air and the heat was suffocating. From somewhere, above his head, he caught the sound of the storm that had buried him, but the noise was so faint that it seemed to come from another world.

'Siro!' Matildet's voice echoed through the darkness.

The hunter turned around. The voice came from the opposite direction. He moved forward little by little, always with one hand in front to avoid crashing with something. He heard someone say his name again, but this time the voice came from somewhere else. The passage bifurcated. He deviated from the path and then, after four steps, the ground ended under his feet. He screamed and fell. He felt the air on his face just before crashing to the ground. It had been like throwing himself off a cliff. He was lucky the ground was soft, otherwise he would have killed himself. He coughed. Something was going up his throat. Suddenly, all the sand that he had swallowed because of the storm came out of his mouth. He hit the ground with his fists in anger.

Enough! He thought, while his eyes reddened and the nausea was gripping him.

His stomach was burning, and he was dying of thirst. He wished he could close his eyes for a while and rest, but first he had to find Matildet.

'Where are you?' He shouted into the darkness.

He no longer heard the Daughter of the Light, only his own breathing.

'Hey, here! Come help me!' Someone called him, but it was not Matildet. It was a male voice.

Siro tried to go back the way he had come, but he ran into the wall. It was impossible to climb it, it was totally flat.

He unsheathed the knife. His hand was shaking.

The voice asked for help a couple of times more until it tired off. Siro moved forward, hoping to find some way to escape the underground labyrinth. He saw a light at the end of one of the corridors coming from a side room.

'Help me, whoever you are! I know how to escape from here, but I need help!' It was the same voice that had called him before coming from the lit room.

Siro got closer with his knife ready. The strangest door he'd ever seen blocked the entrance, it looked like a mixture between a transparent glass and a huge soap bubble. The light inside made the door look as it was bending, but in reality it was only the reflections.

'You there? Yes, I know you're there. Oh thanks! Please, help me, I'm so thirsty... You have to help me, I know how to get out of here, trust me!'

Siro did not move from the spot.

'Don't go, I beg you! They'll return. They'll be back and find you if you do not listen to me. The ones that scare us are nearby,' the voice insisted.

The hunter immediately understood who it was referring to. In the village of Merco there were people who also called them that way.

It must be a person, the hunter told himself, and gathered all the courage to check the inside of the room. But when he looked, he did not see a person, but a Beast.

The creature was tied to the wall of the room with a sort of harness. It was leaning against a bluish, narrow bed, just like the others beside it. It seemed it had been trapped in that row of beds on the wall for a while. The Beast was tall, perhaps as tall as Siro, and wore a torn grey hooded cloak. His face was half covered by the hood but, despite this, Siro could see a large mouth and small and trembling eyes.

There were some glasses on the floor of the room. One of the windows was broken, someone had trampled them by accident. The Beast had something in his arms. The blue and yellow light emanating from the room did not let him see clearly what it was but when the flashing lights of the walls glowed, he realized that they were iron rings, half a dozen in each arm. They were flat bracelets with the same symbol engraved on all of them: three black lines, two of them placed in the form of a cross and the last, thicker, starting from the center and moving up.

Siro had seen those rings before in Merco. Nazeh was carrying them. He had them with him when they met for the first time, during the journey through the desert. When the caravan of people who had fled from Undershell arrived at the oasis where they would end up founding the village of Merco, the first thing that Nazeh's mother had done was to look for a blacksmith who could remove the rings from his son's arms. Siro had accompanied them and seen everything. The blacksmith had had to go very slowly with the pincers and still had injured his arms. Nazeh had screamed and shed tears. Siro witnessed everything with had a knot in his stomach.

Luckily, everything had ended well. Nazeh had gotten rid of the rings safely enough. It was funny to see how the black arms of his friend having white stripes. For a long time, the children of Merco called him Zebra, but he didn't seem to mind it.

The child moved his arms with a freedom he had not felt in a long time.

The fact that his friend had worn rings at some point in his life was something that they forgot rather soon. Only from time to time they commented on it, and they laughed at the subject.

'Only the Beasts can believe that this stretches the arms!' Nazeh used to say, laughing at his own occurrence. And the truth was that Siro had always laughed at that too: 'Extending arms, nonsense! They are crazy! '

He had thought it stupid until he saw the arms of the Beast.

The creature could almost touch its ankles while standing. Siro stood with his mouth open when he saw the deformity caused by the weight of the iron rings. That must had taken years.

'Come in,' said the Beast. It waved one of his arms welcomingly. 'The door melts when you touch it. Go ahead.'

Siro stayed at the doorway. He could not take his eyes off that arm that pointed at him like a spear. It was a smooth pale arm, too long for any piece of clothing to hide.

'Fear not... I'm tied, I can't do anything to you, see?'

'What are you doing here?' Siro asked through the glowing door.

'I was looking for light and I fell into darkness, I'm afraid.' The Beast spoke with a thick, thirsty voice. 'Is not that also your case, Free Child?'

The Beast smiled at him from under the hood with black crooked teeth.

'Answer me!' The hunter shouted.

'Don't raise your voice. We don't want them to come, do we?'

Siro looked at both sides of the passage. He could not see anything in the darkness, but he worried that some funny eyes would shine in the darkness.

Thee quartz stone was still as black as ever.

'It's okay,' the Beast said, pulling him away from his thoughts. 'If you want me to be specific, we could say that I am here because of political discrepancies. I'm too open-minded for the likes of a certain lord whose name I will not mention.'

The hunter looked through the door with a scowl and the knife held high.

'I guess that's not specific either... We could say that it is a work issue,' the Beast kept talking evasiveness.

'You are an Elector,' Siro said.

'How did you...?'

'You called me Free Child.'

'You're wrong!' said the Beast. 'That was ages ago. I try to right my wrongs now.'

Sure, Siro thought.

The Beast buried in silence. It seemed that the hunter had reached a delicate topic. He examined the face of the creature, which hid behind thick hair, as gray as the hood it wore. Siro spotted a detail: the creature was wearing a piece of red cloth that crossed his chest. It was like a band with a white symbol painted in the middle, a four-legged hook. Only the Electors guild wore it.

'I'm coming in,' he announced, after all, he preferred to be in a well-lit place. 'If you touch me, I'll kill you.'

'You have my word.'

Siro touched the shining door timidly. When he put his finger up, it seemed that something inside the door was closing in to wrap it. The door, normally a colour between white and blue, turned purple around Siro's finger and the colour spread. The hand went through the liquid door, but the hunter panicked and withdrew it.

What is this thing? He wondered.

'It's strange at first, but you must not be afraid of it,' said the Beast.

Siro put his hand back in. He noticed how the door caressed his arm: it moved away; letting him in. He took a step forward and crossed the threshold. He closed his eyes when crossing and noticed the gelatinous touch of the purple door. Once inside, the light had changed. The room looked darker and dirtier. The white walls and the ceilings had black marks everywhere. They must had caught fire a long time ago. There were two yellow and blue circles, one on the right and the other on the left. From them bright lines that branched. They seemed to run inside the same wall, but the lines did not stop, they separated and re-joined; they grew or shrivelled; they went back and changed colours. There were symbols on the walls, letters that appeared and disappeared, an invisible hand wrote and erased again and again, spreading their brightness over the floor's broken glass.

'What is this place?' Siro asked without lowering his guard.

The Beast made a sinister smile under the hood. His face was hidden in the shadows, but Siro could see a recent scar around his neck, under the harness that kept him tied.

'It's a place forgotten by time and men, Free Child... Forgotten, but not dead! Can't you see how it breathes?' The Beast shook its head towards the wall.

Siro noticed the yellow circle on his left. It went and came like a slow beat. Thousands of tiny letters were hooked to the ramifications of the circle: they formed words, names... but he never learnt to read, less those signs. For him, all of that was little more than a strange painting that drew itself. A perfect painting, with straight lines and impeccable curves.

He took a cautious step toward the wall and reached out to

touch it ...

'Stop, Free Child!' Cried the Beast. Siro remained motionless. 'I understand you don't trust me, but if you play around too much with this wall you may end up here, just like me. We'll have to wait for someone else to come looking for us... How fortunate would that be?' it added, referring to the harnesses.

The Beast clenched its teeth. There was no noise down there, other than a slow breathing that seemed to emanate from the walls.

The Elector reached down and grabbed the bag it was carrying. It registered its six pockets and pulled out a string of hair bunches tied by strings of different colours. The Elector smelled them one by one, always keeping an eye on Siro.

'I was not wrong with you,' said the Beast, after putting them away, he smelled the air in his direction. 'You are a Free Child... You have never passed through my hands, and yet...' He lifted the last bunch of hair and threw it at him. 'Keep it.'

Siro grabbed him in the air. It was just a few brown hairs tied with a crimson ribbon.

'*What am I supposed to do with this?*' He dropped it to the floor, among the shattered glass.

'I understand your reluctance... But this belongs to you, in a way.'

'Shut up,' the hunter pointed the knife blade between its eyes.

For Siro, the Electors were the most horrible Beasts of all. They decided the fate of the children of Undershell when they were six years old and their decisions were never good. An Elector could turn you into another Beast and make you serve one of the guilds or clans of the city, or send you to a dark mine, or become a servant of some rich merchant... or keep you, if they wanted to. When he was little he had narrowly escaped the verdict. If they had waited another week to leave Undershell, he would also wear one of those Brands on his skin.

The Elector was tied and it seemed that it could not escape. He could kill him if he wanted, but there was something out there, he sensed it.

'Do you know how to get out?' He asked reluctantly.

'My memory is not that good when I'm tied,' the Beast replied.'

Siro hesitated a few seconds.

He passed among the broken glass that gleamed in the blue and yellow light of the walls. He lifted the knife to cut the harness around his neck. The Beast's eyes trembled as it watched the blade approach. And just at that moment they heard the scream:

'Siro! Siro!' Matildet's voice came from beyond the passage.

Then a roar made the walls tremble.

It's a Biter.

Instinctively, he went towards the door for the Daughter of the Light.

'Do not leave me here!' The Elector grabbed him by the cloak and made him fall.

Siro tried to get rid of the hand, but it went from his cloak to the hair. The Elector was dragging him towards him. Pieces of glass scratched his back. He looked for the knife, but it had fallen too far for him... but not for the Elector. The long arm of the Beast went over the head of the hunter to steal the weapon.

Siro grabbed a piece of glass from the floor and stuck it into the Elector's arm. The Beast released him with a broken scream. The hunter picked up the knife and ran out of the room. The curses of the Beast drowned as he plunged into the darkness.

'Matildet!' He yelled back and forth, but there was no answer.

He ran through the corridors without knowing at what moment he could crash or fall again. He was still aching from the last time.

Another roar and a great commotion filled the air. It was like a thousand glass goblets falling. He moved forth towards the rumble.

He saw something floating in the air. It was a giant rounded mass, but he could not distinguish it, only sense it was there. He was no longer in a passageway, but in a wider room.

A light appeared in the distance, accompanied by footsteps. As it approached, the walls of the room lit up, but not in the usual way. It seemed that the light formed strips that filtered through the walls and joined, like thick arteries, then branched into small veins in the form of lines and circles. Siro distinguished the mass hanging from the ceiling, in fact, they were two, a pair of giant spheres floating above his head.

'Siro!' The Daughter of the Light shouted.

From the back of the room, Matildet was running towards him. It was she who caused that glow, it seemed that the lights of the walls followed her wherever she went. Behind her the path went dark again, but not everything was dead. There was something else. A huge creature, with feline form, pursued her.

Matildet grabbed his hand on the run. The two went back into the corridors as they listened as the Biter trampled on pieces of glass and roared behind them. As they moved, the path lit up. They turned right and left along narrow paths, too fast for the hunter to know if he had been there already or not. Matildet's suit shone with a white light that reflected against the walls. The Daughter of the Light jumped through a hole in a wall and Siro followed her.

'No way out!' Siro warned her.

In front of them there was a wall that rose about four meters above their heads.

'Yes, there is!' Answered Matildet without stopping.

There was a passageway that started at the middle of the wall, although it was too high for them to climb. Just when Siro thought they were trapped, a flight of stairs made of light appeared before them, leading them up.

'Hurry!' Matildet was climbing the steps two at a time.

Siro followed her. He did not understand what they were, but thanked the Daughter of the Light for making them appear.

When he reached the top, he turned around and saw the Biter moving quickly in the shadows. The teeth were visible when it approached the stairs. The light illuminated them from below, making them look long as stakes. The animal opened its mouth and licked its fangs. A gush of saliva spattered the bright stairs as its legs propelled it toward the two preys.

Siro raised the knife, ready to receive the animal's charge, but it was not necessary. Matildet touched one of the yellow circles that had appeared on the wall and then a red one inside. The stairs of light disappeared just as the Biter was halfway up and plunged into the darkness.

Matildet made a victory cry.

'There's no meat on the menu today, huh, big cat?' She said, looking down and then at Siro. 'You look awful.'

He did not know what to tell her. She did not look great either. The girl's hair was tousled and full of sand, with the ends twisted all over, from her forehead, sweaty, to her neck. Her suit glowed with its own light, but it had soot stains all over.

'Don't worry. I do not think that thing can move its ass up here,' Matildet said. She took another look down. 'Did you come for me? In the dark?'

Siro nodded.

'Very nice of you,' she said with a relieved smile. 'But...'

The phrase was half-hearted. A noise coming from below put them on alert.

It's like something is chewing on steel, the hunter thought.

A huge claw stuck in the edge of the passage. Matildet shouted and grabbed Siro's arm. The Biter's head came out behind the claws as it struggled to finish climbing the wall. It scratched the ground with frenzy, pulling strips of that strange soft ground. The animal looked at them with bloodshot eyes and showed its viscous and sharp teeth.

This time, it was Siro who pulled Matildet towards the corridor. The Daughter of the Light made the subway come alive. Everywhere there were faint words etched inside the walls. The luminous lines ran alongside him until they reached a red circle, then stopped, like pruned branches.

'Wait, Siro!' Matildet stopped in front of one of those lines and followed his stroke with his finger. 'There's no way out here, we have to go back!'

They had changed path in a few crosses and it seemed that the Biter had lost track of them.

If we go back, it'll find us, the hunter told himself.

The Biter roar echoed throughout the subway, so loud that it looked like it was right there. Siro expected Matildet to have an answer, but the Daughter of the Light was shivering.

'It does not know where we are,' said Siro.

The hunter examined the two entries. He could see almost nothing beyond the room. He did not even know which way the Biter could appear. They had gone around so many times that he could not tell where they were anymore.

'This monster is very quiet, when it wants to...' Matildet muttered, not separating herself from Siro. 'How will we know where it is?'

Siro suddenly had an idea.

What's its name?

With all that situation going on, he had forgotten the word.

He pointed to the walls, the bright lines that ran through it, and then the gleaming suit of the Daughter of the Light. Then he gestured with his hands: first he joined them, then he pretended to open and close them, accompanying the movement with his eyes.

'Have you lost your mind?' She exclaimed. 'Do you think it's a good time to mime? What do you want? Wait... The lights? What's wrong? What do you want me to do?'

Siro repeated the gesture with his hands. Matildet rolled her eyes, she finally got it:

'Turn off?' She said in disbelief.

'Turn off!' He confirmed.

The hunter went to a corner of the room. He accumulated all the junk on the ground. Most of those things, he did not have the slightest idea what they were, but they were made of glass and quite sharp.

Once Siro had collected all the junk and the glass he could, he gave a couple of touches to the wall where the drawing was. He did not understand all those lines and curves, but he knew they it had to be a map of that subway.

'Memorize,' he commanded.

Then he went back to the corner. He lowered his pants and began to urinate on the improvised pile of glass.

'What the...?' The Daughter of the Light articulated, but she fell silent when Siro pointed to the wall again.

'Memorise!' The hunter exclaimed as he tapped his head with one hand and held his penis with the other.

Matildet concentrated on the drawing. The crystal structure vibrated. *Bum, bum.* The floor rumbled.

'Memorise?' Siro kept pointing to his head.

'I'm trying!' The Daughter of the Light rubbed her temples. 'I need more time!'

But we don't have it, the hunter thought.

The Biter came rushing towards them, he could hear it growling closer and closer. He had smelled the stench of urine and trotted like mad at his prey.

'Turn off!' Siro yelled.

She closed her eyes for a second and put her hand to her chest. The walls lost the bluish glow and the letters and words that had been written melted with the blackness. Siro took Matildet to the opposite corner where he had urinated. He grabbed her around the waist and held her close to him to make sure she didn't move. With the other hand he searched for her lips.

'Not with that hand... Gross!' she articulated, but the hunter covered her mouth anyway.

A gust of wind burst into the room. The hunter perceived the stink of the Biter's mouth. A stream of saliva escaped from those huge fangs and splashed his face. Matildet also received her dose, tried to scream, but could not.

The rumble of broken glass mingled with the pained cries of the animal. The Biter was ruthless with the remains of the pile of glass and junk. Sparks appeared every time the claws scratched a metal plate on the wall and projected, ephemerally, the shadow of the monster.

This time it was not necessary for Siro to pull the Daughter of the Light. Matildet led him through the same passage from which the Biter had entered.

The breaking glass noise was left behind little by little. The girl was a couple of steps ahead, but he could not see her. He could only hear the footsteps.

'Siro, I'm lost...' Matildet stopped and touched the hunter's shoulder to know that he was still by her side. 'There should be an exit to the outside... But I can't see it. Maybe the sand has covered it.'

'What is this place?' Asked Siro.

'I wish I knew...' she answered.

The Daughter of the Light shrieked.

'Oh, my... So scared... It's just sand... Sorry. I thought... Siro, look, sand is falling. The exit has to be up here!'

The hunter raised his hand and noticed a trickle of sand slipping between his fingers.

'I have to turn on the lights,' Matildet said. 'It's the only way.'

The Daughter of the Light touched one of the walls. A blue light burst from her hand and extended to the ceiling. The light followed once more the fine lines that someone had engraved inside the wall.

'It's around here!' Matildet shouted.

They arrived at a huge room. It was long and seemed to have circular doors extending further than their eyes could see. Siro realized that everywhere there were strange glass sculptures with rounded shapes. There were also rusted metal machines with car-like shapes, but not like any he had seen before.

'A hangar,' said the Daughter of the Light. The hunter did not know that word.

Matildet jumped between the rubble and the sculptures that had collapsed with time. Now her suit radiated a golden light and it was much easier to follow.

He followed her but could not help checking those strange figures. Looking at the way they were located, it seemed that rather than showing them, they were being stored. A chill went through him.

'This one does not open either! What's going on here?'

The Daughter of the Light placed the palm of her hand on the wall and a greenish light ran through it marking the hinges of the door. The light spread on the inside and branched until all the twigs accumulated at a point, where a crimson shine appeared.

'Siro, the knife, quick!' Demanded Matildet.

The hunter gave it to her without asking questions. The Daughter of the Light hacked the door with the blade and she tore off one of the black plates where the lights gathered together. A black and a white jet poured through the hole.

'Do not touch it,' said the Daughter of the Light, and shook her head in the direction of the two liquids.

Siro looked at the stain formed by the liquids. Tiny cubes sprouted from their surface, growing one among the other. Some were white and with rounded faces; the others were black, and were generally narrower and sharper.

'Never touch them without gloves!' Matildet warned him and showed him her hand. The suit covered her up to the tips of her fingers. 'And be careful, you are walking barefoot.'

'Burn?'

'You wish. They eat you.'

A noise came from the entrance. A metallic disk rolled towards Siro and Matildet, followed by the echo broken glass. Matildet stopped suddenly.

'Not now...' the Daughter of the Light muttered, her voice trembled.

Siro got his knife back and moved between the sculptures and the metal cars.

The Biter sniffed the ground, searching for the trail of its two prey. Siro saw it from afar. He hid behind a strange sculpture: it represented a man surrounded by cubes of emerald and amber colour. The hunter recognized it as a sculpture of Philippe Keerine. It seemed that his legs were melting, but instead of drops, cubes came out. At the foot of the statue tiny ivory figurines represented the Children of Light holding his legs, hugging or trying to climb.

The figure exploded suddenly. The Biter had seen him and shattered Keerine's sculpture with his teeth. The creature had its nose covered with glass and drops of blood.

The animal had a bright scar on one side, where hair did not grow anymore.

Siro backed away with the knife drawn.

The animal jumped with a roar and Siro rolled to one side. The claws brushed his hair, but did not hurt him. The hunter over the sculptures, going through the holes on the largest ones and running with all his strengths to prevent to stay away from the Biter. But the animal did not give up. While the hunter moved, agile, between sculptures and cars, the Teether crashed into everything.

The hunter changed direction as the Biter was about to get him. Instead, it tore off a piece of Siro's cloak, although in his ears, it sounded like if it had ripped off his own skin.

'Siro, I made it. It's opened!' He heard Matildet yell. 'Hurry up!'

The hunter went towards the Daughter of the Light, but the Biter got in his way by jumping over one of the metal cars. The animal slashed, but Siro deflected the blow with the blade of his knife. A rainbow of sparks jumped between the two contenders.

The Biter shrieked and licked its hurt claw. That gave Siro a moment to reach Matildet and leave the door behind.

There was light at the end of the corridor. It was only a dot, but as Matildet and Siro approached, it became a sandy, blue horizon.

Matildet's suit lost its shine with each step as they were leaving the subway. They were about to reach the outside when Siro saw the Biter lunging towards the Daughter of the Light.

The hunter threw himself at the animal.

The crash caused the Biter to bang its head against the wall and become disoriented. Siro got up and saw the animal blocking his way.

The Biter lurked him, jaw tensed and half open. The muscular legs were preparing to jump on him as its claws lengthened. The tongue, thin as a whip, swept over the double row of teeth that filled from side to side. Its eyes looked at Siro greedily.

The Biter pounced on him.

It hit Siro just as he jumped back. The blow was devastating, and both rolled on the ground. Engaged with each other, Siro manage to avoid the animal's jaws. The stinking breath of the Biter surrounded him... But he did not allow him to get any closer. The hunter found the white fur under its jaw and buried the knife there.

The Biter, which had remained on top of Siro, roared with the iron blade protruding from its mouth. The hunter did not release the weapon. His arms were about to explode, but at least he was achieving his goal, preventing the Biter from tearing his head off. Drop by drop, his chest got covered with blood pouring from the animal's chin. The Biter roared again and, with a spasmodic movement, nailed a paw to his arm. Dozens of blades pierced his skin, for a moment he thought he would die of sheer pain. The double row of teeth came closer and the putrid breath surrounded him like a bad omen, but the hunter was still holding his arms up, determined to face it. The knife separated the flesh of the animal. The skin and tendons softened. Siro gathered the remaining strength and gave a final tug just as the animal lifted its paw again. The lower jaw of the Biter remained hanging from the nose and, with a final gesture, the hunter pierced the animal's forehead and laid it on the ground.

'Siro! How...? Are you ok?' He heard Matildet running toward him.

He could hardly breathe. He was exhausted. Had the Biter still been alive, he would not have found the energy to move. He contemplated the mutilated face of the animal, the dropped jaw, the bloody shards piercing its snout and the dead green eyes that somehow still seemed hungry.

He felt a dull ache in his arm, like it were no longer part of him, as if that pain was being suffered by another person. Matildet gagged and began to throw sand and bile, just as it had happened to him before.

Am I that bad? He asked himself.

'Let me help you. We have to go...'

Siro leaned on Matildet to stand up. He put his good arm

around her shoulders. The white suit got bloodstained.

'Don't worry, everything will be fine.'

He looked over his shoulder to make sure the animal was dead. Now he seemed harmless, a spiteful monster that could not hurt a fly. He wanted to rest his eyes for a while, so he let himself be guided by the Daughter of the Light with his eyes closed.

Matildet took him out. The sun bathed his face. He felt the pure air in his lungs and the hot sand between his toes. That revived him a little and he opened his eyes again: desert and more desert, there was nothing else.

'Ok, Siro, take it easy,' said Matildet. The girl was carrying him, although it was clear that wouldn't last. 'Where now? Think. No rush, but think, please.'

The hunter looked towards the sun and then pointed to the east.

Matildet asked him from time to time how he was doing. He responded with monosyllables and scanned the horizon.

We are far away, thought Siro. But he was too exhausted to be afraid. He just wanted to rest.

The Daughter of the Light burst into tears.

'Don't die, Siro... Please. I can't stand it. No more dead...'

The hunter laughed.

'Hey, are you okay? What...?' The girl stopped to catch up her breath. 'What are you laughing at? You are badly injured and I... I do not know what to do... I can't heal you, I...'

'We're lucky,' he said and pointed to a bright spot on a nearby dune.

The Daughter of the Light looked towards the sand and saw the water tank shining under the sunlight.

Chapter 9: Light in the oasis

Sunlight dripped through the swarm of leaves and palm trees. The glow was like a slow beat insufflating life into the dense vegetation. The tall sycamores let the light through their leaves, illuminating the grey pandanus coiled around the larger trees. Huge flowers of shrill colours cut through the vegetation and shared space with vigorous tree trunks that the oasis had nurtured for generations. Vines covered the thickest branches and wilted them without mercy. At the same time, creatures of all sizes ran from one tree to another. They tried to see and not be seen. Squawks and screeches from birds and rodents broke the illusion of calmness.

Siro wobbled among the shadows of that green palace.
The pink camellias descended from the fig trees to the ground, where they merged with the wild vegetation. Siro removed those that crossed his path. The petals disappeared quickly among the leafy grass, where beetles and glowing colourful worms scampered under the gaze of predators. One of those worms slid over his bare foot.

He pushed the tall grass and the orange strelitzias with his legs.

He saw the image of Liduvin at that moment, remembered the movement of her skirt and the noise she made between the tallest stems. She was ahead going deeper and deeper into the vegetation, jumping over the roots of the fig trees and pushing away the enormous turquoise and pink leaves of the alcantares. But the vision of Liduvin came and went. She was not there, and he knew it.

Focus or you will get lost, he thought.

The moisture made him sweaty. His dripping forehead soaked his beard, while long, dirty hair clung to it like slugs. He clung to the trunks with his right arm and thus helped himself to walk. His left arm was no longer bleeding, a sparse scab had formed. Every time he moved it, he felt a wave of pain running from head to toe, as if the Biter was clawing at him again.

His eyes narrowed, and the sounds of the oasis invaded his

mind. The animals were lurking around: the legs and hooves shook the ground; the coats and scales brushed against the nature.

He leaned against a rock half covered by grey and knotty roots.
It was around here, he said to himself.

But *he* had not been around for a while. The oasis paths rose and fell; and from one day to the next, they vanished. Siro descended to an old dry stream while holding onto blackened branches.
Please, do not fall, was all he wished.
He was afraid of fainting if he fell on his left arm.
The floor was muddy and slippery, but that also indicated that he was getting closer. He saw some white flowers and recognized the ulmarias that hid among the highest grass. He pulled out a bush and kept moving.

A trail of drops of blood followed him. The wound had reopened and was bleeding again.

The alchemies were hidden behind a bush of yellowish leaves. Siro pushed aside the dragonflies that surrounded them and plucked the green leaves. He filled the canteen with the pieces of the two plants. He had seen Liduvin mixing ulmaria and alchemilla and administering them in the form of infusions or cataplasms. She always told him her properties: alchemilla for haemorrhages and stomachache, ulmaria for inflammation... And she repeated it to Siro until she was sure she would not forget it.

Now he had two, one down.

Siro found the plant in a pond that had formed below the base of a pandanus. The flower grew in the middle of the bushes, rising more than two feet above the water. The blue and triangular petals of the plant seemed to wait for him. He crouched down and put his feet inside the tiny pond. Tadpoles and frogs hid from the visitor.

Small doses. We want to make a medicine, not a poison, he could Liduvin's voice warning him.

It was said that before the Nightborn cursed them, the flowers of that plant had been white like the stars, but that was a long time ago. Now the blue colour indicated its toxicity. Siro carefully removed the stems. The mere touch could be poisonous. He fumbled with his fingernails until he unearthed a green and white shoot. He squeezed it and two drops of sap fell into the waterskin. He drank a few sips.

Disgusting, He thought.

When he could not take it anymore, he poured the remaining liquid over the wound. His belly was about to burst, an intense pain took hold of him and gradually made him lose consciousness.

'Liduvin…'

Siro opened his eyes a few hours later. The sun was at its zenith. The rays struck the leaves and stems of the plants and gave them a golden hue. His face was covered in mud. The leather canteen floated in the puddle. He was still in the oasis, under the roots of the pandanus. He was quite dizzy, but still in one piece, and the stomach ache was gone.

He wiped his face and sat up in the pond as best he could. His limbs had fallen asleep and it still took a while to get out from under the pandanus.

A small rodent got off one of the nearby branches and rummaged through the litter. The colours of the animal appeared among the leaves that fluttered as it passed. Siro followed the black and beige border he had painted on his back until it stopped. The hunter had not eaten for a long time, and now that the pain had subsided, his stomach was demanding his attention. He threw a piece of giant hazelnut from the oasis. The rodent approached, but immediately perceived the human smell. It turned around and fled with a pair of jumps.

The hunter did not have the strength to follow the small animal, but as he followed its jumps from branch to branch, he saw the black fruits of an acai that he overlooked at first. They were very mature and looked pretty yummy. He climbed a palm tree, feeling his arms and legs trembling. One by one, he took the ripest fruits and left the ones spoiled by the worms.

He was keeping an eye on everything around him. He watched his steps, careful not to crash the red beetles or the snakes that hid among the brambles. He could already hear the murmur of the waterfall when he saw something strange hanging from a tree. Quickly, he hid behind a fallen trunk covered with moss. He stuck his head out and looked at the branches: a white suit hung from it.

The clothes of the Daughter of the Light were full of dust and patches of dirt and traces of blood on the side.

They had seen the oasis on the horizon at dawn, after leaving the underground galleries. They had not stopped to sleep or eat. The had two waterskins and that was it. Siro had been tempted to leave the water tank, but how would he keep living at his cave then? The Sacred Valley was too far from all the oases he knew.

When dark, Siro had collapsed on the ground and the Daughter of the Light had leaned him against the tank. He had woken up with a wet taste on his lips. Matildet had leaned him against the tank and given him water from the waterskin, what little they had left.

'Do not fall asleep here, I beg you,' she had whispered in his ear. 'I'm afraid that the sand will eat us...'

They walked for hours in the dark. Each pulled one of the strings of the tank.

'Is that it? I can't believe it...' Matildet said in a pasty voice. 'It's huge... An oasis, you say? It looks like a jungle!'

As soon as they arrived, they had crossed the vegetation and had thrown themselves to drink water from the pond. Matildet had fallen asleep after the effort of walking all night. He could not afford that. He had to find the plants to heal his wound.

It's been a miracle we made it, he thought remembering the trip.

The hunter heard a splash.

The pond was behind a wall of bushes dotted with blue and green. It was under the shadow of a cliff a few meters high, through which a thin waterfall descended. Among the rocks, grew a single emaciated tree covered with tiny flowers. Below, the frogs swam among the water lilies. And in the middle of scene, a silhouette was moving towards the water.

Matildet was naked, with her back to the hunter. She removed the sand that tangled in her hair. Shoulders and thin arms moved by the effort. That disturbed Siro's imagination. He was dying to see more. The Daughter of the Light dived and the hunter took the opportunity to change his position.

If she sees me, I can forget about Teradam.

And yet, he did not walk away. Matildet stuck her head out from under the water and combed her hair back leaving her breasts in sight. Siro grabbed at the bushes.

Do it. You want it.

He felt the weight of all those years of loneliness. He wanted to grab the girl's hair and kiss her from the neck to the nipples. He wanted to hear the girl's moans.

No. Forget it.

The water slid down her body like the waterfall caressed the rock. The skin of the Daughter of the Light shone under the sun and the drops of water reflected the light making it even more sensual. Siro's senses sucked every moment of that vision: the beauty of Matildet, the murmur of water, the sounds of the oasis... Everything was part of the same captivating essence.

'Siro, is it you?' Matildet covered her breasts and sank into the water.

The hunter held his breath and slipped through the complicit vegetation. The Daughter of the Light scanned the trees, covering herself modestly. Siro's heart ran wild, leaping inside him in a wave of confused sensations.

He retreated into the shade and leafiness of the oasis. The rapture of desire he had felt was appeasing. The squawking of the birds clouded his mind, he felt tired, aching, his whole body crying out for him to rest.

The murmur of the waterfall had been lost among the trees. He looked back, where the Daughter of the Light was supposed to be and then he kept going.

Chapter 10: A Free Child, a Zebra and a Mongoose

'You have to give it a try... C'mon, it's not that hard! Repeat with me: *pond*, Matildet pronounced it slowly and moved her head toward the water to help the hunter. 'Your turn, Siro, say *pond*'.

The Daughter of the Light looked at him enthusiastically. The girl loved to make him practice with words.

The same game every day, Siro thought as he suppressed a yawn. He repeated the word *pond* just as she wanted.

Matildet left the bowl full of stew and gave him a timid applause.

'Come on, don't pull that face. You scare me', Matildet said.

Siro ignored her comment. He pointed to the trees that surrounded them and practised saying their names: pandanus, the one with the green and pointed leaves; strelitzia, with orange flowers; fig tree, the grey bark ...

'Good, good... Keep it up!' The Daughter of the Light was encouraged. She grabbed the flask she always carried in her backpack and put one of the coloured nuts in her mouth. 'Now, with the food'.

'Stew,' said Siro, and lifted the bowl to show the pieces of meat floating on the orange broth. 'Made of... uh... fat rat meat'.

"It's an indigenous capybara...' Replied Matildet.

The Daughter of the Light took another spoonful of stew to her lips.

'Eddo's roots?' Matildet examined one by one all the ingredients in the clay bowl. 'Yeah, I know, they are not very different from a potato, but to me it's just... Wow!', She exclaimed and brought her hand on her heart with a theatrical gesture. 'I love them, you know? I had only tried them once in my life when I was on holidays in... Well, who cares? The name would not mean anything to you either. It was a couple of years ago, when I was still dating Liam.'

'Fiancée?' Siro raised his eyes from the bowl.

'I wouldn't say that... We just dated for a while, until my father sticked his nose in... As always.'

'Do you mean... Philippe?' The young man looked at her expectantly. He had always wanted to know more about the Creator.

'What?' Matildet laughed at the occurrence. 'No, his name is Victor. Philippe? What makes you think that's his name? Are you talking about Philippe Keerine, the Discoverer?'

Siro shrugged his shoulders. Matildet smiled, something clicked in her mind.

'I think I´m beginning to get you, Siro. Tell me. What about you? Do you have family? Siblings?'

Siro shook his head.

'I'm an only child too. Cas always said... Whatever, the thing is that I have an exclusive father, unfortunately... His name is Victor Zalies, so now you know my last name: Zalies... Although sometimes I'd like to forget it'. She started a smile, although seeing the stone-cold expression of Siro erased it. 'Do not stare at me like that, it's... You see, because of him, my boyfriend took off. That's my father. He did not like him, and well, as always, he had to have it his way. He offered Liam an easy way out and he accepted... Yes, in a way that opened my eyes, but, I do not know... There are many ways of doing things, I do not know why he always has to choose the cruellest.'

'He's such an idiot. He should not have offered him freedom in exchange for giving up on me... Anybody would have accepted.' The Daughter of the Light covered her face with her hands. 'Where we lived, not everyone had it as easy as us and it pisses me off when my father takes advantage of that. He is like that, he insists and insists, he does not stop until he gets it his way. And then, he uses it as an excuse to give me a lesson... It was humiliating... He made me feel like shit. It's always been like this, always, even before mom died. I hate him!' Concluded Matildet.

'I did not know you could hate' Siro asked, completely puzzled.

'We hate like everyone else. Hand me that blanket, please.' Matildet pointed to one of the hunter's fur blankets and he handed it to her. 'Thank you, it is impossible to sleep head against rock... Maybe I shouldn't have said that. My father and I don't always see things the same. It could be worse.'

Siro listened carefully to those words. It was funny to think that Children of the Light did not get along well with each other. That possibility never crossed his mind. Liduvin would have loved talking to Matildet. She would have known what to do with that information.

The hunt used to keep Siro alert; he moved without making the slightest noise through wild vegetation of the oasis. He smeared himself with the mud and crushed the bark of the trees in his hands to disguise his smell. A wrong step and the animals would vanish long before he even come to see them. But that afternoon, the hunter was not focused. His head was elsewhere: he thought of Matildet.

When he closed his eyes, he still saw her submerge in the water, he remembered her naked body, her wet hair and the drops of water that slid down her tanned skin.

They had already spent three days in that oasis, three days in which he had not been able to avoid picturing her naked every time they spoke, or whenever she approached him and, that morning, while they were eating, it had been worse than ever. The urge to pounce on the Daughter of the Light was still there.

He tried to push away those thoughts with the hunt. It was a good way to get distracted, although that day was very hard. When he was little and lived in Merco, he did the same. When something troubled him, he went out with Nazeh to hunt insects.

His friend had a knack for it. He remembered that child well enough. He was slightly taller than him, dark-skinned and innocently smiling. They were thick as thieves. Although Nazeh had many brothers, some older and some younger, he always preferred going with Siro. They ran through the woods, played hide and seek among the trunks of the fig trees and chased the kiwi birds that were all over Merco, until the mother of Nazeh called him for dinner or until they both went to the centre of the village, where sometimes Liduvin told tales to the children of the village. They sat in a circle, next to the bonfire that Liduvin dyed in colours to have them all under her spell. That, however, did not happen that often. Only when the parents of Merco insisted a lot, she felt obliged to entertain the kids for a few hours, before sending them home. Most of the times the tales were exclusive for the little Siro, who waited impatiently for the night to come and the two of them to be together under the same tent.

He knew most of the stories she told by the bonfire, even though he realized she did not explain them exactly in the same way. For the rest of the children, the tales had another tone, they were more cheerful and simple, than when she explained them for him only.

Those nights in the centre of the village, Siro did not pay much attention to the stories, but to young Eliria.

For him, she was the prettiest girl in the village of Merco. Her hair was deep red, very dark. He liked the freckles scattered over her nose and cheeks and her green eyes hidden under the leafy fringe. He was a year older than him, half a head taller, missing a fang and damn beautiful... and him, well, he was just invisible to her, apparently.

He knew her since the caravan, after fleeing from Undershell and he had never had the guts to speak to her. She used to sit in the back of her mother's car, staring at the horizon silently. Only once in a while, she would entertain herself sharpening a stick with a silica knife, as if she were thinking about stabbing someone. Everything changed one day when Siro and Nazeh decided to go on a treasure hunt. They found her by chance while she was with another group of children. All of them carried sticks in their hands and pineapples tied to their belts.

'Look, the Free Child and the Zebra!' One of the children pointed at them with his finger and the whole group gathered around them.

'You two, what are you doing?' Rael told them. Siro knew him. The kid was two years older than him, and twice as fat. 'This is Mongoose territory! You can not enter!'

'We are going on a treasure hunt,' said Nazeh.

The gang of the Mongooses had positioned themselves so they would not escape. They had children in front and behind; up on the branches of the trees and hanging from vines.

Rael stepped forward and rested the stick he carried over his shoulder.

'Treasures, huh?' Said the fat boy, rubbing his chin.

'Yeah. Any problem?' Siro stood in front of Nazeh, a few inches from the leader of the Mongoose.

'None. It sounds fun', the kid admitted. 'Can we play?'

The mongoose children looked at them with happy faces. It seemed that everyone wanted to play that game.

'Hey, wait!' Eliria jumped from the branch of a fig tree. 'Weren't we going to crash the Fire Mongoose cabin?'

Siro looked at the girl from top to bottom. She had painted her face with the soot of a bonfire and her hair was pulled back in a tail, except for a flock that fell like a fringe. Her green eyes peered menacingly. She wore the clothes her mother had sewn on, two simple beige pieces that allowed her to run and climb the trees like the other kids.

'Who are the Fire Mongooses?' Nazeh asked, still hiding behind Siro.

'They are a group of very bad children who have a cabin on the other side of the river. They have copied our name!' Yelled a small boy carrying a stick almost as tall as he was.

'And they have just sticked *fire* to the name. What a bunch of losers.' Completed another who was sitting on a branch.

'I see, but, guys… finding treasures is more fun,' Nazeh exclaimed. 'We will…'

'*Ssshh!*' Siro raised a finger to his lips. 'Are you mad? Keep quiet.'

'C'mon, Siro, the more the merrier' said Nazeh. 'There is no need to fight with sticks if we can find glass.'

As soon as Nazeh said *glass*, a great uproar broke out. The children repeated the word *Glass, glass!* Some had released the sticks and were chatting among themselves. They discussed everything they could buy if they found even a small piece. Everyone remembered how valuable that material was back in Undershell. Some adults stated that if they found a glass mine, they would never have to go back to work.

'Sure, a mine of glass… and why not metal sheet one? Or even better, one of talking stone…' said Eliria, incredulous. 'What we have to do is go and kick the shit out the Fire Mongooses!' she added ass he lifted her club.

'No,' said Rael. 'Finding glass sounds better. And I am the leader of the Mongooses! We'll do as I say.'

'I also want to be the leader!' Said the little boy with the enormous club. 'You've been it for a long time, Rael. It's not fair.'

Siro grunted and the little kid shut up. He was tired of that waste of time. He didn't care about all those stupid people. He wanted to find a piece of glass to give to Liduvin, period. If the others came with him, he would have to share the bounty.'

Eliria banged a tree with her club and spat in front of Rael.

'You are the worst leader I've ever seen!' The girl shouted. 'In Undershell you would be deader than dead!'

'Like your father?' Rael snapped, as he sought the complicity of the other children.

There was a terrible silence. The girl winced in anger, her face went red until the freckles disappeared. She raised the club to strike the child, but Nazeh stepped in.

'Please don't! We can all play together! I'm sure he didn't mean it,' he said in a trembling voice. His arms were folded in front of his face fearing she would hit.

'I meant it,' said Rael, from behind. 'Your father is an idiot corpse. He is the king of idiots! Or rather, he was...' and he laughed like a pig.

'Get out of my way!' Eliria shouted at Nazeh and clenched her teeth.

But Nazeh didn't move. He continued with his arms raised. He did not want the girl's club to crack his head opened but neither wished that to Rael, no matter how stupid he was. In the end, Eliria got angry, threw the club to the ground and turned around. Siro took the opportunity to check her ass, which stood out under the pants-skirt she wore.

'*Asshole*', she said as she left.

The children made a circle around Nazeh and they asked him questions about where to start looking for *glass*, who had told him there was a treasure outside of Merco, and whether it was true the Nightborn were protecting it and other nonsense. After explaining that the best place to look was at the bottom of the valley —in the forest of hollow trees, past the blood rocks— Siro approached his friend and shook his head.

'Now they all know where we wanted to go... Happy?'

'No, I want to tell that girl too,' said Nazeh.

'Eliria? But why?'

'She's very pretty. I'd like her to come with us,' Nazeh replied, looking down and shaking his feet oddly.

'No way. That girl is nuts. I don't want her around with that club. And she's not that pretty,' Siro protested.

'Don't you think so?'

'Not at all,' Siro lied and turned his back on his friend. 'Come on, let's go.'

The boy started walking, but Nazeh insisted on fetching her. He pleaded a dozen times until he finally accepted. Nazeh was the best friend he had, if not the only one.

They found the girl perched on a mossy fig tree. She was curled up and seemed to sob. The two children approached quietly. They spent a long minute hiding behind some bushes until finally Siro elbowed his friend.

'Do something. We don't have all day.'

'Excuse me... huh... Eliria, right? We...' Nazeh's voice trembled.

The girl turned suddenly. Her ponytail was dishevelled and her red hair fell over her face. Her eyes shone like a wild animal.

'Leave me alone!' She snapped.

'We wanted to know ... do you want to come with us on a treasure hunt?' Nazeh said hesitatingly.

The girl jumped off the branch and rolled on the floor. She grabbed Nazeh and by the rings necklace his mother had made for him.

'What makes you think I want to go with you, Zebra?' said the girl.

'Well, you're all on your own,' said Siro. He squeezed Eliria's hand until she released Nazeh.

'Mind your business, Free Child!' She replied, raising her fist.

Although Siro was the shortest and youngest of the three, he would not budge.

'Stop behaving like a mad mongoose,' Siro said coldly. 'Rael and the rest of the fools are looking for our treasure and we are here wasting our time. We can't let them get away with it. The idea is ours and the treasure too. You can come with us and get your part or go with those idiots and keep the leftovers. It's your call.'

The girl was placid for a few seconds. Then she laughed.

'What now?' Siro asked her.

'Mad Mongoose, huh? I like it. I go with you, losers, but it's only to kick Rael's butt.'

Siro rolled his eyes and accepted. Nazeh, on the other hand, smiled from ear to ear.

They went through the forest of thin, black trees south of Merco and then turned toward The Thirsty, a dry scree where a river had once passed. They climbed up the vines that fell from a century-old oak tree and jumped between the brown cliffs on the top of the eastern hill. Soon, they reached the blood rocks and the hollow tree forest.

The forest was a strange place. Siro and Nazeh had only gone there once. Siro loved it, but to his friend it seemed a most sinister place. The trunks of the trees were just a carcass, sucked from the inside to the point that some could not stand up and broke with the gentlest touch. It was not uncommon to find more than two meters long bark sheets lying on the ground, just as it was not unusual to find a snake or rat somewhere in between. The few trees that stood were rising above the bark of their companions, which dyed the ground brown.

When they arrived, Eliria pointed out the Mongooses band, who were already prowling around raising pieces of bark to see if they could find a glass underneath.

'Man, I really want to punch Rael in the face!' The girl muttered.

The three children were lying under a piece of gigantic bark that had fallen to the ground long ago. The fragment was curved and large enough to fit even a couple of children below. More than a piece of tree, it looked like a tunnel.

'Please, let's skip the fight. If I wanted to see that, I would go with my brothers,' Nazeh explained.

'Whatever, Zebra,' Eliria said, at his left.

'Could you shut up, Mad Mongoose? What is wrong with you?' Siro snapped from the right. He was tired of her messing with his friend.

'I wasn't speaking to you.' The girl stuck out her tongue. 'My mother says you are Liduvin's fake son. And that it is her fault that we all had to leave Undershell.

'Your mother is dumb. Screw Undershell! We are better off here,' he said.

The two children looked at each other with hatred, but suddenly Eliria's eyes softened a little and her lip trembled, as if she were going to laugh but did not want to. Siro thought that perhaps she was ashamed to show her teeth because she was missing one.

'What's up?' Exclaimed Siro.

'Nothing... You're funny,' Eliria answered.

One of the boys of the Mongoose band came close to their hideout. He was a very odd child, wearing a red scarf on his head and the skeleton of a lizard hanging from his neck. Siro had seen him once in the town, his name was Merli. At that moment he licked a piece of bark, as if that helped him follow the trail of the treasure. Luckily, he had not seen them.

'You see that big tree?' Nazeh pointed.

'Which one? The one with the branches down instead of up?' Eliria asked, getting up a little.

'Yes, exactly! It's that tall tree,' Nazeh confirmed, glad to finally have their attention. A week ago, Siro and I came here and saw that the interior of that tree was empty...'

'...There is a hole in the ground, inside the stump,' Siro finished, his voice monotonous.

'And you think that there is glass inside?' She asked.

'Of course! We saw reflections inside the hole!' Nazeh replied but lowered his voice for fear of being discovered. 'We need to think how to get there'.

'Easy,' said Siro, and with a wave of his hand told them to follow him.

The boy's plan was to gather three pieces of bark large enough to be placed on them like shells. Once they had found them, they impregnated some lianas with resin to join them to the bark.

'We look like giant tortoises,' Nazeh said, amused.

'We look like idiots,' Eliria corrected him.

'You think the same about everyone,' Siro snapped, still hurt by what she said about Liduvin.

The discussion was over at that point. For lack of a better plan, the three crawled among the trunks and the broken bark of the fallen trees. It was easy to dodge Merli, who kept licking things randomly; but Rael stood at the top of the hill of oak and holm bark. From there, he gave orders to all the children so that they would not stop working. 'It's not so different from when we lived in Undershell,' thought Siro. Maybe Rael would be happier if he lived with the Beasts.

It was impossible to go over the surface and not be seen. The children picked up and threw pieces of wood non-stop. Some did it with real diligence, expecting to find a real treasure at any time. Others, on the other hand, were throwing pieces of bark or breaking entire sheets on the head of their friends just to have fun.

Siro instructed Eliria and Nazeh to follow him through a tunnel opened at the foot of the hill. They got rid of the improvised shells and entered through the opening. The interior smelled of mud and resin. It was dark, although you could see some light coming through the slits of the pile of logs.

'Go ahead,' said Siro.

'Are you afraid, Free Child?' Eliria scoffed.

'Not now, I beg you!' said Nazeh implored them. 'Eliria, do you mind if I go first?'

The girl looked indifferent. Nazeh passed by and she followed him. Siro got in the last one. He crawled like a snake through the bark. He was careful not to cut himself since some of the sheets had ended up in sharp shapes when splitting. He got a couple of scratches, but he was already used to that. Whenever he went out to play, the same thing happened. He used to always go ahead, in case snakes or rats appeared, he could kill them with the silica knife, but this time he had a plan and he needed to be the last one in.

'Is that it?' The girl asked, as she exited the tunnel.

'Yes, look, that's the hole we were talking about. Hey, Siro, what are you still doing in the tunnel?'

Siro came out with a piece of vine in his hand. He had tied it to a log he had found in the middle of the tunnel. The vine passed through a thick branch like a pulley. He sat down next to Eliria and gave it to her.

'Help me pull,' he asked.

The girl grabbed the vine with a malicious smile and between the two of them they pulled it once and again, until they could hear a creak. And suddenly, the pile of hollow logs and pieces of bark sank and became a wave. The Mongoose band screamed as they fled away. Rael was dragged by the tree tide to the blood rocks while he begged for help.

Eliria laughed at the top of her lungs and Siro smiled at her. She gave him an affectionate blow on the shoulder and the boy noticed that she was blushing.

'Siro, that was not ok. What if they hurt themselves?' Nazeh scolded, in the same tone his mother used.

'A mongoose less to worry about, so what?' He answered. Eliria laughed with his comment.

'You should think a little before acting,' Nazeh looked angry. 'Go fetch the vine. We need it to go down.'

While Nazeh tied the knot, Siro noticed that his own hand was on top of Eliria's. She had her hand on the ground, on a piece of grass that had entered the inside of the hollow trunk and he had two fingers on it. A soft, soft hand that reddened with touch. Siro looked at Eliria, but she looked away; either she didn't realize, or she didn't want to.

'Me first!' The girl snapped. Siro withdrew his hand at once.

'Are you sure?' Said Nazeh, his eyebrows rose almost touching his shaved head. 'Look, you have to go down while you're sliding with the rope. Hold it tight and try to keep your feet against the wall all the time. If it truly is a glass mine, you could cut yourself...'

'...The legs, I know. I'm not stupid, Zebra.'

You try to tell her everything to look more mature, but this girl is miles better than you, Nazeh,' Siro thought. There was something in the attitude of the girl that he liked. Maybe he could even get used to it.

'I can't see anything.' Eliria looked down the hole in the floor and tilted her head, worried. 'I can't go down like this. There could be worms. I can not stand the worms!'

'I do not know about glass, but worms you'll find for sure,' said Siro. A chill ran through the girl's spine and he laughed. 'Wait a minute.'

He took out a flame stone he always carried on him and grabbed a piece of small, parched bark.

'What is this? It smells familiar,' Nazeh exclaimed.

'Liduvin uses them to light the bonfire when she tells stories,' Siro told them, without losing focus on what he was doing. 'She calls them phosphorus stones, although people know them as flame stones'.

'Does she know that you take her things?' Eliria asked.

Siro didn't reply. Instead, he rubbed the stone against the bark a couple of times. The piece of wood caught fire with a blue flare.

'Not bad,' said the girl. She tried to be condescending, but the tone gave her away. He knew she was impressed.

'Look,' he said.

He grabbed the piece of bark at one end and threw it through the hole. As it descended, the walls of the tunnel glowed. When it reached the bottom of the hole, the flame suddenly went out and a trickle of white smoke rose through the hole.

'It's full of glass, Siro! The treasure is ours! We are rich!' Nazeh was jumping with emotion.

'Yes, but we have to be careful. I think there's water at the bottom,' he said.

'No worms, no problem. Water does not scare me,' said Eliria.

Siro was going to say something, but the girl went ahead down the hole. Se went in feet first against the wall, just as Nazeh had told her.

'Hey, you two! I just saw a piece of glass as big as your head, Free Child,' Eliria shouted when she had already dropped a meter and a half.

Nazeh laughed as he covered his mouth. Siro ignored his friend and pulled his head in the hole to see if she was speaking the truth.

She was. Eliria held a heavy and huge piece of glass with both hands. Many things could be done with it: recast it to make containers, jewellery, glasses, binoculars...'

How much should it be worth? In Undershell we would have taken a good price, but here in Merco... What is the value of things now? The boy asked himself.

In the village people didn't use money, but exchanged what they had. Sometimes it was quite chaotic, but people were afraid to go back to using the same system as in Undershell. Now that they had finally escaped, who would want to go back?

'Impressed, huh?' Eliria told him, while she was swinging down there. Your dummy face gives it away.'

'Careful with the worms...' said Siro, with malice.

'Worms? Where... where are they?' Eliria screamed and the rope moved violently.

'Eliria, stop!' Nazeh brought his hands to his face. 'You are going to break the rope!'

Siro was about to tell her to be quiet when he saw that the girl had a long, viscous earthworm crawling from her forehead to her reddish ponytail. The words stuck in his throat. 'Relax, there are no worms. You stand still, we'll get you out right away...' he wanted to say all these things, but how could he, if he himself had gone mute when he'd seen that monstrosity?

'You, Free Child! Are you getting me out of here now or what?' Exclaimed Eliria, who seemed not to have realized what was on top of her hair. 'I can't wait for you and the Zebra to finish kissing each other. I want out!'

'Yeah... We are on it, but be quiet, huh? Stay cool...' Siro replied. He could not take his eyes off the little animal that crawled, calmly, through the girl's hair.

'I'm cool, dumbass!' she replied. He rubbed a hand over her forehead and inadvertently pushed the worm a little away, which ravelled by the side of his head, just above the ear. 'Just pull the rope! Don't you want the glass?'

'Sure, yeah...' Siro answered.

'Hey, what are you doing, guys? -Nazeh approached at that moment to see what was going on down there. 'The rope is tight, there is no risk that... Oh, boy! What a piece of worm!'

Everything happened very quickly. Siro remembered that he had not been able to do anything. Eliria ran her hand over her head and the worm got tangled in her fingers. She screamed so loudly that the boy thought she was going to pass out. She moved, the rope tensed, brushed against some of the glass on the wall and there was a click before Eliria fell into the depths of the hole.

They heard water splashing and the children looked at each other not knowing what to do. Nazeh's face was distorted in fear. It seemed that he would never be able to close his mouth again. His eyes trembled, as he always did when he was about to cry. Siro shouted the girl's name, but she did not reply. Only the murmur of water came from the bottom of the hole.

'We have to go down!' Nazeh snapped, moving his hands and covering his mouth while. He was breathing in fits and starts.

'How?' He asked. The hole was too deep and the rope was cut in half.

'What if she drowned? What if he is dead? What do we do now?'

'She has not drowned, ok? Listen, you can hear the water flowing, right? It's a river! We just have to find the end.'

Siro rose to his feet and stomped out of the trunk on which they stood. Nazeh followed him.

'Where do we go? Eliria is down there! We can not abandon her!'

'Follow me!' replied to his friend.

It was hard to walk among the pieces of bark on the ground. His feet sank like if they were quicksand and there were treacherous splinters everywhere. Siro detested them. It took him hours to remove the stuck ones, but there was no room for hesitation. At the limit of the hollow trees forest, there was a cliff full of white stones. Seen from above, the arrangement of the rocks made it look like a spiral and that's why they called it the Snail Leap.

At the bottom of the pit there was a pond from which a stream meandered into the depths of the forest. Siro often asked Nazeh to follow its course, but his friend always came up with a good excuse: 'We do not know how long we will be' or 'What if it gets dark while we are out of the village?'.

So, they had decided to postpone that excursion until the days got longer. They had never gone down to the bottom of the pond. The Snail Leap rocks were slippery. One had to pay attention to every step, but Siro was in a hurry. If he was right, Eliria would have gone down there. If not... he didn't even dare to think about it.

'Siro, be careful!' Shouted Nazeh, who had been standing just on the edge of the leap. 'You can break a leg!'

But Siro wouldn't listen. He took light steps and jumped from one place to another, without hesitation.

One wrong step and I'm dead, thought the boy; but even that could not stop him. A part of him was having a blast. He felt alive, his heart was beating harder than ever... until he lost grip on one of the rocks. His foot failed him and he lost his balance. He fell with all his weight on a bent stone and noticed how his body slid towards the cliff. He grabbed the ledge just in time. His legs hung in the air. He tried to climb, but he couldn't.

Nazeh's hand caught him just on time when he could not take it anymore.

'Why don't you ever listen to me?' The boy scolded him, as soon as he had managed to raise his friend. 'If you run like that, you will kill yourself!'

'Your girlfriend is down there,' Siro replied.

'My what? No, I... What are you talking about?' he stammered. 'She is not...'

'Ok, Nazeh. Let's just hurry up' He said, as he saw his friend blush.

The two children kept descending, only this time slower. Siro checked for loose stones before committing to the next jump.

It's higher than I thought, He told himself when he saw the pond it is full extension. Sharp and white rocks he could not be seen from the top of Snail Leap were surfacing in the water.

'Eliria!' Shouted Nazeh. 'Where are you? Eliria!'

Only the echo of his own voice came as a reply.

'What can we do now?' He asked, as he looked around.

'You see all those holes in the stonewall?' Siro pointed to one of them from which a stream of water fell. The whole wall was full of them, but the one he pointed out was lower and wide enough for a small child to fit in. 'She must have gone out from there.'

'What if she's stuck?'

Nazeh grinded his gears with all his doubts. Siro opted to move closer to examine the hole, which was four meters above the pond, instead of listening to his friend's complains.

If she's up there, that's it..., feared Siro. He hoped it was not like that, though. He didn't want to face her mother.

A weak cry was coming from behind a porous rock formation. Little trees on top of the rocks, sneaking their roots through their cracks to the point that the rocks seemed to have tentacles. Eliria was crouching underneath them. She was sobbing and staring at the wound on her leg. When she saw Siro, the girl hastened to dry her tears. She had scratches all over her arms and her pony-tail was a mess of wet hair. She was soaked from head to toe and her dress was half torn, baring one of her shoulders.

'I've lost the glass...' she muttered, feeling the wound in her leg.

'I knew you would fail,' he replied. The girl gave him a killing glare.

Siro sat down next to her and looked at the wound. It was long and swollen, but it did not seem deep. It would heal. He had seen them worse.

'I've seen strange things in there,' Eliria said. It seemed like she came from another world. 'I've gone down a very strange tunnel. It was not rock, it was something soft, and it was full of lights and colours that followed me... And I heard voices, many voices that spoke at the same time... Maybe they were talking stones, but... I don't know... They seemed so real...'

'C'mon. Don't tell me a mad mongoose like you is afraid of a few lights' Siro said, although that was not funny either. And less if she had really heard voices.

'You're stupid,' she answered and punched him when he least expected it.

Eliria laughed and her tears disappeared. When Nazeh

arrived, he found Siro writhing on the floor, with his hands on his stomach and the girl grinning fiercely.

'The poor boy. He can't stand blood,' he heard her explain to his friend.

It took them almost an hour to climb up to the Snail Leap, and two more hours to return to the village of Merco. Eliria limped slightly and Siro and Nazeh took turns to help her walk. Whenever it was Nazeh's turn, he chatted with her about a lot of nonsense: she asked him what his favourite colour was —beige—, he told her the name of all the flowers they found, and about the many adventures he and Siro had lived in the forest —all of them exaggerated, ready to make Nazeh look like the bravest of the brave— and launched a flood of questions to learn more about her.

On the other hand, when it was time for Siro to carry her, the argument was endless: 'Hey, don't pull me like this, it hurts me,' said Eliria, 'Be careful, why do you have to go that fast?' She complained all the time and Siro either ignored her or messed with her. And whenever he called her a mad mongoose, she hit him in the ribs.

'I should have left you there,' Siro told her. The girl had her arm over his shoulders.

'And why didn't you?' She said. The girl's green eyes were staring at him with a strange shine, a different look as she used to.

'Hey, you two... I just saw a piece of glass as big as your head, Free Child' said Siro, doing an impression of the girl's voice.

Eliria chuckled. She did not want to admit that she had been amused, but he knew. Nazeh was ahead removing the branches that crossed them on their way.

He sure listens to us all the time, Siro thought. He lowered his voice and spoke into her ear:

'Why did you say that about Liduvin before? It's not her fault that we had to leave Undershell.'

'I do not know. My mother says so. She says it's her fault that my father stayed in there.'

'That's not true. It's the Beasts' fault. They did it,' replied Siro, angrily.

'If my mother says so then it's true. She knows everything.'

'Your mother is stupid. That's why he had a mad mongoose instead of a girl.'

She punched him again, but that time it was not so strong. Siro had the feeling that this was the girl's way of caressing.

It was already night time when they made it to Merco. The houses were lit up, with warm lights shining through their windows and reflecting over the river. The smell of dinners mixed with the smell of the jungle and the mud that penetrated everything. In the middle of the village, the Council House stood above the rest of half-built huts and stone houses. The House, which was nothing more than a tent made of skins and various fabrics, shone with different colors due to the inner candlelights. That meant that the adults were together.

Unfortunately, not all adults were up there. As soon as they set foot in the village, the welcome committee formed by Liduvin and Nazeh's and Eliria's mothers appeared.

'Oh, my little boy. What happened to you? You are all bruised.' Sailia, Nazeh's mother, brought her hands to her mouth.

'Mom, what are you doing here?' Nazeh asked, and hurriedly let go of Eliria.

'Rael's mother told us that you had gone play in the hollow trees forest,' she said. 'You know I don't fancy you going over there. There are snakes hidden under the bark!'

The mother hugged her son. Sailia was a plump woman, with dark skin like her children, and her hair pulled back in braids.

'Eliria, let's go home,' said Debra, the girl's mother.

Siro was always surprised when he saw them together. They were a perfect copy of each other. Looking at the mother, one could know what the daughter would look like in a few years, but he hoped that she would not have that sad look that always accompanied her.

'You should watch more closely what your child does,' Debra told Sailia, taking her daughter by the hand. 'Any day a misfortune will occur. This is goes also for you, Liduvin. Children do not grow on trees... Well, not for most of us at least.'

'Have a good night, Debra,' said Liduvin with a forced smile.

Mother and daughter took the path to their house. Siro heard Nazeh sigh. He looked for the last time at the girl's red hair and grimaced, not willing to admit that deep down he also wished she wouldn't leave.

Liduvin and Sailia chatted for a while. The two boys waited impatiently for the women to get tired of talking, although it seemed that would never happen. Finally, they pulled both of them up their skirts until they were able to separate them and each one went home. Liduvin did not ask where he had gone that afternoon. She only reminded him that there were dangers when the night fell that she preferred that he never had to meet,

'Come back sooner next time, little Siro,' she cared for him, but at the same time he let him do whatever he wanted. He was lucky to have her. He could not imagine having a mother as protective as Sailia, and much less as cold as Debra. It had been only a year since he had met Liduvin, but he had already considered her as his mother.

After that day, the three of them were always meeting to play. Eliria no longer returned with Rael and the Mongoose band, but preferred to go with them both. The first days, Nazeh did not stop looking at her and behaving like a fool, but eventually things calmed down. The kids devoted themselves to exploring every corner of the woods and the oasis that surrounded the village of Merco, from sunrise to sunset, but they never returned to the hollow trees forest or to the tunnel of lights and voices where Eliria had fallen.

Years later, Siro still remembered the day they had met, and how, in the following days, Eliria became part of his life, just as Nazeh had done before. He thought about her all the time when she was not around. He liked to play and mess with her. He would wait for the night to come and all the children to gather around the bonfire to see her while Liduvin told her stories.

Those nights, she also stared at him. Sometimes they looked at each other and quickly turned their eyes away, and other times, they grimaced at each other. No wonder they ended up kissing under the lilac palm trees in the garden of their house.

He often thought of Eliria and Nazeh. He had them in his mind, just as Liduvin. How could he not think of them, with the years he had spent alone in the desert? He missed them, he had cried for them more days than he could count. But the Night of Fire had changed everything.

Suddenly the hunter was no longer feeling well. He was distracted, the hunt no longer mattered. He was not hungry nor thirsty. He just felt empty. He curled up beside a tree covered in blue moss and looked at the strelitzias. The orange petals of the flowers swayed in the wind, as did the tall grass and the tree leaves. That place was not so different from the village of Merco. But that village was gone and so were his friends.

His breathing quickened and he felt a prick in his chest. He put a hand to his forehead and felt soaked.

What's wrong with me? Why am I like this? I know they are gone! I know! Why do you torture me? I do not... I've forgotten them! Enough, I do not want to think about them anymore...

Siro pulled his hair and hit right and left, but nothing calmed him.

Liduvin, I have to find you, I know you're in Teradam... I know you're there... We'll meet soon, I swear.

Chapter 11: Stop when I tell you to

Finally shaving his beard was one of the things Siro enjoyed the most when visiting the oasis. With the water up to his wrist, he removed his beard and rinsed the knife from hairs in the pond.

As he finished, he dove a couple of times and swam among the fish. After giving a few strokes among the pink water lilies, he felt that the pain easing on his arm and his whole body relaxing for the first time in days. He ripped the dirt from his hair and the sand that stuck on his body. He saw himself reflected in the water and wondered if Liduvin would recognize him. His face had changed a lot since he was a child, not only because of the years or the scars that crossed his eyebrow and cheek, but because of something subtler. His eyes had a different light, they had become cold as the dew on the dunes.

What will she think of me? He wondered. It had been a while since he assumed that the age of the bedtime stories was long gone. He was about to put on his pants when he saw, out of the corner of his eye, that the Daughter of the Light had already woken up. She was lying down, blankets on top, but her eyes were wide open, and she was staring at the hunter's naked body.

Pretend you haven't seen her, thought Siro.

He put on his pants as fast as he could, but suddenly, the image of Matildet nude crossed his mind.

Shit, not now! He prayed as he pulled up his pants.

What shall I do? He thought. His brain gave contradictory indications: go away, stay, look at her. He turned to see what she was doing and found her standing right next to him.

Matildet was there. Her hair was disarrayed from sleep and her eyes looked tired.

'You look younger,' she said, seeing his face shaved. 'I used to think you were almost thirty, but now I'd say you're twenty something... How old are you?'

'I do not know,' he replied dryly.

He turned around, but the girl grabbed him by the arm.

'Siro, wait, I need...' Matildet halted in mid-sentence and decided to change the subject. 'What you did for me the other day... in the desert... I... I appreciate it, really... If it hadn't been for you, that monster would have killed me'.

He was silent. He wanted to know where that was leading to.

'They hurt you because of me and I'm sorry...' she said and pointed to the injuries the Biter had made on his shoulder.

The Daughter of the Light ran her finger along the hunter's arm. While she was doing it, her mouth was half open with an incredulous gesture. Her finger stopped at the first of three scars that streaked his forearm.

'How did you get this?' Matildet asked, although they were not the only one she could see.

The hunter had three scars on his right forearm; two on the side, just at the beginning of the ribs and engraved in parallel; four in the legs, one of them turning around the calf; and finally, two vertical scars on the face, one on the left cheek, usually hidden under the beard, and another crossing his right eyebrow. Most of them, especially those of the arms and side, had been made by animals. Siro could not easily forget the first night he spent alone in the desert, when a pack of hyenas chased him.

'The desert is dangerous,' he said to Matildet. 'These three...' He pointed his forearm. 'Four years ago, a jackal... He tried to eat. Me asleep.'

The Daughter of the Light swallowed and looked away.

'What a wonderful awakening... What about these on your legs?'.

'Playing... Kid,' said Siro, shaking his head. 'No remember how...'

'Oh, so you had friends? Where did you play?'

'Oasis... Like this one'.

'Did they have a name?' Matildet insisted, excited.

'Eliria and Nazeh,' he answered, though he hoped he would not have to talk about them much longer.

'It must be nice to grow in a place like this. When I was little I was always at home. A whole mansion, yes, but always on my own. It would have been nice to have someone to hang out with.'

Matildet looked at the sky for a moment, remembering

something.

'When I told Liam that my friends were the dolls in my room, he did not believe it. He laughed at me...'

The girl grinned sadly and looked at the hunter's legs.

'Oh, wow. That scar below the knee. Oh, my... That's a burn, isn't it?'

'A trap,' said Siro, and with mimed and choppy phrases he implied that a snare had caught him, and he had been hanging over a hole full of stakes. 'The pull... *Zas*! Burn me.'

'Uh, yes, I see the rope marks,' Matildet grimaced. 'Who made the trap? Do you know?'

Siro shook his head. Sometimes hunters' traps were placed and fallen into oblivion. Other times they were stocks that the Beasts themselves had put to hunt people. He did not know if in his case it had been one or the other.

The girl was examining the hunter's torso and the dark lines that ran along his ribs. She avoided asking, it was obvious they were the deeds of wild animals. She caressed the new scars on his shoulder made by the Biter. Siro felt the warmth of her hand on his skin. He wanted to tell her to be careful, that they could reopen, but he could only think on one thing:

She has seen me naked.

'Does it bother you, me asking?' Said the Daughter of the Light, gently touching his wounded arm.

'No...' he murmured.

The Daughter of the Light stared at the hunter.

Why does she look at me like that? he wondered. *Oh, right, it's because of these two... The scars on the cheek and the eyebrow.*

'The first night I was alone' said Siro anticipating the question, but the Daughter of the Light did not want more explanations.

She ran her hand down his cheek and removed the wet hairs but did not release them. The girl approached him until their bodies were touching each other. Siro noticed Matildet's white suit against him.

'You do not look like Liam at all.' The girl's voice had filled with air and seemed to caress the words instead of saying them. 'And, yet, there is something in you that reminds me of him...'

She put her arms over his shoulders.

'Hold me,' she said. Siro wrapped his arms around her waist, felt a smile on his lips. She was smiling too.

'Why are we here, Siro?'

He had Matildet's lips inches from his.

She is a Daughter of the Light...

'We're both so unlucky,' she said, her eyes fixed on the man's lips. 'Many times, I think it would be wonderful to start over. Be born again and decide knowing what we do. We could choose better how we use our time, who we are with and not...'

The face of the Daughter of the Light withdrew. She was on her tiptoe, running her hands over his chest and descending until she wrapped her arms around his waist in a hug. She leaned against him seeking for consolation.

'I can't, Siro, I'm sorry... I don't know what got into me... I feel stupid... I have too many things in my head... I'm sorry'.

Matildet moved away, but before she could leave, Siro pulled her. She was so surprised that she did not react when the hunter pressed her against him, his hands on her ass. The faces of the two were so close that he almost did not dare to breathe. She took him by the cheeks and stroked him with her thumbs.

'I want you to stop when I tell you,' the girl said in a broken voice and kissed him.

The tongues touched inside the Mouths. A wave of heat ran through him. What was that? How could it be so different from the kiss that had given to Eliria when they were little? Was this how the Daughters of the Light kissed?

Matildet was rubbing against him without any regard. She pressed her breasts against the his chest and their parts brushed fleetingly through her clothes. She grabbed him by the hair at the back of his head and bit his lower lip before playing with his tongue again. Siro noticed how little by little he lost control. He stuck his fingers into her buttocks and the girl let out a moaning of pure excitement. 'All right, enough, enough!' Said the Daughter of the Light as he kissed her neck, unable to stop. 'Stop, please!'

Matildet pushed Siro and he stopped, suddenly confused.

'I'm sorry, but it's not a good time,' she said as she fled. 'I'm going for a walk...'

The Daughter of the Light shot through the vegetation of the oasis and Siro stayed there, as lonely, and hot as he had never been in his life. And, not knowing what to do, the hunter dove into the pond again to remove all the excitement that was on him.

I screwed up, he thought and sank underwater.

When the Daughter of the Light returned, the hunter had lit a fire and cooked a couple of fish he had caught in the pond. Matildet sat on the other side, a little farther from where she used to.

'It looks tasty,' she said, not daring to stare at him yet. 'Every day I like your food more. I think I could get used to it. Forgive me for not helping you, cooking is not my strong point... You should teach me to light a fire. I would like that. I find it very interesting how you do that with the stones... Yes, it's very...'

Matildet chatted for a long time. She jumped from one topic to another, with no coherence. Siro turned the sticks, so the fish would brown on both sides with the voice of the girl in the background.

'What do you want to do...?'

'Pardon? What do you think I want? No! Nothing!' Matildet blushed. 'I'm fine like that! We do not need to do anything! We can just be here and talk... and...'

'...with people,' Siro finished, as he served the grilled fish. 'What to do... with people? When you find'.

The Daughter of the Light went from nervous to serious in the blink of an eye, like if she had forgotten about it but, after all, that was the reason why they were together. She expected him to help her find other people, if there were any.

'I want to give them a better life than the one you've known,' she said solemnly. 'I still do not know how to do it. I want to take them with me to Teradam, just like you.'

Siro nodded but at the same time thought there was something that did not feel right. Why after so many years of seclusion would the Children of the Light want the Tear-City to be filled with humans?

'Tomorrow morning, we leave,' said Siro.

Matildet smiled when she heard it.

That afternoon they had to prepare, so after filling the tank and the few waterskins that had survived the desert storm, they went into the jungle for provisions.

'An acai, huh?' Said Matildet. She had taken one of the purple fruits that Siro had collected the day before. 'You know what? I had never tried it before... and what is this?' She pointed to a flower with three-colored petals, hoping that Siro would know its name.

After the days they had spent together, the hunter had become accustomed to the endless questions of the Daughter of the Light. While they walked through the corners of the jungle, she was interested in everything they found: sometimes they were turquoise leaves, sometimes, bushes of twisted trunks, bearded lizards or even scarlet dragonflies that flew swiftly close to the ground. And each new discovery was accompanied by a shout or a string of comments that Siro almost never understood.

She insisted that he had to tell her, one by one, the names of everything they gathered: giant datils, white and yellow bananas, ground coconuts, bark chameleons... and if he did not pronounce it correctly, he would repeat it. In doing so, Siro realized that words flowed more and more easily

The Daughter of the Light kept asking her questions about everything around them in the oasis but he did not do anything but check her ass, her slender waist or her round breasts, tight under the white fabric of her clothes. He wondered what she thought of him. He heard a commotion among the bushes and motioned Matildet to shut up. She reacted immediately.

'What is it?' Muttered the Daughter of the Light after a long minute of silence.

The hunter shook his head, he thought he had seen some heavy mammal among the trees, but it had vanished from his sight.

'Let's go back,' he said.

They ate with ease. They both knew that a hard day was waiting. Matildet struggled to eat everything he cooked for her. In a few days she had got used to eating all kinds of reptiles, to get them off the sticks as the hunter did and had even learned to peel the rock beetles, a sort of gray insects the size of a fist and with hard skin, but easy to remove. Even so, there was a detail that Siro never missed to notice: every night, Matildet opened the flask she kept safe in her backpack and had one of the colored nuts before getting under the blankets.

That night, after Matildet fell asleep, Siro stared at the backpack, where she kept the nuts.

He got up, careful not to make a sound, and grabbed it. Quietly, he held the flask near the embers.

What will they taste like? He wondered, checking the nuts inside. He removed the cap from the flask and took out a smooth walnut, or that's what it looked like to him. It was green and red, but the ones inside had other colors: blue and white, black and yellow; even three colors together. He imagined each of them having a different flavor. They had no smell.

If I eat one, she won't notice.

He raised his hand and opened his mouth, but just then he realised it would not be right to steal from a Daughter of the Light. She would not do that to him, at least that was what Liduvin always said: the Children of the Light are good by nature.

Reluctantly, he returned the nut to the inside of the flask and put everything in the bag without Matildet waking up. He murmured the prayer that Liduvin had taught him when he was little, and that he always repeated to himself: 'To you, who have been born of destruction and hatred, I give you this world. Forgive us and live.' And when he finished, he got under the blankets and fell asleep with the image of the mane of the Daughter of the Light.

The journey through the desert was hard, but not as hard as the previous time. Matildet volunteered to help Siro drag the tank and he thanked her: it was not the same to drag the tank full as dragging it empty. They walked for three days. They covered as much distance as they could when the sun was low and camped at dusk, to avoid running into the Nightborn. Siro always left a lit torch near the awning so they would not get close. He knew it was no guarantee. A strong wind would have sufficed to extinguish it, for that reason, every time he saw the flame tremble, he would hold the necklace with the quartz stone. Luckily, the Nightborn did not show up and the journey passed placidly.

Matildet talked a lot and urged Siro to do the same. Every now and then, she complained about her father, how he always managed to complicate her life.

'He always told me what to do... And look at me now!' Exclaimed the Daughter of the Light as she raised her arms and showed her bright smile. 'Living adventures in the desert! Who takes the calls now, uh, dad?'

Her speech seemed endless. Sometimes she talked to him about what she would like to eat, sometimes dishes Siro already cooked, and sometimes recipes he had never heard of; she would tell him at least twenty times a day how annoying the sand was... and how happy she was to have left Teradam.

'I'd love to think that in the end, it was a right choice,' she said. 'I have a good feeling, Siro. You and I are about to make history.' Those were three days that he would remember as marvelous, despite the heat and the hardness of the journey. After so much time alone, he thought he had forgotten how it was to have someone next to him. A part of him had become used to it, while the other enjoyed like a madman being in the presence of someone else, not just his own shadow, in that endless desert. Everything was fine until she realized that they had returned to the cave.

Then, everything changed.

Chapter 12: What do you want?

'Why have you done it?' Matildet asked.

The Daughter of the Light had not spoken to Siro for hours. Since they reached the cave, the conversations had been gone. The girl's smile had been erased and now there was only a gesture of regret. She looked at the horizon, towards the sunset. The crests of the dunes had shed to a bright orange, like melted caramel. The night would fall soon on the Sacred Valley.

'You get me to the people and I let you into Teradam. That was the deal, wasn't it?' She said. 'At least I thought it was. But here we are. At the cave.'

'Why now?' Siro asked, he needed to know. Why after so many years of imprisonment, the Children of the Light wanted to make peace with humans? 'It's too late. Why now? Nobody left.'

'My ass there's nobody left! You hear me? Just use your head for a change! How can you think we are the only ones? People survived! There has to be someone in this shitty desert and I will not give up until I find them, do you understand? I can't go back empty-handed!'

'Why not?' Siro was more and more certain that she was hiding something.

'It was not easy to get out of there!' The Daughter of the Light pointed towards the mountains.

Teradam rose somewhere behind the sandy peaks that surrounded the Sacred Valley. From where they were, at the threshold of Siro's cave, they could not see the huge tower that jutted out from the centre of the city, but the Great Light would soon appear above the mountains.

He had not seen it in days, since they had left for the oasis and he needed to see it. That absolute whiteness comforted him. Every time he looked at it, he thought that there, somewhere, Liduvin was waiting for him.

'Maybe you can afford to come and go from the oasis to the

cave as many times as you want,' Matildet reproached him. 'But not me! See this? You see it?'

The girl took out the flask with the coloured nuts from the backpack and shook it in front of the hunter's nose.

'What do you think they are, huh?' She said loudly. 'Do you think they are candies? Are you that stupid?'

Her eyes reddened little by little, and each time he shook the container, her chin moved with more uneasiness.

'This keeps me alive, Siro! And there's no more! Just the flask and that's it. I'd better be back inside before they're over!'

Matildet crouched on the sand and grabbed her legs. She cried. Siro looked at the floor, suddenly feeling bad. Could the little mischief he had been about to do the other night have cost her life?'

I almost ate one, he recalled, and was glad he had not.

'You obviously do not want to help me', Matildet murmured. 'You only care about yourself and whoever is waiting for you inside! Who is she, Siro? Tell me!'

'Liduvin is my business,' he shouted. He was tired of all that show.

'Oh yeah? Liduvin, right?' She repeated, the tears stopped for a moment and she burst in a sad laugh.

Siro grabbed her by the chin. She looked at him, surprised by the nature of the move, but did nothing.

'Is she in or not?'

'I know everyone in there... And there is no one called Liduvin' Matildet said. Only a trickle of voice came out.

The Daughter of the Light cried again, and Siro let go of her face.

'It's over,' he said. He turned around and went back to the cave. Matildet sat on the dunes, but now he did not care what happened to her.

He entered through the crooked gap the cave had for an entrance and found it full of junk, just as he had left it. He took off his cloak, threw it at the piece of tree trunk that he used as a hanger but fell to the ground. He glanced at the twigs-made cages that had taken him so long to build, grabbed his double-edged spear and broke them to pieces.

Worthless, he thought.

He dropped one of the glass jars he had found in the Mirror

Rocks. The glass shattered and the green spices within spread over the stone and the sand.

Yelling, he went to the shelf where he kept the wise stone and threw. A couple of them bounced off the water tank and gone missing through one of the many slits in the cave.

You promised me, Liduvin. You told me you would wait for me in Teradam!

How could he have fooled himself all this time? It was impossible that Liduvin had made it, on her own, to Teradam. How would she have crossed the desert? It was too dangerous to venture into it. He himself had needed years to find the Sacred Valley, years! And he already believed that he would not succeed when he finally saw the Great Light. But now it did not matter. Everything had been in vain. She had not made it, period. The Beasts, the Nightborn, the animals of the desert... it was impossible that she had overcome all those obstacles. She was dead, now he saw it clearly. The body of Liduvin must had been rotting for years under the dunes.

I must get out of here; I have to leave...

Outside, Matildet was still sitting. She had stopped crying, but her cheeks were still red.

Don't look at me, Siro wished when he saw her raise her eyes. *Do not do it, I do not want to see you anymore.*

'Siro, where are you going?' he heard her ask. He kept walking, but Matildet got up and grabbed him by the shoulder. 'I did not want to lie to you. I was hoping I could help you.'

He got rid of her hand, but she wasn't planning on giving up.

'I want you to come to Teradam anyway. It doesn't matter if she is there or not. I'm sorry for what just happened. It's all this stress... I can't barely think. Help me look for the others, please, and if we fail, it does not matter... I'll let you in. But we must try! There are too many things at stake.'

'No,' he said and turned his back on her. 'Deal is over.'

'What do you want, huh?' He heard the girl yell at him from the bottom of the hill.

It's the last time.

He knew that there was no point in seeing the Great Light if there was no hope of seeing Liduvin too. He sat on the top of the mountain. His feet hung from the edge of a small precipice, but he did not care. The wind dragged the tiny sand whirls towards the valley and the tower of Teradam.

The Great Light did not wait. The tower lit up little by little and everything was filled with white. Siro raised his hand to cover his eyes, but it was inevitable to go blind for a few seconds. A mixture of sand and mist rose to the sky. The two together formed a yellow spiralling cloud that filled the valley. Siro was looking to the narrow path drawn on the rocks. He had known it for a long time, but he had never dared to take it all the way down at night. The Light was so intense that it did not let him see anything, and the so-called path was little more than a narrow line with cliffs on either side. The smallest mistake, and he'd end up cracking his skull open.

I'm going to enter Teradam, He said to himself. *I don't care about the Children of the Light! If Liduvin is not there, I want to see it with my own eyes.*

They would open the doors of Teradam, or else he'd find a way in. The tower had no access during the day, but at night? What if it was when the Children of the Light came out?

He jumped up and started off. Teradam's light was diffused, veiled by the sand cloud. It was hard to see where he put his feet. It was like falling into a murky lake, full of dust instead of water. After a while, the ground lost its incline and he assumed that he had reached the bottom of the Valley. The wind now scratched him. Every time it blew, he felt it stinging his face. He wrapped in his cloak and went on. His eyes burned, he could only open them from time to time. The Light became increasingly warm. Little sweat drops formed on his forehead. Then he noticed something that grazed his arm. For a moment, it felt like someone else's hand.

It's just the sand, he told himself.

He kept on, although it was getting harder by the minute. Somehow the light was growing thick, suffocating him. He noticed again that someone was close to him and drew his knife.

He turned around and brandished the weapon against whoever was there, but there was no one. He brought his hand to his face and realized that he saw it perfectly, just like his feet, and his whole body. His eyes weren't itchy, though he had them wide open. He was surrounded by white. There was someone running, he could not see it well, but he could see the shadow he was casting, infinite, because of the Teradam's Great Light.

'Nazeh!' He shouted, although he could barely believe his eyes.

The boy ran past him and Siro could not help but observe the dark, rounded features of his face. He had not seen it coming. And suddenly, another child appeared. No, not just a child, it was Eliria. He recognized her reddish hair. She moved like blur. Siro could see her as the infinite white It was gradually deforming and filling with flames. He ran, because he knew what it was. He followed the children while he smelled the smoke behind him. Palm leaves fell from the sky, leaves burning. The trunks fell on his way. The screams of animals mixed with those of Merco's people.

What do I do here? What is this nightmare?

Now he was not running through the desert, but in the middle of a jungle. He ran away like his friends did, while thousands of tiny animals fled between their legs. Everyone wanted to escape from the fire and the Beasts. Siro followed the two children closely. He pushed aside the leaves and vineyards, and when he did, they melted, they were nothing but sand. He saw them approaching a crossroad and swallowed. He recognized that place.

'Don't go right!' He shouted to Eliria and Nazeh, but they did not listen. They turned left. He heard their cries resounding in the jungle. 'Don't go! Come with me!'

Siro bumped into something. The jungle melted, the trees crumbled turned into dust, and the ground and everything else rose up and was blown away by the wind. It was hot, very hot, but he could not move from the ground.

'Very good, little Siro,' he heard a voice saying.

'Liduvin!' He cried, ignoring where his steps had let him to.

'I'm proud of you, little one.' He heard the voice again. It was her, he had no doubt. 'See you soon…'

After so many years, he was listening to the voice of Liduvin. He was looking around, trying to find her, but it was hard to distinguish anything in that blurry mess. He could only see his own shadow casted long and thin behind him.

Teradam is in the opposite direction, he said to himself, and headed for it. But as he went, his eyes ached more and more. A tear slipped down his face, but when he touched, he saw it was blood. He closed his eyes and stopped walking. Although he was dying to reach the City-Tear, he knew he would not get it. The Children of the Light would use their tricks to blind him before he got even close.

'Liduvin!' He shouted towards the Great Light. 'I'll see you later. I know how to get in! Matildet will help me! We have a deal!'

Indeed, they had it. Now he saw it clearly. Maybe Matildet did not know every living-form inside Teradam, or maybe... what if Liduvin had spent all those years hidden from the Children of the Light?' He did not know. The only thing he was sure of was that he had heard the woman's voice. That had been real. The jungle, Nazeh and Eliria were not, they were all memories of the Night of Fire, he was certain, but the voice...

Siro took a long time to climb the mountains that closed the Sacred Valley. He felt a chill as he escaped from the hot sand cloud, but at the same time he felt relieved being able to open his eyes. His eyesight was alright, nothing had happened to him or at least he thought so.

He burst out laughing and felt strange. He went down the slope with a smile on his lips. They had to find the other people no matter what. The desert was huge, but there were more oases and remains of ancient camps everywhere. It was not impossible for someone to live there. Then he remembered the Elector, the Beast he had abandoned in that strange underground.

Those monsters are always looking for people to brand them, Siro told himself. 'If he searches, it's because there must be someone left! He concluded, and he felt stupid for not having thought of it before. He could have asked the Beast, but by now, it would already be dead. If neither the Biter nor the Nightborn had killed him, surely hunger would have done it.

That Beast makes no difference, he told himself. *I can do it, I can find someone with no help. I will do my part.*

He quickened his pace to get to the cave as soon as possible. He wanted to see Matildet. He would tell her that he had heard Liduvin in the Sacred Valley, that he was wrong, and above all, that he would help her, regardless of the cost.

As he approached the cave, he heard a clang of metal. He approached it prudently, knife in hand. He entered through the gap and saw the Daughter of the Light. She had the double spear in her hands and she stuck it into the water tank again and again. Siro sneaked in to see the disaster. The water tank had holes everywhere, but there was no water on the floor. Next to Matildet, there were half a dozen full waterskins. The girl noticed the hunter's presence and turned around. She pointed at him with his own spear.

'The deal does not end until I say so,' Matildet eyes sparkled with rancour. 'Take me to the oasis.'

Chapter 13: The Beasts

The journey across the desert happened with no incidents. No storms, no dangerous animals. Just three calm and quiet days. Very quiet.

Matildet had crossed the line and now the hunter couldn't stand her. He would find people, whoever, someone, even if he had to track the whole desert, but he would not trust that innocent-looking blond girl again. The only thing that had kept him from strangling her that night was the certainty that Liduvin was waiting for him behind Teradam's gates. He had the picture of the leaky water tank burnt in his mind.

Maybe she wanted to fix the whole situation, but he didn't give a shit. He would do his part and so be it. Pity her, if she ever thought on betraying him again.

Once at the oasis, in a much shorter span of time than the previous journey, they went straight to the clearing next to the waterfall. Siro wanted to take off the sweat and drink some fresh water, but when he got there, his whole body froze.

There was someone at the oasis.

Beside the pond, there were the remains of a bonfire. There were traces everywhere, some of boots, others of bare feet: one, two... Siro counted to three different traces. Hanging from one end of the stick was the skull of a boar. One could still see the flesh of the gums inside the jaw of the animal, the rest was peeled to the bone. He had found a leather bag, with one of the animal's eyes inside.

Beasts love to eat them, he thought.

He thought that Matildet would understand that they had to leave, but she had refused outright. He had tried to make her realize that they were not people, but she was damn stubborn. Siro was worried. The more she complained and argued, the more noise they were going to make. If someone was listening hidden in the vegetation, they could be in big trouble, but she was getting more and more excited, desperate to find the other inhabitants of the outer world. She told him he did not have to follow her, only wait for her, if he wanted to. She thanked her for everything he had done for her and apologized —he supposed for ruining his water tank— but that did not matter to Siro. The danger was imminent.

She does not know Beasts, he thought.

'I promise I'll be back,' she said at last. 'We have a deal.'

The Daughter of the Light stood on tiptoe and kissed his cheek. Siro restrained the instinct to press her against himself, as he had done a few days earlier in that same place. Matildet moved away from him with a light step.

Don't go... stay! Thought Siro.

The girl disappeared into the bluish bushes following the footprints trail. When he lost sight of her, he realized that he was back on his own.

She will not find the trace, he told himself as he glanced at the footprints in the mud. *She will get tired soon and will come back here. Probably the Beasts are already gone. The boar seems to have been here for a few days and these monsters never camp for too long.*

Years ago, Siro had found an abandoned camp in the desert on the top of a high plateau. He did not remember exactly where he was —perhaps to the north, near the ravines— but he kept a vivid memory of what he had found. The camp was little more than five tents of fine canvas that fluttered in the wind. There were tools thrown on the ground, a wrecked wood car, trampled fruit and a trail of blood that carried to the remains of a bonfire. There were five bodies tied to the ground, each with an iron ring around his neck. They were arranged so that they formed a circle with their heads in the direction of the fire. The bodies were naked, and their Brands had been crossed out. The skulls were scorched, the bones protruding from the slimy flesh that had melted from the fire. The stench of oil, burned flesh, and blood made him throw up. He must had been eleven or twelve years old when he made that discovery, he was not sure, but that was not what struck him the most. In one of the tents there was a woman still alive. She was sitting in a corner, her clothes stained with blood. Her eyes had been removed and she was murmuring something he could not understand. The woman had a silica knife in her fist. Every now and then, she stabbed herself in the cheek, chest, stomach... but she did not die. She was bleeding and sobbing, but that was all. If he had noticed that Siro was looking at her, she pretended not to, or simply did not care. The boy didn't remain to see the end of it. He took the little food left in the wooden boxes beside the store and left the plateau, with woman's sobs and the sound of the knife against the flesh in his ears.

That's the Beasts' way, he reminded himself.

And now Matildet had decided to go find them.

What could he do? Wait for her to fail and come back empty-handed? How long would that take? He spat on the ground. That stupid girl always had to get it her way. She'd regret it, he knew that. But if something had to happen to the Daughter of the Light, he hoped it would be after she opened Teradam's gates.

I hope the Beasts are gone, he wished.

Siro narrowed his eyes and repeated the prayer that Liduvin had taught him in a murmur. He opened them again and noticed two things that didn't fit. The first was that they had forgotten about the leather bag --the Beasts use to value the treasures they find-- and the second was that they had come back to the oasis much sooner than he anticipated. That was not part of the routine.

He knew it was not the first time that the Beasts visited that very same oasis. Siro had deduced how often they pilgrimaged by the traces they left: embers, tattered gourds, hyena skins ripped out and set to dry, and collections of knives of bone-made tools. Thanks to these signs, he had managed to avoid them for months, maybe years. He had never seen them, nor they him, because he was cautious and only returned to the oasis when he knew there was no danger of finding them.

He knew they came often, but he did not expect to run into them so soon. It was very weird. The first time he had gone to the oasis with Matildet, the Beasts had been gone for at least two weeks: he had known right away as he had seen those acais so ripe the day he chased the small rodent with the valance on his back. Those ripe fruits wouldn't go unnoticed by the Beasts; they would have eaten them. That meant that the last time they had come, the acais were still green. Siro knew that it took about two weeks to ripe, the same timespan the Beasts have been away.

But there was yet something he didn't quite understand. Siro had assumed that the Beasts had come back to the oasis in the when Matildet and himself were not there. He knew his routine well enough, and that was why it was so strange to him that they had returned later than usual.

While he was thinking all this, the hunter dug absentmindedly into the leather bag. Apart from the boar's eye, he found two small, pointed darts with red feathers on the end. Beside him was a greenish flask half full with thick liquid. He uncovered it and smelled an acidic scent, like rotten lemons.

Snake venom, he said to himself and sniffed again. *Desert yellow skin snake venom. This snake lives only east of here.*

Whoever they were, the Beasts came from far away. He touched something else inside the bag. It was smaller than the wild boar's eye. It was smooth and soft, and as soon as he pulled it out of the bag, he realized what it was.

He had one of Matildet's nuts in the palm of his hand.

As he held it, the ashen leaves and screams crossed his mind again. He could see the face of Eliria again, the fire reflected in the girl's round eyes, burning the village of Merco; the very same fire the Beasts started amid crazed howls. He felt again the fear of that distant night, too young to do anything, alone in the middle of the jungle. A spell of dizziness washed over him. Nausea rose from his stomach because he knew that the Beasts had come to get them. He had no doubt: the nut was covered with remains of the same muddy soil that was near the pond. The Daughter of the Light must had lost it and the Beasts found it.

The hunter ran down the same path Matildet had taken.

I must find her! He said as he pushed away the vines that crossed his path.

He heard a buzzing sound and threw himself into the bushes out of pure instinct. Two feathered darts got stuck to the ringed trunk of a pandanus. Someone was shooting at him with a blowgun. The hunter looked around, but the leaves and branches did not allow him to discern where the attack was coming from. He came out of the hiding place with a jump and two more darts crossed the air. Whoever shot him was hiding there and if he stayed still, it would not take long for him to hit his target.

Siro zigzagged between the fig trees. He could hear the buzzing of the darts flying by and see a blur of red feathers trying to reach him. He jumped and launched himself into a dry stream. The yellowish leaves at the riverbed cushioned the impact and flew when he landed on his feet.

The stream was sufficiently deep and narrow so that someone

looking from outside would not see who was in there, but Siro did not think that was enough. He followed the path of leaves, towards the depths of the oasis. He climbed the steep riverbed and stopped when he felt that his legs could not take him any further. He hid behind a sturdy tree and with its trunk split in two.

He had changed his route often while fleeing from the shooter, to try and guess where the darts came from: when he did not hear the buzzing behind him, it meant that his pursuer had no angle to shoot him. With that, it was enough for the hunter to imagine what path he would have taken to get to him.

It will appear right away, he thought, confidently.

But time went by and the hunter snorted with impatience.

Where is it? Come on… What are you waiting for?

Nothing. The oasis remained calm, only the rustle of the branches and the sound of some untimely frog hopping in the grass could be heard. His chaser either had vanished or had managed to mislead him, he did not know; but Siro could not waste all day to find out. Matildet was in danger. Judging by the footprints beside the bonfire, there must have been at least two more Beasts in the oasis.

If they have not come for me yet, it's because they're going for her, he realized.

He came out of his hiding place only to realize that there was a dart stuck in the tree bark.

A hoarse, metallic voice came from somewhere in the oasis. It was the voice of one of the Beasts.

'It's rare to see a man without a Brand these days…' it said, dragging an annoying echo between word and word. 'Who removed it, wildling?'

Siro unsheathed the knife. He could not see who was speaking to him, but he was on guard.

'I can't see how you are going to stop the darts with it…' said the voice. Siro had the feeling that it was laughing. 'Tell me your name, wildling. Those who remove Brands bother me… Wait… No, your smell… I smelled dirt and blood on you, but you're no slave… There's something about your smell… Who are you, wildling? What is your name?'

'Show yourself!' Siro snapped as he turned on himself. It seemed that the voice came from several directions at the same time. The Beast went quiet for a moment. The hunter didn't know what to do, whether to stay or run. If he was still alive, it was because the Beast had not wanted to kill him, but he had no guarantee it wouldn't change its mind.

'You think yourself so special, huh? A free man...' the voice continued. 'What a catch! If Adon knew...'

Siro took advantage of the fact that he was halfway through the sentence to sprint off, but the Beast's voice was chasing him.

'Where's the fire, wildling? Running won't help you... or your friend... Oh, what a joy. She's beautiful, isn't she?' The Beast swallowed loudly with the last phrase. 'Is she who I think?'

Siro did not care what the Beast said. He was not going to answer the questions.

'Your silence tells me more than your words. Oh, wildling, you are blessed! How did you manage to deceive a Daughter of the Light?'

The hunter had a bad feeling, as if he had already lived that situation. The Beasts had returned once more to take everything away from him.

'Wildling, is it me or your friend is really gorgeous? I can't stop thinking about her... You must feel the same, right?'

'Shut up and get out!'

'Oh, I'm afraid I can't, wildling. The vision of the Daughter of the Light has shocked me too!' He added, playfully. 'It turned me so much seeing her naked by the pond... Oh, boy...'

The provocations were making him mad. That monster had known about them since the first time they arrived at the pond and, instead of taking its chance, it had decided to wait, with the certainty they would be back.

'Actually,' the voice went on almost reading Siro's mind, 'I got so aroused, I decided to come back with two friends... Now they must be with her... Oh, wildling, they've seen her too, and they love her! And between you and me... I don't think, ah, how to say it... I don't think they'll behave.'

The Beast had Siro cornered, unable to know where it was hiding. For some reason, the voice didn't seem to come from a precise source but bounced off among the myriad of trees.

'Don't worry, wilding, she'll make it in one piece. Adon wants to see her... But that doesn't mean they can't have some fun. Sure you wonder why I haven't gone for the Daughter of the Light myself...

Well, wildling, I must confess, but don't tell anyone, huh? This has to be something between you and I...'

Siro listened carefully, crouching behind the broken trunk. He did not want to do it, preferring to occupy himself by trying to determine the Beast's hideout, but that voice was hard to ignore.

'I am more interested in *you*,' and when the Beast pronounced the 'you', it swallowed again.

'What do you want?' Exclaimed Siro.

'Oh... wildling, you can't even dream about the things I'd do with you,' the voice sighed, with a metallic hint. 'This body of yours... so strong, so full of scars! I can't get it out of my head since I saw you bathing in the pond... Ah...' It swallowed again. 'Tell me your name, wildling, or do you prefer me to keep calling you that? Wild...

'Shut up!' He shouted as he clenched his fists.

'I suppose you've already looked inside the bag,' the voice said, it was having a blast. 'And I shall assume you know what the yellow queen's poison does to a man... It leaves you very, very soft, just as I want you.'

Just remembering the snake poison, Siro shuddered. The attack could come from anywhere. If he heard a dart buzzing, he'd roll and run, but until then he could only wait.

'Unfortunately, wildling, I only have one dart left... The rest are in your hands... You still have an opportunity to get away, so to speak. Can you imagine it? What if I miss? You would have saved yourself, you could get out of here! Damn, you could even go and look for that gorgeous little thing that travels with you,' the voice filled with joy to immediately switch to a lugubrious tone. 'But what if I hit a bulls-eye? What if I make it and you lose your strength, your muscles relax and this delicious body of yours falls flat on the ground? Ah, that'd be perfect. You could see me... Yes, you could SEE me!'

Siro tensed, with sweat drops trickling down his face. He had noticed something odd when the Beast had pronounced that 'see'. What had it been? It was like a twitching in his hand, no, not in his hand, but on the knife, on the metal blade! He did not understand what it was, but he had felt it: the blade had oscillated for a moment.

'Yes,' The voice swallowed a couple of times. Siro was becoming uneasy. 'We would see each other. The yellow queen's poison paralyzes you from head to toe, but it leaves your eyes wide open, wildling... Oh, I want you to see me... I want to know what you think of my body, when I'm ON TOP of you.'

The knife twitched again. Siro arched his body, ready for the Beast to come.

It's only got one dart left. He told himself.

It all went down to his sheer reflexes: his survival, Matildet's... As soon as she'd came across the Beasts, she'd realize what a mistake.

'Shoot already!' Siro shouted.

'Oh yeah! Have no doubt, that's what I'm going to do, wildling. I hope you're READY,' another vibration ran through the blade. 'If I hit... you will be MINE! And I'll do all I want with you. For me it will be a dream, wild, but I assure you that for you it will be...'

'Shoot!' Siro roared.

'Not even the vultures will want to taste your MEAT when I'll be done with you. I'm going to tear you apart! Get ready, wildling. I know you believe you can dodge the DART, but it's impossible... TOTALLY Impossible! Specially if you don-t know I'm BEHIND you...'

It's a trick, Siro told himself. He didn't turn around but remained in stance. *The voice came from behind that crooked tree. I'm sure...*

He felt a prick on his back: brief, almost painless, and cold, as cold as the sweat that bathed his forehead. He tried to reach his back and felt the dart's feathers. He tore it off and saw a drop of blood falling from the tip.

A metallic laughter filled the oasis.

Chapter 14: Those who know us

I'm dead, thought Siro when he saw the dart between his fingers. The Beast had won and now he could do anything that crossed his mind.

He still felt good. The yellow-queen venom was not instantaneous, he knew that, but it would not be too long before the arms and legs turned soft and could not stand.

And while he waited for that moment to come, the metallic voice of the Beast had faded among the palm trees and vines. Tension stirred deep in the pit of his stomach.

The hunter closed his eyes and thought of Matildet. The Daughter of the Light was also in danger. Siro imagined her in the narrow jungle paths, with the two Beasts chasing her eagerly.

'Where are you?!' Siro was determined to find the Beast, even if he did not have much time left.

The voice did not respond.

'Why are you quiet?' He asked. The unbearable verbiage of the Beast had stopped when it'd known himself victorious.

Why is it quiet if I can't find it either?

He looked at the knife, the blade gleamed in the sunlight that fell through the leafy treetops. Except for those timid light beams, the place was swamped in shadows and hiding places. He wouldn't be surprised if the Beast were very close. It sure was, counting every second until the hunter would fall numb on the ground.

He looked at the knife again; the answer was there, he sensed it. There was some connection between the voice and the vibrations of the blade.

I need the Beast to talk.

'Your friends... leave without you!'

The voice did not respond.

'You are a coward, show yourself! Fight face to face!' He yelled, knife in hand, but the provocation did not help either.

Siro did not know what the hell he could tell the Beast to speak with its horrifying voice. He had to think of something very quickly but could not think of anything. He screamed in all directions, hurled insults, and threats; defying it again and again, but the Beast was too smart to fall for it... Until he thought of something:

'I'll close my eyes...' Siro muttered. 'I'll close my eyes, so I do not see you! He shouted everywhere. The poison will not let me feel, huh...' He got stuck a little, but suddenly he found the word he was looking for. 'Pain! No pain! And besides, I will not have to see you, because I'll close... eyes.'

He heard a noise, very brief, someone had snorted. Siro laughed loudly, to make sure he heard it.

'I will not see your disgusting face, nor your rotten body!' He laughed again, louder this time. 'Dying like that is not so terrible. Worse deaths in the desert... If I had to see face... I'm sure it makes you want to throw up...'

'SHUT UP, WILDLING!'

The oscillation ran through the knife. Although Siro could not grasp the full reason of that phenomenon, he was aware that the knife was not common since the day he had taken it from the Forgotten Grave, but he had never done anything similar. The vibration dissipated quickly as Siro moved the knife. That was not good enough, but suddenly, as he shifted its position, the vibration returned, amplified. He pushed the knife away and the vibration disappeared; lifted it and quivered again.

It is the direction, the knife guides me towards the Beast!

'I got you!' He shouted and ran blindly to where the vibrations were stronger.

The Beast let out a panicked scream. The metal sheet resounded again and Siro oriented drifted towards it.

'What are you doing, wildling?' The voice came from all directions. 'That will not do you any good. You're dead! You are mine!'

'No, you are mine!' Replied Siro, the cries of the Beast did nothing but help him. 'I see you! I see you!'

'LIAR!' The Beast's voice denoted pure terror. 'GET OUT, wild! Get out, tell you! If you run away now I'll leave you in peace, I promise. I will not harm you.'

There was someone running in front of him, a shadow blowing the leaves and vines away. He was closing on it.

'Leave me, wildling! I'll KILL you, I swear I'll kill you!'

A silhouette ran clumsily before him, stumbling over the roots in its path. It was taller, much taller than Siro. From what he could see, his back was painted with black lines. The Beast no longer shouted, but its snorting echoed throughout the jungle.

Siro drifted its path, jumped over a puddle, and sneaked through a clearing packed with colourful birds, which took off immediately. The Beast ran parallel to him, on the other side of the treeline. The hunter charged and just as he was about to sink the blade of the knife in its neck, the Beast bent down, grabbed him by the arm and kicked his legs. Suddenly, Siro found himself flying. He fell on the ground like a dead weight.

The counterattack was something the hunter certainly didn't expect. Siro stood up quickly. His head was pounding, he had hit himself on the back of the head and heard a whistle in his ears. Next to him, the monstrous face of his adversary was revealed at last.

The Beast had a large metallic appendage on its face, a rare mask of sorts, covering its mouth. It reminded Siro of a flower, a rose perhaps, an iron-made sinister rose. At the centre of the mask, there was a hole through which grapples passed down the throat of the monster. Its left eye was sewn. Most likely, the Beast would had lost it in a fight, but Siro had the feeling that there was still something moving behind the closed eyelid.

He had the body of a well-muscled man, tense and hard as a rock, although scarred by dozens of burns and cuts. The black lines that Siro had seen before were nothing more than the blood of the boar they had devoured.

A tall, strong Beast... and with Siro's knife in its hands.

'Hello, wildling. I was starting to miss you,' he scoffed. 'And I bet you missed me too... That's why you came so fast, right? You can't live without me, oh, I know. Such a good knife you have. It's good quality... I wonder how it will look... stained with BLOOD!'

The Beast lunged toward the hunter as the words flooded the air. Siro dodged the first blow, but an unexpected kick made him fall on the ground. The Beast laughed with sadism.

The hunter searched the tall grass until he found something to use against his opponent. As the Beast came closer, he raised a fist-sized stone, and slammed it into the knife's wielding hand. The weapon flew off. A metallic scream deafened the hunter. The birds and rodents that remained in the clearing fled away.

But the Beast did not give up, it struck back. The hunter endured a few kicks, strong as iron bars. A surprise headbutt made him lose his stone. The Beast grabbed him by the neck and slammed him into a tree.

'Oh, wildling... what do you have here?' He whispered in his ear, his fat fingers squeezing his throat.

The half-shattered hand of the creature went up his arm and Siro noticed how its dirty yellow nails pressed the Biters' wound. An intense pain ran through his body. For a moment, he felt his legs numb.

No, stop! Siro thought, as the fingers tore the scab and the blood burst out again. *I'm dying! Stop, you bastard, stop!*

'Wildling of mine, don't you think we make such a good couple?' He said as the nails sank deeper and deeper.

The Beast brought his body closer to Siro's and rubbed against him. The hunter noticed the stench of blood and sweat. The breathing of the Beast became that of an excited animal.

The hand that squeezed the wound came down his pants. Siro was in great pain, but he could not let the opportunity go by. While the Beast was rubbing his dick over the pant's fabric in a futile attempt to excite him, Siro fought the disgust he felt and reached into its leather bag. Before the Beast noticed it, two darts got stuck in its wrist.

The Beast left the fun for a better time and punched him in the stomach. The hunter's face reddened. The air escaped his lungs.

'Ouchy, wildling. Do you think this is going to stop me?' Said the Beast, as it greeted him with yet another punch. 'Make us a favour and let me do my part, darling.'

Siro grabbed the flask full of poison and stuffed it into that monster's mask. The Beast finally released him and coughed violently. Siro fell on his knees. His stomach and the wound in his arm burned.

The tall grass hid him as he crawled away.

It's going to kill me, he said to himself. He heard the Beast stop coughing and spit something.

'This isn't over, wildling,' he said matter-of-factly, catching his breath.

The Beast kicked his stomach. Siro did not see it coming. He lay on the ground, curling and pleading for a truce.

'Now, this is how I like it,' said the Beast. Siro did not see it, but he felt it sit on top of his ass. 'I hope the poison has not yet taken effect, wildling, I want you to FEEL it!'

And just as the Beast said *feel*, something twitched in the tall grass. Siro reached out and felt the handle of the knife. He grabbed it decisively and, with his remaining strength, stuck it in the Beast's calf.

The creature howled, so intensely, that the hand where Siro carried the knife shook uncontrollably, as if the blade had come to life. The wound in his leg got bigger, and so did the screaming. The hunter allowed the hand to dance madly, while the knife sank deeper and deeper into the flesh due to sheer vibration.

Siro stood on his knees, eyes swamped in tears, and looked at the Beast and the thick vein pulsing in its forehead. He kept the knife stuck in the leg.

*I'll kill you! Now you are mine, you fucking Bea*st! But at that moment his arm became limp.

The poison, Siro realized.

The Beast stared, madness shining in its eyes.

'Oh, wildling of mine, you were so close...' It said sarcastically, tore off the knife and pinned it to the ground, all covered in blood.

No, not now! Siro though, and suddenly he lost his temper. Rage as he had never felt before reached him from within. His gaze blurred and his mouth burst into a fierce, animal cry. The Beast was still kneeling when the hunter pounced on him. He grabbed him by the bright, monstrous mask that covered its face, put the sole of its foot on its neck and yanked it off. The cries of the two adversaries mingled.

The Beast rolled on the ground, spasming from top to bottom.

Siro looked at the artifact in his hands: the metal flower was preceded by long, bloody tubes. The mouth of the Beast had been torn by a thousand cuts. It spoke, it moaned, but without the mask, it sounded different.

Siro dropped the mask with disgust.

'Don't kill me, wildling... Pity me, I beg you!' The Beast curled on the ground, trembling like a frightened puppy. 'You don't have to do it, wildling... You're good, I can see...'

'Shut up!' Siro shouted, out of control.

The hunter did not have the strength to pull the knife from the ground, so he went for the stone.

'You're right, wildling, you're absolutely right,' the Beast said as blood poured from its mouth. 'You're not good... From the moment I saw you I knew it. You are like us. You are not a poor lost soul in a world that doesn't love you. You are a cruel and bloodthirsty monster, oh, yes, you are... But does it matter? No! You know why? Well, that's because I love you, wildling! I really love you and I want to prove it...'

Siro raised the stone. He looked in the Beast's only eye, the brown iris trembling. Every word that Beast spat was like a rude and detestable vomit to the hunter.

'Oh, I see, it's because of her, right?' The Beast's chapped lips drew a macabre grin. 'Do you think she will see you as a hero? Surely you think that one day she'll lay eyes on you, poor bastard... You are only dust to her. Only dust...!'

He did not let him finish. Siro lowered his arm and the stone hit the creature's skull. The Beast fell on its back, with open arms.

The voice was gone, giving some sort of unnerving relieve to the hunter. The Beast had fallen with its mouth open. It lacked most of the teeth.

They were ripped off to put the tubes and hooks, Siro deduced coldly. He should be disgusted but felt nothing.

His gaze lingered to the Brand the Beast had on its arm.

'I've seen it before...' Siro recognized the three intersecting black stripes: one blade and one stripe pointing upwards. It was the same symbol the Elector wore on the rings. 'This is odd. Brands tend to be more detailed,' he remembered. Sometimes they represented animals or tools, it depended on who the masters were and what they did for a living: if they owned a mine, the slaves would likely have a peak tool's Brand; if they dealt with cattle, an animal's head. This Brand, however, did not make sense. It was obvious that this Beast and the Elector were not involved in the same activities. There was only one explanation by which the two creatures could have the same Brand, and that was that they had a master in common. Someone wanted to make clear where the authority came from.

He said a name before, he recalled. *Adon? Yes, I think Adon was the name. Is he the master of these Beasts?*

But he didn't have the time to think about it.

Matildet.

She was somewhere in the oasis, with two Beasts going after

her. He picked up the knife and wiped it with an alocasia's leaf.

He stopped feeling his left hand when he was on his way to the waterfall. His body was getting numb little by little because of the yellow queen poison. He had managed to outlast the confrontation with the Beast. He could consider himself lucky, but that was not enough.

He knew that it would have been wise to look for a good hiding place and let the poison do its thing; after all, it would not kill him, but knock him out for a few hours. If he did, however, the Daughter of the Light would have to deal with the other Beasts by herself.

Maybe she does not need me, thought Siro, and he remembered, painfully, that Matildet had pierced the water tank and threatened him with his own spear.

Surely you think that one day she'll lay eyes on you, poor bastard..., the words of the Beast echoed in his head.

It's not that! What will you know, disgusting Beast? You are dead and you have nothing to say! Shut up!

He climbed the slope full of twisted, grey trees that led to the waterfall. He felt a tingling in his toes, and thought it was some insect, but when he looked down, he saw nothing. It was the poison again. He was running out of time.

From the top of the waterfall, the water flowed, lazily, down the rocks. The hunter had ended up next to where he and the Daughter of the Light had camped, just a little bit higher. Beyond the lonely little tree rooted on the waterfall rocks, he could see someone next to the extinguished bonfire.

It's Matildet! He thought, gladly. *She is alive!*

But his enthusiasm vanished immediately. The Beasts were just behind the Daughter of the Light. It was strange. It did not look like they wanted to hurt her. They talked, no idea about what, but they talked. He could not hear from so far away.

He watched the Beasts, the gestures they made, the distance between them and Matildet. *What's going on?* The hunter asked himself. These creatures were sly, but not compassionate. If they had not attacked her, it was because they knew that she was a Daughter of the Light. They were afraid of making a wrong step.

From that distance, it was difficult to assess whether he could face the two Beasts or not. Their presence was not as imposing as the previous one, and none wore a mask. One of them, the shortest one, laughed. He could hear and see it. It wouldn't stop bowing before the Daughter of the Light.

The short one was no threat for him, but the other one was a different story. It was fat yet strong and, more importantly, it carried a stone axe hanging from his back.

If I go around them, I might have a chance, he thought.

But before Siro decided on which path would be best to go down, the wind ruffled the hair at the nape of his neck. The seedling tinkled and a few dry leaves fell downstream. The wind carried a stench within, a mixture of sweat and blood.

It can't be... This smell..., he told himself. *It can't be!*

'Oh, wildling of mine, this love of ours will kill me...' he heard the Beast whisper in his ear.

A thick hand twisted his arm and knocked him to the ground. Siro's head sank into the mud and grass. The creature lay on top of him and licked his face with a bloody tongue: from the scar on his jaw to the beginning of his hair.

'You taste like desert, desert and terror!' Exclaimed the Beast as it stole the knife again.

Siro could not move, the Beast squeezing his face harder and harder against the mud. In that position, he could only see from one eye. Between the stems, the rocks and the insects that ran to hide, the hunter saw Matildet, very small and far away... and talking back to the Beasts.

Flee! Get away now that you can!

The Beast was getting excited again. Siro noticed how a hand ran through his body from top to bottom.

'Bring it to me, bring it to me. I want it now... Quiet, they're coming, quiet, I say! He is mine, the girl is yours... It's too hot in here.'

The Beast bled and talked nonsense. The knife slipped from its hands. Siro headbutted its chin. The creature moved away and the hunter tried to get on his feet, but his left leg did not respond. He remained on his knees. The Beast seemed absent, looked around, like seeing everything for the first time.

Siro contemplated the results of his aggression. The creature had its skull slightly sunken on one side, and its entire face smeared with blood. The stitches that covered his eye had fallen, revealing a lively and curious eye pupil spinning inside an iris that had once been brown, but now looked whitish.

'She is not like us. She can not understand our pain,' said the Beast. 'It's hot... I want to go.'

Siro was tired of hearing the delusions of that being. He did not want to listen to a single more word, he wanted it dead and be eaten by the vultures like the carrion it was. He picked up the knife from the floor and squeezed it until the leather covering the handle began to tear. He despised that creature, he could not stand its dirty teeth and its stitched eye. Everything in that being was screaming for him to end its existence.

But before the hunter sank the knife blade in its flesh, the Beast said something he could not have anticipated.

'Mom, no, take me...' the Beast stammered in a child's voice. 'I want to go with you, not Siro. He hurts me.'

What? The hunter was paralyzed. He felt slapped, he did not know how to react.

'Siro is bad. He squeezes my hand. Mom, please! Take me with you, it's hot! Where do we go?' The Beast kept going, his eyes lost in the blue, cloudless sky.

What is it talking about? Who is it? He wondered.

'Siro, don't pull so hard. I'll tell mom,' The Beast was still rambling, its eyes spinning. 'Siro, Siro, Si-ro, Si...'

The Beast was halfway through saying his name when the eyes stopped twitching and focused on the hunter. Siro, still wondering about its adversary's delusions, did not realize that the spark of malice that brutalized the Beast's eyes was back.

'Siro... No, not Siro... My wildling... Oh, my wildling! You are here with me, you haven't left me! Do you know what this means? This must be love, what you and I feel for each other... Yes, this love will kill us!' The creature raised its arms and lunged itself headlong at him.

The hunter reacted too slowly. The Beast rammed him with its body. It was a strong, dry blow that sent them tumbling down the cliff. The small tree, thin and lonely, broke under the weight of the two contenders. The hunter and the Beast fell into the pond.

The water surrounded Siro as he sank. The algae brushed his face and the water lilies floated above him, like dark, round stars, in a glassy sky. The arms, the legs... his whole body was slowly numbing. He had the temptation to close his eyes and let himself sink to the bottom, but he knew that if he did, he would never rise again.

Bubbles escaped through his mouth, hurrying him to go back to the surface. The effect of the poison was more and more evident: no response from his legs and he could not have opened the fist with which he held the knife even if his life was in stake... and indeed it was.

As he struggled to get out of the water full of seaweeds, he saw a large silhouette swimming towards the pond's edge. His blood boiled, he gritted his teeth and forgot that he was running out of air. He swam towards the prey.

The creature uttered an agonized weeping when it noticed it was being stabbed in the back. The cries of pain followed each other until they reached the shore.

'Do not ever say my name again!' Siro shouted, raising and lowering the knife, his face deformed into a merciless grimace. 'Do not say it again!'

He stabbed the Beast, the water, everything he could reached. *Shut up, Beast, shut up and die at once!* He thought as he let himself be carried away by the frenzy. *You have not said my name, you haven't!* He buried the blade between the water and the flesh, he wanted that metallic voice, that mad voice, to never pursue him again. He wanted the annoying noise to disappear.

You have not said my name... You do not know me... I've never seen you before! How did you know my name, Beast? How?

But he did not want to know, he just wanted it to remain forever at the bottom of the pond.

And so, with each thrust, the water turned redder. Siro noticed the taste of blood on his lips and realized that enough was enough. This time, it would not come back. He came out of the water, wheezing and limping because of the poison. He looked up from the damp shore and saw Matildet and the Beasts.

The Daughter of the Light covered her mouth with her hands. The other two Beasts were by her side and had seen it all.

'By the Great Shell, where does this slave come from?' Exclaimed the short Beast. 'Is this Ubald's blood...?'

'Count how many we were, and how many we are...' answered the plump Beast with a tenor voice that contrasted with the shorter one.

'Guido, your lack of empathy will never cease to amaze me...'

said the short Beast. It looked at it with disdain and then laid its eyes on Siro. 'Hey, you, wildling, stay away! Don't dare coming any closer!'

Siro observed the Beasts and said nothing. He had mud stuck in his face. His black hair was full of blood and seaweed. His whole body weighed on him.

'Look at this lame wildling...' The short Beast said, and looked towards the pond, where there was still some blood. 'Ugh, so gross! Guido, can you see him? It's still floating... Oh, no. This is just too much for me, I can't even... Ugh, this wildling makes me sick! He's killed...!'

'Put the obvious aside, Junal. It bores me. And stop pretending that you care,' the Beast called Guido answered without changing the tone.

Guido ran a hand over his shaved head, like if it were all that the others Beast's death deserved. He held the axe, a half meter weapon from top to bottom, and stared at the hunter with indifference, as if he were a bug.

'Ubald is dead and you tell me to stop pretending? Do you listen when you speak, Guido, or can't you with all the shit pouring from your ears?' Junal snapped.

While the Beasts argued with each other, Matildet approached Siro. She got behind the hunter and grabbed him by the shoulders.

He was exhausted, hurt and paralyzed. He forgot about the Beasts, who argued among themselves, and let himself be carried away by the gesture of the Daughter of the Light.

Only Liduvin had held me like this, the hunter thought. He suddenly felt the weight of all the years that had passed since he had last noticed that warmth and wished he could move his limbs to hug the Daughter of the Light back.

'What do we do with the wildling? Shall I chop it to pieces?' Guido asked, unaware of Junal's fuss.

'You quiet! Nobody kills nobody until I say so. You got it, sack of faeces? Junal said.

'Then it matters or not, that he's beaten Ubald to a pulp?' Said Guido.

'Just... You... Shut up! Do you... Seriously, can't you just shut up, you witfuck?' Junal was angry, but then changed his tone to address the Daughter of the Light. 'Miss Daughter of the Light, please... if you allow me, could you tell me what you are doing with the wildling?'

Junal drew a crooked, yellowish smile that pretended to be flattering. The face of the Beast was small and sharp. Wrinkles on his forehead and jaw exaggerated his already excessive gesticulation.

Matildet ignored what it said. She brushed the hair from Siro's forehead and looked at him with a worried expression.

'Siro, are you okay? Where have you been? Answer me, please.'

'The wildling does not move...' Junal whispered, its smile frozen.

'What have I said about acknowledging the obvious?' Guido muttered.

'Oh, for the Great Shell, the Children of the Light and all the snakes of the desert, Guido,' Junal turned red with rage. 'Why of all the servants of Adon, of each and every single one of his Beasts, did I end up with you? Was there really no one else available to go and look for the Daughter of the Light? Why, huh? Answer me, foul-smelling sack! Why you?'

'Siro, answer me!' Matildet insisted, shaking the hunter's body. 'Siro... What have you done to him?'

'Nothing good,' Guido added. 'You know what Ubald uses this poison for... Well, used...'

'Will you shut up?' Junal yelled.

'Adon did not say a word about the wildling,' Guido said. 'That's it, I'm chopping him down.'

Siro looked sideways at the fat and huge Beast. From the ground, and backlit, he could not see the face of the creature very well. Its belly, as big as it was, casted a shadow on his feet. The Beast wielded the stone axe menacingly. It had the same Brand on its arm as the late Beast: the blade and the vertical stripe.

Guido reached out to grab Siro, but Matildet pulled the hunter's numb body even harder.

'Guido, stay still, you fucking retard! Don't provoke the Daughter of the Light!' Said Junal. 'Please, Miss Daughter of the Light, if you were so kind... If you would allow us the audacity... If you do not mind, could you leave this wildling on the ground and leave with us? Our Lord Adon is dying to meet you...'

'What have you done to him? I command you to explain it to me!' Matildet was not fooled.

'Time to chop,' Guido said.

'No, Guido, son of a brainless hyena, stand still!' Junal jumped on the bigger Beast's arm, but that did not stop it.

Matildet raised her hand open in front of the Beasts and suddenly a glow appeared in its palm. The light intensified, as the rest of the dress darkened. An aura of sheer brightness and heat grew stronger and stronger, leaving Siro and the Beasts open-mouthed.

'Do you really want to see the wrath of a Daughter of the Light, Guido?' Matildet asked. 'Is it really what you want?'

Siro only saw the girl's arm. Her hand shone like the Great Light in the middle of the Sacred Valley, but beyond the elbow, the dress had turned black. He knew that Matildet had the ability to play with light, he had seen it when they had fallen into that strange underground, but it had never seemed to him to be as terrifying a skill as at that very moment... and the Beasts thought likewise.

'It never crossed our minds, noble lady!' Junal exclaimed. Its face paled. 'It would be the last thing we would want, for you to be mad at us. In fact, we thought that it was getting late, and we might as well get going, yes, that'll be the best.'

Junal pulled Guido by the arm and this time did not say a word.

'Where's your lust for chopping down stuff, huh?' They heard Junal say, as the two Beasts left.

'Always stating the obvious...' Guido responded and then the voices melted with the sounds of the jungle.

When she was sure they were far enough, Matildet lowered her hand. The light disappeared and the dress recovered its usual whiteness.

'Are you okay, Siro? What happened to you?' The girl asked, shaking him. 'Siro!'

But the hunter could no longer move his jaw. His tongue had fallen asleep inside his mouth. Exhaustion spread all over his body, so he closed his eyes for a moment to rest, but he did not open them again.

Chapter 15: Men like you

It felt like he had only slept for five minutes, but the light of the oasis had changed. The green plants were no longer outlined by a golden glow, but an orange hue that contrasted with the navy blue twilight shadows. He was lying on the floor, face up and with his head cocked. He could hear the murmur of the pond behind, but he could not turn his head to see it.

It was a strange feeling. He felt trapped in an unresponsive body that felt not his own. He tried to shake his fingers, but they did not respond. Even the eyelids opened and closed slowly. He wanted to scream, but his tongue was as dead piece of meat in his mouth.

It took him a few moments to overcome the initial panic and realize that it was poison.

The Beast, he thought. It would still be floating in the pond. He tried to move his head, but his muscles didn't respond.

'It leaves you very, very soft, just as I want you,' the masked Beast had told him.

It knew me. It knew my name. Did it hear Matildet say it while spying on us? He wondered, but then he realised that the first thing the Beast had done was asking what his name was.

It's dead, he tried to convince himself, but he wouldn't be at ease until he looked at the pond. He could picture the big hand of that monster closing around his neck and dragging him to the water.

You are like us, the metallic voice echoed in his head.

Something was moving in the nearby bushes. Beneath the green and pink leaves, two brown kiwis fled away. Matildet showed up behind them.

The Daughter of the Light had completely dirtied her dress. It had mud stains all over, tiny leaves and feathers filled her hair, and a strand of spiderweb stuck together like a braid. On her belly, red finger and handprints on his belly completed the picture. Matildet was dragging a black and white feathered pheasant tied with a rope. It was an impressive specimen, about four spans from head to tail.

She carried the two halves of the double spear that Grinat had given Siro on her back. The silica tips were little stained, as if she tried to clean them after the hunt. The girl picked up a few dry branches and put them on the coals of the previous bonfire. She removed the head of the boar from the stick where it was nailed using her foot, and then came back, stick in hand, for the bird.

'Now comes the worst part,' she said to herself. She lifted the bird and the stick, but did nothing. 'This is so out of my league…'

She picked up the bag and took out Siro's knife. The hunter watched her pull it out of the scabbard and examine the blade before beheading the bird. He heard Matildet gag, but she covered her mouth and waited a few moments.

'Ugh, that was close,' Matildet said when her stomach calmed down. 'Come on, Dr. Zalies, proceed with the operation,' she said to encourage herself.

The Daughter of the Light struggled to impale the animal. She stopped three times during the process while repeating that she could not do it, that she preferred to die of hunger, but in the end, she got it.

At the time of lighting the fire, she took out some flame stones from Siro's bag. She rubbed the two red stones, as she had seen him do, but it took a long time to get the fire lit.

When the whole process was over, she realized that she had not plucked the bird and then tried to remove the feathers with the knife while the pheasant roasted. Had his mouth not been paralyzed, Siro would have laughed.

The sun was setting, and when it seemed that everything was going as it should —the pheasant was browning little by little and giving off a mouth-watering smell—, it had already got dark.

Siro was still on the ground. He had forgotten about the Beasts and all his fears. For the first time, he had not devoted himself to reviewing the curves of the Daughter of the Light but had been attentive to the whole process. It was a play just for him.

The girl left the pheasant for a moment and Siro saw how her white-clad legs approached.

'Hey, Siro...'

He wanted to respond, but not his jaw.

'Siro, can you hear me?' The Daughter of the Light squeezed his hand, or so it seemed, he could hardly feel anything. 'If you are pretending, it's not funny, ok?'

Like if I had nothing better to do than play dead, he thought.

He tried to sigh, but not even that gesture came out. The yellow queen's poison was more effective than he had ever imagined.

'Let's try something,' Matildet removed two feathers from her hair. 'If you hear me, blink once, ok?'

And so did Siro. The girl's mouth widened with a smile.

Matildet ran her fingers through his hair in an affectionate gesture.

'I do not know what that guy did to you, but don't worry, I'm taking care of you.'

The Daughter of the Light tried to maintain a dialogue based on questions and answers with his eyes, but it was a failure. The only positive result was when she asked if he was cold and then dragged him closer to the bonfire.

The warmth of the embers comforted him. The weather had turned cold at dusk. Matildet stared at the fire, thoughtfully, while waiting for the pheasant to roast. She had put one of the nuts from the flask in her mouth and swallowed it with a sip of the waterskin.

The pheasant smelled very good. Siro's stomach roared and that made him laugh.

I can laugh, he realised and that seemed to him even more funny. His body shook on the floor. The Daughter of the Light raised her eyes and gaped at him. Siro realised that he had finally made a sound. He focused on the fingers of his hand. They moved!

'You're back!' Matildet exclaimed. 'I was about to put you in a heroic position and leave you like a statue,' she teased him. 'Do you fancy some pheasant?'

Siro was hungry, but he still had something to do. He leaned back and turned his head towards the pond: no one in the water, no sign of the Beast. An intense pain ran through his body. Every bruise, every cut, every scratch, every blow he had received burned. Siro bent on the ground and Matildet pounced on him. She wanted to help him but didn't know what to do. After a while, the pain subsided, although it kept bothering him for the rest of the evening.

The Daughter of the Light hugged him and he returned the gesture without thinking. They sat, Matildet between the legs of the hunter, with her head resting against his chest. For both, this was so natural that they did not need to say a word. They were alone. Who else could they trust in that place?

The body of the Beast had disappeared. *It sunk*, thought Siro.

Matildet returned with a pheasant leg for each. Siro took the box of salt and spices and showed Matildet how he scattered them over the meat.

The oasis pulsed with life. Stars shone on the calm water, frogs drawing little circles in its surface until they reached the waterlilies and the bulrushes. He heard the animals, large and small, sneaking among the vegetation. That noise reassured Siro, because it meant that the Nightborn were far away from that place. The night air inspired him: the mixture of flowers, grass, water and grilled meat transported him to childhood, when he lived in Merco. How happy he was then, when all the worries he had were to get Eliria's attention and find treasures with Nazeh.

'They left,' said the Daughter of the Light when she had finished eating.

'They'll be back,' said Siro. 'And they will come with more. We have to leave right away...'

'It's not the first time you kill, right? We have seen you fall. You've stabbed that man until...'

'It was no man,' repeated Siro for the umpteenth time.

The Daughter of the Light didn't insist.

Siro breathed in and out.

'First time I killed; I was in the white desert. I saw a Beast. Wounded. It crawled over the salt and shouted. He asked me for help.'

The hunter still remembered the face of that creature. It was full of scars and burns. Its dark eyes were just two lines, unable to open them due to the sunshine and salt. Its clothes were torn and loose, probably stolen from someone. 'Water... Please, water...', it implored. 'Have mercy of a man who can no longer walk.'

A man? Thought the boy. He saw the Brands, the scars on the arm, self-inflicted to count its victims. What if he had taken part in the Night of Fire? What if he was one of those who had taken Eliria and Nazeh? What if he had killed Grinat in combat and that was the reason why it was so badly wounded?

All those possibilities stacked little Siro's head and, in the end, he did what he had to do.

'I stabbed it in the neck. I felt nothing.'

'You did not feel anything because he was a Beast?'

Siro nodded.

'He was a man!' She snapped. 'Just like the other two, they were men, like you! You have no right to kill them like animals! What kind of monster are you?'

'You don't know them! They would have killed you! A Beast was trying to kill me! It poisoned me. Beasts are like that! They are all like that!'

Without realizing it, Siro had risen to his feet and was shouting at Matildet. The girl, though, was far from scared. She stood up and replied:

'They wanted to take me to their city! It was the only chance I had to find other people! I hope you know what this means... Maybe they were bandits, yes, but if you had listened to me we would have solved it. No one needed to die!'

It seemed that the Daughter of the Light was about to say something, but Siro went ahead.

'Tomorrow we look for people,' he said. 'Tonight, we sleep here. But tomorrow go somewhere else.'

'Where?'

Siro knew another place beyond, to the northeast, where they might have a chance, but he did not relish going back.

'The lagoon,' he said.

Chapter 16: Our secret

'Siro, I don't think it's a good idea,' Nazeh murmured. 'My mother will notice I'm not home.'

'Don't be a such a coward! We can't go back,' Siro replied. 'Don't you remember what I told you? Beasts are close.'

Nazeh's face was a swamp of questions. Siro was afraid his friend would chicken out any time; but if he had managed to get him out of bed, he wanted to believe Nazeh would make it until the end. The two children were hiding behind one the curly sycamores that grew beside the hill of roots. It was late at night, and the village of Merco had turned off the lights and gone to sleep.

It had been Liduvin's words that had brought little Siro and Nazeh to the hill of roots. Siro had heard her speak with Grinat, when the two adults thought he was asleep. The guardian had sworn never to speak in front of anyone who was not his protege, but that night he did not know that the child was listening to them.

'If you speak the truth, we will all be dead before long,' Liduvin walked up and down the side of the store, accompanied by the tinkling of her bracelets. 'How can I open Firla's eyes? She's so stubborn! No wonder they have chosen her as the leader of the village. I must do something... I'll talk to the council.'

'Do you think it's wise?' Grinat asked.

Siro was surprised every time he heard the man's voice. It was a phenomenon as rare as finding a Child of the Light wandering in the jungle.

'They have a meeting tomorrow,' said Liduvin. 'What future awaits us, otherwise? May the Light of Keerine guide us...'

Siro had not been able to sleep that night. He had thought for hours on the day of the Exile: the Beasts charging at them; spears and darts flying past him; the cries of the people and the dead bodies piling up against the wooden palisade.

Not the Beasts, please. Not again, he repeated. *I do not want them to come back!*

He had told everything he had heard to Nazeh after making him swear three times he would not tell anyone: not his mother, not his brothers...

'What about Eliria?' The child asked him, his voice trembling because of his friend's revelations. He grabbed his arms, and Siro remembered that not so long ago his friend wore steel rings on his arms by word of the sadistic Electors.

'No one! I'll see you tonight, by the river.'

As they agreed, the two children had left the beds shortly after going to sleep. Liduvin had kissed Siro goodnight and left the tent, where Grinat was waiting with a grim expression. The man looked like the sculpture of a giant god rather than a person. Under the light of the stars, the green irises shone like a mountain that had come to life. Siro had huddled under the blankets and pretended to sleep.

He had spent a long time in silence, until he was sure that the two adults were already far away. He came out from under the blankets and went to the river. It didn't take long before Nazeh arrived. Siro saw him walking shily, checking no one followed him.

'Looking for the Nightborn?' Siro greeted him.

Nazeh had a good scare, pretty close to turn into a shriek. Siro chuckled and his friend scowled at him. The two crossed the marketplace and continued along the northern road to the foot of the hill of roots sheltered by the night.

It had been two years since they had reached the oasis and now the houses stretched from the hill to the riverbank. At first, Firla and the rest of the council members had ordered to mark on the floor all the places where the houses would raise, the fields where the crops would go; later on, the a square for the market, and even a park of coloured paving stones for the children to play —although none of them did, everyone preferred to run through the jungle— but careful planning had led to the haste and the enthusiasm of the people to have a home where to start over. And so, what had to be a well-thought, ordered village with wide paths quickly turned into a spiral of houses piled one on top of the other.

The hill where the Council House stood was a compact net of roots, branches and brambles that grew around a thousand-year-old tree stump. The trunk measured more than ten meters in diameter. Siro could not imagine how high the tree should have been before it fell. The vegetation that covered the hill was so dense that one could not distinguish whether there was soil or not between the branches of that arboreal monstrosity. At the top, on the flat part of the stump, the adults had built the Council House, a tent supported by thick trunks and covered with animal skins. Inside, the lights shone and casted the shadows of dozens of women and men against the walls.

'Are you sure you want to climb up?' Said Nazeh. 'We will get in trouble.'

'Don't you remember what Liduvin said? The part of "we will all be dead before long" Do you think it's a joke?'

'My mother says that I do not have to believe the Liduvin tales. She says she's sick in the head.'

'Your mother is the one sick in her head!'

'Why do you get so angry? She's not even your mother.'

Maybe Nazeh's intention was to apologize, but if it was the case, it didn't work. Siro ignored his friend's statement and moved toward the Council House. Thousands of moss-covered roots tangled among them and covered the hill making it hard to spot. The adults had built a path made of stone and logs that led to the top, but it was guarded by a pair of sentries. They were not very good: they played with the lucky stones and pretended to do their job when someone approached. Siro knew that they would not bother to go around the hill to check that there was no one ducking behind the tall grass and the sycamores.

He put one foot on the root covered with wet moss and then another one, keeping his balance lifting his hands. He ascended a few meters on all four to avoid falling through the gaps. Nazeh was still hiding behind the tree, he could feel his eyes asking: *Do I really have to follow you?*

'Come!' Siro snapped.

Nazeh came out, unconvinced. Siro crawled over a trunk stuck in the web of roots and took a leap to a better position. When it was almost there, he heard a scream and a loud noise behind him. Nazeh sobbed. His leg was trapped between the roots.

'*Ssshh...*' made Siro. In two leaps, he got to his friend. 'You'll wake the whole town!'

A man with a torch was approaching from the other side of the hill. He was one of the two guards. Siro swallowed. He pulled Nazeh's leg out of the hole.

'It hurts...' the boy moaned.

'The Leg? I barely touched it!'

'No, my nuts...' Nazeh brought his hands to his loincloth. Each leg ended on each side of the thick root had hit squarely in the crotch.

Siro pulled his friend once more, until his leg was set free. His skin was full of little bloodspots. A bramble had stuck in his ankle. Siro took it off carefully, while Nazeh bit his fist to keep him from screaming.

The sentinel was almost there. He walked lazily, as if hearing a scream in the middle of the night was not his business. He looked at the jungle and the hill and kicked a stone that had crossed his path. But despite the apathy with which he acted; he would soon run into the two children.

'Time to hide,' thought Siro.

The boy encircled one of the thick roots with his legs and went headlong into the artificial hill. Inside, the mountain was hollow. Among the darkness, one could appreciate how thousands of roots, trunks and stones had stacked on top of each other forming a singular mixture. It looked like the skeleton of a mountain.

Nazeh did the same and the two remained hanging upside down, with their legs and fingers clinging to the impossible ramifications of that vegetable hill. It was not necessary for Siro to tell him they could not make a noise. If they were discovered, they would be grounded for centuries.

Siro's hands were illuminated by an orange light, as were the roots that shielded them. It was the light of the torch. A tall, thin figure, with dark complexion and sleepy eyes, was approaching on the road. He wore a headband made of animal ossicles and his hair tied in dreadlocks.

'Good thing it's your silly brother,' Siro murmured. The sentinel was Cairu, the second eldest brother of the Muhara family.

Nazeh's older brother glanced quickly up the hill, but saw nothing. The torch made him more visible than the two children. He propped the silica spear against one of the yellowed palms and pushed his loincloth aside to urinate at ease. When he was done, Cairu returned to his spot in front of the stairs whistling a song.

'He's the worst guard I've ever seen,' Siro exclaimed.

'My mother says we all have to contribute,' Nazeh shrugged.

When Cairu was far enough, they climbed the remaining

stretch until they reached the top. Siro was surprised to see the flat surface at the top. Moss and lichens had covered a good part of the tree.

The light of the Council House lighted up the brown rings of the stump. They were concentric slender rings that were interrupted constantly by cuts, dark knots and showy plants that had rooted there. Liduvin had explained to him that counting the rings would tell him how old the tree was, but Siro could not count up to such big numbers.

The House was a tent made of fabric cuts and skins of zebras, mongooses, tapirs, and boars sewn together. The shadows of the people were projected against them. The two children huddled next to it. Siro untied one of the ropes that linked the fabrics to see through. The tent was full of candelabra and spicy scented candles. The red and purple carpets, all stolen during Undershell's escape, covered the floor, but it was an elegant solution. Any sense of refinement was lost by the dozens of oil and grease stains, the cluster of fruits and vegetables that hung from the ceiling or the sacks of wheat and tools.

There were women and men sitting and standing, all in a circle. On one side there were the council members: people who had been rich and powerful in Undershell, and managed to keep things the same way in the outer world. 'People have abandoned everything except loyalties and fear,' Liduvin used to say when talking with Grinat about the exiles and the council. Both adults were inside the tent. The silent guardian stood imposingly beside Liduvin. He was one of the tallest men in the village and, no doubt, the most fearful. He scrutinized the sour faces of the councillors and the other inhabitants of Merco, without saying a word. He had his hand on one of the handles of the double spear, ready always in case someone decided to swap words for weapons.

Only a madman would face Grinat, thought Siro. The guardian's precaution seemed completely unnecessary.

'That we are in danger, you say? Hah! Why should we listen to you two?' Siro recognized the Firla's voice, Merco's widow. 'In the eyes of the Council, you do not have any credibility.'

'Firla, we can afford such risks,' it was an old woman's voice, it could only be Quela. Siro had talked to her a few times, especially when they were traveling in the caravan. She was nicer to him than most adults.

'Do I have to remind everyone why we had to run out of the city? Don't you remember why the Dugol's Beasts were trying to kill us?' Firla spat the words with anger. 'It seems that you have forgotten because of whom my husband died, just as so many others!'

Siro shifted his position until he saw Firla's crimson clothes. The leader of the village was a wiry, average height and inquisitive-looking woman, former hunter of the Bindagi tribe, just like her late husband. Her arms were as strong as those of a blacksmith and it was whispered that she could take down any animal, no matter how big it was, with a single spear thrust. There were even those who said that she had slayed the legendary Worm of Nacra all by herself. Siro had spent weeks imagining her fighting a giant worm, with poisonous tentacles sticking out of its mouth and a gleaming sting at the end of the tail; until Liduvin had told him that the Worm of Nacra was actually a sort of giant bird from Undershell's far east. But all of that had been before the day of Exile. Now that woman's explosive temperament was more well-known than her skill as a hunter. Many feared her, and even more spoke badly at her back; but all the inhabitants of the village knew that if it had not been for Firla and Merco, none of them would have escaped the Beasts massacre. Even Liduvin said it, when she didn't criticize her...

The circular room was filled with stone and wooden benches covered with hyena skins. Firla's seat was an austere throne covered by the skin of a huge Biter, no doubt the one who Grinat himself had killed during the last expedition the hunters had made.   T h e Biter's teeth had also been a goodwill offering for the leader of the exiles. Firla had accepted them and had herself made a more than sixty pieces necklace out of it. But the grudge she held toward Liduvin and Grinat had not diminished the slightest.

At the base of the throne, Taurus, one of the new husbands of Firla, looked at all the attendants with a restless look, as if some agent of Dugol, Lord of the Beasts, could leap out of the crowd to kill his wife. Firla's second husband, Jahisel the Crafty, was leaning against Firla's seat, and struggling not to fall asleep. Tersian, the last husband, was not there. If someone in the town felt ill, it was he who had to attend them, consuming most of his time. The three had married Firla at a simultaneous wedding within two weeks of arriving at the oasis. The ceremony had been held inside the river, with water at ankle height, as dictated by the customs of the Bindagi tribe. The women had thrown red petals at them as they made the three traditional offerings: a dress, a bird hunted the day before and a bow with buzzing arrows. Firla had plucked the bird's head off with a bite and poured its blood into the river. The three husbands —Taurus, Jahisel and Tersian, although the latter was not Bindagi— sang a deep simple melody, but one that sung by the three of them at the same time left everyone astonished, not used to the rituals of the nomadic tribe. The bride had shot the three arrows. The wind flowing through hollow wood arrow tips caused a buzz that little Siro had never heard. And after the ceremony had been concluded, the traditional celebration banquet begun.

Siro wondered many times how was it possible that Firla had three husbands and Liduvin none. Although Grinat was always by her side, the silent guardian had married Zuria during the trip through the desert.

'What's going on, Siro? Tell me what you see,' Nazeh tried to poke his head through the same hole, but it was not big enough.

'Not now!' She scolded him, though shared some of the space so his friend could see.

The commotion of the room suddenly vanished when Liduvin stepped forward.

'Firla, I can understand how you feel. We all lost someone when we left the city, but...'

'Understand?' The town leader interrupted. 'Traitors like you? What do you know about our suffering? I barely remember the reason why I let you in here. I'm sick of your lies...

'We can not remain,' insisted Liduvin. 'They are very close and far more numerous. Grinat has seen their trail.'

'And now I have to believe the word of someone who does not speak?' Firla mocked the man's vow of silence. There was some shy laughter in the Council House, but it stopped quickly. Nobody wanted problems with Grinat.

'Look, I do not trust these two either,' said the man who sat at her right, on one of the stone thrones of the councillors. 'And yet I think that if they are looking for us we have to leave immediately. I propose we send scouts.'

The man speaking was Infidas. Back in Undershell he was a merchant, although he did not know exactly what he traded with. He was too rich and too young, which generated both allies and detractors. According to what women said in the marketplace, he should not have been more than twenty years old. He had a cropped beard and a pair of dreadlocks with jade ornaments reaching down his amber dress. He had heard that he had escaped from the city with all the money he could —quite a fortune according to the gossips— and that the Beasts with which he had dealings did not keep too much sympathy for him.

Firla weighed the option with a sour face. Her forehead was wrinkled and her eyebrows, thin and deep black, tensed like the strings of a bow. She held her chin in her hand and had her eyes on Liduvin, who stared back calmly.

'It's too late to send anyone,' Liduvin proclaimed. 'If we don't leave, they will find us. And this time, no one will escape. You all know what Dugol is like.'

'You better than anyone, I suppose...' added Firla.

'And when should we go?' Quela interrupted the Merco's leader before the situation escalated.

'Tomorrow,' said Liduvin.

People bursted again. Men and women stood up. The same people who entrusted their children to Liduvin now booed and insulted her. 'We have needed months to build this town! Why should we go now?' Some said. 'Traitor!' They shouted. 'Do not listen to her! Now we can't leave!' Roared those who were closer to the two children. The adults were fighting and it seemed that the whole tent was going to fall down. Siro and Nazeh looked at each other, wondering what would happen next. Grinat stood before Liduvin with his hand always ready on the spear handle.

'Quiet! Women and men of Merco, this is the Council House!' Infidas managed to restore the order. 'We are not here to shout at each other, but to talk. Who listened to us when we lived in Undershell? Who? Nobody, right? I think this is the main difference between living there and living in Merco... apart from the whips, of course,' he said as he unbuttoned his tunic and showed a white line across his chest.

Some of the attendees laughed, but for others the memory of the Beasts was still too recent. Infidas smiled at the people of Merco and raised his arms, showing them there was nothing to fear.

'We listen to each other in this House,' he said a couple of times, to make sure the message reached everyone. 'We listen and let talk. Let this woman speak before judging her!'

Infidas cleared his throat and pointed to Liduvin.

'Liduvin, we are too many to wander aimlessly through the desert. Where can we go? To the east there is only Undershell and the stony hamada. To the north, the ravines... To the south, who knows what? And to the west..'.

'West,' said Liduvin.

Infidas was surprised but gestured so she kept talking. Firla, sitting to his left, was about to explode. Liduvin took a couple of seconds. For the first time all night, she did not seem so sure of herself.

'The Great Light is to the west, in the middle of the Sacred Valley. The Children of the Light await us. It's time to go home.'

An older man gave a sharp and broken laugh and the laughter spread like the fire in the summer fields. Infidas shook his head from right to left. Firla went pale for a few seconds, but quickly regained her breath to strike back.

'So the best idea you have is to follow a children's bedtime story to save us?' The leader scoffed. 'Do you think that Keerine himself will come to take care of all of Dugol's Beasts? Why don't we sell our souls to the Nightborn?'

Grinat took a step forward, but Liduvin put her hand on his arm. Taurus, at the foot of the throne, did not take his eyes off the silent guardian.

'The Tear-City exists. My mother saw it and explained to me how to get there before she died. If we find the Children of the Light, they will help us,' argued Liduvin.

'The only thing that will help Merco will be the spears and the Firespreader!' Cried Firla, her face flushed. 'It will be our courage that will carry us through victorious and not your delusions. We will end each Beast that dares to set foot on our town!'

Some men applauded the idea and shouted 'Bindagi! Bindagi!'

'This is easy to say when you have nothing to lose,' said one of the attendees to the meeting. 'But what about those of us who have children? And those who can not brandish a weapon?'

'You will kill us all, Firla,' old Quela whispered in her ear, but it was too loud and everyone heard it.

The discussion caught fire and soon everyone had something to say. The tent turned into a cricket cage. Couples shared their concerns, looking for each other's support, some attendees just shouted at the Council members and the smartest of them sent messengers to their homes to start packing.

Nazeh stopped looking through the hole and Siro asked him if he was okay.

'I don't want the rings back. I don't want to be a Zebra again.'

'Who said anything about rings? Liduvin has said that the Children of the Light will help us if we go west. That's all we have to do!'

But Siro's words did not have the desired effect. Nazeh burst into tears.

'The day they told us we had to leave Underhsell,' he explained, sobbing. My father, mother, Baru and I were at home. My other brothers were in the fields, working. My father faced the Beasts, told them they had no right to that... They took him away. Baru went to look for him the next day at Dugol's palace,' he said as he wiped his tears away. 'He did not come back either.'

'They locked them in the dungeons?' Siro asked.

'I asked my mother the same thing,' Nazeh replied.

'And?' Siro asked in a soft voice. He wanted his friend to stop crying.

'She told me...' He tried to stay put, but his chin trembled, and the words were cut off. 'She told me that now my older brother was Cairu, that I shall forget about Baru.'

The boy remained silent for a few seconds, until he was shaken by an unstoppable crying. Siro covered his friend's mouth to keep the noise from giving them away. Tears slipped between his fingers. He held his friend while watching the few lights were lit in Merco. The river ran quietly, down below, indifferent to any dispute. It was a town that came out of nowhere and was now about to return to it. If they left, all those houses, all the effort of the people would have been in vain. They would go back to the cars and through the desert.

Why can't the Beasts leave us alone?, the boy asked himself.

The uproar in the Council House had diminished until there was only one voice left.

'People of Merco!' Infidas said. 'There is something we can not ignore, the Beasts will come sooner or later. We have built a town, yes. It hasn't been easy, I know. But what is more important?' He paused briefly and made sure everyone paid attention. 'Some huts or our lives?'

'Easy for this one to say, he got his house built...' a man whispered to his wife, just across from where Siro and Nazeh were.

'I left Undershell for a reason...' the merchant said. 'And although it's hard for me to recognize it, it was not because things were bad for me, but because I was tired of seeing how the Beasts did what they wanted with us. And I am happy to have left everything, because now I see that nothing of what I had in Undershell, nothing at all, brought me closer to the happiness I feel now, among you... And I am happy to see that the village of Merco goes on!'

There was some isolated applause. Firla, always full of anger, relaxed. She listened to every word that said Infidas, entranced.

'I would give everything to be able to stay in this oasis,' the man declared, his voice vibrating. 'I have seen your faces during the journey though the desert and I have seen them now, after two years. I know that you also want to stay, I know! And that's why we have to think...'

Infidas descended from the place where he was and approached Liduvin and Grinat. Liduvin's protector interposed and the merchant raised his hands in peace.

'We have to think about what our comrades tell us,' said Infidas. 'They know Dugol first-hand, and so do I. We know what he is capable of and believe me he has no mercy. If he wants to find us, he will. So, as much as it pains us, we must accept the fact that our trip is not over yet.'

Liduvin looked at the merchant with a surprised expression on his face, she did not expect to find an ally in this man dressed in luxurious clothes. The whispers grew back in the room, but Firla cut them short.

'I will not allow this village to surrender,' said the leader of Merco, but she no longer spoke with the conviction she had before.

'And I do not want it either,' said the merchant. 'What I want is for you to keep going! This oasis will not disappear, no matter how many Beasts walk on it. A town can be rebuilt, but what about the people? Let's move forward, Firla. Guide us!'

'Westward?' The village leader asked, for once it seemed that she did not reject the idea fully.

'As long as it's not to the east...' said Infidas with a smile.

There was laughter scattered in the room.

The people applauded the idea of Infidas. Merco's leader stirred on the throne, bit her fist. She looked at Quela, seeking advice. The old woman nodded sternly, whatever it was decided, she would agree.

'The people of Merco will travel...' the leader declared.

A triumphant smile appeared on Liduvin's face, but it did not last long. Firla had not finished giving the verdict.

'But it will not be tomorrow, but five days from now, when everybody will be ready... And I don't know if it will be west or south, that will be decided by the council once the explorers return,' he added, looking at Liduvin. 'We will be guided by what is more prudent, not by superstitions and tales.'

'We must leave tomorrow!' Insisted Liduvin. 'They will be here in five days.'

'That you do not know!' Retorted Firla. 'And the decision is already made. The meeting is over!'

The Council House emptied. People pushed themselves to exit through the tiny entrance while chatting about everything that happened. Siro stared at Liduvin for a moment. She had remained quiet in the middle of the tent, her fists clenched, and her gaze lost.

Why don't you listen to her? The boy was outraged. *She knows more than you all!*

Grinat surrounded Liduvin's shoulders and guided her out of the tent while whispering something under his breath. That was when Siro realized that he had to get home before them.

They're supposed to find me asleep! He told himself.

He grabbed Nazeh by the arm and made him follow him down the slope of the hill of roots. He thought he would not, but as he went down, he saw that Infidas had stopped Liduvin and Grinat halfway down the stairs of the hill and spoke to them under the torchlight.

What does he want? He wondered, but he had no time to eavesdrop.

When they reached the foot of the hill, the two children said goodbye. Nazeh looked scared, but he could not do anything to help. He told him to go to sleep right away and that they would talk about it all the next morning.

He arrived at Liduvin's tent with plenty of time, but he could not sleep. He had heard and seen too many things to just close his eyes. His head was resting on the blankets when he heard the two adults arrive.

'I know you don't trust anyone, Grinat,' said Liduvin. 'But Infidas is the only person who can help us.'

Grinat whispered in her ear.

'Firla does not need to know anything about all this,' she replied.

Liduvin said goodbye to Grinat with a long kiss and a hug. When the man had left, Liduvin entered the tent without making a sound. From the bed, Siro pretended to sleep.

'You can open your eyes any time, little Siro,' said Liduvin as she undressed. She took off the bracelets and some and the cloak, the good one, she decided to bring to the Council House. 'I know you just arrived.'

'How did you know I was awake?' Siro asked.

'I didn't know,' the woman said, brushing her hair. 'But you have left leaves everywhere. It is obvious where you have been. Have you heard everything?'

'Firla is stupid,' Siro answered as he covered himself with the blankets. 'It is not your fault that the Beasts seek us.'

'She lost her husband that day, Siro.'

'And I, my parents,' the boy objected, although there was no trace of grief or resentment in those words. It had been a long time ago. 'She can't be so selfish.'

Liduvin kept the wise stones that had been thrown across the carpet and went to bed next to Siro.

'Well, well, little one. Maybe we should give you a seat in the council,' She ran a hand by his hair and kissed his forehead. 'You have become a little man since we arrived.'

'But you still treat me like a child...'

'Get used to it,' she said as she started a tickle attack under the boy's armpits. 'It will be like that for many years, you know?'

The boy laughed and grabbed the woman's hands. She finally gave up, and just gave him a hug. Siro noticed the warmth of her body and the scent of jasmine with which she had perfumed.

'Why does Grinat go every night?' He asked suddenly.

'It's because of the twins, Bartus and Axelai require attention.

It's hard for them to go to sleep,' explained Liduvin as she settled into the bed. Each time there was less space for the two. 'Zuria needs Grinat more than we do.'

'That's why he's her husband?' Siro asked as he imagined Grinat kissing Zuria under the sheets, just as he did with Liduvin.

'It's one of the reasons... Do you remember the wedding, little one? We stopped all the cars in the middle of the desert just for that! And with the heat...'

The boy nodded. It had been old Quela who had married them before the eyes of the rest of the exiles. Zuria was single and had two three-year-old twins to take care of. She was younger than Liduvin, only eighteen.

Siro saw the whole ceremony sitting in a car, in the shade, but the couple had to sweat under the sun. He had listened to people's conversations without even noticing. Some commented that Zuria needed a husband no matter what; others that they made a very strange couple, she so short and he so tall; and some more sinister voices insinuated that the father of the twins was a Beast, and that Zuria had been one of his slaves. Siro had not understood why they had married until they reached the oasis and had seen how Grinat helped her build her house and took half of the prey she hunted. 'But what about Liduvin?' He always wondered.

'I just do not understand why you're not his wife too,' Siro asked, not sure what went on between the three adults.

'No, it's different,' she said, with a smile that did not let him see what she really thought. 'But we could have married if we had wanted! A man can have several women and vice versa, you know, right?'

'Yeah, sure!' Exclaimed Siro, he was offended that she still took him for a small and ignorant child. 'Firla has three husbands. Why don't you two get married? You are always together. And Grinat only talks to you! Not with Zuria, nor with the twins...'

Nor me, he was about to say, but he bit his tongue.

'Our story is different. Now we are together, yes, but we may not always be together. There will come a day when Grinat will have fulfilled the promise he made to me, and then he will be able to talk to Zuria or whoever he wants. And who knows...? Maybe that day will no longer need me,' she stroked his hair slowly, with the same cadence with which she spoke.

They were silent for a while, while Liduvin played with Siro's hair. The stars shone through the window. He felt a chill when he saw the night sky. He pulled up the blanket and noticed that his eyelids heavy.

'Will we go to Teradam?' He asked with narrowed eyes. 'Will we see the Children of Light?'

'Yes, little Siro,' he replied sweetly. 'Although I'll need your help… But you must promise me that you will not tell anyone,' said Liduvin. 'It has to be our secret.'

'I promise,' said the boy.

Chapter 17: The lagoon

'What is this place?' Matildet asked as she entered the grotto.

Siro watched the darkness from the threshold. The sunlight timidly crept into the cave, shining on the lagoon's surface. He could feel the humidity of the floor under his bare feet. The air was cool. A drop of water fell on his shoulder. The ceiling was full of deformed stalactites dripping at odd intervals.

A black-scaled lizard with glowing eyes went by the hunter's side and climbed up a stalagmite. He stuck out his tongue twice, mocking him, and then disappeared in the shadows.

I wish I could hide myself too, he thought. He did not like being there, but if they wanted to fill the waterskins, there was no choice. He sank one of waterskins under the lagoon and then another. Matildet was by his side, handing him the empty ones.

'I found this place a few years ago,' explained Siro. Since the last two days, he noticed that the words came more easily.

'A cave. It fits you... I bet someone else lives around here, Siro,' exclaimed Matildet. Her voice echoed through cave's vault. 'It's not the oasis, but one could live here...'

'I don't think so,' he replied, keeping his eyes at the bottom of the lagoon.

'Always looking at the bright side...' the Daughter of the Light added, sarcastically. 'Do you think those two may have come all this way? You know, Guido and Junal, I think they were called...'

Siro gestured to Matildet to be quiet. The girl shut up and listened. A single wave reached the waterskin that the hunter kept sunk. It came from the furthest side of the lagoon, but it was so vast, and the cave so dark, that the exact origin could not be distinguished. Siro reached out and grabbed the girl's arm.

'Out, now!' he ordered.

'Really, now? It's boiling outside...' The Daughter of the Light complained.

A deep roar made the whole cave tremble. Matildet shrieked

and ran even faster than the hunter. They went out into the sunlight without looking back for a second.

'What was that?' Matildet asked, catching her breath.

Siro shook his head left and right. He did not know what it was, never did and didn't intend to ever find out. They had filled four of six waterskins.

It could have been worse, he told himself.

They had walked for four days until they reached the ravines of the southeast, where the lagoon was located. The wind and sand had accompanied them for the first three days, and on the fourth, when they reached the canyons, they recovered their strength under the shadow of the walls of silica and granite.

The Labyrinth, as Siro called that place, encompassed hundreds of natural paths that scarred the earth. It was very easy to get lost. Luckily, the hunter had learned to orient himself over time. The walls of pearly mica were sculpted by the onslaught of the wind, and Siro knew the paths he had gone by thanks to these marks. Each turn was a contrast of light and darkness. There were hiding places, holes and caves where it was better not to get close to. Bushes and some withered orange trees that folded under the weight of their own fruits rooted among rocks. It was not uncommon to see green and arid areas less than a meter apart. Everything depended on the capricious turns of the canyons and the angle of the sunbeams.

The lagoon spread below the surface of the Labyrinth. One could access it through many caves, but some were dangerous: as access to them was too high or just above the water, and once one was in, it was not possible to go back. Once, Siro had fallen into the lagoon entering through one of those openings. He had swum for hours without knowing where to go or if he would find solid ground. During that journey through the black waters of the lagoon, he had heard the monster for the first time. Helpless, he heard the monster growl growing under his feet. He had hoped that thing had died of old age. He was wrong.

'Now I get why you left,' said Matildet.

The two sat behind a half-holed rock, sheltered from the sun. Siro handed her one of the waterskins. She took a few sips but didn't look away from the cave's entrance.

'Shall I suppose... you've never seen anyone around before, have you?'

'I saw two girls.'

'Really? Who? When…?'

'Two girls,' repeated Siro. 'I was fifteen or sixteen, and they… about the same, I guess. They looked alike: black, braided hair. They wore purple dresses. Very dirty. They saw me and pointed at me with spears. We said nothing. They left after a while. I looked for them… for days. I never saw them again.'

'Do you think they had a hideout around here?'

'They had a basket full of oranges. They must have left that same day.'

'What were they afraid of?' Asked the Daughter of the Light.

Beasts, he was about to say, but instead shrugged and took a sip from the skin. The fresh water felt good, although he regretted not having drunk more when he was by the lagoon.

'I hope they did not run into anything in there,' Matildet added and pointed to the cave's entrance.

After resting for a while, Siro decided it was time to go hunting. Matildet accompanied him as usual. They arrived at a spot full of small holes. They were the size of a fist and scattered along a silica wall. Siro saw a trail of tiny droppings. The Daughter of the Light was ready to receive a new hunting lesson.

'If you put your hand in the hole, it will bite you. If you want the badger to come out…'

'…You need a bait,' Matildet completed. 'But I doubt they like to eat twigs. You will have to look for something tastier.'

The hunter scratched the ground and pulled out a handful of worms. Matildet turned pale as she watched them writhe between his fingers.

'I don't like where this is going to,' Matildet asked.

Siro kicked them against the stick and rubbed them hard, until the blood and entrails of the worms stained half its length. The girl looked away.

'You done?' She asked, still turned.

Siro brought his hand close to the girl's head without making a sound. Then he said yes, and when Matildet turned, she let out a cry of disgust when she saw the hand full of blood and bits of worm a inches from her face.

'It's not funny!' She shouted.

Siro laughed at the top of his lungs and Matildet slapped him on the arm, but she also laughed.

'Eliria did not like worms either.'

'Do you know anyone, other than yourself, who does like them?' Matildet exclaimed. 'How old was she?'

'Who?'

'Eliria.'

'One year older, nine,' Siro replied.

'Did you like her?'

'Yes,' he replied, feeling awkward, though, why should he hide such a thing? There were days when the memory of the girl was painful, but those days were long gone. 'Nazeh like her too.'

'Oh yeah?' Said Matildet, amused. 'And which of the two got the girl? Or were you too young to think about these things?'

Siro smiled mischievously, like the Daughter of the Light just did.

'I expected no less,' she said as a compliment. 'Can you show me how?'

The comment caught Siro off guard.

'I mean the badger,' she clarified. 'I'd like to have something for dinner tonight, you know?'

Siro nodded and approached the rock wall. He introduced the bloody stick as he pulled the knife from the scabbard with the other hand. Matildet observed the whole process with expectation. The hunter raised the weapon and, suddenly, something pulled the stick from the other side. He held and pulled unhurriedly. The black and white furry head of the badger came out of the hole in the cave and then Siro pounced on him. After a quick movement, the animal was beheaded.

'How can you get used to this?' Matildet asked.

'You could too.'

'Sorry to disappoint you,' she added. 'Death and I do not get along too well. I'm afraid of killing. What goes around comes around. Did you hear this saying before?'

'I'm hungry.'

'Sure. Let's go,' Matildet forgot the subject right away.

'I want to explore the caves,' Matildet said as Siro chewed on the roasted badger. 'There's water and food in this place. It's very likely that there is still someone left. I bet you they are hiding somewhere around.'

Siro was opening a stripped pineapple he had picked at the oasis. He almost cut himself with the knife.

'I know, I know… Let me elaborate. We must find a way to get in there unseen. Just think about it. If those girls lived in this place before you came, it's possible they've been hiding from you all this time, right?'

'Dangerous,' Siro replied.

'I think it's worth it. If we are careful enough and… what the hell? Siro, look down there!'

Siro turned and glanced at the bottom of the gorge. Below, a pink and white-feathered ostrich was messing with the luggage of the travellers. The bird pecked the fruits that were inside one of the hunter's sacks carelessly.

'Hey, what are you doing!?' Matildet yelled. The ostrich lifted its long neck, looked at the Daughter of the Light for a moment, and carried on with its own devices.

The hunter descended the path slowly. He did not want the bird to eat the little supplies they had left, but he did not want to break a leg either.

'Oh, shit…' he heard Matildet say from the camp where they had lit the fire. 'It's got my backpack, Siro! Hurry up!'

Yeah, yeah, I'm on it… Thought Siro. He stood beside the ostrich and was surprised to see how big it was. With its neck stretched, it was more than two meters high. The tail feathers opened like a fan when the hunter approached it.

The ostrich had Matildet's white backpack ravelled between the beak and the neck. It was shaking its head, trying to get rid of the backpack, but all it achieved was for it to slip down the neck, like a saddlebag.

The small bird eyes stared at him with an awkward look. Siro saw the curved beak stained with pulp and hesitated whether to jump on it or not. And in that instant of hesitation, the ostrich turned and ran off.

'The flask!' shouted Matildet. 'I need it!'

Siro did not wait any longer and went after it. The bird turned in the narrowest recesses of the Labyrinth, as if there were a perverse logic inside that tiny head. At one point, it jumped an obstacle thanks to its short wings leaving trail of feathers behind.

Damn bird! The hunter complained silently. He climbed one of the rock walls with his bare hands and reached out to jump the rock that blocked the path.

The bird was nowhere to be seen, but not the trail of feathers. Siro moved among the rocks, slender as columns, that populated the place.

They are like bare trees, he thought as he passed by. He noticed the higher parts of the monoliths and saw that some of them bent and joined together. The lush, dark vegetation of the oasis came to mind for a fraction of a second.

After the forest of monoliths, the path ran alongside a ravine that Siro called the Breach. It was the deepest precipice of the whole Labyrinth, so much so that one could only see the bottom thanks to the silver shine of the river running in its depths. Siro had to move carefully to avoid falling. All the grey rock of the Breach was streaked with reddish granite that rushed to the bottom of the valley and making it look like the mountain was bleeding.

There were blue and yellow streaks on the other side of the cliff. The wind carried the characteristic sulphur smell in it. Just below the veins, halfway up, there were a few openings in the rock. Some were little more than protrusions that might had served as shelters long ago. The two girls he had met could have lived in one of those caves, isolated from the rest of the world, yes, but also safe from the Beasts and perhaps the Nightborn.

The wind was blowing so hard through the Breach forcing Siro to grab on every rock and small trees he found. Occasionally he would find a pink feather filling him with hope to find the ostrich again.

I really hope it has not fallen down the ravine. Else we can forget about the flask and the backpack, he told himself.

He went around the entire precipice until at last he found himself back into the Labyrinth's bright walls. A couple of hares hid in the bushes as he passed. They took a long time to react. They were not used to seeing humans in that place.

'C'mon, be good. Give me the backpack back. Don't you see it is not made for you?' Siro heard the voice of Matildet coming from somewhere nearby.

He arrived at the same place where they had camped, but came out from below, after crossing a natural stone arch. The Daughter of the Light was standing on a rock and kept the attention of the pink ostrich with the remains of a pineapple.

'The backpack! The backpack first, then you get food' Matildet negotiated, although the bird did not listen to reason.

The Daughter of the Light shrieked every time the animal approached the beak to remove the fruit from her hands. Siro watched the show until it stopped amusing him. He took one vein-braided rope he had made back in the oasis and made a lace to catch the ostrich. As the animal was being distracted, it was not hard to tie it around its neck.

'It was high time,' Matildet exclaimed. She jumped off the rock. 'You had a good time wandering around, huh, while I was here fighting for my life? Have you seen the way it looks at me? I know its herbivorous... but I'd bet it wanted to gauge my eyes out.

'Not herbivorous. Eat everything,' said Siro. 'Hand me the pineapple.'

The hunter lifted the fruit and held it close to the ostrich, which was fighting with the lasso. The animal forgot its problems and focused on the food. Siro tried to grab the backpack, but the bird got nervous and pecked him in the head. The hunter gave him an angry slap in the face and removed the backpack with a jerk.

'It got confused with your pineapple-shaped head,' she said, holding back her laughter. 'Did it hurt you?'

Siro pointed his head.

'Hard,' he replied.

With the ostrich well tied to one of the monoliths he had seen beside the camp, Matildet told him the fear that had experienced when she saw the bird return and without Siro. By the way she related it --how she had hidden at the beginning, how she slowly had found the courage to climb the rock, and the determination with which she had used the fruit-- it seemed that she had had a worse time than when they encountered the Beasts in the oasis.

We are all the same for her, the hunter was disappointed. *For the Children of the Light, Beasts and humans are the same.*

When she finished, it was Siro's time to explain what he had seen on the other side of the Breach. Matildet wanted to know more about the caves on the other side and asked they could make it there one way or another. The hunter shrugged.

While they talked, he realized he was getting better at understanding Matildet's words. She spoke fast, sometimes too much, and often arrogantly, but he did not care. By her side, downtimes had changed. Meals were no longer a silent ritual interrupted only by the monotonous noise of his chewing, but an ever-meandering conversation from one subject to another. Matildet loved to complain about the things she did not like about living in the desert, like not being able to bathe whenever she wanted. Every day, she'd wrinkle her nose at her own smell, although Siro still noticed her unmistakeable moon flowers aroma, when she was close.

'I can't believe I used to shower twice a day! Twice!' Exclaimed the girl. 'Do you know how hard this is for me?'

Siro pictured her in the Tear-City, bathing under a brilliant waterfall, not like the oasis, but much wider, with the crystalline water flowing down her breasts to the tip of her pink nipples. He could well see her and the other Daughters of the Light, all together, just like the women of Merco bathed in the river; although that other picture suggested very different things to him.

Sometimes, when he chatted with her, he focused so much on her lips that the Daughter of the Light realised and asked if he was still listening to her because he seemed to be miles away. She certainly understood why he looked at her that way, but never made any sign that it bothered her.

Surely you think that one day she'll lay eyes on you, poor bastard..., a metallic voiced whispered in his ears.

That night, while trying to sleep side by side, Matildet got up and put her hands to her face. They had moved the camp to higher ground, slightly above the cave overlooking the lagoon. The stars filled the night sky, which shone with a navy-blue hue, like Matildet's eyes. The ostrich cackled somewhere below. Siro had thought that it would serve as a sentinel if someone approached while they slept.

'You good?' he asked her.

The Daughter of the Light wiped away the tears that ran down her cheeks.

'I was thinking of my colleagues at Teradam,' she explained.

'Miss...' Siro stopped and pushed himself to say it right. 'Do you miss them?'

'Yes. Mostly Cas. I never imagined I would befriend someone like her... We are so different.'

'And your father?'

Matildet took a few seconds to answer.

'No,' she said dryly. 'Since my mother died, we are like ghosts to each other. We rarely coincide. We don't talk. It's a weird situation, but I can't change it. Sometimes I feel that I move, I breathe... but I do not think, you know? It's like I'm not even alive. It seems that nothing is worth it, that the only thing that remains is her memory. I guess he feels the same way about mom, and that's why he pretends nothing matters...'

The Daughter of the Light fell into silence. Her sad eyes settled on Siro, who noticed how the hair on his back stood on end.

'And the worst part is that no matter how hard I try, I can not leave it behind,' Matildet finished. 'You know what I mean?'

'Maybe.'

'Do you feel this way when you think of your parents?'

'No.'

'What about Liduvin?'

Siro found himself speechless and suddenly ill. He remembered how Liduvin used to kiss him goodnight after telling him a tale.

All of that is behind me, he told himself. *Even if I see her again, nothing will be like before.*

He did not want to say anything else to the Daughter of the Light. He covered himself under the blankets and turned his back to her, but she made him turn again and snuggled into his arms. The girl's golden hair stayed under his chin and he kissed them instinctively. She did not say a word.

Nightmares had chased him since they left the oasis. The Beast chased him. The location changed every night: sometimes it ambushed him in the jungle, other times it cornered him in the Nest of cages... It had even chased him through the streets of Merco! And in all those nightmares, he ended up killing it. He cracked its head open with a stone or stabbed it, but when he looked at the corpse, the being lying on the ground was no one but himself.

'Mum, not with Siro, he hurts me,' said his own bloodied face.

He woke up with the same questions swirling in his head: *Who was it? How did it know my name? Did we meet before? In Undershell, perhaps? In Merco?*

Its face was completely strange to him, and he was positive he would remember! In his mind he could still see the scar covering its eye, the shaved head, the rose-shaped mask, those horrible Brands. No, it did not look like any of the children in the village, and it was impossible for any of them would have ended like this. Its companions had called it Ubald, but the name did not say much either.

A hand shook him. Siro turned under the blanket. Matildet stared at him, with a full smile.

'I have an idea.'

'What?'

'An idea to dodge the monster and explore the cave. C'mon, get up!'

Siro frowned.

'What if it is bigger than us?' Siro asked as he followed the Daughter of the Light. He pictured a giant fish with black scales that swallowed them in one bite.

'Is that what you're worried about? You faced a giant lion...'

'A Biter,' said Siro.

'Whatever...' She continued. 'It was three times bigger than you! And now you tell me you're afraid of what? A fish?'

'What if it's an eel or a snake?' Siro protested. 'Or a...'

Unconsciously, he wrapped his hand around the quartz stone hanging from its collar.

'A what?' Asked the Daughter of the Light.

'One of your enemies,' Siro said hesitantly. 'The Nightborn. What if they live in the lagoon?'

'Nightborn...? Do you mean the bad guys in Mother Snake's story? Those who like to kidnap little girls and transform their mothers?'

The hunter nodded.

'Fear not, Siro. I assure you there is no Nightborn in the whole gorge.'

'How do you know?' he asked. He glanced at the quartz stone in his necklace, still black.

'I know. As long as you are with me, the Nightborn will do you no harm… Listen, it might be dangerous. But I have good news. I know how to minimize the risks. In fact, it is an idea that you have given me. Let's say the monster is a seven-meter-long eel,' Matildet said, snapping her fingers to get Siro's attention. 'Would not it be good for us to have a bait in case things get tricky?'

Siro looked at the bird. He could see where she was going.

The humid air and the thousands of stalactites and stalagmites that populated the cave made the Siro shudder. He could already feel the danger. Matildet stepped forward, carrying the two halves of the spear hanging from her back, in one of the pods that Siro used to keep them.

Matildet raised a hand in the air and it shone with a clear light, just like Teradam's. The cave lit up and Siro became uneasy seeing the shadows casted by all those grey stalactites. They reminded him of the Biter's teeth.

After pulling and getting pecked in the head, Siro had manage to tie the rope around the ostrich's neck and take it with them. He guided the ostrich to the edge of the lagoon and tied the bird to a stalagmite while it drank, oblivious to the danger that lurked under the water.

The two travellers hid. The hunter had the knife ready for when the lagoon's monster appeared. Matildet's gloved hand shone like a torch.

'What is it waiting for?' she whispered. They had been hiding for a long time.

'The bait. It has to be closer,' replied Siro.

They approached the ostrich with discretion and pushed it by surprise. The bird cackled and fell into the water. The two rushed back to the hiding spot. The ostrich floated quietly in the lagoon, rocking left and right, like a small boat.

'It can't get closer than this,' exclaimed the girl.

The waiting went on for ages. The ostrich was very happy in the water and the monster was nowhere to be seen. The hunter was scanning the edges of the lagoon, looking for some trace on the underwater creature, but the seconds lengthened, and nothing happened... Until a sharp noise emerged from the darkness. The spear slipped from Matildet's hands, but Siro was ready to go. The waves followed one another at the bottom of the lagoon. Some were so violent that they crashed like hammer blows on the nearest stalagmites. The ostrich squawked at being shaken by the tide but did not move from the spot. The noise increased in intensity. The whole grotto trembled, about to crumble.

It's going to eat the three of us in one bite, he thought.

'Time to go,' Siro said.

'No, wait!' She said. 'It's about to end.'

And just as Matildet had announced, the noise disappeared. It had lasted a little more than a few minutes.

'Did the monster run away?' The hunter asked.

'Sorry to disappoint you, but there's no monster here. It's something else.'

She raised her hand and the brightness beaming from it spread throughout the cave. Water became clear and some ghostly fishes fled into the abyssal darkness of the lagoon.

Light spread along the rugged ceiling beyond they had seen so far. The lagoon was huge, at least a hundred steps wide, under the mountain.

The vision did not last long. The glow of the Matildet's glove lost intensity. Siro noticed that the bottom of her dress had blackened, just as it had done in the oasis, when he had seen her use the light to scare the Beasts away.

'There's a water extraction plant down there,' Matildet explained. 'All we hear is the drill against the rocks. I can't believe it still works, but it's got to be that. This means that there must be some of our facilities up here. How is that possible? Do you have any idea of how many years have passed since someone put their feet there for the last time? Follow me, Siro, time to swim.'

The Daughter of the Light got into the water with her dress on. She made sure she had the spear securely tied on her back and sank into the lagoon.

'Siro, come! Don't you see it? It's the chance we were waiting for!'

Chapter 18: Listen to the voices

Wait! Thought Siro. Matildet dove into the water as she hadn't a second to spare. Siro removed his cape and tightly fastened his belt as he slipped into the lagoon. The ostrich floated indifferently over the dark water. It moved the tail feathers, saying goodbye to the hunter.

I don't know who the bait is now, he told himself. He hoped that the Daughter of the Light was right about the origin of the noise.

He dived into the cold water and followed Matildet's trail of light. The girl looked like a star in the middle of the night sky, a fallen celestial body sinking deeper and deeper.

A school of silverfish passed by Matildet, who lit the seabed around her. Siro followed closely, holding his breath. As they descended, the outline of seaweed-covered sea rocks waved at them like hands begging for help. An eel swam by the hunter and slipped between two rusty plates that someone must have screwed down there a long time ago.

The Daughter of the Light suddenly changed course and ascended. Her gloomy silhouette moved near a thick steel-made column, with a sharp relief spiralling upwards.

Siro swam as fast as he could. A whistle reached his ears as he pushed his way up. His body could no longer hold on without breathing and his fingers and toes were numb from the cold.

Matildet's light was standing still. The water was already coming through his mouth, but he made a final effort, his eyes shut with pain, and finally he felt a breath of fresh air.

The air got in his lungs too quickly making him cough. The girl floated next to him, clutching to the steel column. Her face was red, teardrops showed under the eyes.

'I am sorry, I'm truly sorry. I didn't know it was going to be so long... I... We almost didn't make it, huh?' Said the Daughter of the Light and violently coughed. 'We can't stay here. The drill can get back to work any time and I don't want to end up like mashed potatoes.'

Siro swam towards her and grabbed the steel column. His heart was pounding. The air refused to enter his lungs fast enough.

The girl's hand still shone and illuminated everything around her. The features of the Daughter of the Light were bleak in that light. The marked cheekbones and wet hair attached to his face gave him an emaciated appearance.

'Look, we have to go up. Can you see those ladders?' Matildet pointed out.

Above their heads was a network of metal platforms. A fly of stairs descended parallel to the column. Siro gathered that they were about ten meters up. It seemed they were at the bottom of a well.

Matildet climbed up the column, clenching her fists around the grooved sides. Her white suit dripped as he climbed. Her lit hand revealed a messy patch of rusty metal plates on the walls. Some of them might have fallen into the water long ago. Black tubes run the walls from top to bottom.

They climbed the ladders reaching the circular platform the drill was built on. The floor consisted of perforated metal plates, giving that uneasy sensation it could all fall apart with a breeze.

Matildet's light went from yellowish to bluish. The place suddenly woke up, and blue sparks swept across the ceiling and sparked the top of the drill. Then, those same lights scattered everywhere, and the hunter was awed to see that there were five identical metal columns far beyond.

In between columns, one could see a series of metal platforms that formed rings around the columns in all directions, like a spiderweb.

'What's this place?' Asked Siro, with anguish in his voice.

'I bet this is the 'Third,'' Matildet replied as she twisted and pressed her hair to remove the water.

'The third what? Does it belong to the Children of the Light?'

Matildet leaned against the railing and Siro took a spot next to her to contemplate the metal paths that ran over the lagoon.

'I don't know when it was, but... at some point in history we went nuts. But don't worry, I won't let it happen again.'

'I don't understand.'

'This is pure greed,' Matildet pointed to the five columns. 'The drills bore the planet and destroy it. Who knows for how long this has been going on...'

'So, Nightborn built it?'

'I wish I could say so,' Matildet bowed her head. 'They are ours. But now we are here, and we must stop them, there has to be a way to do it.'

The Daughter of the Light pointed to one of the rock walls with a huge door. A metal walkway led to it, but it would not be easy to get there. The roads until that last section were damaged, the metal had bent and some bridges between ring and ring were cut. Even so, Matildet seemed determined to make it, and Siro followed her.

The hunter watched where she stepped. He felt the cold pierced metal sheet under his feet. Through them, he could see the large fall to the lagoon.

'Why... build?' The words getting stuck in his throat again.

'We forget the consequences of things easily, Siro. We think ourselves unique and look for excuses to stumble upon the same rock...'

'I thought the Children of the Light were all good,' he said.

'That makes as much sense as thinking that all the people you call Beasts are bad.'

Matildet stopped for a moment and turned to Siro. The bluish light of that place made her even more mysterious and sensual than she already was.

'Sorry, I shouldn't have told you that. Sometimes I talk like Liam...' Matildet said wistfully. 'And sometimes I do it like Cas. Whether you like it or not, people change us. You yourself would be different if you had not met Liduvin, perhaps.'

'I would be dead. By the Beasts.'

Siro followed the steps of the Daughter of the Light along the crumbling path.

'Let me ask you something,' Matildet said. 'Let's say you have someone you love very much like, I don't know, a son. You would do anything for him, right?'

He did not know what to reply, the possibility of having a child had never occurred to him. He had been alone most of his life. Where did the idea of being a father fit in all that?

'I guess,' he said simply.

'Of course, it's normal,' Matildet said as they circled the second drill in search of a safe path. 'But everything has a limit, right? And even if we think we would go further, without no person or law being able to stop us... Don't you think we might be wrong?'

'Why should we be wrong?' Said the hunter.

'Well... Our view of what is right and what is wrong would be distorted, wouldn't it? What kind of moral compass can you have if you have no limits? What happens when our actions become a weapon instead of a shield?'

'What do you mean?'

'You can see the result. This is what happens when instead of protecting your children you use them to attack others' she explained.

The Daughter of the Light pointed to the three drills ahead of them.

'Someone built these to protect their children from misery, thirst... They forgot about the rest of the world. They told themselves there was no choice but to break this world. They repeated it over and over, until they believed it. They needed an honest reason under all that greed... but there wasn't one. Those people... They were people like my father.'

Matildet stayed in the middle of one of the gangways and looked down. The lagoon was pitch black from that height, the mild echo of the tide rising from the depths. The girl's eyes stared at the black tubes connecting the drills.

'Liam opened my eyes...' she said. 'It's all my father's fault. All of it.'

Siro felt he had to say something at that moment. He closed in and put a hand on her shoulder.

'What do you want to do?'

'We'll stop this place,' she declared and struck the railing that rang through the cave. 'Cas and I already tried, but it's not possible from Teradam. It must be done from here, somewhere. Look at the lights, they all end up at that rusty door.'

It was true, Siro noticed that all those threads of blue light would come together around the door, waiting for it to open and sneak in. High-pitched shrieks raised from the darkness below them. The hunter grabbed Matildet's hand and pulled her to help her cross the gangway.

The shrieks intensified and a cloud of bats engulfed them. The creatures flapping their wings furiously above their heads. The bats flew between the metal bars of the railing, circling around the intruders. Siro pulled the Daughter of the Light to get to the next ring.

Bats were everywhere. Their wings shone under the blue lights and turned that dark cloud into a thousand sharp faces that filled the vault of the cave. 'You taste like desert, desert and terror!' He heard suddenly. A bat hit his legs and fell face first on the gangway. 'Down here, wildling, you know where I am.'

A body floated in the water.

'Get out of here!' Matildet's voice rose above the bats' fuss and a whitish light filled the grotto. The winged creatures returned to the shadows. 'Siro, where are you?'

He couldn't talk. He was staring at the bottom of the lagoon. *It's the Beast... It's down there. How?*' He wondered. He recognized his huge silhouette, the Brand around his arm and the bloodied skull from the blows he had given him. He noticed that someone was grabbing him, and the contact brought him back to reality.

'Ok, ok. This time was my fault. I was being noisy,' Matildet apologized. The bats left her dishevelled. 'What if we leave before they decide that my light is not that scary, huh? Siro, are you alright? Why are you so quiet? Did you get a bat in your mouth, or what?'

The hunter scanned the lagoon for a trace, but there was nothing there.

I've seen it, He told himself. *The Beast was down there.*

The hunter followed Matildet, trying to keep calm. As they moved along the rings surrounding the drills, he repeated to himself that there was nothing down there, that it was all his imagination. The Beast was dead in the pond, not there.

It did not know me and now is dead, he thought while holding the quartz stone. *I crashed its skull, stabbed it and let it sink in the water... No one survives that.*

Matildet put her palm on the rusty door. Straight threads of light left its centre and spread along the door. Each of the white threads joined with one of the blue lights gathered around the door and the lines changed colour. Even so, three of the threads did not find their pairs. Siro noticed that the light of the door was channelled through glass tubes. Three of them were cracked. Under the tubes, on the side where they were damaged, a black and white crust had emerged, formed by tiny cubes. They were the same cubes he had seen in the desert underground base before but, at that time, with the Biter chasing after them, he had not had a moment to share his thoughts.

'What is it?' He said, as he pointed to the polygonal crust.

'This, Siro, is one of the greatest discoveries in our history,' Matildet said in a solemn tone. 'They are high voltage bioelectric generators. How to put it? Well, I think the white liquid is the superconductor and the black one is the generator, or the other way round, not sure... Anyway! In contact with oxygen they grow in a fractal pattern, as you can see.' She pointed to the crust of cubes coming out of the tube. 'That's why they are kept locked in reinforced methacrylate tubes. There's xenon flowing through and...'

The Daughter of the Light halted the explanation. Siro looked completely puzzled.

'Ugh… I don't know how make you understand. Let me try again. If I say that this is what makes the lights turn on and off and the doors to open, is that enough?'

Siro thought about it for a second.

'Is it blood?', he asked.

'A very romantic way to put it. But yes, we could say that it is the blood of this whole installation… And I think this door has been bleeding for too long.'

The hunter had a hard time assimilating that the old rusty door was alive, but the drills also turned on on their own, as Matildet pointed out before. It was incredible that the Children of the Light were able to build such things. There were so many secrets he couldn't even grasp...

'Who built this place?' He wanted to know.

'You mean names and surnames? No idea. Maybe if I had been in Teradam a little longer, I might have found out, but things don't always work out the way we want,' she said.

Matildet placed her hand on the door and a stream of lights, thin as strings, appeared over the remaining methacrylate fragments. Yellow symbols, remnants of lost characters, shone on their surface. Siro ignored the meaning of the writings.

The Daughter of the Light followed the door lights with her free hand. The lights turned away from her and changed to darker tones. The more she tried to catch the shiny strings, the more branches burst out. Matildet grimaced. She didn't seem to find what she wanted.

'You can give life to the drills, the walls,...' Siro murmured.

'Can you give life to people?'

'Sure,' said the girl, who increasingly moved her finger more frantically, as the lights played with her.

'How?' he asked, awed. Would she reveal that secret?

'Well, as usual, I suppose,' she said. 'How did your parents give you life?'

The Daughter of the Light giggled and looked at him with roguish eyes. He knew her enough to realise when she was just teasing him.

'Sorry, I was being mean,' Matildet apologised, though the smile was still present on her lips. 'You make it so easy sometimes... How do you want me to give life to anyone? I can't even open a damn door! Oh, screw this!'

The girl detached her hand from the door and the branches of light cringed to disappear.

And now how do we go through? Asked Siro. We have risked our lives to get here. *That can't be it.*

'I am BEHIND you...', the hunter heard the metallic voice of the Beast. He turned in a hurry, knife in hand, but behind there was only the decrepit web of catwalks. 'No, it is not,' he told himself. 'Take it easy...'

'More bats coming?' Asked the Daughter of the Light.

The lights had gone out in the distance. The drill they had climbed up was out of sight. The only illuminated part of that cave was the threshold of that impenetrable old door, the rest was all darkness. The distant shrieks of the bats and the murmur of the water kept Siro on edge, and yet the squeals of the catwalks had him baffled. It seemed someone was walking in the shadows.

'Hey Siro, it's only you and I down here,' Matildet told him, as if reading his thoughts. 'You should know better than me. Can anyone survive feeding off only bats?'

Before Siro responded, the rusty door opened by itself. A stream of air dishevelled the Daughter of the Light and made her stagger inward, but it was over immediately. The blue lights surrounding the doorframe sneaked through the opening.

'I swear *that* wasn't my doing,' the girl exclaimed.

'Light!' Said Siro.

The hunter crossed the door without thinking it twice. He entered a wide passageway full of even older doors. The outer wall must had served to hold the mountain in the past, but now more than half of its length had crumbled, granting an unpayable window to the outer world. The passage ran right next to one of the many ravines of the Labyrinth. Beyond the edge, scattered waterfalls sprouted from the wall of mica, flowing into a river full of sharp stones that ran along the bottom of the Breach.

They followed the passage upwards. The floor, made of white cobblestones, was dotted with weeds and shrubs that had made their way over time. The lights followed them, glued to the wall, as usual, as they branched and re-joined in coloured beams. Siro watched the entire precipice, and the blue sky.

'We come from the other side of the ravine,' he told Matildet. 'I've been up there before.'

'Oh yeah? When?' The girl asked, although she was only paying attention to the shiny drawings on the glassy wall.

'When I was looking for the ostrich.'

Clinging to one of the few remaining columns, Siro leaned into the abyss to see what was above. The rock wall was painted by veins of crimson granite. *Yes, these are the caves I've seen before,* he told himself. Below them, there was a natural path meandering between the rocks. It was possible to get to the river if one walked very carefully, and from there, get to the other side of the ravine. That was an unnerving thought. If there was a passage to the river, it meant that someone could be roaming the cave.

The Daughter of the Light put her hand on an opaque glass door. The door lit and disappeared by some sort of charm. Once inside, they plunged back into darkness. They were in a passage leading to a circular room. Siro followed Matildet in silence. He glimpsed at the black tubes that stretched and braided with each other. The blue lights passed over the heads of the two, and when they reached the circular room, they ascended. The room was like a tower built inside the mountain. There should be five or six meters to the ceiling, but the circular room's diameter would barely reach two meters.

The bottom of a well... again, Siro thought.

Matildet stood in the middle of the room and looked up.

'Wait for me here,' she said. 'I'll be right back'.

Suddenly, the Daughter of the Light's feet took off from the ground. The girl's body floated to the top of the well. He passed through the dark tubes and the lights shone brighter when Matildet passed by, dying her in blue.

She is flying! Siro looked at Matildet's small performance with his mouth open.

The girl disappeared as she entered a dome on the top. Hidden gates closed behind her and leaving Siro down there, alone and in the dark.

So now what? He wondered.

He waited for a while to see if Matildet would return, but that did not seem to be the case. He thought of exploring the path that led to the river instead of looking upwards. Perhaps he would find some trace of the two girls he had met so many years ago, although what he really wanted was to get out of there.

And while he was considering what to do, the black tubes shook. An odd gas escaped from one of them whistling. The floor returned the echo footsteps. There was someone else. A silhouette stood still at the end of one of the passages. It was dark, yet Siro could only tell the visitor was a tall being with something hanging from its face. Siro was astonished when he saw that it was a metal rose-shaped mask.

The misty gas surrounded him. A blue light came down from the roof dome, but the passageways and the silhouette were still dim.

'Why you follow me?' He shouted into the darkness. He didn't know how, but the knife was in his hand.

The silhouette did not answer. The hunter's hand was shaking.

'Go away! I'll kill you again!' He snapped at the shadow, but it remained silent.

The mist dispersed and exposed the dark walls, where thousands of red flowers had sprouted... or that's what Siro thought at first glance. He realised soon enough they were the red feathers attached to the darts that the Beast used. He felt moisture in his feet, looked down to find himself in the middle of a puddle. Water rose to its knees. Flaming leaves fell from the top of the well landing on the water and remaining lit. He saw himself reflected in the water, not as he was now, but as an eight-year-old boy. He ran through a burning forest and heard the cries of Nazeh and Eliria behind the line of bushes.

'No! Enough!' He shouted. His voice echoed throughout the passage.

Siro looked away from that vision and ran away from the

Beast, but the water had become thick and already reached his waist. A marquise leaf fell burning beside him. The water had become blood.

What is all this? His mind buzzed as he backed away. In a panic, he reached out and grabbed the first thing he found so as not to sink into that muddy blood. He was clenching to a series of long, thin tubes. *They are the mask ones!* Thought Siro, in horror. The image of those tubes ripped out through the Beast's throat repulsed him so much he had to open his hand. He fell into the blood up to his neck.

Bubbles appeared on the surface and a frightening face slowly emerged. Ubald's shaved skull and stitched eye popped out. Siro tried to scream, but the blood ran into his mouth. The rose-shaped metal mask came out of the pond. It shone liked the blood was enamel.

'Siro is bad,' said the metallic voice.

'I'm sorry,' he stammered as tears mixed with the pool of blood.

'It hurts, mom,' he insisted. The sewing of the eye was undoing on its own.

'I'm really sorry,' said the hunter between sobs. 'I didn't want to leave you. Ubald, I promise you.'

'Where are we going, wildling? Where?' Asked the Beast. His eye had just broken off and it revealed three bright yellow irises.

Siro had never seen anything like it. Three irises and three pupils in the same eyeball were staring at him with a terrifying depth. His breathing stopped. He could not blink, he could only look at that eye.

'Forgive me, Ubald,' was the only thing he could say and then he sank.

Dead fish floated in the blood. Viscous seaweed rolled up on his feet and hands and dragged him towards the bottom. The Beast's body floated above him, farther and farther, until a bright light passed through the pool and Siro opened his eyes. Matildet's silhouette descended from the dome.

What's just happened? He was on the floor of the circular room. His hands were shaking. He felt weak and dizzy. He had a nasty wound on his forehead. He had fallen, but he didn't remember when.

The Daughter of the Light burst in questions, but he was too confused to answer. He was looking for the Beast, the blood, the flower-shaped darts, but there was nothing there. Only black pipes and metal panels bolted to the floor and walls; and steam, steam everywhere.

Have I dreamed it all? Siro wondered. *How can it be? It was real, the Beast was here, it was right in front of me. He could... he could have killed me, he was really drowning me.*

'Where are we going, wildling...?' Murmured the hunter. Why did it say that?

'Siro, are you alright?' He heard Matildet say.

The Daughter of the Light had him by the arms. Her eyes shone with real concern.

'I think... Yes, I'm fine,' said Siro. 'I've had a vision.'

'You were lying on the floor. What have you seen?'

'The Beast... It was here. It came for me.'

'Here's just you and me, Siro. Calm down, okay? This place is already creepy enough to give you a heart-attack,' she joked, yet she looked worried.

The hunter took a while longer to put himself back together. Matildet gave him some space and went to the wall in the circular room.

'You take it easy. We'll be gone in no time. I stopped the machines, but still got an ace in my sleeve. I found this,' Matildet touched the wall which filled with green shiny lines. A tiny gate opened, and a red orb floated through the air.

Siro was impressed to see that miracle, but he was even more impressed to see that the orb projected images on the air. They were views of the desert, the Labyrinth and beyond. The hunter was in awe, what kind of powers did the Children of the Light have? Liduvin had never told him about it, but perhaps he would not have believed it if she had told him. *They are images in the air,* he had to repeat himself to be sure he was not still hallucinating.

The floating images were a pleasant distraction. Gradually, the idea of having dreamed everything seemed more plausible. The Beast was not there, it died in the oasis. He himself had killed it and its companions had left the body to be eaten by the fish. Despite everything, the question remained, 'where are we going?', the Beast had said. That made Siro's mind go back until the day of the Exile, when the same Beasts that had expelled them from Undershell, had all of a sudden decided to kill them. He remembered the darts and the arrows whistling in the sky, the people falling in the mud, his parents fleeing from the crowd without looking back. And he, a six-year-old, on his own, grabbed by the hand of…

Ubald, it was Ubald, Siro put his hands to his mouth to suppress a shout.

He glanced at Matildet, but she didn't pay attention to him, she was watching one of those images in the air.

'Siro, have you seen that?' She said jovially. 'Come on, what's with this face, huh? It's just holograms, they aren't dangerous. Check this out. We made it. We have found them!'

What are you talking about? The hunter wondered. The floating image was a view from the top of one of the highlands of the Labyrinth. It had to be one of the tallest, since the rest of the gorge looked like paths for ants. The view showed the salt desert, as well, and something else beyond. There was a cloud of smoke emerging from beneath the ground. No, it wasn't from under the ground, but another gorge.

Matildet touched the red orb, and the image widened. Siro distinguished the entrance that sank between the fields of crops and the wooden palisade. He recognized the Great Shell standing at the end of the gorge, the little houses, the lights between the rocks and the blackening clouds, and at the end, just where the vision ended, a dark palace with tall and crooked towers.

'It's eastwards, three or four days away at most. Let's get ready and leave right away. A city no less, Siro. We found ourselves a whole city,' Said Matildet as she threw herself into his arms. 'Do you know what this means? You'll go to Teradam! We did it, we did it!'

'We can't go there.'

'What? Are you kidding? It is very close and there's people. I thought we wouldn't make it!'

'No, Matildet, they are not people. We can't go. That's where the Beasts live.'

The Daughter of the Light separated from Siro and looked him in the face, surprised.

'What are you talking about? We're about to…' Matildet separated her thumb and forefinger less than a centimetre to show him how close they were to their objective. But the hunter shook his head. 'Wait a moment, have I heard correctly? Did you say that is where the Beasts live?'

Siro fell silent and stared down at the floor. When he looked back at the Daughter of the Light, her blue eyes were filled with anger.

'You always knew. You knew this city existed. Answer me!'

The hunter looked at the floating image once more. Yes, he would never forget that palisade of sharp logs. Never.

Chapter 19: Give me a reason

Siro rubbed the flame stone a couple of times against a beech branch and a reddish flare spread along the bark. He put the branch on the chips he had cut with the knife and closed the bonfire circle with one more stone. He blew the ambers with his cloak. The beech always lit with a generous flame. It was the best for cooking, but Siro rarely had it within reach. Near the river that split the bottom of the Labyrinth, beeches grew in abundance, more than the orange trees or any other. In a few minutes they would have the badger roasted and they could eat… That if Matildet spoke to him again, of course.

The Daughter of the Light was close to the edge of the plateau. She stared at the horizon, beyond the Labyrinth.

She doesn't trust me, he thought as he looked askance at the whitish silhouette of Matildet. After what had happened in the cave, when she had shown him all those floating images, she had become furious. 'Do you think this is a joke? How could you? I trusted you!', she shouted.

She had stormed out the circular room. Siro had reached her while crossing the river, at the end of the narrow path. 'Don't follow me, leave me alone!' Matildet yelled at him. Yet, he had followed her to the top of the plateau and then he had lit the fire and prepared the food while waiting for her to talk to him again.

I must do something, he thought.

She still needed him if she wanted to get to Undershell, but did he want to go? The question itself seemed absurd. Going back there meant death. The Beasts would not let him out a second time. And yet, he wondered what he would discover if he returned.

The Daughter of the Light stopped scanning the horizon and grabbed her white backpack. She took out the flask and put one of the nuts in her mouth in her daily ritual. For some reason, seeing her do that reminded him of something she had said the first night.

'I think I saw you one day,' The hunter repeated the words Matildet had said that night before falling asleep.

She was convinced that she had seen him from Teradam, and that the event had opened her eyes, but what did she mean?

Is she here for me? Siro wondered. *Does she really want to help me?*

'The day I left the city was very hot,' said Siro, Matildet still looking away. 'Many years ago that day... but I still remember the heat. We had to leave the city. Not only me and my family, but many...'

The Daughter of the Light ignored him. He had ceased to exist for her, but Siro did not give up.

'Mother said it wasn't fair...' Siro remembered. In all honesty, she had said much more than just *fair*, but decided to spare the exact words. 'I asked her why they kicked us out, and she said that we were too many mouths to feed and... and...'

Siro fell silent for a moment. He had not thought about his mother in a long time. He didn't like to do it. She always had that look, those brown eyes, the same as his, pressing him. 'Why don't leave, kid?', the eyes said, 'Why don't you go away forever?'.

She was nothing like Liduvin.

'So what?' Matildet snapped. The story didn't matter to her in the least. She wanted him to shut up and leave her alone.

'Nothing. My mother... I don't think she ever loved me,' said Siro. 'My father... I don't know. He spoke very little and when my mother was around, he didn't speak at all. I not, uh... get to know.'

'I don't think I got to know him,' the girl corrected him.

'Yes... On the Exile Day, we left home and gathered in front of the city's palisade. There were so many people... I'd never seen so many people together. There were cars, caravans, oxen, horses, camels... We waited and waited under the sun and then... The Beasts attacked us... My parents were the first to flee. They knew that if they left me there, I would die, they knew it, and... they left, they didn't look back... But I survived, Liduvin and Grinat saved me and took me with them to Merco's oasis.'

His parents had abandoned him but Liduvin had taken him by the hand and had not released him until they were on the other side of the city gates. She had told him not to look while she pressed his head against her skirt, but how could he not look? Beasts jumped on men and women. They ripped off their clothes, stabbed them until they were nothing more than a crimson stain on the sandy ground. They threw ropes around children's necks and took them away, dragged over the bodies of their own relatives.

Luckily, Grinat was amid the battle. The silent guard had speared their way through. Siro had never seen anything so extraordinary. No Beast that crossed his path could stop him. Grinat impaled them or cut their neck, without hatred, without rage. He killed them without hesitation and moved on, towards the wooden wall that prevented everyone from passing.

Liduvin had hugged Siro and told him not to worry when they realized they were surrounded. All the exiles were trapped between the wall and the Beasts, the same Beasts that until recently wanted to kick them out to the desert, where many of them would die of hunger and thirst. They were hundreds of families. Siro had recognized some faces, but most were all unknown to him. Grinat had stepped up between him and the Beasts, just like many other slaves. He remembered hearing a farmer brandishing a hoe shouting something like: 'Come here! We will bust you all! ', But after the Beasts' first barrage of arrows, the voices had quieted and only the cries of the dying were left.

Grinat had covered him and Liduvin, and it had worked. Around them, all was screams and cries. Siro had seen the farmer, who was still alive despite the arrows, was crawling to escape. But the Beasts were thrown at him right away. He was beheaded with his own weapon.

Then the city gate had opened, and people had started pouring out towards the exit. They were stepping on each other, the cars wanted to pass all at the same time and collided. It seemed that they would not succeed, but the three made it through the gate with death behind them.

Siro had raised his eyes before crossing the Undershell's gates. He had crossed the wall, something he pictured himself doing. He had seen two silhouettes above the palisade, facing the Beasts who dared to approach them. One of them was Firla, but then Siro didn't know her. Fighting by her side was her first husband, Merco. They had opened the gates; it was thanks to them that they still breathed.

As Liduvin pulled him, Siro saw how the couple teared the Beasts apart, making them fall down the palisades. They were very different from Grinat, they did not keep calm: they were fast, frantic and had their faces distorted by rage.

He had watched the couple's struggle until the end and wished everything would end well. They seemed invincible, on top of the wall. But an arrow pierced Merco in the chest and the man fell into his wife's arms, still battling the Beasts, who kept coming. He was not sure if it had gone as he remembered —he was already far beyond the walls, in Liduvin's arms— but he had had the feeling that Merco had pushed Firla from the top of the palisade with his last breath. Shortly after, Undershell's gates had closed with half of the slaves still inside.

Siro told everything that had happened on the day of Exile to Matildet. The girl had finally turned, but her arms were crossed.

'The city was... It *is* called Undershell,' Siro continued.

'Why do you tell me all this? Matildet asked. 'I know you don't want to go, you don't have to...'

'No. I want you to understand why *you* don't have to go. The Beasts massacred us, killed everyone they could, and would have killed more if it weren't for Firla and Merco.'

'Who?'

'They were Bíndagi, a nomadic tribe from the east,' Siro explained. 'Firla was the leader of the village that we founded next to the oasis. Merco died on the day of Exile, and so they named the village after him.'

'I see.'

Siro nodded. Judging from the Daughter of the Light's expression, he guessed she wanted to know more.

'They killed everyone they could. They have no mercy; they are not human. Beasts are Beasts. You won't get anything talking to them. Going to Undershell is a bad idea.'

'So what then? Keep looking? Where? Where can we find more people, more cities? Tell me!'

'I don't know...'

'You don't know or there isn't?' Matildet grabbed him by the cheeks and forced him to look her in the eye. 'You don't know... or there isn't?' She repeated.

Siro remained quiet. She snorted and went to the bonfire. She turned the stick where the badger was nailed and sat there, eyes lost in the fire.

Although it was hard, he sat next to Matildet.

'What happened to your parents?' She asked after a long silence.

'I do not know. Dead, I suppose. Beasts only capture children.

They put the Brand on them and make them work until to death... or turn them into Beasts, whatever happens before.'

'What is the Brand?' She asked. 'You don't have any, right?'

'No. If we had stayed two more days in Undershell, they would have taken me to see the Elector and branded me.'

'An Elector... Is it a sort job title or something?'

The hunter nodded. He recalled the Elector with whom he had met in that underground hideout in the middle of the desert. He had no idea how it could have gotten there. Matildet hadn't seen it, and now he didn't think it was a good time to tell her.

'I didn't know anything about it,' The girl curled in her hair. 'You should have told me before.'

'I could not...'

'Why? Don't you trust me?'

'I...'

'Siro, you and I have been through thick and thin! I would never have imagined that...' The girl chuckled. 'I mean, look at me! I am in the middle of the desert! I eat filthy animals from the top of a stick! If Cas knew! She would say something like that: *Look where the princess has decided to go out for a picnic!*

The Daughter of the Light grabbed one of the sticks with one of the badger legs and took a bite. She chewed with her mouth open and swallowed it.

'And worst of all, I like it!'

She took another branch and offered it to Siro.

'The desert has literally *swallowed* us. We have run away from a giant lion with the jaws of a shark. We have fought with strangers who, as you would put it, could have killed us without thinking it twice,' Matildet enumerated. 'And you still wonder if you can trust me? Is that it? We are here, Siro! You and me, together!'

The hunter looked at her without knowing what to say. The girl smiled again and that made him happy.

Matildet stood a little closer to Siro. He had not even tried the food, he was absorbed by the girl's face: those beautiful eyes, the golden mane, those lighted lips he was dying to kiss again.

'You think there are only bad people left, but I have to go,' Matildet continued as she put a strand of hair behind her ear. If there is even a good person, I must find it. That's why I'm here. And, you know, do not come if you do not want... It's fine. You will enter

Téradam too, if that is what worries you so much, I promise. And... And look, if you want to take me to the entrance of Undershell and wait outside, that also works, if not, well, it doesn't matter, I...'

'I want to go,' Siro interrupted.

Matildet raised her eyebrows.

'Oh. Cool.'

Siro left the stick with the badger and watched the fire for a moment.

I need tell her. I need to tell her or it will haunt me forever.

'The day we left Undershell, just before my parents ran away, Liduvin took me by the hand, but on the other... With the other I think I was grabbing someone else.'

'Huh? What do you mean?' Asked the Daughter of the Light.

'I was grabbing a child.'

The words slowed on Siro's lips, but he did not plan to stop. He had come too far, he had to tell her everything.

'I think the child was Ubald,' he murmured.

'Ubald? You mean that...'

Beast, he thought. She had been about to say it but rectified in time.

'...The man in the pond?'

'I don't know who he was, I can't remember,' Siro explained as he looked at his hand. 'But I know he was in that place and he trusted me.'

Chapter 20: I've seen them

'Nazeh, wake up!' Siro shook his friend's arm vigorously.

'No, please... I'll put the rings back on, I swear!' The boy shouted as he opened his eyes. He grabbed his arms checking he had nothing on them. 'Siro? What are you doing in my house?'

Nazeh looked at him, puzzled. His dark skin melted in the night shadows. The only light reaching the cabin where the Muhara family lived came from Merco's street torches.

'I've seen them. The Beasts are here, they have surrounded the whole village!' Siro said.

There was noise in the house. A curtain made of vines pulled away and Mohaki, Sailia's fourth son, appeared.

'It is not time to play,' he said with a yawn.

Mohaki put a hand on his little brother's shoulder and told him to go to sleep, or he'd tell mother. The two brothers were almost identical: same nose, short hair and the look of perpetual uneasiness; but Mohaki was a year older and it showed. Siro had never seen him play with the other children in the village. He was too serious for his age.

'Siro's seen the Beasts,' said Nazeh, his voice trembling like a leaf.

'So, the storyteller's boy likes to make up stories, huh? What a surprise...' said Mohaki.

'I'm not making it up, idiot!' Siro snapped.

Nazeh's brother raised an eyebrow, unsurprised for his lack of education.

'I'm going to sleep, tomorrow I have to get up soon. Someone must take care of Wangari and work at the dam. Not all of us can be kids...' said Mohaki, shook his little brother's shoulder and turned around.

'Go back to sleep if you want, the Beasts will kill you anyways' Siro said. He noticed a fuss in the nearby houses. Some dogs barked in the dark. The boy delved into the bag he carried and took a necklace made of human teeth.

Mohaki paled.

'You know what kind of Beast carries this, don't you?' Siro told him.

Mohaki's face was an open book. Electors loved teeth necklaces. They would select the children and decide their fate in Undershell. If they were lucky, they'd become miners, farmers, porters... or Beasts; and if they weren't, they would end up with as the private toys of the aristocracy or the Elector himself, if such was its desire. Mohaki caressed the Brand on his abdomen. Nazeh had told Siro that the Beasts had branded his brother with the laborers symbol a month before leaving Undershell, then he had been bought back and the Elector had crossed out the symbol and replaced it with the Brand of the heart and the tear. Siro didn't know what it meant. He had asked Nazeh but he didn't know either. His friend made the mistake of bringing it up to his mother once and she had slapped him. How terrible had that change of destiny been? Whatever it was, it had to be way worse than having to plough the muddy ground all day or get your arms stretched. The clutter had awaken the rest of Nazeh's family. Cairu, now the older brother after Baru's death, and Sailia came out in the torchlight. Nazeh's mother wore a white robe that covered her bulky silhouette. Siro always saw her covered with colourful clothes and glittering bracelets, it was strange for him to see her so poorly dressed. She pulled and angry face and looked at the three of them. Before she could say anything, Siro repeated the same thing he had said to the others.

'No... Have you seen them? Siro, tell me the truth, this is very serious,' the woman leaned down to catch up with the boy.

'Mother, he brought this,' Mohaki pointed to the collar of teeth on the floor.

Sailia did not react much better than her son, but for once she was determined. She addressed his eldest son, still bleary-eyed.

'Cairu, go chime the village bell,' she ordered. 'Mohaki, I want you to wake up everyone, tell them the Beasts are here. Hurry up, don't waste your time.'

When they saw the face of their mother, the two brothers ran up the path that led to the centre of Merco. Sailia followed her children with their eyes, who ventured into the streets lit by torches and stars and then looked towards the river on the south side of the village, as if she expected to find someone there. The woman put her hand on her neck and scratched her jowl frantically.

'We will also let people know,' said Siro.

'No, young man!' Shouted Sailia. The nail marks looked white on that jet neck. 'You and Nazeh will prepare Wangari's gurney, we will have to cross the river and I don't want to...'

'What about Liduvin?' Shouted Siro. Wangari was not his brother, he didn't understand why he had to stay to take care of him. 'I'm out of here. Nazeh, come.'

'Do not even think about it!' Said the woman. She tried to grab him, but the boy sneaked through her fingers.

Siro pulled Nazeh and they ran. The mother's screams faded before they reached the colours square, but then his friend suddenly stopped.

'My brother needs help,' he said. He didn't even dare look him in the eye. 'I can't come. I hope you find Liduvin.'

That felt like a smack. He didn't dare to say it in front of Nazeh's mother, but it was not Liduvin he was after.

'What about Eliria? She lives on the other side of the Council House, right next to the forest. Where do you think the Beasts will come from?'

Nazeh looked down at the red, blue, and green cobblestones that formed the colours square. The mosaic that symbolized the freedom of the people of Merco looked bleak and sad in the light of the dozen tall torches that surrounded it.

'Take her to the marketplace,' Nazeh said. 'Please do not let anything happen to her. Promise me.'

Siro saw the tears climbing up in his friend's eyes. He nodded. He was going to repeat himself that Nazeh had a brother who could not walk and had to help him. He would have to.

They didn't say goodbye, they just walked in opposite directions. Nazeh ran to the river, back home, and Siro went up the narrow, steep streets. Eliria's house was on the other side of the hill. He could circle it going east and stop by his house to check if Liduvin was still there, but if he went west, through the Marketplace, he would be much quicker.

First Eliria, I have promised Nazeh, Siro told himself as he hurried.

Something shiny passed in front of his eyes and made him fall on his ass. It had seemed to him that it was a kind of bright bat that was thrown at him, but when he got up, he saw that it was the broad leaf of a marquise burning at his feet. The flames devoured it from the inside out. The outline of the leaf shone with the orange hue of the embers and then turned ash. The sky was no longer covered by stars, but thousands of blazing leaves that were swept away by the wind. Like birds of fire, they fell down their paths and houses, while the smell of burning mixed with the river's. The bell chimed breaking the night calm, and Siro knew that Cairu had reached the Council House, as his mother had ordered.

'Wake up!' Siro shouted as he echoed with his own hands. 'The Beasts are here! Wake up!'

He didn't know if the people in the houses would hear him or not, but he had to try. If the blazing leaves had reached the southern part of the village, that meant that the Beasts perhaps already roamed the streets of Merco.

One of the thatched roofs caught fire with the arrival of the leaves. The whole family, the father, the mother and two small children left half-naked. The mother held one of the children, a baby, in her arms, and blamed the father for that unexpected fire. Siro told them it was the Beasts deed and that they had to go to the Marketplace. The father must had recognized him because he gave him that look he had seen so many times since he arrived to Merco. 'He is the Liduvin's step-son,' said his face of disbelief. 'He sure tries to deceive us.'

Why does nobody trust me? I'm not lying, this is so unfair! Whatever… It's their call…, he thought, and left them behind.

About fifty people filled the Marketplace when Siro arrived. He had a hard time believing that Mohaki and Cairu had managed to warn everyone. He recognized the figure of Firla, dressed in her crimson clothes, in the middle of the crowd. The village leader shouted orders all over the place. The children distributed spears, two-meter-high sharped hangers, knives and axes among women and young men. The mothers and grandmothers counted the children and made sure they did not lack the provisions of arrows they had prepared for months in case the Beasts appeared.

'Bring in the cars! The barriers!' He heard Taurus, one of Firla's husbands, shout above the people's bustle and the loud bell.

The market square had been built so that it could be closed

with wooden barriers that were camouflaged behind the houses and little shops that configured it's shape. The barriers were five times higher than Siro and were not thought to allow anyone passage. If the Beasts wanted to reach them, they would have to climb above the houses, but that was exactly what Firla wanted. Siro had once heard Liduvin criticize her security measures. 'This woman is crazy!' She had told Grinat. 'Filling the houses with Firespreader, what's she thinking? Can't she see the whole village can blow up?' Liduvin had a very particular sound when she talked about Firla.

'Siro!' He heard a voice calling him.

Zuria had arrived with the two twins holding hands. One of them, Bartus, cried nonstop, while Axelai glanced at him, his chin trembling.

'What are you doing here?' Asked the mother.

Grinat's wife was quite young. She seemed like a good person, although very reserved. The truth was that they had never come to speak, although the two knew of each other's existence.

'Yes, you have to do me a favour.'
The girl's voice quivered. She looked side to side, worried to see the Beasts at any moment. 'They need help bringing supplies to the centre of the square, I want you to watch the twins. Will you do it for me?'

The boy looked at Bartus and Axelai with objection. In the village there were people who said that Zuria had become a widow the day everyone escaped from Undershell, but there were also those who said she had never had a husband, and that the two children were the fruit of two Beasts that had raped her. Be as it may, she loved them, and Siro wished them no harm, but he had no time to babysit. Eliria was in true danger.

Zuria was about to give him the children, but Siro reacted quickly.

'Where is Grinat?' He asked as he stepped back.

'He has brought us here and gone again,' said the girl. 'I thought he had gone looking for you and Liduvin. Come on, watch them, please.'

'I can't now. I'm looking for Liduvin,' he lied. He didn't have time to explain why he was heading to Eliria's house first.

Zuria kept the answer on her lips. The boy rushed through the square. He avoided adults, who moved from side to side carrying buckets of water, sacks of grain, ropes, spears and shields.

'Leave the south door open!' Firla ordered the men around her. Among them were their husbands and other Merco guards. 'I want two rows of men behind each barrier and be sure to shoot only when they are close.'

'Firla, what do we do with the east gate?' Asked Eder, he was one of Merco's most beloved guards. During the trip through the desert he had become friends with everyone thanks to his sympathy.

'No gate closes until I say so!' Blasted Firla. 'We are not all here yet. I want you to place stakes inside the houses. If the Beasts climb up the roofs, they'll sink.'

'Let's see how they like having a few stakes up their asses,' one of the guards joked, although no one else laughed.

'Everyone who is on the northern barrier must have a bow or sling!' Said Firla, pointing non-stop. 'Each squad must have a messenger child, so look for it! And someone tell Cairu to stop chiming the damn bell! I'm going crazy!'

Firla's neck veins swelled with each order. If she did not run into any Beast soon it was likely she would kill some of her men instead.

Siro saw Rael and a few more children —the whole Mongoose band— gathered in the centre of the square. The were being instructed by a man with grey hair.

'I hope you got it, kids,' said the man. 'You, girl, quit crying or I'll smack you!'

The crying girl was the daughter of Eineran Crownmaker, a young man who boasted of having made crowns for all the important merchants and slave traders of Undershell. His old relationship with the Beasts had not made him too popular in Merco, but during the desert journey he had promised Firla that he would forge a crown for her, and that had prevented him from being beaten to a pulp. His daughter had not had an easy time trying to get along with the other kids. She was a small and shy girl who always wore a crown made of yew branches and adorned with firekiller pink petals. Everyone called her Crownie, and Siro had never bothered learning her real name.

'My father's not back...' Crownie said between sobs.

'Your father is sure licking Dugol's balls to spare his life,' the man said. 'At least he's been smart enough to leave his useless daughter here.'

The girl burst into tears and the man forgot about her too.

'How is it that you're still here?' He told the other children. 'To the barriers! Now!'

Rael and the rest of the Mongoose dispersed in all directions.

'Why does the Free Child not help us? So unfair...' Siro recognized the voice of the little boy who always made Rael mad.

The man shook his head when he recognized Siro.

'If you are smart, you will not turn your back on the storyteller's stepchild,' said the man and went away to take care of other things.

The northern barrier was already closed, and it was the shortest path to Eliria's house. The guards stood with bows and slings in the loopholes, ready to shoot. Beyond the wooden wall was the winding road that led to the Council House and behind, between the rows and rows of trees that surrounded Merco, fire tongues lighting the night. The entire forest burned, and Eliria's house was right on the edge.

Siro found Taurus next to the west gate of the market square. He had gathered three men and a woman to accompany him to look for stragglers. Of all of them, only Firla's husband wore a leather breastplate and protections around his legs, the rest were almost naked, only a bunch wore reinforced shirts and rough cloth pants. The guards distributed spears and rectangular hemp and wood shields to the expedition. As they did, Siro saw his chance to sneak past the gate, but just when he was going to, Crownie stood in front of him.

'Siro, you dropped this,' The girl handed him the silica knife he always had on him.

She was nervous, the Beasts had surrounded the village and she had lost sight of her father. Before he could reply anything, the girl said:

'I like your non-mother's stories.'

It seemed to Siro that was the nicest thing he had been told all night. For a moment, he regretted not having talked to that girl before and tried to be her friend. Surely they would have gotten along, but now it seemed too late. Would there be another night after that?

'Hide,' he said before running away.

He rushed between the sentries. They yelled at him to come back, but none of them chased him.

The streets beyond the Marketplace were deserted. Most people had already left their wood and stone houses. The ground had been cluttered with tokens that the inhabitants of Merco had lost on their way to safety: pieces of clothing, pots, a hen that was walking around as if the world was hers, the broken wheel of a car, looms, fishing rods. Siro recalled the day he had fled from Undershell: the people falling dead around him; darts and arrows that struck everyone, both old and young, men or women. If it hadn't been for Liduvin and Grinat, he'd be just another corpse in the mud. If he were to bump into a Beast, he'd run. He knew that. But how many of those creatures were around Merco? And how many would have reached the north of the village?

Siro soon discovered it. Four Beasts had surrounded the blacksmith's house and had the whole family cornered. The smithy was a two-story house, with the ground floor open on one side to evacuate the fumes. An unpleasant smell, like burnt hair, reached him. Black feet stood out of the smithy's main furnace.

'You know the game: Oven or Brand. Your call,' Said one of the Beasts, as he spun an iron rod with the red-hot tip between his fingers before the family.

'The blacksmith burns quite well, why don't we try with his wife?' Proposed a small Beast with bulging eyes.

The other two Beasts watched, amused by the cries of the blacksmith's family. The mother hugged her two daughters —who were to be Siro's age—, while the eldest son, a teenager, looked dangerously at one of the bamboo-cutting swords hanging from the wall.

Don't, wished Siro.

The Beast with the bulging eyes grabbed the woman. The son got up and punched the creature in the face. The other two Beasts launched themselves forward while the son pounced on the sword.

Siro was hidden behind an overturned car on a side of the path. He tried to see more, but the fourth Beast left the house and had to hide to avoid being seen. The last Beast had long black hair and a red ribbon on the forehead. It was tall and muscular and wore bronze protections on the legs, while its chest was exposed. The black-haired Beast whistled merrily as the screams boomed inside the smithy. When it turned on its back, Siro glimpsed a Brand he had never seen before under the Beast's neck: it looked like a bird, perhaps an eagle but with bull horns, pierced by six spears. The boy backed away a little more until he could only see the feet. The Beast's boots had bronze inlays on top in the shape of Biter claws.

On the other side of the road a great uproar arose, and Taurus and his explorers appeared ready to stand up to the Beasts.

'It's my brother!' Shouted one of Taurus's men. 'These motherfuckers have burned my brother!'

Without further thinking, the man pounced on the Beast. Siro saw that the spear moving straight towards the heart of the creature, but the wood creaked, and the spear fell to the ground splintered.

Siro took advantage of the skirmish to slip through the window of a house and move under its protection. The inside of was in total darkness. *Careful...*, he told himself. If he stepped on something and made the slightest noise, the Beasts would hear him.

Luckily, the owners of the house had left it empty before leaving. Siro found a half-open door that overlooked the backyard and left the house. Outside, the screams were over. The sobs of the girls raised above the fire crackling. The voices of the men had died out. Although he knew it was not a good idea, the boy poked his head around the corner of the house to see what had happened.

Taurus explorers were dead on the ground. The long-haired Beast had finished them all. He had the boot protections bloodstained.

'It's always the same with you, Shahrokh,' The Beast with the bulging eyes came out of the smithy and addressed its comrade. 'All the fun for yourself, huh? What about us?'

'I thought you *were* having a good time,' replied the Beast of the bronze protections. 'I love the puppet you made. Really classy, guys. Why don't you show it to the fugitive?'

Siro saw Taurus was still alive. The man was on his knees, right in front of the Beasts. He had a bruise in his eye and one of his arms fell lower than normal, dislocated. Despite the pain he surely was in, he said nothing. He squeezed his shoulder, trying to put it in place.

'Sick bastard,' said the other Beast in laughter. 'Belasar, Irad, bring the puppet!'

The two Beasts left the smithy. One of them carried the red-hot iron in one hand and the blacksmith's sword in the other, soaked in blood. The second carried the head of the blacksmith's son in his hands. The Beast that carried him had put his hand through the neck of the body and moved his mouth like a puppet.

Siro looked away and covered his mouth.

No, please, no, he thought. *Keep it in.*

All he managed was to vomit through his clenched fists staining his clothes. He curled up and sat down while the chills ran down from head to toe.

'What do you think, Hyena? Like it or what?' Asked the Beast that shook the corpse's head.

'Give it to me, you'll end up breaking it!' Snapped the so-called Hyena.

The Beast removed the head from his comrade's hands and addressed Taurus:

'Hey, look, you piece of shit. Look closely!' The Hyena exclaimed and adopted a sharp tone, like a ventriloquist. 'How can I help you, sir? Do you want me to forge a sword and stick it in your ass?'

'I think what he wants is to put his arm back into place,' Shahrokh replied. 'Why don't you give him a hand?'

All the Beasts laughed at that.

'Oh, Shahrokh, give him a hand!' said the Hyena. 'Next time leave the puppet's arms on! What good is a blacksmith apprentice without arms?'

'Arms go to the oven. They are the most tender part,' said the Beast that played with the burning iron stick.

'Belasar, you and your fixation on eating all the crap you find. You'll get sick,' the Hyena replied.

Siro didn't want to hear one more word. He got up from where he was and ran. He decided to take a detour. If he continued along the main street, he would run into many more Beasts. Now he moved between houses staying away from open spaces. He heard their footsteps and mad howls. They were everywhere. They had taken the village and hunted for the stragglers. At one point, a group of Beasts broke into the house where Siro was. He thought they had discovered him, but the Beasts carried four women with them. Three were thrown on the beds and one of got tied by the wrists to the ceiling beams. The women defended themselves at first, but the Beasts beat their will out of them. They ripped off their dresses and jumped on top of women.

The one who was tied to the ceiling saw Siro. The boy was petrified. They looked at each other for a long time, while the Beasts abused the other women. The tied girl would not be twenty yet. Her dress was torn, her breasts hung in the air and her cheeks were scared by tears. She moved her lips, but didn't dare making a noise. Siro understood the word she articulated: knife.

She's seen I have one on me, the boy thought.

The girl looked at the rope that kept her tied. He couldn't take that risk. What would happen when he cut her loose? The Beasts would realise and kill him. The same that happened to the blacksmith's son.

I don't want my head cut off, please, anything but that... can't help you, I can't, it's too dangerous, I'm sorry...

He shook his head, but the girl was desperate. Her face deformed into a bitter grimace and shouted:

'A kid! Look, there's a kid!'

Siro reacted before the Beasts moved. He passed by the tied girl's side. She kicked him. It hurt, but a part of him felt he deserved it. He left the house. He did not turn to see if the Beasts followed him or not. He ran for a long time, changed direction between the alleys and wished those creatures had forgotten him.

The blazing leaves still fell from the sky like an endless rain. The fire crackled in the distance and the wind hooted in the alleyways. Merco seemed numb, but it was an artificial sensation, shattered by screaming and intermittent cries.

The Council House burned on top of the hill of roots. Someone was running up the stairs, with two Beasts on his heels. Siro had the feeling that it was Nazeh's older brother, who had gone there to chime the bell.

Cairu is very fast, he'll escape for sure, he told himself, yet he lost sight of the chase as soon as they got down to the houses.

Almost there...

Siro was breathing heavily. He had tun around most of the village and was now very close to the woods. There the houses were scarcer, and it was harder to hide. A trail of impaled and burned corpses covered the roads, witnessing the advance of the Beasts. None of them was Eliria.

Please, be well, Siro wished. But when he arrived at his friend's house, there was only rubble.

The place was charred. There was nothing left but the foundations and the skeleton of the burning thatched roof. Siro got as close as he could. The heat was intense, so much so that the air burned his nose as he breathed it. He saw a piece of clothing on the ground. It was Eliria's skirt, half scorched. It shook with the wind.

No, Siro's eyes got moist.

I should have gone home. You told me to come back right away. But I couldn't, Liduvin. The Beasts. My friends. It's too late... I'm too late.

He coughed because of the smoke and sat on the floor, just in front of what used to be his friend's house. There was nothing left of the garden. The two palm trees under which they had kissed for the first time were no more than two black columns. Nazeh didn't know anything about it, nor was he going to tell her, but he really liked Eliria. He was crazy about her. He had crossed the entire village to find her, but he was late. She no longer...

'Free Child! Are you mad in the head? What's wrong with you? The Beasts will see you!' He heard a familiar voice tell him.

When Siro turned, he saw Eliria's freckled face. The girl threw herself into his arms. He hugged her back.

'Yikes, Siro! Have you thrown up or what? You smell like shit.'

'Shut up, you rabid mongoose,' he ran a hand over his face to hide the tears, but only got soot stained. 'Beasts are everywhere. Firla has taken everyone to the marketplace. Come, we have to go!'

'Wait,' said the girl. 'It's my mother, she's hurt. I can't leave her.'

Debra..., thought Siro. For a moment, he had assumed she had died and not had a second thought. She didn't like that moment in the slightest. She always seemed so cold... The night in which Liduvin, Sailia and Debra had caught coming back from the hollow trees forest, she had looked at him with those eyes that said 'I know you are the one to blame for this'.

Eliria led him to a rectangular house, smaller than the few that were still standing. The house was empty. There was only a crooked counter, some burlap sacks piled in the back and the smell of cinnamon mixed with coal in the air. Siro had already been there before. It used to be a shop full of exotic items, stuff that couldn't be found in the oasis. The business owner was a nice man, always wearing a cloak with drawn animals. He'd let Siro and the other children come in, even if they never bought anything. He couldn't remember the name of that man, maybe he had never known. All he knew was that he had gotten feverish for some time and closed the business. The man used to have the rarest species stored inside dozens of glass bottles along the mahogany shelves, but the goods had disappeared. There were only traces of broken glass at the entrance and in the oval window, at the bottom. The Beasts must had stolen them as soon as the fire started. They were evil, but not stupid. They knew glass was expensive.

Siro followed Eliria behind the counter. The girl set aside a few sacks and a trunk with the inlays torn off and exposed some descending stairs.

The basement turned out to be bigger than the house. There was a very weak light casting shadows on the reliefs engraved on the grey rock wall. Someone had carved a mural, or at least started it: tiny women and men who clustered around a faceless man. The man pointed to a distant sphere, on the other side of the wall. There were indefinite forms in between. Siro distinguished eyes and claws between the traces of the escarpment, but the drawing was not yet finished.

At the back of the room, Eliria's mother rested on a quilt. When Siro approached the candlelight, he saw that Debra had a horrible burn on her left leg. It had bits of meat, red and black, suppurating, and large blisters swollen like mushrooms on the foot and on the hip.

'What is he doing here?' Was the first thing she said to her daughter, with her usual coldness.

'He's come for us, mom. He can help us.'

'It is true?' Asked Debra. 'Do you want to help?'

'Yes, ma'am,' said Siro.

'Then why don't you go to your house, grab a good knife and chop off Liduvin's head?' She said emptily. 'It's all that whore's fault.'

Chapter 21: The tomb of the Forgotten One

Siro was sick of walking through the white desert. His feet were swollen. Matildet, on the other hand, couldn't cares less. She strolled calmly. Her only concern was to pull the rope they had tied the ostrich with, whenever the animal got distracted.

'I really don't know how you orientate yourself here,' the girl said. 'Don't your eyes hurt?'

'It's the salt,' the hunter explained. 'It's in the air. Don't talk, it'll make you thirsty.'

Matildet raised her thumb —'got it'— and remained silent.

The girl and the ostrich were a few steps ahead of him. Siro watched the animal hungrily. They carried just enough food to make it Undershell. He couldn't rule out having to skin the bird. It was useful, though. The animal carried Matildet's backpack, the canteens, the double spear, a handful of beheaded snakes and a dozen oranges on top. In the end, they had been lucky to find her. They had seen her in the morning, before leaving, just as they discussed how to distribute the luggage and Matildet had the idea. To the surprise of the two, the animal had been much tamer than the day before.

'You got scared at the lagoon, huh? Now you want to come with us, you chicken head?' Matildet had joked, while tying the canteens to the bird's side.

It had been four days since they had left the Labyrinth and the truth was that the ostrich was behaving herself, although it was easy to see that her favourite was the Daughter of the Light —Siro still got pecked from time to time— that's why she was the one in charge of feeding it with beetles.

Siro estimated that they had already done more than half of the trip. They had first passed through the hamada, a place where instead of sand there were stones and cracks; and then, at the southern end, the Mirror Rocks, where black quartz rocks and glass sources abounded. It was dangerous to enter. The rocks were treacherous, and although the chance of stocking glass was tempting, it was also very easy to stumble and fall through some of the natural wells. Siro had explained a little of what he knew of that place to Matildet. A few years back, he had gone in search of a refuge before venturing across the white desert. There he had found whole glass bottles and other recipients that he had carried with him to his cave next to the Sacred Valley. The Daughter of the Light had listened to everything he had said, and had corrected him every time he was mispronouncing a word, but when he had reached the end of the story, she had stared at him with those dark blue eyes that he liked so much and had asked:

'Do you really want me to believe that there are glass mines? I am not an expert, but it seems to me that the glass is made from silica, or sea sand... You need an oven at a thousand degrees. No matter how hot it is here, I don't think you can possibly find it in its natural state.'

He had insisted that it was true, but she had not believed him until she had seen the sun reflected in a field protruding from a wall of reddish stone. She had pulled that face of not understanding anything. She asked no questions.

'Hey, look at that,' Matildet said suddenly, sinking her boots in the white sand. 'Is that a wheel?'

Siro came forward, leaping because of the salt, and found that, indeed, it was a carriage wheel. It was old and in bad shape. One of the spokes had broken and it was abandoned there.

'I've seen it before,' said Siro.

'Oh yeah? Did you have a car and you hadn't told me? Don't tell me you had it hidden in the cave all this time...'

'When we left Undershell, we fled in a caravan.'

'We have to work in your sense of humour...'

'We wandered for a long time... I remember going through here, it was... ' Siro put a hand to his forehead to think. 'It was Rael's car, well, his parents'.'

'Who is Rael?'

'He was the leader of the Mongoose...' Siro explained, although he realized immediately that this was no longer important, it was just a child's play. 'He was a kid who lived in Merco.'

'You two were friends?'

'I don't know.'

Eliria, Nazeh and himself had competed with the Mongoose

band to find the treasure in the hollow tree forest. At that time, Siro saw Rael as an adversary, but those disputes were already so far back that he could only remember them with nostalgia. Last time he'd seen him had been in the market square, with the other kids. The Beasts must had captured or kill him during the Night of Fire.

'Rael's parents had a car,' Siro told her. 'They were wildebeest breeders in Undershell. The father took care of them and the mother sold them. That car cost them a fortune, but they didn't mind sharing it. They took turns with two families throughout the trip.'

'They were good people,' Matildet said.

'I didn't get to know them well. One day a wheel broke and they needed someone strong to change it. They called Grinat,' continued Siro.

'Grinat was... Liduvin's guardian, wasn't he?' Matildet tried to remember the hunter's vague explanations. 'He must be very strong.'

'He was the strongest man in Merco. And he was the best with the double-headed spear, even better than Firla and her husbands.'

'I still can't get my head around the idea of a woman with three husbands,' she said with a smile.

'Doesn't it happen in Teradam?'

'In Teradam? Well, over there everything is more... complicated.'

'Liam was your only fiancé?' Siro was suddenly curious. How should that Son of the Light be?

'Yes... No! Fiancé? No! You are wrong. What I had with Liam was different, I... Look. Why don't we keep moving? I think the ostrich's feathers are melting.'

When the sun was descending through the distant mountains of the Labyrinth, the two had already left the salt desert behind. The landscape was as empty as hours before. Wherever they looked, an endless desert surrounded them.

Siro had decided to take a turn before getting to Undershell. He had been through that same landscape when he was little, he knew it by the sharp profile of the mountains and the black bushes that tried to take root in their shadow.

It was around there, he told himself until he saw it. The hunter stopped and grabbed the quartz stone from his collar.

Matildet pulled the ostrich's rope and turned back to see what was happening. Siro pointed to a dark shape protruding from the sand. It was a metal monument, not more than a meter high. It was made of rusty steel bars bended to form a cylindrical pillar.

'The altar marks where the Forgotten One rests,' said the hunter.

'What a strange thing...' replied Matildet. 'It reminds me of something.'

'The night I escaped from Merco I found this place. I was chased by a pack of hyenas... I found a hiding place, just below the altar.'

'Hyenas, you say? I have never seen any. Are they very big?'

'Very,' Siro confirmed.

Some nights I still see their eyes, he thought. He had encountered them shortly after leaving Merco. The choppy laughter of those hyenas had haunted him for hours. Those animals had not confronted him, but had followed him in the dark. Occasionally, they would bite him, but not insist. They came and walked away, as if eating a human child was a game for them. They were in no rush. They knew he would fall. They were taller and thicker than him. When they looked at him, he saw two lights close together and a malevolent smile on their furry faces, but when they stood next to him, they disappeared. It was then that they were most dangerous. He had cried all the way in silence thinking that although he was the only person who had escaped the Beasts, he would die by the fangs of the hyenas. Without knowing how, he had bumped into that skeletal pillar in the middle of the night and had slipped through the hole next to it.

Matildet was curious about that altar and went over to examine it. Siro did not know if the it was the work of the Children of Light, but from what he had seen inside the shelter, he doubted it.

'One can hardly see it from above,' said the Daughter of the Light as she examined the hole. 'It's quite narrow, I don't think you fit, right?'

'Do you want to come in?'

'It will only be a moment. Keep an eye on Queenie, would you?'

So now you have a name…, thought Siro, and looked at ostrich. The animal also looked at him, with who knows what intentions.

The Daughter of the Light went through the hole.

Should I tell her not to disturb the Forgotten one? He wondered. *No, sure she already knows how to deal with other gods...*

Matildet screamed so loudly, it made Siro jump.

Then hunter tied Queenie in a hurry. The ostrich pecked him all over his head pulling a few hairs.

I will remember this one, the hunter told himself, but revenge would have to wait. He threw himself to the ground and stuck his head through the hole. The girl was inside, with her back against one of the metal walls of the shelter. Siro knew why: the body of the Forgotten One hung on the other side of the hiding place, its torso wrapped in black cloth, the face covered by a giant dark crystal mask.

When Siro saw the Forgotten One for the first time, he was only a child, and had been afraid more afraid of it than from the hyenas. He had tried to run away but, in the dark, he had not found a way out of the hole. The Forgotten One seemed dead, although little Siro had heard enough of Liduvin's stories to know that this could be a performance An effigy that could rise at any moment, just like in the stories of the times when it still rained.

He would never have approached that figure had it not been because a hyena had followed him into the hiding place. The animal had taken him by surprise and scarring his face with three lines he still had today on his cheek and eyebrow.

The presence of the animal had made him ignore the fear of incurring the wrath of the Forgotten One. He had pounced on him as he fled the predator. Then he had seen the handle of the knife, hidden under the black clothes, and had pulled it without hesitation. In a single gesture he had cut the hyena's claw and, while the animal backed away, cornered it and stabbed it again and again. It had been the first time that little Siro killed to survive, but it would not be the last. The steel of that weapon seemed unbreakable, nothing to do with the fragile sheets of silica he had used until then. He was even able to get through the skin of a Biter.

And a Beast's, he thought, and felt a wave of guilt. *Ubald.*

'I'm done!' Shouted Matildet from the inside. 'You could have told me about the surprise.'

'Have you found anything?' Asked the hunter while helping the girl out. He glimpsed the white backpack.

'Beetles, snakes, dust and a lot of crap,' she replied.

After plucking a few black bushes, Siro lit a fire at the feet of the hills.

Matildet asked him to teach her how to drive snakes into the sticks so she could roast them, and the hunter had taken up the challenge.

'The best way to do it is by nailing them three or four times per side, so that they were bent over themselves. But before, you gut them…'

The Daughter of the Light had set the limit at *that* point on other occasions. Although that night, she replicated the hunter's movements regardless of the bloodstains in her hands.

'Did Liduvin teach you all of this?'

'Eliria did.'

'Are you telling me that an eight-year-old girl has more stomach than me?'

'Don't you starve in Teradam?'

'Oh, nice, Siro, real nice. Just when I lower my guard… *Boom!* I was starting to think you would never find a comeback… Too bad it took you so long. I won this time.'

'I don't understand,' he said.

Matildet brandished the snake that had stuck in the branch in front of Siro's nose.

'I've learned to do what you do first,' the girl explained, and stuck out her tongue.

'I could never be a Child of the Light,' said Siro. 'And I will no understand why you want to be hunter.'

'And I will *never* understand why you want to be *a* hunter?' She corrected him. 'Because I find it very useful. Much more than anything else I've learned before…'

As he was recovering his ability to speak, he felt more confident on teaching and expressing himself. He wanted to tell her things… and he wanted more than that too. Sometimes he stared at her for long periods. He could not forget that moment they had shared in the oasis, when they had kissed. Was he doing well thinking about that or did he cling to a burning nail? After the encounter with the Beasts, everything had become so odd between the two, that he had buried the thought… but that night it had surfaced again. For Siro, Matildet was no longer a divinity that had been lost in the middle of the desert, nor any irascible goddess to be feared. Matildet was his friend, his only friend in that whole bloody desert.

'So… Grinat changed it or what?' Matildet asked as soon as

they finished dinner.

'You mean the wheel?' Siro had almost forgotten that he had not finished telling her the story. 'Yes, he did. After that everyone asked him for favours. He married Zuria.'

Siro explained to Matildet that Zuria was a young woman who had escaped from Undershell with her two children. The men did not approach her because they believed that the father was a Beast and they were afraid to wake up one day beheaded if they slept with the mother. Liduvin had asked Grinat to marry the girl to better integrate with the other families that were part of the group of exiles and he had agreed without protest.

In the caravan, supplies did not abound, and the desert offered nothing but sand and thirst. There were many wounded among the exiles, mostly because of the Beasts that had attacked them while escaping. Siro remembered the screams, and the fights shaking the first nights. In the morning, when the caravan resumed its way, he saw the bodies of the dying abandoned on the sand, and the clouds of vultures that roamed overhead, ready to finish off the task. He felt alone those days. Liduvin cried every day for no reason and did not leave the back of old Quela's car.

'To integrate, you say...' Matildet repeated. 'It sounds like there was a problem with him.'

'People feared him because he was strong and didn't speak. Liduvin did it for him.'

'Was he mute?'

'No, he was forbidden to speak. He could only speak to Liduvin.'

'How so?'

'I don't know... It was an oa... ah...'

'An oath?'

'Yes, an oath. He made it when the two lived in Undershell. All silent guardians must swear the oath.'

'I see...'

Siro shrugged. Yes, it seemed strange to him now that he said it out loud. When he was little, he had accepted things the way they were, but now that he was older there were many questions he would have liked to ask.

'But he did talk to his wife, didn't he?'

'No.'

'Shut up… Who could endure such a husband? And what about the twins? Tell me he spoke to them at least…'

'No.'

'And with you? He never spoke to you?'

'No…'

Not even in the Night of Fire had he spoken to Siro.

Chapter 22: For Eliria

Siro didn't believe what Eliria's mother had just said.

That I should cut off Liduvin's head? What is all this about? He wondered. *Why? Why does everyone in this village hate Liduvin so much?*

It made no sense. She was everything to him! She was the best person he had ever met in his life. He had adopted him and treated him with much more love than his real parents ever did, and she didn't have to! But wherever he went in Merco there was always that feeling in the air, a like cloud of murmuring chasing after Siro.

'Mom, Siro wants to help you!' Eliria shouted. 'Don't talk to him like that! Don't you see we can carry you between the both of us?'

Debra ignored the girl and grabbed Siro by the wrist. The boy tried to get out of it but the woman was stronger.

'Don't go near my daughter. You and Liduvin have brought them here... It's your fault,' she said as the nails dug. Her moves were violent, but her voice calm. That gave him goose bumps.

The woman was drenched in sweat. The leg wound looked awful, but she didn't seem to care. She was more worried about Siro's presence than the battle outside.

'Tersian or any of his shamans could see your leg, mom,' said Eliria, but Debra ignored her.

Siro slipped his free hand to the silica knife in his belt.

'Let go of me...' said the boy. He wrapped his hand around the handle.

'Your hands and face are stained with soot...' Debra said. Her gaze was empty, but her hand still gripped him with the same strength. 'We should have abandoned you when we were in the caravan or killed you, it would have been more pious. I knew this would happen; we all knew. I wish you were dead, Siro. You, Liduvin and the promiscuous idiot that follows her around. The three of you should be burning out there.'

'Let me go!' Shouted Siro at the top of his lungs.

He raised the knife. Eliria shouted. And then they all heard the footsteps upstairs. The echo of some metallic boots came first. Others joined the din. A cloud of dust fell between the planks of the upper floor. The three fell silent.

They are here, thought Siro.

Eliria was frozen right next to him, not believing what was happening. Her green eyes trembled under the candlelight. Siro saw a couple of shelves with hammers, escarpments, and bowls with dye powder behind the girl. Between them, there were two domed jars, large enough for a child to fit into.

'Siro…' The girl's voice was trembling.

'Eliria, hide yourself,' he whispered, nodding in the direction of the jars.

'Eliria, you better stay here, dear,' said a voice in the dark.

The two children screamed. Debra remained unperturbed. A tall silhouette appeared through the hole in the stairs. Its steps rumbled. Siro recognized the boots with bronze details and full of bloodstains. The Beast called Shahrokh approached the candlelight followed by its minions.

'Interrupting something, partner?' Shahrokh asked when he saw Siro with the knife in his hand and Debra grabbing him.

The other Beasts looked bad. They had cuts and bruises all over. The looked recent. One of the Beasts covered its eye with one hand. Its arm was stained with blood to the elbow.

The blacksmith's son's, the boy recalled. He felt nauseated.

'Screw them, Shahrokh! I need to get high,' the Beast of the wounded eye sat next to Debra. 'What are you looking at, bitch?' He said to the woman, but she didn't really look at him.

Debra had not looked away from Siro for a moment. She was still holding the boy's arm. She didn't mind the bloodthirsty creatures. From what Siro knew about the Beasts, they captured the children to take them to the Electors, so he still hoped he and Eliria would come out of that basement alive. *But she…*, the boy thought as he looked at Debra's blank face.

She will not leave, and she knows. Why is she not afraid?

It was then that it crossed his mind that Debra was not going to let him escape either.

The woman looked away for a second at the silica knife Siro had in his hand.

While the boy realized the imminent danger he was running into, the Beast sat next to Debra too, on the other side. The Beast lifted the blanket that covered her and whistled at the sight of the wound.

'Gross,' it said. It laughed and then a rough cough. 'Shitty smoke... What's wrong with these fugitives, huh? What?' It looked at Eliria. 'Listen, girl, you won't believe it, but one of you has managed to gauge an eye out of the famous Hyena, the Manhunter. That's brutal...'

'Shut up, Irad!' The Hyena bellowed, sitting on the other side of the mother. The Beast rummaged through a cloth bag that he carried in his belt.

'Yes, girl, like you hear it. The whole eye out in the blink of a... well, you know,' continued Irad. 'From now on, he's going to need a patch so the wind does not blow through,' it said and showed its decayed teeth.

'Shut the fuck up, Irad!', said The Hyena. 'I swear, I'll gauge you one of your frog eyes out and put in my eye socket. You better shut the fuck up, you piece of shit...'

Siro had the feeling that neither Beast had noticed that he had a knife in his hand and, if they had, they considered it as dangerous as a wingless fly. He wanted to stab them both, but especially The Hyena. That bastard still had the blood of the blacksmith's son dripping from its arm.

'Partners, before you surrender to your passions, I would like to draw your attention to one detail,' Siro heard Shahrokh's deep voice just behind him.

'You're not getting any?' Asked Irad.

'Only those who fear remorse need it,' Shahrokh replied.

'What now...?' Said The Hyena.

Shahrokh knelt beside Siro accompanied by the metallic row of the boots. The Beast had no recent injuries —unlike its *partners*— but had white lines on the face and chest. Old scars. The Beast moved the hair that went to its face and Siro saw that he had a bronze earring that represented the mouth of a Biter covering half his ear.

'Give me the knife, boy,' Shahrokh said. 'It's not okay to stab your mother, don't you think?'

'She is not my mother,' replied Siro.

The Beast is very close, he thought. He doubted he would be fast enough. What if he failed? Did he really expect the Beast to forgive his life after that?

'Then it must be her mother,' Shahrokh said and pointed at Eliria with his thumb. 'Would you really do this to your friend?'

The Beast reached out and gestured for the girl to approach. Eliria stepped back hitting the shelves behind her. The bowls above clinked.

'As you wish...' Shahrokh shrugged and turned to the mother. 'Ma'am, that wound doesn't look good. Luckily, my trade has made me an expert in burns, cuts, bruises, amputations... and other injuries that I'd rather not name. If such is your desire, and let go of the child, I can take a look...'

'Firla will kill you all. None of you will live another day,' Debra replied. She was still staring at the boy.

'I don't think so. Plus, she doesn't know we're coming,' said Irad, as he removed a piece of ginger from between his teeth.

'We are acquainted with Firla,' Shahrokh replied.

'Indeed,' Irad said. 'And Merco. Belasar and I choked his body into the bloodpit. What a monster...'

'He was a true Bindagi,' Shahrokh said.

'You mean not all Bindagi are monsters?' Asked Irad.

'Fuck off you all! Fuck off!' The Hyena exploded. Its spit fell on Debra, but the woman didn't flinch. 'I lost a fucking eye! An eye! I'm about to kill everyone in this basement. Yes, starting with you, Irad! You'll be the first one down! Can you all shut up at once and let me get a line? Is that too much asking, you, fuckwits?'

'Patience, partner,' Shahrokh replied. 'Listen to me, Eliria. As I said, we can heal your mother. She needs it. If we do nothing, the wound will become infected and she'll die.'

'Then do it,' said Siro, who was sick of the whole situation. He didn't understand why the Beast would do such a thing, though. Beasts didn't help, ever.

'If you touch me, I break his arm,' Debra pronounced the threat the same way she would read a recipe.

'What the...?' Said Irad. 'Sorry, boy. And I thought my mother was bad...'

'Why can't you get in your thick skull that she is not his mother? Damn asshole...' The Hyena said.

'Please, don't let her die,' Eliria burst into tears.

That brave girl, who always messed with Siro and fought with everyone who looked for trouble, was scared to death. Siro noticed that the knife was getting heavier in his hand.

'Well, Siro, what have you decided?' Said Shahrokh.

He couldn't hurt Debra. If he did, Eliria would never forgive him. He gave the blade to Shahrokh.

'I knew you were his accomplice,' said Debra. 'I knew right away.'

'You've done well, boy,' Shahrokh ran a hand through his hair, in a gesture that Siro would have considered tender if it did not come from a Beast. 'Girl, come closer, I'll show you how it's done.'

Shahrokh asked The Hyena for the bag, and took out a few flasks with herbs. He uncovered one full of a greenish ointment. Siro recognized the smell of marigolds mixed with the faint aroma of witch hazel.

This is for the burns, Siro recalled. Liduvin had explained it to him long ago.

'Would you please apply this ointment to your mother?' The Beast asked the girl. 'Spread it well.'

Eliria looked sideways at Siro and he nodded.

'Mom, I'm going to rub this on you... You're going to get well.'

Debra didn't answer but let her do. For a while, everyone watched as the girl spread the ointment over the wound. Siro thought that must had hurt, but she didn't look away from him.

She's nuts, Siro thought. This woman was more afraid of him than the Beasts that surrounded her. At any time she could completely lose it and break his arm, or steal the knife from Shahrokh and stick it again and again in him until he was a pulp. She was up to something, he knew that much.

'Very well, Eliria, you have done very well,' The Beast congratulated her, ran a hand over her shoulder and patted her. 'Partner, would you mind serving now?'

'It was high fucking time,' The Beast retrieved the bag and took out a jar full of white powder. 'Where do I make the lines?'

Shahrokh pointed to Debra and The Hyena smiled. It threw the blanket aside, pushed the mother's skirts off and extended three lines of that dust on her thigh.

'If you shake them off, I'll kill you in front of your daughter.

I don't give a shit,' The Hyena drew a flat-pointed sword, a bamboo-cutter.

'Hey, Hyena, I'd like to say a few words to Belasar,' Irad said just before its comrade lunged itself on the line.

'For all the Nightborn, I really can't believe this is happening...' The Hyena gritted its teeth.

'These are for Belasar. He was a legend. It's a shame he had such a tragic end,' Irad said as it raised its eyes to the basement ceiling. 'I can't believe that dying bastard killed him.'

'Screw Belasar! He let him take his sword. And because of him I lost an eye. If he's dead, it's because he was an idiot. Now let me do my thing. This pain is unbearable... It's like I have a fucking snake nest biting my face.'

'One of the best has fallen today,' Shahrokh proclaimed. 'Belasar was never afraid of anything. He put passion in everything he did.'

'That's why he had little bastards in all the brothels of Undershell,' The Hyena murmured.

'...A father and a friend have died today, then,' Shahrokh added.

'Yes, a very special son of a bitch...' the Hyena concluded. 'Let's get high!'

Hyena and Irad went over the woman's leg. Just then, Shahrokh lowered the silica knife and stabbed it into Debra's wound. Eliria shouted, but not her mother. Her upper lip trembled a little, and that was it. The hand with which she grabbed Siro loosened for the first time and the boy noticed that his blood was pumping again, but that feeling of freedom did not last long. Shahrokh jerked him away, just like Eliria. The Beast got up, as tall as it was, and put them under its arms like two tiny kites. The Beasts trembled with excitement and shouted. Siro saw for the first time the bloody hole where The Hyena's eye used to be. It didn't hurt anymore. The Hyena jumped and swinged the sword from side to side.

'I leave her to you,' Shahrokh said as he took the children upstairs.

Eliria called her mother and kicked. She reached out to her, but it was useless. Debra remained silent on top of the quilt, between the two Beasts that already ripped off her dress and turned her upside down. Siro knew that she was looking at him, even at that moment, when she knew that she would never see her daughter again, she watched and thought about killing him.

Oddly enough, he was glad that Shahrokh took them from that basement.

He knew it would have been terrible to tell Eliria, but he hoped it was the last time they saw Debra.

Chapter 23: Undershell

'Is that it, Siro?' Matildet pointed to the horizon, below the plateau.

He nodded.

The city of Undershell grew stacked up inside the gorge of the Cross. The yellow crop fields were still spreading through it up to the city gates side by side with the open mines at the foot of the mountains. Beyond, behind the wooden palisade that closed the southwest entrance of the city, the beige and white houses of Undershell stood out until they reached The Mouth, a hollow mountain from which black clouds like coal sprouted. Further east, the twisted towers of the palace rose under the shadow of the Great Shell, which split the gorge of the Cross in two. Its gigantic metal structure was shaped like a broken eggshell. No one knew where it had come from. According to Liduvin, the Great Shell had been a gift from the Children of the Light before the day of the Excision, but there were also those who believed it was a sort of slab thrown from the sky to mark the place where the bones of the first Nightborn rested. Siro explained it to Matildet hoping to know which of the two versions was true.

'I know nothing about bones, sorry,' The Daughter of the Light said. 'And about its origin... I think I'll tell you more things when we get closer.'

Whatever the true story was, the inhabitants of the city had never seen the Great Shell as an object of worship. Over the years, they had not hesitated to tear off parts of that structure. Roads had been opened in its base to pass to the valley's east end. Siro's father had told him that, for a time, people used fragments of the Great Shell to make valuables —metal parts to reinforce windmills, cars axis; or more small things, like cuttlery, and gears so that the hourglasses flipped on their own— although all that ended with Dugol. The Lord of the Beasts had decided to build his palace right next to it to prevent anyone but him from taking advantage of that relic. Now that he was older, Siro understood that the reason that a city like that could survive at all was the Shell itself. Thanks to it, Undershell was in the shade during the early sun hours, and that allowed plants to grow and animals not to die of heat.

'Well, are you ready?' Asked Matildet. 'If you have changed your mind...'

'No, it's fine.'

Siro pulled the ostrich's rope and descended from the plateau with a sad step.

Queenie shook the feathers. The hunter fed her beetles, but it was clear that the bird did not want to go down.

We have something in common, he thought.

The crops were strips of dry land separated by stone walls where wheat claps, cabbage and eddo roots grew. A wide road ran through of the gorge, scarred by car wheels and hundreds of peasants. As they moved on, the Daughter of the Light noticed the skinny silhouettes of the slaves who worked the barren land. They were almost naked, most were adults, both women and men. They looked exhausted, but they were still lifting and lowering the hoes under the gaze of their foreman, a big Beast with its lips painted black. It had two small and rowdy Rapids tied to a stake. The foreman punished them from time to time with a cane, so they'd stay still. The Beast watched with a smile as the slaves worked under the sun and licked its lips each time a woman passed by.

'You, move your ass!' It shouted to an old hunchback man. 'You'll rest when you die!' it added, sheltered from the sun under an umbrella made of feathers and hemp.

The old man it was giving grief to had a Brand in the shape of a hoe under the neck. He dragged a sack full of stones, but it showed that he could not take it any more. He stood up with the remaining forces, but instead of continuing to work, he turned his head and Siro had the feeling that the old man was watching him. *No, not me. Her*, he thought, checking on Matildet.

And he was not the only one. In the fields, on the roadsides, people stopped working. Some whispered with discretion, others pointed them out.

'Holy Maker… She is a Daughter of the Light!' Said an old woman who took care of the goats.

'Is it me or am I the main attraction here?' Asked Matildet.

'They've recognized you,' said Siro.

They kept the pace up. The slaves did not worry him as much as the Beasts that guarded them. If any of them realized that a Daughter of the Light had just arrived at Undershell, they would have problems.

We should have entered more carefully, Siro thought, but Matildet had insisted on going straight ahead. He hoped she also had a good plan to get out of there alive.

At the end of the fields, the Beasts had dug a huge pit that prevented them from reaching the palisade. *It wasn't there before*, Siro recalled. In the background, there were dozens of tunnels leading to the mines. Down there, the slaves were chained together. There were hundreds of them, and there were also many more Beasts than in the field. They were easily distinguished from slaves: full bellies, aggressive Brands, spears on hands and shackles on the belt. Siro saw a boy walking in the middle of a column of adults towards the digging wells. The boy was a sack of bones. His hair was not growing, and he certainly couldn't hold a pick with his hands, but he was tiny enough to get into the smallest places.

It could have been me.

'Siro, don't turn around, but we have like fifty people following us,' Matildet said. 'How about we keep moving?'

They crossed the wooden bridge over the pit. At each step, the boards creaked, but still the bridge was wide and strong enough to let a couple of cars at a time. The sharp tips of the palisade cast a long shadow over the two travellers. The last time Siro had looked at it, Firla and Merco kept Beasts at bay so that the exiles could escape.

A score of slaves crossed the bridge behind them, but most stopped on the other side of the pit. Matildet looked at them from time to time. None dared to speak to them. They looked at Matildet with a mixture of fear and respect, just as it had happened to the hunter when he first met her.

'Siro, are you sure they know who I am? *Totally* sure?'

The hunter nodded. He had no doubt. He stroked the knife handle just to make sure it was still there. Matildet had insisted on carrying the double spear herself, although he had warned her that, if they had problems, the best thing she could do was give it to him.

At the palisade's gate, there was a group of Beasts guarding a mountain of barrels and wooden boxes. The Beasts laughed as they watched two girls in their tens or twelves fighting with each other.

'Check this out, man! Look she goes at it!' said a squalid Beast. Every time it opened the mouth, the two front teeth stood out. 'I think she likes you, Reshna.'

'Everyone likes me, Taralban,' said the Beast who drank from a wine boot. 'But I prefer the other one to win. Have you seen her tits?'

'Well. She's not putting much of a fight. The skinny bitch will kill her.' a third Beast added as it sharpened the tip of a spear.

The thinnest girl clearly winning in the fight. She hit the chubby girl everywhere and gave her no chance to dodge or run away. It was a petty fight, neither of them had any technique, but the thin one put all the edge and seemed to win. Her rival tried a weak push, and the girl took that chance to scratch her face. The Beasts howled, some of them even applauded.

'Enough, stop!' said Matildet.

The Beasts paid attention to the two strangers for the first time.

The Daughter of the Light grabbed the thin girl and pulled her away from the other. The two girls were crying, although only one of them was injured. The Beasts were not amused by that. They grabbed their weapons. Siro had counted eight Beasts at first, but now that he was closer, he had seen that they were thirteen, all armed with spears, neckcutters —very sharp flat swords, those creatures' favourites—, bows, darts and axes. Only one of them, the so called Reshna, kept sipping wine.

'Slave, I think you haven't understood how the *Captain or Dozen* game works,' it said.

'Do you think this is a game?' Asked the Daughter of the Light. Her voice oozed hate. Siro feared that his words would lead them to the grave.

Reshna put the wineskin on the floor, belched and combed its black crest back. Siro recognized the same Brand that Ubald wore, the two blades and the ascending line, tattooed on the chest.

'Of course, it's a game. It´s a game and has three very simple rules: first, the winner has the honour of being shagged by the captain, in this case, the great Reshna,' it said and pointed itself with the thumbs.

'You mean Reshna the Fast,' said another Beast.

'Or Reshna the Lightning,' added another.

The Beasts laughed and elbowed each other.

'Enough, assholes!' said Reshna. 'I don't want you to ruin the expectations of these beautiful ladies. Where was I? Ah, yes, second rule: the one who loses, has the dishonour of being fucked by all these idiots that you see here. We always do that.'

The Beasts booed Reshna and made obscene gestures to the girls.

This is not going well, Siro thought.

'They're only girls...' Matildet said.

'Ah, wait!' Complained Reshna. 'You haven't heard the third rule. Do you want to know it?'

'You can shove your rules up in the ass!' The Daughter of the Light shouted. 'Open the door, do as I command!'

The Beasts stopped laughing and exchanged complicit glances. Reshna was serious for a moment and then smiled again. Its eyes reviewed Matildet's body from tip to toe.

'The third rule, slave, is that if you interrupt the game, you start playing. So, you know, beat the shit out of the little bitch and we'll have a good time. Hurry up. I have something very special for you,' he added with a wink.

Matildet seemed about to lose control, but before anything happened, the Beasts began to talk to each other, restless. Reshna was looking over the travellers. Siro turned to see the miners and farmers approaching the door.

'The fuck are you doing here?' Shouted Reshna. 'Where are your foremen? Go back to your hole, or you'll regret it!'

'She is a Daughter of the Light,' said the old hunchback they had seen at the entrance of the gorge. 'Even you should know what that means.'

The man had forgotten the sack of stones and had followed them there, just like a hundred slaves who had gathered whispering about the Great Light, Keerine and their children. At the top of the palisade, Beasts were also arriving. They pointed at them with their bows and arrows.

'Reshna, look at her clothes. She doesn't look like a slave,' said Taralban.

'Excuse me, ma'am... are you a Daughter of the Light?' A woman asked Matildet.

People had gathered around the girl. They tried to touch her, some even knelt before her and implored her blessing. On the other hand, the Beasts were becoming impatient. Siro knew what would happen next. If the slaves did not leave, it would be impossible to avoid the bloodbath.

'I'm Matildet, Daughter of the Light, and I command you to open the gate,' she said and raised her hand. A bright light surrounded it, just as it did in the oasis.

The slaves knelt around her as they contemplated that miracle. The Beasts looked at each other doubtfully, but did not move from the place. Reshna showed a confident smile.

'Yes, whatever you say, sweetheart...' It waved so that the Beasts would not move. 'I've seen better tricks in The Mouth. Some of them even made my magic wand fly, if you know what I mean.'

It took a long drink from the wineskin. A stream fell down the corner of the lips, then it turned to the thin girls that were fighting.

'You, little shit, your name,' it said almost not looking at her.

'Maia, sir, I'm the daughter of...' the girl answered, keeping her head down.

'Shut up, I couldn't care less... Now, listen, Maia, I have decided to add a rule to *Captain or Dozen*. If you win two consecutive rounds, you can go back to your miserable life.'

'What about me, sir?' Said the chubby girl, she had blood on her eyebrow and a bruise that grew on her cheek and prevented her from opening her eye wide.

'Shut up, cow! You should have tried harder,' Reshna threw the wineskin at her head, but missed. 'You, Maia. Do you see that impertinent slave? Beat her and you are out.'

'You don't expect her to...' Matildet said, but before she finished the sentence, the girl pounced on her with a high-pitched scream.

Siro tried to remove the girl from her, but she had grabbed the hair of the Daughter of the Light and kicked her in the ribs. Matildet just covered herself. The Beasts laughed out loud.

'Quiet,' Siro ordered as he lifted the girl with one arm. She was lighter than air.

The girl stirred for a while longer, but when she saw the hunter's eyes, she realized that she was playing with fire. She stood still, not knowing what to do.

She is scared to death. The hunter knew. He felt like burying his knife in the Beast's belly to see what was inside.

'So a Daughter of the Light, huh?' Said Reshna and clapped to the short fight. 'And that's how they fight in Teradam. Keerine would be proud.'

'The Children of the Light seek peace,' protested a bearded man who had knelt beside Matildet.

'Taralban, I want you to hang that one by the balls. Go get him,' Reshna ordered. 'The rest if you, servants of Adon, you have five seconds to head back to your jobs. Whoever stays is going to earn a free trip to the gallows.'

Matildet looked at Siro for help, but the hunter was only watching Reshna. Beasts like that were the ones that had swept Merco. Reshna's gaze was glassy —the Beast surely drank from sun to sun— but its voice didn't tremble if it had to order someone's death.

'And you two, what a waste of time. Now you will know why you don't have to fuck around with great Reshna. Archers, shoot!'

Siro stood before Matildet in the blink of an eye and pushed her to duck with him. He closed his eyes, waiting for arrow that was going to pierce his back, until he realised that nothing was happening there. The archers held fire. Two more Beasts had popped up on top of the wooden wall.

'Reshna, open the gates. Let them through,' Junal ordered.

'Now he will tell you that you cannot give him orders,' Guido said, beside him.

'You can't give me orders, you, asshole!' Shouted Reshna, from below.

'You are not helping!' Junal scolded Guido and then turned back to the gatekeeper. 'It's a direct order from our beloved lord Adon. Open.'

Reshna a combed its crest and winked at Matildet.

'We'll leave it for another day,' it said.

Reshna's Beasts turned gave the sign to open the gate. A pulley system pulled the wooden wall to open in half in two movements. The bowels of Undershell were at sight. Matildet didn't move until Guido and Junal came down to greet them.

'Lady Daughter of the Light,' Junal said with a bow. 'It is an honour that you have accepted our invitation. A shame you could not get rid of the savage.'

Siro pulled a face.

'I haven't had the reception I expected,' said the Daughter of the Light. Her hand no longer shone, and she looked nervous.

'My most sincere apologies. Our beloved Lord Adon is eager to meet you, milady,' said Junal.

Matildet was tempted to move forward, but then she thought of all the people who had gathered there because of her appearance.

'What will happen to them?'

'Oh, they will be punished and returned to their masters. Don't worry, milady, they're not worth it.'

'I want them to come in with me. Everybody.'

Reshna laughed behind the group. It had opened another wineskin.

'Well done, Junal,' said the gatekeeper. 'Lord Adon will love to see the palace full of rats.'

Chapter 24: Two Lights

Siro's feeling as he crossed the palisade was like entering a world he already thought lost forever. Undershell had changed, just like himself, but deep down it hid the same cruel face. The main street where hundreds of people had been killed years ago during the day of Exile remained as dirty and muddy as ever, but now the line of houses had gained territory and almost touched the palisade. Crooked and narrow buildings and limestone shelters were the places where entire families huddled at bedtime.

They kicked us out because there wasn't food for everyone, Siro recalled. *And now there's even more people...*

Along the street there were more wells than before, but that didn't solve the problem with the queues waiting to fill buckets of water. As a child, he was tasked to carry buckets home and had a very vivid memory of that feeling of thirst mixed with the anguish of queueing under the sun.

As it entered the gorge, the city became a succession of little shops and stables: on the one hand, merchants and slaves that bargained for everything and anything; and on the other, the nervous fuss of wildebeest, horses and poultry on sale. A mixture of cinnamon smell and apple jam welcomed them to the market of the Cross. Siro's stomach was roaring. He had often gone to the market running errands for his parents; or play hide and seek with other children whose faces and names he no longer remembered. Now he could see over the sideboards instead of seeing them from below. The world seemed much smaller than it used to. People were no longer giants that he had to avoid, but scared and silent slaves who moved aside as they saw the Daughter of the Light's entourage, which grew more and more as they made their way through Undershell. Many slaves left what they were doing to follow such an unusual event. Siro looked at them with suspicion, but Matildet didn't seem worried. She was talking to the two girls who not long ago were fighting each other to death. After the Beasts let them pass through the doors, she had addressed the two and asked them their names.

'I'm Matildet. I know that your name is Maia. You have a very bad attitude, girl. Change that, ok? And you?'

'I don't have a name, but they call me Olive,' the chubby girl replied, touching the scratch the other one had made her.

'Olive is a very pretty name.'

'They gave me the name because my father sold me to the Beasts in exchange for a sack of olives. I don't like it.'

'Ah. Then I'll find you a better one,' said the Daughter of the Light as she checked the bruises. 'I have a friend named Cassandra, Cas for shorting. Do you want it to be your name?'

The girl named Oliva nodded, excited to get rid of her nickname.

'Well, whatever it is, I don't want you two to fight anymore. From now on, I want you to be friends,' Matildet made them promise and they both gladly accepted. Maia even apologized for the blows.

'I didn't want to do it,' she said. Her chin was shaking, about to cry.

The chubby girl put an arm over her shoulders to comfort her. Soon, the two girls walked a few steps ahead of the group, chatted animatedly and peeked at Matildet.

'I think Cas sounds better than Olive. You're lucky,' Maia said to her friend, who suddenly smiled, as if there wasn't a single problem in her world.

'Thank you. Matildet, do you know you have very pretty hair?' said the chubby girl, who had mine dust in hers.

'Thank you very much,' she said, and looked at Siro, trying to guess whether he thought the same, but the hunter was only half listening to the conversation.

The hunter wanted to know where they were going. Junal and Guido were guiding them, but they hadn't said a word since they had crossed the palisade.

They take us straight to the palace, he realised when they left the market behind.

They continued eastward, towards the Great Shell. He was worried about what would happen once they were there. In the past the palace belonged to Dugol, but the name that all the Beasts seemed to have on their lips was Adon. The Beasts were not usually loyal. Each one for itself, and although they could have a leader from time to time, it was like trying to reason with a pack of Biters: most wouldn't make it out in one piece. The siege of Merco was a prime example: the looting and rapes had begun almost before the offensive.

But this time was different, Adon inspired some respect. Would Dugol's name have stopped someone as mad as Reshna?

And yet, despite the respect the Beasts felt for that name, the entourage of the Daughter of the Light were increasing. It had become so large that the streets could barely cope with it. From the top of the roofs, dozens of curious faces poked their noses to see the Tear City's herald. Perhaps it was the most amazing thing any of them would see in a lifetime.

'Look, I live there,' Maia pointed to a house with a garden hidden in one of the turns of the gorge. 'We used to live in The Mouth, but my mother remarried a very rich merchant and we moved here. Now I have a window in the room.'

'Yarei is not rich,' said the newly baptized Cas.

'No, not anymore,' Maia had to admit. 'The Beasts stole all his chickens to play *Hide or burn.*'

'What is *Hide or...*? Matildet was about to ask but remembering the rules of *Captain or Dozen* made her take a step back. 'Anyway… And where do you live?'

'Me? Out of town,' Cas said indifferently. 'In the barracks, with the miners.'

Matildet nodded and then turned to Siro.

'Do you remember where you lived?'

Siro knew there was a road from his house to the market, but he wasn't exactly where. He had never considered it a home, not even on the good days. For him, the tent in Merco he shared with Liduvin was more a home than anything else.

'Do you want to go later?' The Daughter of the Light insisted.

Siro shook his head. *Why would I want that?*

'Maybe your parents still…' Matildet tried to say, but the sentence ended halfway.

A man and a woman had approached her with a boy in their arms. The boy must be just over two years old; his jaw was crooked, and his head was elongated. The eyes were only two tiny dots he could barely open. The Daughter of the Light raised her hand to her mouth when she realised that the kid was blind.

'Please, Daughter of the Light, heal our son,' said the mother.

'It's hard for us to keep him. What will happen to him when we'll be too old to work? Help us, please,' the father added.

'Leave the Daughter of the Light alone!' Said Junal. 'Guido...'

'I know,' the fat Beast stepped in and pushed the mother, also bringing the father and the blind child to the ground.

Matildet was about to stop the entourage to reprimand Guido, but Siro was faster.

'Keep walking,' the hunter whispered in her ear. 'If you stop, slaves stop and we have problems.'

'He's just a child. He could be hurt...'

She looked for the family, but it had been swallowed by the crowd.

'If you help them, the others will ask for help too,' said Siro.

'Then I should.'

'You can't help them all. What happens if you fail? They will doubt that you are a Daughter of the Light and will kill us.'

'But...'

'Can you heal the child? Can you make him see again?'

'I can't. Not here,' she admitted. 'I'm going to get them out of here. I have done well coming.'

I hope you are not mistaken, thought Siro.

The Daughter of the Light's entourage was under the shadow of the Great Shell when they stopped. Matildet looked up at the sky to contemplate the vast metal structure.

'It's ours, Siro. The Great Shell is ours. It is incredible that it's been preserved, it must be about four centuries old...'

'What is it?'

'It's part of a larger structure. I can tell by the beams and anchors left at the ends... Do you see them? And you were right, it fell from the sky.'

The gaps and holes in that structure let in the sunlight that lighted the crooked towers of old Dugol's palace. The place had seen better days: one of the towers, the southern one, was leaning in such a way that it seemed it could fall any time. The slaves had tied dozens of ropes from the tower to the Great Shell to secure it. They had begun to build a wooden scaffold to make repairs, but they were in no rush to finish. The rest of the palace did not look much better, but at least the central nave remained solid, with its characteristic black walls and sculptures of ancestral creatures intact. Siro distinguished the silver outline of Mother Snakes statue, the obsidian composition of the Nacra Worm and the Water Scorpion, made of glass and lapis lazuli.

The palace had a dry pit full of stakes that surrounded the wall of limestone and mortar. The sentinel Beasts had been made aware. Even so, Junal called them three times to lower the drawbridge.

Matildet told the girls to stay and take care with Queenie. She gave them the sack of beetles in case the ostrich got annoyed. Then she and Siro and crossed the bridge preceded by Junal and Guido.

The entourage stopped there too. Undershell slaves knew very well the palace was off-limits without a work order.

As Siro and Matildet waited in the parade ground, one of the sculptures caught the hunter's attention. It was an exact replica of the one he had seen when Matildet and him had gotten into that strange basement: a representation of Keerine surrounded by emerald and amber cubes and hundreds of ivory figurines. The Beasts had placed it on a water fountain to make it more elegant.

They have been there. They have gone through the underground.

Beasts were venturing farther from Undershell.

He'd bet the Elector he had met in that strange basement, was part of an expedition who had had the misfortune to end up down there, just like them.

Sooner or later, they would find the Sacred Valley.

The palace doors opened, and from the top of the long staircase a squad of brawny Beasts came out carrying wide and grey swords. A Beast dressed in black then went down the stairs accompanied by a swarm of well-dressed jugglers, jesters and Beasts that formed a most eccentric group.

Siro recognized a single face but refused to believe he was there. He was much older, the dreadlocks he had always worn showed strakes of grey hair. He had not lost his taste for jade jewellery and garish-coloured clothing. The old merchant looked like he managed to recover his fortune. *What's Infidas doing here?* He thought, still struggling to believe he was up there. *What have you done, rat? How did you escape from Merco? Was it you who brought us to the Beasts?*

Siro felt a crazy desire to climb and strangle him, but there was an army of Beasts between them.

Infidas did not notice him, maybe he didn't even recognise him. It must had been ten years they had last seen each other. Like the rest of the Beasts, his eyes were set on Matildet.

The Beast dressed in black bowed before Matildet. The bow was so exaggerated, like the rudeness with which it ignored Siro. The Beast wore a blue mask with an engraved smiling face, although it seemed more sinister than cheerful.

'Dear Daughter of the Light,' the masked Beast announced in a distorted tone. 'It is an honour to have your presence. Allow me to introduce you to the master and Lord of the Beasts of Undershell, son of Dugol and bearer of the blood of Keerine, the light that guides us, our beloved and adored Adon.

A boy descended the stairs. His clothes were white, except the cape, which showed crimson shades and the symbol that almost all the Beasts carried: the cross and the vertical line. He had a delicate face, no Brand in sight, no scars, nor that ruthless look so typical of the Beasts. He could have been just another slave... if it weren't for those light blue eyes and the blond hair that fell on his shoulders.

Siro remained with his mouth open, not believing what he was seeing.

'Welcome home, sister,' said Adon with a perfect smile on his lips.

Chapter 25: Walk, don't stop

When they left the basement, an explosion surprised all three. A column of fire and ash rose to the sky, far from there, in the marketplace. Shahrokh dropped Siro and Eliria to the floor.

'If you run away, only one of you will live. If you stay, you'll both live,' the Beast warned them. 'Follow me.'

Siro grabbed Eliria's hand. The girl looked back at the old shop all the time. Tears fell down her cheeks.

'Mom... Siro, I can't leave her there. Siro, come on... Let's go back, please!'

'We can't,' he replied in the softest tone he could use.

He was pulling the girl to leave behind the basement where they left Debra and not to think about what Irad and the Hyena would be doing.

It took him a while to convince her, but in the end she relented. Siro knew they couldn't believe in Shahrokh's promise. The Beast was very likely to kill them when he no longer needed them, but if they fled at that very moment, they would only speed up the process. He had to find a way to escape.

You will not put your hand on Eliria, he promised himself as he followed in the footsteps of the Beast.

Shahrokh made them go up a half-collapsed watchtower down the path. The tower was not too tall, only a couple of meters higher than the houses that surrounded it. It was designed to be a water tank and a lookout at the same time. It had taken two months for them to build and a few hours for the Beasts to destroy. The part of the wall facing east was in ruins and exposed the skeleton of beams that held the building.

'Look, children,' Shahrokh said and pointed through the opening of the tower. 'Down there, the future of your village is being decided. Future looks grim.'

In the distance, a huge fire burnt beside the west barrier of the market square. Several rows of houses had disintegrated, and a black and grey smoke covered the night sky stars. Armed shadows moved through the ruins, while a rain of burning arrows fell on them from the sieged square. Firla's idea of using the Firespreader had slowed down the Beasts, but they had already destroyed a good chunk of Merco. The explosion had opened a huge crater. Siro knew that it was impossible that the women and men who defended the walls had come out unharmed.

'Firespreader,' Shahrokh muttered. 'This woman has no boundaries. She'll fight to the end.'

The two children held hands under the Beast's gaze.

'Take me to the marketplace and I promise you that nothing will happen to you,' it told them. 'I'm sure you know the way.'

'What about my mother?' said Eliria.

The Beast stroked the girl's shoulder and then hugged her. Siro stood still next to them. He felt like punching the Beast, but what would have been the next step? Shahrokh was much older than him. He could not prevent the Beast from touching her. He squeezed Eliria's hand to show her he was still there.

'I'm really sorry for everything that happened down there,' said the Beast. 'But I have done it for the sake of your friend.'

'What? Why?' Asked Eliria.

'He knows why,' Shahrokh released the girl and looked at Siro.

...Why don't you go to your house, grab a good knife and chop off Liduvin's head It's all that whore's fault. Debra's words had been burned into his brain. What had happened to that woman? Everything about her was strange and perverse. *Did you know?* Siro wondered. *Did you know that Debra wanted to hurt me so you stabbed her?* She had threatened to break his arm, but surely the Beast had not believed that... or had he? Siro didn't know what to think. The Beasts did not save anyone's life. They were cruel and bloodthirsty. Sure it would have had a great time if Debra had broken his bones. The three Beasts would have laughed and encouraged her to continue. But then why had he done it? Was it possible that this Shahrokh was different? For a moment, Siro doubted what he knew about those creatures, but then the memories of smithy came to mind, the family of the blacksmith who screamed and cried, the eldest son killed and cut up like an animal... No, he would fall for that. A Beast was a Beast, there were no exceptions.

'Eliria,' Shahrokh spoke to her warmly. 'I'm sure your friend can explain you everything as soon as this is over, but now I need your help...'

'No way,' said Siro. 'If you want to get to the marketplace, you'll have to do it alone. Have fun with the Firespreader.'

'This is not a game, child. I have to get there before Dugol and the other Beasts do it.'

'You want to kill Firla,' said Siro. The Beast scared him, but he didn't want it nor Eliria to notice.

'You couldn't be more wrong...' he replied, but then he heard howls and the three fell silent.

Shahrokh made them hide inside what was left of the tower and then went down the stairs. Siro pulled his head through the embrasure to see what was happening. A group of six Beasts ran through the streets. They threw torches inside the houses that remained standing. Among them was a naked man wearing an iron ring around his neck. One of the Beasts was pulling him so he wouldn't be left behind. Siro recognized the man they had captured: he was Eineran Crown, Crownie's father.

'Shahrokh! Look what we have here, do you think Dugol will like it?' Said the Beast that dragged Eineran.

'I think rats are not to our beloved lord's taste, but a king needs a crown, doesn't he?' Siro heard the Beast answer.

The Beasts asked Shahrokh what it knew about the battle and if there were women in any of the houses. Shahrokh chatted the comrades, but with the rumble coming from the centre of Merco, the words did not reach the two children.

'Siro, what do you see?' Asked Eliria.

'I see it's time to escape,' the boy replied.

If they went downstairs, they would run into Shahrokh and the Beasts, so they had to find an alternative path. Under the tower, through the sunken wall, the thatched roof of the surrounding houses was visible. They were a little far off, but if they gained momentum, he thought they could jump on them.

'Are you crazy?' Said the girl when Siro proposed the idea. 'What if the roof sinks? Don't you see we'll die?'

'Ok. What about that fruit stand?'

'Do you think melons and watermelons are soft? We will split our heads!'

Siro couldn't believe they were trapped there.

There must be a way out! He told himself. *I will not help Shahrokh! Nor will I let it take us, never!*

He had to hurry. The Beasts little chitchat would not last much longer. Inside the tower, there was a ramshackle table and a closed oak trunk. He rummaged through it, but only found the remains of a pie, a pair of ropes and a rabbit skin with the tower plans wrapped inside. On the shelves there were hammers, nails and planks in case an emergency repair had to be done; on the floor, were a pair of bloated sawdust bags. Siro noticed a drip against the wooden floor and directed his eyes toward the ceiling: the water tank was held two meters above their heads, surrounded by the stone structure and held by four aged cherry wood beams.

'If we tie the two ropes to one of the beams, we can go down,' Eliria had had the same thought as him. 'Come on, help me! Hurry up!'

The boy was glad that it was Eliria, and not Nazeh, who was with him in those circumstances. His friend would surely have been crying in a corner; she, on the other hand, was not one to give up.

'Make sure they are well tied. I heard rabid mongooses have no idea of making knots,' Siro teased. 'It must be because they have no fingers.'

'Free Child, I knew how to tie knots before you learned to walk,' the girl said and smiled for a moment.

Since they had left basement, Siro thought he would never see that smile again. But the girl became serious again, maybe feeling guilty for smiling just after what had happened to her mother. They tied the other end of the ropes to the waist, but when they were ready to go, Shahrokh had already returned and blocked their way. Standing in front of the sunken wall and with the glow of fire trimming his dark silhouette, he looked like the Nightborns Liduvin always spoke about.

'What is this?' Said the Beast. 'Tying yourselves to the tower will make no difference. You are coming with me.'

'Eliria, now!' Shouted Siro.

The boy grabbed his friend's hand and jumped towards Shahrokh. The Beast raised his arms and told them to stop, but they ignored him. The three flew through the void through the hole in the wall. Siro felt the acceleration in his stomach as he fell, followed by a very strong pull. The children hanged in mid-fall, but the Beast went through the thatched roof below and disappeared inside the house. They heard a crunch above them and the watchtower sank. An avalanche of stones went down the slope, crashing house roofs and the fruits on the stand. The ropes gave way and the two children fell.

Siro got up coughing. He was inside a house, surrounded by shattered furniture. His head was spinning, and he had scratches all over. Wherever he looked, he only saw straw floating in the air. A tall silhouette clinked in the background, holding its head.

That's Shahrokh, he told himself, although the Beast was just a blurry stain in his eyes. He left the house, limping, through what was left of the door before it saw him.

'Siro!' He heard someone yell at him. 'Wait for me!'

Eliria was on top of the remains of the roof. She seemed she had been luckier with the landing. She climbed down the sunken roof and the two fled down. The path was half flooded with water from the tank that had burst after the watchtower collapsed.

'Siro, run! It's coming!'

She put the boy's arm around her shoulders to help him walk.

The Beast limped behind them.

'I'm glad you decided to show me the way. Next time, you don't need to be so enthusiastic,' Shahrokh told them as he brushed the dusty mane from his face.

'Walk, Siro, don't stop!' Eliria encouraged him.

The houses they passed by were stained with soot. Dense smoke floated in the alleyways. Night had fallen and there were no lights on the street. The only thing that guided them was the trail of the Firespreader and the small fires that rose around the square. Siro saw bodies in the distance that moved with frenzy: the Beasts were trying to climb the walls.

Eliria stepped on something. When she saw what it was, she gave a high-pitched squeak that scared Siro. There was a charred arm in the middle of the street.

'You two... walking around at night can be dangerous,' Shahrokh said.

There was a dry thud just behind the two children, like a wooden plank splitting. A man had left one of the houses and faced the Beast. Shahrokh had received a blow to the head and was swaying from side to side, about to fall.

'Especially for you, son of a bitch!' Siro recognized Taurus's voice. 'Get out of here, kids! Run to the square, fast!'

Firla's husband was badly injured. His arm hung grotesquely. The wooden board was the only weapon he had, and now that it was broken, he was left alone to face the Beast. Siro closed his eyes when Shahrokh kicked Taurus under the ribs. The man groaned like a dying animal.

The children fled from there, not waiting to see how the fight ended.

The ruined houses and the orange light of the fires created a bleak landscape. The floor was full of strange shapes, human fragments, bodies wrapped in scorched clothes. Siro noticed that his snorts were not the only noises there were. A chorus of agonizing voices hid among the ruins.

The shadows followed them. Silhouettes appeared and disappeared. People or Beasts. Siro didn't know. Someone grabbed Eliria's ankle, but the girl got away and stepped on the hand that was looking for her.

'Help me!' Shouted the woman who was crawling on the floor. Siro saw that the girl had broken her fingers with the stomp. 'Don't hurt me, don't let them take me away! No, please no!'

Two more silhouettes approached, tied a rope around the woman's neck and pulled her into a house. While the children escaped from there, they heard the trail of cries and insults.

'I can't do it, Siro! I can't anymore... I don't want to see anything else,' Eliria sobbed.

'We must keep going,' he said and pulled the girl tighter.

The slope descended as they approached the square. They surrounded the craters that the Firespreader had left. There were no bodies. No one approached them. The Bindagi's secret weapon had made its effect. The acid smell of the flammable liquid filled the air as a reminder of what had happened.

'Filling the houses with Firespreader, what's she thinking?' Had said Liduvin, and now he understood why. The explosions were out of control, killing Beasts and people alike. Worst of all, there was still much more of that liquid stored in the houses.

An armed group approached them. They carried spears and shields that shone when they moved near the fires. Siro counted a dozen.

'Look, there is someone on the other side of the crater!' He heard one of the soldiers shout.

'Are they ours?' Asked another. Siro glimpsed a bow, ready to show.

'Stop! We are not Beasts!' The boy shouted. 'We need help!'

The group of soldiers approached them. Eder led them. The guard wore a bandage on his forehead and torn clothes. A red spot stood out above the white cloth.

'Siro, Eliria, for all the Children of the Light!' Eder's eyes were wide open. 'Where have you been?'

'Taurus is in danger,' said Siro. 'A Beast is attacking him, you have to help him!'

'And my mother!' Eliria added. Her words trumpeted. 'Beasts have her trapped in a basement. You must go get her out of there, please!'

'Ok, children. Cool down,' said Eder. 'First of all, are you hurt?' He turned to two of his soldiers. 'Asteria, Laonice! Take these two children to see Tersian.'

'Taurus is very close!' Siro insisted. 'He has saved us. You must go look for him!'

'Eder, the Beasts are coming back! They are about twenty… No, more!' Shouted the man who carried the bow in his hands.

The guard spat on the ground when he saw those creatures approaching from the other side of the crater. They ran and howled towards them. The Beasts were not afraid of anything. Already from a distance they threw stones and axes to see if they reached someone. An arrow came flying and got stuck in Eder's shoulder.

'Captain, are you all right? Captain, answer!' Asked one of his men, as he grabbed Eder so he wouldn't fall.

The two soldiers the captain had called appeared at that moment. They seemed very young, of the age of Cairu.

'Take the children and warn the others. Hurry!' Eder ordered as he rose again. He grabbed Laonice by the back of his neck before he left. 'Don't forget, tell Firla they have Taurus!'

'Come with me, children,' Asteria told them in a motherly tone, although the fear of the approaching Beasts was reflected in her eyes.

While the four fled from that place, the rest of men and women who formed Eder's group stayed outside the crater, ready for the the Beasts' attack.

As they followed Asteria, Siro saw a strange movement. He tried to say something, but before he could do so, Laonice, who was ahead, had already fallen to the ground. He had a rope tied to the foot. The Beasts dragged him to the crater.

He saw more ropes flying towards them and Asteria covered the two children so they wouldn't catch them. One of them grabbed the girl by the arm and made her fall. The rope dragged her, but before she disappeared forever in the darkness of the crater, she cut the rope with her sword.

'Go on, don't stop!' The girl shouted.

Three Beasts climbed to the top of the slope. Asteria did not hesitate for a second and lashed out. Swords and axes collided. The girl's arms shook every time they stopped a blow, but she didn't lower her guard for a moment. The Beasts surrounded her and the small silhouette of Asteria disappeared beneath the huge bodies of her adversaries.

I will not see them again, thought Siro. *I will never... Liduvin... where are you?*

Chapter 26: One More

'You won't escape, wildling!', 'Look, up there!', 'Seven jade moons for his head!'. The Beasts chased Siro as he fled through the roofs of Undershell, which rumbled under the stomps of the pursuers. Siro ran through the windmills that populated most of the rooftops and dodged their turning blades. Further down, in the streets, the Beasts got mixed with the slaves, growing in number. A stone brushed his head and slammed into the wall of a house. It raised a cloud of white dust and left a hole the size of a fist. The slings whistled as they spun in the air.

The roof ended in a wall and Siro had no choice but to climb it. He was getting further from the ground level. He doubted that was a good thing. At his side stood a windmill with four blades of cloth that turned above his head at a steady pace. From that height, he could see the whole city, from the wooden palisade where they had entered the city to the Great Shell hiding the sunlight.

Two hooks crossed the sky and got a hold on the edge of the building where the hunter was.

You won't have it that easy, he thought. He cut the two ropes with the knife, but by then it was too late. Two Beasts had cornered him.

'Do you think Junal will pay us better if we bring him alive?' Said one of them, while spinning the sling. At any moment the Beast could shoot the stone and crack his head open.

'I don't know, but I want to tear his face away,' said the other one, a creature with a scar that broke his lower lip. It swapped the butcher knife from hand to hand.

Siro was ready for the attack. At his back, he had a ten meters free fall to the main street and, in front, two Beasts that would not let him go anywhere. The creature with the scar on its lip brandished the knife as if Siro was nothing more than a chicken to be dismembered.

Stay away from the slingshot, he told himself. *Don't get in the fire line.*

While the butcher and the hunter exchanged lunges, a barrage of hooks crossed the sky like black snakes and got hooked to the edge of the roof. One of them tore one of the mill blades. The rope got caught and spined at the mill´s pace. The Beasts climbed up the wall, while four more of Adon's henchmen peeked through the same place where the other two had come from.

Now there were four Beasts trying to gut him. One of them grabbed him by the cloak, but Siro released it in time to avoid the butcher's cut and counterattacked by splitting the flesh from its ankle. The creature rushed into the void with a gasp. But that didn't help, because an even stronger Beast, with a neckcutter sword in each hand replaced it.

'Congrats. You killed a butcher... Let's see how you manage against the best warrior of Undershell' The Beast swinged the swords around Siro with a monstrous force, but the attack did not last long.

The hunter threw the cape to its face and, at almost the same moment, threw the knife at him. By the scream he knew that he had hit him in the stomach. He lunged himself against the self-proclaimed best warrior and the two rolled over the roof, until Siro got up with a bloody-stained knife in one hand and the cape in the other, prepared for the next contender.

There were half a dozen Beasts already on the tiny roof, and there were even more climbing up the wall. *How many can I kill before they tear me apart?* The creatures approached him more carefully, groped him with spears, and shot him with slings. He was crouching down to make it much harder to hit him. *They can't shoot downwards*, he reminded himself, but he knew that the Beasts, no matter how stupid they were, would soon realize that the best they could do was attack him all at once.

Siro saw what could be his only escape. In one of the blades of the mill the rope of one of the hooks was still there. The blade turned slowly over the heads of his adversaries and in a few seconds he would have it within reach. Meanwhile, he swung the knife back and forth. He earned time for the rope to get where he was.

Just a little more... C'mon!

A hand sprang out of nowhere and grabbed his ankle. Siro fell face first, slipping to the edge of the roof. The Beast clung to his leg to avoid falling and laughed. Siro held the weight with all his strength, clinging to the wooden edge. The shadow of another Beast got closer holding a spear.

'Release me, we'll both die!' He yelled at the creature that grabbed him by the foot, but there was no answer.

He glanced at the rope attached to the windmill blades

It won't arrive on time, he thought seeing the spear getting closer.

He let go of the edge. The tip of the spear broke against the place where his hand had been. His stomach went up to his throat the moment he felt that nothing was holding him. He noticed that the Beast forgot his foot and screamed in terror. He could have done the same, but instead he reached out and grabbed the rope. His hands slipped over a meter when he clenched his fists around it. It was like hugging a cactus, but he took the pain, and with one hand on the rope and his feet against the wall, he ran down the facade of the building under the incredulous gaze of the Beasts. He turned around the building and took advantage of the momentum to jump into the adjoining building.

Cherry wood planters stopped his fall. Siro ended up landing on the moss of a private garden. His back was bruised by the blow and his legs were full of scratches from the times he had slipped running down the wall.

The garden had a rectangular water channel that ran along the floor, decorated with circular tiles and varnished in ochre tones. Siro, a little dizzy after the crash, sank the hand with which he had grabbed the rope in the water. The feeling of relief was so pleasant, it made him sigh. He would get a huge blister.

'Insolent slave!' He heard a voice growl. 'You will end your days as a eunuch!'

A fat man and an old woman looked at him from across the garden. Siro had not even realized that they were there because of the pain. The woman was sitting on a white wooden bench, under the shadow of a palm tree with turquoise leaves on one side and purple on the other. The fat man was standing and had drawn a saber so shiny that Siro was sure it had never tasted blood. He wore a dress that reaffirmed his belly rather than concealed it, but didn't seem to care.

Probably a merchant, thought Siro. He tore off a small splinter that had stuck in his back and shook off the remains of petals and vines with which he had collided, without paying much attention to the other two.

'Helos, I think he is not a slave,' the woman said timidly. 'I can't see his Brand.'

'Then I'll send him straight to the Elector... In slices!' Was the man's response and he gifted the hunter with a few juggling moves of his shiny saber.

I don't have time for this, thought Siro. He ran next to the man, but he was faster than expected and gave him two blows. The first one, he blocked it with the knife, but the second touched his left buttock. Siro noticed a frightful pain that almost made him fall.

While the woman applauded the merchant's bravery, the hunter jumped into the next building.

Siro landed at ground level after going down a wall. It wasn't hard. The plastering of the wall was old and falling apart, there were plenty of gaps between the billets. He was in a dark and narrow alley. Something moved beneath a pile of garbage gathered between the two buildings. Under a cloud of flies and filth, an old, ragged man came out.

His stench was worse than the garbage itself. Flies roamed his lips and between the hairs of his beard feeling at home.

'A coin, good man?' Said the old man in a voice so scratchy that it seemed to be drowning.

'Give me your clothes,' ordered Siro. *I will regret it*, he also thought, but if he didn't change his appearance, the Beasts would find him right away.

'My clothes? And what do you want them for?'

'It's none of your business,' The hunter drew his knife and didn't need any more arguments. 'Hurry up.'

The clothes smelled like piss and mould. At some point it must have been a luxurious enough dress, with ornaments and watermarks, but they had been torn away long ago. It could have been the clothes of some wandering merchant in the southern Mirror Rocks, but now it was little more than four badly sewn fabrics full of grey and brown spots.

'Will you give it back to me?' The beggar asked, now that he was naked, he was nothing but a sack of bones. The slavery Brand on his neck was so wrinkled that Siro would not know what it was: a coiled snake or the blade and the vertical line?

'No,' Siro replied.

Beyond the shadow of the alley, the Undershell market extended left and right. A fog of exotic scents filled the place: cinnamon, incense, hot spices and fruits in syrup mixed with the fumes that emerged from the forges and fires and candles from the wandering wizard stops. Fruit-filled cakes and freshly baked breads made his stomach roar. How many years had it been since he had seen something so delicious? People bought them and moved on, but for Siro that meal was as incredible as if the Creator himself had appeared before him.

There were greengrocers, pens full of chickens, goldsmiths with the rarest jewels and instruments he had ever seen, blacksmiths and artisans, usurers and farmers carrying sacks full of wheat. They all shouted prices, bargained, and made offers to everyone who walked by. Golden suns, jade moons, iron triangles, mother-of-pearl coins and even raw glass... any currency was valid in Undershell's market.

The square was full of slaves, all of them with their Brands on the skin. Siro counted a score for every Beast he saw. Some bought food and clothes for them, others for their masters... and others were bought and sold as just another commodity.

Siro joined a group of slaves. The Beasts were still looking for him. They patrolled in small groups, of three or four, but they didn't go unnoticed to anyone. Every time he heard a scream from a slave girl or vase shattering on the floor, he knew they were closer.

'Show me the Brand!' He heard a Beast shout at a slave carrying a wildebeest; but he was not fast enough, and two other Beasts tore his cloths in front of the entire market.

'The Agate Shepherd Brand,' one of those unscrupulous creatures announced. 'You'll live another day, worm.'

Siro put on his hood and changed direction. He noticed that the dress itched on his back and legs. He was getting tired of running. He had escaped the palace of Adon, just before they lifted the drawbridge... but Junal's Beasts were waiting for him outside.
He hadn't heard what they were saying, but he hadn't needed it. It was obvious. 'That's him, he is the wildling who killed Ubald,' he imagined them saying. 'He stabbed him again and again until the pond was red.'

That damn Adon had said nothing, he had only looked at him with his blue eyes, like Matildets'. Those were the eyes of a Son of the Light. 'Sister,' he had called her, but was it true? Did she know?

He had refused to accept it at first, but now he saw it clearly.

Matildet had mocked him, betrayed him and made a fool of him. Every time he remembered the face of the Daughter of the Light on the staircase, he wanted to scream and break everything. *She had known from the beginning!* He told himself. *That's why she insisted so much on coming here.* He could forget about entering Teradam and seeing Liduvin again.

It was all over.

Adon had invited Siro to enter the palace. In fact, he had referred to him as 'our wild friend'. Even Matildet had begged him to accompany them inside. But he knew very well that once in he would not go out again, and he had run before the guards reacted.

The entourage that the Daughter of the Light had left on the other side of the drawbridge had prevented the Beasts from catching him right away, but surely the slaves would have preferred not to find themselves in that situation. How many people would have died simply by following Matildet to Undershell's palace? Did the Daughter of the Light really care, or did she just pretend?

'I'm going to get them out of here,' Matildet had said when she had seen how slaves were treated. Now he didn't know whether to believe those words.

A group of Beasts grabbed a young man of the same height as Siro. He was pulled to the ground and one of the Beasts put the tip of its sword on his neck while the others searched his arms and legs.

They are checking the Brands, he thought. Luckily, the clothes he wore covered his body enough and it was hard to recognize him. If he had kept his worn pants and the cape, they would have caught him already. He wondered if the old homeless would find something to put on that night. He looked fragile.

He may die because of me.

I knew it, wildling, you are like us, Ubald's words echoed his head.

I am not. I don't kill innocents! I don't rape women! I don't burn children alive! I am a free man, not a Beast.

He ducked behind a barrel of Ardent and pretended to beg to fool a squad of Beasts approaching him. None of them paid attention, except the last one, who spat in his hand.

'There you have your coin, rat!' It snapped and forgot he even existed.

Siro wiped his hand with the sandy ground and held back the urge to fight back. The rest of the slaves turned away when they saw Beasts. They didn't even dare to raise their heads when they were close. If they could have become invisible, they would have.

The houses where he had climbed to flee his pursuers were east of the square. It seemed to him that he still distinguished the rope he had used to escape hooked to the mill. Next to it, the outline of the merchant's garden was visible. The cuts that the old fart had inflicted him with the saber burned like coals. Further east, the Great Shell hid the sun, although not for long. The hour of the Birth, remembered that they called to the moment in which the sun rose above the metal structure, would arrive soon. Undershell had a short time of gloom before the day became was bathed in sunlight.

'If I don't take this opportunity, I can never escape from here,' Siro reflected. But the options were not too good. The east was ruled out, he was not going back to the palace; and to the west, an impassable palisade and an army of Beasts awaited.

Around him, merchants rushed to close deals. In Undershell, not everyone was a slave or a Beast; there were also rich merchants, priests of hundreds of different temples, bounty hunters and looters who had made their fortunes with their adventures and aspired to be someone more respectable. Some were from the city, but most were just stopping by. 'Undershell is nothing more than a market of lost souls,' his father had once told him. The merchants and the rest of the foreigners came to make deals with the Beasts, to take a pretty woman or buy a strong man who could be useful during their travels. Siro had no idea where they came from. Not from the west, he was positive. He had never met anyone on the way to the city of the Children of the Light. His father had once told him that there was a city somewhere among the northern ravines, a place called the Jade Valley, where many merchants came from. 'Nobody knows if the city really exists. Also, its inhabitants are cowards. Always hiding...,' his father used to say. 'Why?' The boy had asked. 'Why do you think? They have the beautiful Jade Valley, and the Lord of the Beasts has… well, thousands of blood-thirsty Beasts' he had added with a click of his tongue. 'Will we go there one day?' He had asked, excited by the idea of seeing a valley dyed in bright green, and not that monotonous limestone colour of Undershell. His father's answer had been short: 'No,' he had said, and he had sounded so defeated when he said it, that little Siro had lost his wish to ask for anything else.

'Forty golden suns, I've heard! Who gives more?' A woman's

shouts took him out of his thoughts. 'Have I heard forty-five? Fifty? Fifty five? No, we don't want that, Micah, your painted brass is worthless!' She scolded one of the men around her.

The people attending the auction laughed and moved on. The auctioneer wore a purple dress that left her shoulders exposed and looked at the audience with a big smile. Beside her, a Beast with red Brands around its arms could not take its eyes off.

The true master of the business, Siro thought as he moved from the barrel of Ardent to the crowd around the stage. There were about twenty men and women who were bidding to take three amphorae of white jade. The amphorae were as tall as the hunter and, as the woman said, they were filled with stuffed olives up to the top.

The square was getting swamped with Beasts. A group of Adon's henchmen searched in a post where they had caged roosters. They broke the cages they could and took what they wanted without their owner opening their mouths. Right next to him, a couple of Beasts grabbed a boy by the neck and interrogated him.

He had to look for another hideout. He passed a post where a merchant bargained with a slave for some dyes for clothes. The man looked at him with a look of contempt. The woman covered her nose. It gave off a terrible stench, and it was increasingly difficult to go unnoticed. Even the slaves pulled away or pushed him past.

The Beast hunt pushed him north, pushing him to The Mouth.

The smoking hill was rising at the end of the market, so large that it could almost compare to the Great Shell. The Mouth was the name that received the opening where you could access the endless galleries that spread out inside. The massif was full of holes and windows excavated from inside the rock. Most were chimneys for the forges and businesses that were inside the mountain. When Siro was little, he used to think that when the mountain was fuming, it was because he was thinking. That made him feel funny, but when he asked his father what was inside, he had become serious. 'You should never go, even if your friends go and insist. Never, you hear me? Never!'.

A group of chained slaves carried sacks full of charcoal in the direction of The Mouth. Siro approached with his head down, so they wouldn't notice him.

'Give me a sack,' he murmured to one of the slaves, a skinny teenager, with his face and shoulders tanned by the sun.

The boy hesitated. The two advanced little by little behind the tail of slaves and cars that had formed at the entrance of The Mouth.

'No, go,' he said.

'I need to get in,' Siro insisted.

'Master Querz will whip me to death.' Go away please! The boy pleaded.

The slave was tied by the ankle to the rest of his companions and did not want to waste time with a wanderer. They all carried a Brand on their left shoulder, a kind of winged snake curled up into a human skull.

At the entrance of The Mouth, a pair of Beasts arrested all who approached and required something. They had a small mountain of treasures: burning pitchers, sacks of apples, pears and oranges; and a pair of caged pheasants. One of the boys in the row of slaves left one of the sacks of coal at his feet. The Beast removed him with a sharp sword and then pointed to one of the chained slaves.

'I'll keep her too,' he said, amused, as he grabbed her arm. But the smile was erased when another slave buried his fist in his face.

Everyone stood still, holding their breath. The slave, a tall boy, hesitated a few seconds, and then threw himself on the Beast with the intention of finishing what he had begun. When the other sentry drew his weapon to put an end to the dispute, chaos broke loose. Half of the slaves in the chain chose to flee, while the other half decided to stand up. All of them fell to the ground, made a mess of chains. One of the oxen pulling the cars became nervous and began to move. The catwalk that led to the entrance to The Mouth was filled with shouts and shoves as the car moved and crashed into people, animals and other cars. Siro wanted to turn around to get out of there, but Adon's minions were waiting for him at the end of the line. The Beasts banged the slaves and brandished spears and scourges above their heads. Behind everything, was Junal, shouting orders, and Guido by his side.

A push made him fall to the ground. For a moment he felt like the helpless child who had been the day of Exile, but this time neither Grinat nor Liduvin would appear to save him. He crawled between people's legs in search of a hiding place. Along the way, someone stepped on his hand. He shouted in pain. He tried to reach the ankle of those who had trampled him, but it was useless. It was a matter of time that some runaway animal passed over him or that any of Adon's henchmen caught him while he was helpless.

'The car, I have to get to the car!', He told himself, and crawled as people fell under the steel of the Beasts. Once under the car, he advanced at the same speed as the vehicle. From his hiding place, he watched the pitched battle unleash around him. A man fell to the ground and the car passed over his arm. He bent in a grotesque gesture and then fell back, inert. The wheel of the car left a red line. Siro couldn't look away. A couple of children tried to hide under the car next to Siro. He reached out to help them, but before they arrived, someone grabbed them and they disappeared. People fell trapped by the chains and the fury of the Beasts. A part of him wanted to go out and face them. He was now a man, not a child, like when Merco had been attacked… But he remained under the car.

'Just a little,' he said as he crawled. 'Don't look, and move, you're almost there.' The sunlight suddenly disappeared, and he knew that he had crossed the threshold of The Mouth.

Chapter 27: Whom I really wait

Inside he Mouth, the screams from the outside echoed like furious spirits. Row after row of torches lit the galleries carved into the rock centuries ago. Beasts were much more numerous in there. Siro had them all around him laughing, joking, hiding in the shadows, doing business, and drinking until they could no more. The air was impregnated with the smell fumes, strong liquors, and women's perfumes.

Siro move along the galleries, glancing over his shoulder.

The floor of the gallery was paved with bright hexagonal slabs. The ceiling and the columns that held the vault had reddish engravings, bronze inlays and iron reinforcements. Most engravings depicted some legend: Siro recognized the outline of Mother Snake on the ceiling; and the figures of two metal women in a column, probably the Copper Sisters. He had heard their story once, from the mouth of one of Merco's fishermen, who had no issue telling the tale, unlike Liduvin. The two sculptures breasts were shinier than the rest of the bodies. Every time a Beast passed by, it caressed them. They thought it brought luck. As he passed by, he doubted whether to imitate the gesture or not, but not seeing any slave doing it, he kept his hands off.

In the gloom of the galleries, it was hard to distinguish slaves from Beasts. Even so, their way of walking and their sad looks gave them away. Siro covered himself as much as he could with the hood and avoided the eye contact. He didn't know where he was going, only that the road led up. The smell of roast got to his nose. He saw food stalls on the sides of the gallery. Each business was a hole dug in the rock, with a counter and a door inviting to enter. Sellers had their signs with fireflies flapping in them to lit the glass letters and symbols. Each sign had a different colour, and the movement and light of the fireflies made the sea of signs that stretched along the gallery wave above the passers' heads.

'Two jade moons? Are you crazy?', He heard a Beast

screaming. Its eye was stitched. For a moment, Siro had the feeling that it was Ubald.

'Crazy me? Look at her again! How long has it been since the last time you saw a pussy? I promise you that nobody has tried it yet,' the being who negotiated had a girl grabbed by the neck. Around it, two Beasts had offered iron and mother of pearl coins as a payment.

'This little bitch isn't worth shit,' the Beast of the stitched eye complained. 'She's split lips and doesn't even have boobs. She'll die as soon as I take it out my pants.'

The girl looked at everyone who was passing by. For a moment, her eyes fell on Siro. 'Somebody help me,' they seemed to say. One of the Beasts put its hand under her skirt and then nodded to its partner to make a better offer. Siro forced himself to look away, but he could feel the girl's eyes fixed on the back of his neck. And she was not the only one. Throughout the gallery, other girls and boys, older and younger, were sold the same way.

Four Beasts bargained for a fan-shaped sword. The vendor assured them that it had been forged with steel from the Great Shell and that, if they wanted, they could try it with his slave. Beside him, two merchants shouted at each other to see who had the deadliest poisons. A Beast dragged two half-naked slaves, chained by the neck, towards a circular door. Just ahead, a gathering of those creatures betted on the result of a fight while a scribe wrote down the amounts on a wooden tablet. The hunter went through it all, crestfallen. He wanted to be invisible, just like the rest of slaves.

Even if I don't have the Brand, I'm like them here, he told himself, and he felt more uncomfortable than ever with the clothes he had stolen from the beggar.

He itched all over. His elbows and knees hurt after crawling under the car; and the sword's wound stung him with every step. *I must get out of here,* he told himself, but every time he looked back, he was afraid to see Adon's henchmen about to catch him.

The main road branched into dozens of secondary galleries. Siro did not feel like entering them. The gallery he followed seemed sinister enough. As the smell of roasted meat, wine and Ardent intensified, so did the fights. The Beasts beat each other with no apparent reason, just one look was enough to make them jump. Siro did the impossible not to get in the middle, but the gallery was too narrow and he knew that sooner or later he would receive a blow not meant for him. The path widened until it reached a circular cavern, with the roof full of sharp stalactites.

'Keep searching! He must be close!' Junal's voice rose somewhere in the galleries.

'Search... We know, Junal. What else have we been doing all day? Obvious, always obvious stuff...' Guido replied.

The two thugs headed a squad of Beasts armed with neck-cutting swords, flagellums, axes and metal claws. The group had dispersed and traced every corner of the cave.

'Hey, slave, get out of here. Don't you see that you scare the clientele with your stench?'

Siro turned to see who had spoken to him and met a voluptuous woman wearing a red dress that covered her nipples, crotch... and not much more. On one cheek she had the Brand of a heart with a tear. Siro had the feeling that he had seen it before.

It's the same as the one Nazeh's brother had, he realised. He had never dared to ask him about Mohaki's Brand. It seemed that it was a taboo in that family.

'I'm no slave,' he replied.

'Whatever you say, honey, but if you don't pay, forget about the Palace of Dreams,' the woman shook her head in the direction of a fly of stone stairs leading to a gallery lit by blue fire torches. In the background, there was a double door painted red.

'Take me,' he ordered. He could see the thick silhouette of Guido getting closer and closer.

'Of course, honey, in exchange for your gold, jade, copper... oh, wait. You have nothing, haven't you? Such a same... Have you left everything in the house you don't owe?'

Siro searched the homeless' pockets. He found only half chewed rat. He dropped it to the ground, disgusted. He reached into his pants, hopeless, and found something he had long since forgotten he had.

'Have you heard that a Daughter of the Light has arrived at the city?' Siro dropped.

'...And also that she is prettier than any courtesan that's ever lived... But those who say that have surely never been to the Palace of Dreams, I promise you, honey.'

'This is yours,' he showed Matildet's coloured nut. It was the same one he had found inside Ubald's bag, next to the pond. 'It's her food. It's what makes her so beautiful.'

The woman hesitated for a few seconds, pulled a reluctant face, but for Siro it was more than obvious that the rest of the potential clients who walked around were no longer interesting to her. She took the nut from his hands.

'Follow me, honey,' she said, and they both climbed the stairs leading to the red door.

Am I still in Underhsell? Siro wondered as he took the first steps inside the Palace of Dreams. The birch wood decoration covered the cavern vibe the rest of galleries had. The lights on the walls and tables shone in a sky-blue fire expelled by the copper burners. Inlays of pink mother of pearl reflected the light of the flames like mirrors.

The Palace of Dreams had a large room below the entrance level and a dozen luxurious boxes on the second floor. The boxes were adorned with overloaded sculptures of naked women and men who chased each other. At the bottom, a multitude of coloured robes moved and talked in an endless muttering. Music came from somewhere, but Siro was not looking for musicians. His eyes were on the tall girl who had approached him.

'Welcome to your palace, prince,' She greeted him from behind a silver mask. Her voice sounded as she wanted to rip his clothes right there. 'What colour may I offer you today?'

'Colour?' Repeated Siro.

She showed him three different robes.

'The black one if you're looking for ladies,' she explained with a smile. 'White if you prefer men... and red, if you believe variety is the spice of life.'

Siro remembered the disgust he had felt when Ubald had rubbed against. He chose black.

At least with it they'll leave me alone, he thought.

'As you wish. My friends call me Meres. And you, my prince, are already my friend. Please, let me be your guide.'

Siro continued the merry walk of Meres, not knowing what else he could do. He admired the white statues sculpted on the ceiling of the room, around a gigantic mirror. He hadn't seen himself in a mirror for years. The only notion he had of his own appearance came from his visits to the oasis when he could see his reflection in water of the pond. In the middle of that place, wrapped with a strange black robe, he hardly recognized the man who looked back at him. He had a long, thick beard and his hair almost reached his shoulders. Behind him, a lot of robes chatted animatedly. he felt insignificant and out of place in the middle of all those strangers. A part of him missed the desert.

Most people wore rounded masks, although there were also many who did not bother to hide their hungry faces. For each robe, there were two slave girls and a slave male who walked half-naked. They served high quality Ardent and let the attendees grope them. In the centre of the room, there was a performance inside a circle of colour-changing flames. Two jet-skinned girls wielded ice sabres in a dance where bodies rubbed, and the blades dripped with each spin.

A man with a bird mask approached him by surprise, drew white powder from a sack and blew it in his face. Suddenly, the world was spinning around him, the smells became more intense, as if he had two noses instead of one. The aroma of cinnamon and incense was so sharp it burned. It seemed to him he could see the smell of the bodies, that he heard the drops of sweat falling on the floor. The noise was much louder than the music; and conversations, like glass exploding. He experienced all the bright colours like flares: the painted masks, the silver trays, the ornaments of the women, the bronze protections on the legs of a Beast in one of the reserved ones, the snake-shaped necklace of a slave girl who bended down to serve a table. And he sweated, and felt the drops, and his brain about to explode.

I see you, wildling, repeated Ubald's metallic voice. *You and I are made for each other.*

'What may I get you for a drink, prince?' Asked Meres.

He was sitting in a booth. *How did I get here?* He wondered. Meres looked at him, amused. She was waiting for an answer.

'I'm hungry,' was the only thing that came out from his mouth.

'We have sweet pork or hare with caramelized carrots. Should you wish something more exotic, we have snake stuffed with plums and dates with a side of watermelon dices from the Splashes. Delicious, if you like watermelon, of course,' Meres recited the menu like a poem.

I'd kill for a watermelon, he thought. His throat was dry, but he was also starving, and in the end, he chose the pork.

'And watermelon,' he added. He did not plan to leave without trying it.

Meres nodded and disappeared.

Siro ran his hand over his face. He felt his heartbeat in his temple, like a drum that wouldn't stop. The show of the dancers had changed since the last time he had looked at it. In a rehearsed movement, the girls had clashed their sabres and they had broken into pieces. With what they had left of the ice weapons, they had rubbed their bodies, from the shoulders to the buttocks to rise again to their dark and hardened nipples, and end up kissing with a more than convincing passion.

A masked man had climbed onto the platform. He exposed an imposing erection that wobbled at every step. He grabbed the two jet-skinned girls by the hair and forced them to kiss his neck, then the torso and lower and lower.

'Do you like it?' A girl had appeared at his side. He hadn't even seen her enter the booth.

'Who you are? Asked Siro. The girl had an intense look and wore a pair of yellow feathers that contrasted with the black of her hair.

'Who do you want me to be?' Was her answer. She put her hand under his clothes.

Matildet, he thought, but said nothing. He couldn't. His eyes were lost on the show. The man in the mask made the two girls moan, and their sounds echoed above the sea of white, black and red robes.

A second slave girl entered the booth and left a tray with smoking pork on the table. Siro's stomach roared and that brought him back to the real world.

'Leave him to me, Vela,' the slave said.

Siro noticed that the girl was removing her hand from under his clothes. He barely cared, he only had eyes for the smoking pork.

'The boy is not from the city,' Vela murmured. 'Do you think he comes from beyond the Cross?'

'Go away. He's mine,' the other one said.

The girl nodded and left the booth. Siro looked sideways at the way she shook her ass and then returned to the pig. Where could he start?

'Come with me,' the slave ordered, and before he could reach the pig's tooth, she had taken him by the hand, and pushed him to follow her.

He obeyed without questioning. He had trouble moving his mouth, everything was too bright, too intense. He said goodbye with his hand to the smoking tray and almost cried of hunger.

The girl's hand guided him to the other side of the room. Siro felt ridiculous running around. He hadn't realized until he had stood up, but all his excitement was focused in a lump under his robe. He crashed with people at every step he took. He thought he saw two Beasts biting a slave's fingers off, but he told himself that it was tomato juice or a piece of watermelon. That couldn't really be happening. A door opened and closed behind him. The music had stopped, the light was no longer so blue and the room was no longer full of people but dirty stacked dishes.

Before he could say anything, the girl pushed him against the wall, stroked his face and stuck her tongue in his mouth. Siro did not resist, he enjoyed that furious kiss as if it had to be the last one. The girl hugged him and whispered in his ear:

'Did you miss me, Free Child?' Said Eliria.

Chapter 28: Firespreader

'Ready the Firespreader! I want the Beasts to shit their pants!' Shouted Firla. 'I want them all dead!'

The few inhabitants of Merco that remained in the square rebuilt the wall with cars, furniture, sandbags and all they could find. People ran from place to place, put out fires, moved the wounded or joined the rows of soldiers behind the barriers. The leader of the village was at the top of a mound of ruins, commanding and pointing with traditional spear of the Bindagi tribe.

If she grabs it any harder, she's going to break it, Siro thought.

Despite the pain, the fatigue and the tears, the children had arrived at the square, just when the inhabitants of Merco were preparing to defend it from the Beasts final strike. Jahisel the Cunning, Firla's second husband, looked side to side, expecting an imminent attack.

No one paid attention to the two children, abandoned in what had been the marketplace a few hours earlier. The wounded and the dying moaned, lying on the floor, while Tersian's apprentices struggled to bandage their wounds. Beyond the barriers, the Council House burned with a terrifying glow.

'Siro, what do we do?' Murmured Eliria.

The girl had her eyes on a man who had lost a leg: he was on the ground, still, but couldn't tell if he was dead or alive. Siro didn't know what to do, but he knew he didn't want to stay there. Neither of them was really hurt, there was no point in going to see Tersian, the shaman. On the other hand, someone had to tell Firla that Taurus was in trouble, and they were the only ones who knew. Siro slipped through the people who had gathered in the square, without letting go of Eliria's hand. He was about to get to where Firla was, when Quela got in his way.

'Siro, Eliria, what are you still doing here?' Asked the old woman. 'Go to the river, quickly!'

'No, we can't! Taurus and Eliria's mother are in danger, the Beasts have them... ' Said the boy, but the woman ignored him.

'Liduvin is waiting for you at the river, Siro,' Quela said, when she saw that the boy was about to run away.

Liduvin! He recalled. For a moment he had completely forgotten that she would be suffering from his absence. But she can't be there, he told himself. *Why should she be in the river? It is not where we were supposed to meet.* He had to go home, just as he promised.

'What about Grinat?' Asked Siro, raising his voice above the commotion of the soldiers.

'He is there too. Everyone is by the river,' Quela insisted.

'That's bullshit!' Siro replied. He knew that the silent guardian was not in the river. Liduvin had told him. He had to go home no matter what. 'Grinat is not there and Liduvin isn't there either! You don't know where they are!'

Quela grabbed him by the arms and looked him in the eye. She trembled from tip to toe. One could tell she had a hard time standing on her feet.

'Please, Siro, go and cross the river,' she begged. 'Do it for Eliria. Please, leave.'

The boy was speechless. That woman had always treated him well. She had been kind to him when they were in the caravan, lost in the middle of the desert. She was one of the few people who spoke to him when nobody else did. Why did she lie to him?

Angry, he grabbed Eliria by the hand and left in the direction of the river without saying goodbye.

Liduvin is waiting for me, he said to himself.

Tears poked in his eyes. He wiped them as fast as he could

so that Eliria wouldn't see them, but the girl was absent. People ran around him and the two children moved with care not to bump into anyone. Drums echoed beyond the wall. For a moment, Siro feared that it was one of the signs of the Nightborn, as Liduvin had explained, but he immediately understood that it was the Beasts. They were getting closer. He sped up to reach the south gate, but just when they arrived, Firla's soldiers locked the barrier.

We're stuck in here, he realised.

'We're still in!' Eliria shouted to the men who moved the wooden barrier.

'Open the door, we have to get the wounded out!' Said one of Tersian's assistants. He dragged a stretcher with a man who had lost a foot.

'If we leave it open, they'll kill us all. Don't you see it, idiot?!' Answered a man who, despite having a wound in his forehead, wielded a spear against the Beasts.

Siro did not see who started it, but little by little the shouting and pushing gave way to blows and weapons. A man fell to the ground and, suddenly, the blade of a sword flew past the boy's face and pierced the ribs of another man. A stream of blood stained his face. The men had forgotten about the Beasts and killed each other to escape their own carnage. Spears and arrows crossed the sky. The dying crawled to escape. Before he could do anything, someone grabbed Siro under the armpit before the fight swallowed him and Eliria. When he turned around, he saw that it was Quela who had gotten in the middle of the danger to get them out of there.

'Stay with me. I need to sit down,' the woman told them when they were far enough.

She had a red spot on the dress, just below the chest. It was growing. The two children looked at each other for a moment and then sat next to the old woman.

'You have to wait, whatever happens, you have to wait,' the woman told them.

And what do you want us to wait for? Being killed? Siro wondered. They were trapped and it wouldn't be hard for the Beasts to enter the square if they made it that easy.

'They kill each other,' said Eliria.

Quela hugged her against her chest so she wouldn't look.

'They are scared, that's all it is. I've seen it so many times...'

the woman said. The wound was bleeding more and more.

'I will bring Tersian,' said Siro. He didn't want Quela to die.

'No, boy, stay...' the woman replied, but she no longer had the strength to grab him, and Siro broke free.

He passed through the rows of the wounded gathered in the middle of the square but did not see the shaman anywhere. The few men who defended the north ran away. The wooden barrier shook with the charges of the Beasts.

The smoke rose. It dragged the smell of wood and burned flesh like a bad omen. Thousands of blazing leaves filled the sky. The screaming of the Beasts and the noise of their drums were getting closer and closer.

We can't win, the boy told himself. *We are not enough, why do they stay here?*

'Siro, let's go...' Elirira said.

'But Quela...'

'Quela has told us to leave.'

Siro said nothing more, he just had to look at the girl's teary eyes to know that it was too late.

'They've closed the barriers,' he said after a few seconds of silence.

'We could jump them,' she said.

'No. The Beasts are on the other side. The only exit was south.'

'So what do we do?' Eliria insisted.

'I don't know...' he replied.

A few meters away, Firla and Jahisel organized the rows of soldiers.

'Shields to the front line! Spears behind! Prepare to replace those who fall!' Jahisel shouted hoarsely. 'I want you to do it as we rehearsed, you hear me?'

The remaining soldiers did not reach a hundred. They were not enough to fill a quarter of the marketplace. They were supposed to fight and push back the Beasts, but at that time they were nothing but dirty and terrified faces. They were too few and too inexperienced to stop them. All of them knew that those creatures would not just kill them. Behind their fragile lines was the field of wounded that Tersian and his assistants struggled to heal. If they failed, the Beasts would slaughter them all and move on towards river.

They won't leave, Siro understood. Firla did not plan to retreat. She would endure the attack until the very last man. Siro checked on Eliria. The girl trembled every time a soldier passed by. She had left her mother trapped with two Beasts and, on top of that, she had had to help him get to the square when he couldn't walk on his own; but seeing what had happened to Quela had been one too many. Her gaze was absent, her mind had flown away from that dark and smoke-filled place. Would she be thinking of her mother? Siro did not dare to ask.

It's all my fault, the boy thought. I *have brought her into a trap. I wanted to help her and now we will die here.*

'We have to hide,' he said with all the stillness he could muster.

That message woke Eliria, if only a little.

'There?' The girl proposed.

Good call, he thought. The two headed for the platform where the preys that the hunters brought to the village were auctioned. The platform had been partially cannibalised to reinforce the northern barrier. The few parts that were left served to store and distribute the soldiers' weapons. No one guarded the place, and Siro and Eliria had no problem sneaking under. They stood still, side by side. They watched the soldiers, the wounded, all the inhabitants of Merco. These people had been his neighbours for two years, men and women who worked for each other, who struggled to build the houses with their own hands, who yelled at their children to come home before nightfall. And now they were in a dark and destroyed square, surrounded by the dying and not knowing if their families would be safe and sound, and everyone knew what was about to happen.

Firla passed by the platform, with Tersian behind, reaching to her.

'This is crazy, Firla!' Said the shaman.

The village leader turned around, with her back to the platform. The adults could not see Siro and Eliria.

'If they can stand, I want them with a spear in their hands,' she told Tersian, and showed him how she did it herself. 'We have lots of weapons, we lack people.'

'They're injured!' He exclaimed.

'The Bindagi die fighting.'

'They are not Bindagi,' the shaman replied. He wasn't either, maybe that was why he didn't understand what the difference was between dying with spear in hand or begging for mercy. 'They are not even soldiers!'

'They'll fight. They know why they are here. They'd rather die than letting the Beasts reach the river.'

Tersian grabbed her arm to force her to stop. She stood still, which surprised even the shaman himself.

'Cut the crap, Firla. I know very well what you expect to happen, and it won't be like that,' he snapped.

'I won't stand you speaking to me like this. I am your wife and your leader…'

'…A naive one if you think Dugol will lead the attack.'

'How dare you…'

'Merco is dead. Don't make us die for his memory.'

Firla smiled for a few seconds, put the spear against the platform, and with a ferocity that Siro had only seen on the Exile Day, grabbed Tersian by the throat.

'You think yourself very smart, don't you?' She told him. The spark of madness shone in her eyes, as she choked the shaman.

'Firla... they'll kill us,' he tried to say. He moved his arms to escape, but it was in vain. 'Let's run away... you and me.'

'What?' She said, a thick vein had swollen in her forehead. 'Are you telling me to run away? Now? They... they killed Merco!'

If it had been Jahisel or Taurus, they would have easily got loose of Firla, but Tersian was not as strong as the other two husbands. He was not a Bindagi, but a delicate boy with talent to heal people.

'They killed him! Dugol did it, and no one batted an eye…' The woman spat each word as she squeezed her husband's throat more and more. 'None of these rats you try so hard to save did anything. They would abandon us all! They are the same scum as the ones on the other side of the barrier. They just expect someone to save them in exchange for nothing.'

Tersian's face turned red. Tears slipped down his cheeks. Siro, crouched under the platform, stared at the floor to see no more, but still heard Firla.

'No one will come to save us! We are every drop of blood, every spear you see here and nothing else! This is what we have, and I intend to avenge Merco even if I must sacrifice every single one of them, you hear me? Do you hear me?!'

She dropped Tersian on the floor. The boy sucked the air and coughed. He had Firla's fingers engraved on his neck like the Beasts' Brands.

'The river...' he managed to say. 'Let's go to the river.'

But Firla had already returned with her men and had forgotten her husband. Tersiano turned and saw the two children hidden under the platform. He began to cry, sitting on the floor, and not knowing what to do.

'Don't move,' he said after a while, in tears. 'Don't make noise... don't let yourself get caught.'

That said, he got up and returned with the wounded, to take care of them.

The noise of the drums and the fire was getting closer. The northern barrier rumbled with the onslaught of the Beasts. Firla's screams echoed across the square. Her voice encouraged the soldiers, who beat the spears against the shields as if they had any chance.

'People of Merco!' The woman shouted. Jahisel handed her a burning torch, which she held in the air, as a sort of banner. 'Do you hear them? Do you hear the Beasts of Dugol? They think they've won... but they have no idea of what awaits them!'

'Remember the training!' Repeated Jahisel, who patrolled the line of soldiers with a severe look.

'Listen to me well, town of Merco!' Firla said to the soldiers. 'Listen to me! Do not let even one of these Beasts step on this square! Not one! This square is ours! We built it! It's ours!'

'It's ours!' Jahisel repeated, and the rest of warriors joined the shout.

The northern barrier was shaking, the first hooks had appeared on its top, the Beasts would be crossing over any time soon, but Firla looked calm, smiling ecstatic at the prospect of what she was going to do.

'It's ours!' Shouted Firla once more.

Spears and shields echoed, shouts of 'Bindagi!' and 'Firla!' interspersed with the clamour of the soldiers.

'Behold, children of Merco, the power of the Bindagi fire!' Said Firla. 'Firespreader!'

Firla lowered the torch and a trace of the lethal liquid ignited. A line of fire crossed the square towards the barrier, passed between the Beasts that had just assaulted the place and slipped through a tiny hole in the base of the wall.

'Shields!' Jahisel ordered.

All of them were covered, except for Firla. She looked past the barrier, clenching her teeth. A few seconds passed. The silence between the soldiers was palpable. None of them breathed.

A light bright like the sun itself appeared before Siro's eyes. The barrier, the cars, the houses, everything blew up into the air. A shower of blood and splinters fell on the soldiers after a deafening roar. A burned hand fell from who knows where right next to where the two children were, and a burning car wheel rolled by, fleeing from that place as well. Then, a cloud of fire and ashes engulfed the square. The sky was no longer black or red, it was all brown and full of a thick, acid stench that burned when breathing.

Chapter 29: In another life

Nazeh looked at him with the same scared eyes as always. He sucked his finger, which seemed childish even for him and, cherry on top, he had a shabby stuffed animal toy under his arm.

Something is wrong here, thought Siro. *Why is he a kid... and me an adult?*

He was inside a bath, with his knees jerking out of the water and his arms hanging. He had no idea where he was. He had a terrible headache, an invisible hand squeezed his brain.

It can't be Nazeh, but he looks just like him, he told himself. The boy stared at him from the doorway while he stuck another finger in his mouth.

'Are you hungry?' He asked.

For the Creator. He even sounds like Nazeh.

The boy disappeared through the door and ran back with a bowl with a hare leg and a few chopped carrots. It wasn't much, but Siro was starving. When the boy approached him, the hunter snatched the bowl from his hands.

'Do you need cutlery? Mom says older children use cutlery,' the boy asked as Siro grabbed everything he could with his bare hands and put it in his mouth. Some carrot pieces fell into the bath.

Siro finished eating it all and then looked around the room. The grey rock walls made him think he was inside a cave, and the wet carpet and the soap bars on the furniture, that it was an inhabited one. He hadn't seen that place before, and the worst part was that he didn't remember how he got there.

The boy still looked at him with wide eyes. The face, the hair, even the way of moving and speaking, everything in him told him it was Nazeh; but it was not possible.

What if he's not here? He wondered. *What if he's a vision, just like Ubald? What if it's just inside my head to torture me?*

'What are you doing here?' He asked. The boy said nothing. 'You should be...' *dead,* he thought.

The boy was sucking his finger in silence. A thread of drool fell from his lips.

'I told you not to go to the right, Nazeh,' said Siro. 'Why did you ignore me? Everything would have been different. You could have escaped with me...'

'My name is Ranzeh,' said the boy, offended. 'Nazeh is my dad's name, not mine. You have made a mistake... or you tell lies, but surely you have made a mistake, because you don't look like a liar, no. You don't look like it. I know how a liar looks like.'

No way, Siro felt a surge of joy upon hearing that. *Is he really his son? Is Nazeh here?*

'Where is your father? And your mother? Who is she? What's her name?'

'I call her mom because she is my mom,' Ranzeh said. 'But the elders call her Mrs. Muhara or Eliria. You are older, so you can call her that, but not mom, no, only I can call her mom.'

The image of Eliria's fiery kiss lit up in his head. His mind suddenly cleared. He remembered the Palace of Dreams as just that, a misty dream where half-naked women and Beasts disguised in colourful robes swirling around him. He had in mind the table where he had sat, the exquisite delicacies that had enticed his nose —the tray with the smoking pork—, the girls who danced with ice sabers on the stage, the receptionist's caring smile and the the way she called him prince... and Eliria's lips.

'Do you know my dad?' Asked Ranzeh. The boy dried his fingers full of drool with the stuffed toy.

Siro was speechless. What was he supposed to tell him about Nazeh? That he had not seen in ages, perhaps? That for years he thought the Beasts had killed him? He couldn't tell that. The poor kid looked four or five, maybe younger judging on his behaviour.

'Yes... He was my friend,' he said. It was the easiest option, but it seemed empty and he added: 'He was my best friend.'

'Oh,' the boy exclaimed. 'I did not know. Well, my best friend is Segis, but don't tell Daina, because she is her little sister and she gets angry, because she thinks I'm her best friend, but it's not true because Segis is my best friend.'

'I won't,' said Siro, after the boy's speech.

A red-haired woman walked into the door. Siro didn't recognize her at first, he had changed a lot since he had last seen her. Eliria was no longer a girl. Her hair fell below the shoulders, much longer than he remembered. Her face had also changed, her cheekbones had become more prominent and with a much more mature expression, and her body... Yes, her body was also that of a woman. He could guess her seductive curves under the beige dress.

She approached, and Siro saw the spark of her roguish eyes, just like when they played together along the jungle of Merco, but that time there was something else: while she surrounded her son with her arms, she cast unpolite glances at the hunter's submerged body .

'Are you friends already?' Eliria asked Ranzeh. Her voice had changed. She sounded like her mother, but her tone was warm, unlike Debra's.

'I don't know his name because he hasn't told me his name,' said the boy, enjoying his mother's cuddles.

'His name is Siro,' Eliria said, and winked at him. 'He's a friend of mom's... and dad's.'

'I know that because he had already told me, but I didn't know he was your friend, too,' said the boy. 'And why had I never seen him? Didn't you want to invite him because he eats without cutlery? I told him to use them, but he didn't want to use them.'

Eliria laughed and kissed her son on the cheek.

'Ranzeh, listen. Irenda needs you to help her raise the buckets of water to bathe, would you you be so kind to help her?' She asked.

The boy snorted and crossed his arms.

'Can't she do it alone? I do it alone,' he complained.

'When you have a child in the belly, everything is more difficult. Besides, I do help you raise the cubes. Do it for me,' she insisted.

The boy accepted reluctantly.

'Goodbye, Siro!' he said before leaving in rush.

The hunter responded with a vague gesture and realized that he had not said goodbye to anyone for a long time.

'Goodbye,' he replied.

I have been able to talk to Nazeh's son thanks to Matildet, he realised. The Daughter of the Light had struggled to make him talk again, day after day, and now he could see it had been worth it.

Will she be alright? He wondered. He trusted neither Adon nor his Beasts.

When the boy had left, Eliria knelt next to the bath and rested her elbows on its side. Siro had never felt so aware of his own nakedness. He noticed how he was getting excited.

'He likes you,' she said, as she showed him a smile he had not seen for years. This time, she had all the teeth. 'He doesn't have too many friends, and he's always surrounded by the girls of the Palace of Dreams. It is good for him to talk to men from time to time.'

'He looks just like Nazeh,' said Siro.

'Like water drops,' Eliria admitted and laughed out loud.

The girl's hand slipped into the water and stirred it, pretending it was normal.

'Where is he? Is he here?'

'No, Nazeh… He's not with us anymore,' she replied, and withdrew her hand from the water. 'He died four years ago.'

Siro fell silent. For a moment he had hoped that he would see his best friend again, but the days of playing in the jungle were over.

'What happened?'

'The beasts. It's always them, Free Child. They finished what they had started years ago… That night, when they attacked Merco, I… Do you remember?'

Siro nodded.

'I don't know if you ever think about it. I still have nightmares… There are so many things I can't understand,' she said.

'It's ok,' Siro knew exactly what she meant, but wondered if she would be mad at him too. Although nothing in her behaviour indicated so, she probably blamed him for what had happened to her mother.

'Eliria! How much longer will you be in the bathroom? I need to bathe!' Shouted a voice on the other side of the door

'It's Irenda,' Eliria rolled her eyes. 'The bigger the belly, the worse the mood. Here, take the towel.'

Siro left the bath and covered himself. His body was seized, as if he had slept for hours in that tiny bathtub. Eliria ran the hand through his hair and snorted when she saw Siro's sharp beard. She stroked the scar on his jaw, which was the only place where hair didn't grow, and felt he got goosebumps. She had that look again, as when they were kids and met under the palm trees. Eliria did not see the lonely man he had become but the rogue boy who had stolen her first kiss, the one who called her rabid mongoose and got away with it.

'It was hard for me to recognize you at the Palace. I couldn't believe it was you. I still can't believe my eyes. You know, Nazeh always hoped that the three of us would meet again one day.'

'He was very much in love with you,' Siro replied. It was something he had buried inside him for years.

'And I came to love him with time. He was always good to me, much more than I deserved. For Keerine and the Great Light! I treated him so bad…' Eliria's face reddened.

'Classic rabid mongoose,' said Siro.

Eliria slapped him on the chest and then gave him a rogue smile, like the girl she used to be.

'He made me happy, Siro, much happier than I ever thought I would be.'

She took him to the common room, where two girls laughed sitting by the wooden table that took most of the space. They gave him a sidelong glance and then continued chatting. Siro wore a grey robe that Eliria had given him. 'It was from Nazeh,' she had said. His friend must have grown a lot in all those years he had not seen him. He had to roll up his sleeves to get his hands out.

'Let me introduce you to Vela and Renilda. They are my colleagues in the Palace of Dreams,' Eliria told him. 'He is Siro.'

'Call me Reni, please. Renilda makes me feel old,' said one of the girls, wearing a gleaming dress and painted eyes.

'Your face rings a bell, have we met before?' Said Vela.

Siro recognized the girl's voice. She was the one that had entered the booth with him. 'Who do you want me to be?' She had asked jokingly as she put her hand under his clothes. She looked very young.

'No,' Siro lied, hoping she would let it go.

'Do you know who else is pregnant?' Said Vela. She was jumping, eager to tell what she knew.

'The fatty's wife will walk her belly again…' Reni said.

'Really?' Asked Eliria. 'How do you…'

'Because this morning, after you left, she threw up in the dining room,' Reni explained with a raised eyebrow.

'She couldn't reach the latrine,' Vela added.

'It was gross,' Reni said.

'Did you clean it?' Eliria was inspecting the ground looking for the disaster.

'Who, me?' Said Reni. 'Please…'

'Then who…?'

'Meres,' Vela and Reni said in unison.

Siro didn't know what they were talking about. That situation was so strange to him.

'Meres, poor girl,' Eliria shook her head. Then she turned to Siro. 'You'll see. She also works in the Palace. I'm sure you've met her already. She works at the reception. She's so good…'

'She calls them princes,' Reni added. 'That's all men want to hear.'

'They are not men,' said Siro. 'They are Beasts.'

'It's harder for me to distinguish them by the day,' Reni raised his eyebrow and sighed.

She gave him a condescending look. She had a certain appeal, but it showed that she was older than Eliria and, of course, than Vela. There was a moment of silence until Vela clapped.

'This Rael… How will he manage to provide for three kids?' She said.

The name didn't go unnoticed by Siro. He glanced at Eliria and she nodded.

'Yes, Rael, from Merco, the… the leader of the Mongoose,' she confirmed, and remembering the nickname made her rolled her eyes.

'Does he live here?' Asked Siro. He barely remembered that kid, only that he was fat and that he was messing with Eliria.

'With his wife and two children who can't be quiet for their lives,' Reni replied. 'How did you two know each other?' She added pointing at them.

'Well…' Eliria began, not knowing where to start.

They ended up sitting at the table by the candlelight while the day was coming to an end. Eliria gave them the details of how they met. Vela listened to her holding her cheeks with her hands and Reni laughed and cast a sidelong glance at Siro every time she told something about him.

'I promise you, the first thing I thought when I saw he was that… He was a total idiot,' said Eliria.

'You weren't too nice either,' replied Siro. He was having a good time.

'And what about the way you spoke to me? You talked to me like if I were rubbish.'

'Didn't you do the same?' He retorted, unable to look away from her immense green eyes.

A door opened, and a boy and a girl ran in. They greeted Vela and Reni, but when they saw Siro they turned shy. Behind them, a short woman with her hair pulled back entered the room. She carried a bag full of turnips on. She scolded the children, ignoring Siro's presence.

Behind her, Rael got in. He was much fatter but had the same face. He wore a humble robe, quite worn out. He looked tired. He stared at Eliria's Palace colleagues for a bit too long, oblivious to the ongoing dispute, and then set eyes on Siro.

'For all the Nightborn, where have you been hiding all these years?' He exclaimed. He had recognized him right away. 'To my arms!' Siro let himself be hugged. That enthusiasm was odd. 'Have you seen, Eliria? It's the Free Child!'

'I know, Rael,' she said. 'I brought him.'

The former leader of the Mongoose asked Siro questions relentlessly. He sat at the table, while Vela and Rael's wife served a broth of capybaras and malangas to all the guests. Siro had just eaten but wouldn't refuse any food. One never knew when it could be the last time.

Ranzeh then appeared, exhausted according to him, after helping Irenda bring the water buckets upstairs. He sat between Siro and Eliria. With everyone at the table, Rael introduced his wife, Mirna, and their children, Segis and Daina, who were pushing each other to sit next to their mother.

Siro looked at the two girls who worked at the Palace, Rael, his family, Ranzeh and Eliria.

This could have been my life, he thought. *If I had only turned right that night...*

They talked about how hard it was to raise the children and the nonsense that the girls had to endure in the Palace. They had to soften the language a lot so that the children wouldn't understand it, but it was clear that Rael enjoyed those anecdotes, unlike his wife. Siro did not realise how time went by until Mirna lit a second candle and put it on the table. No light entered through the window carved into the rock. He supposed they were somewhere in The Mouth.

'What about you, Siro? Where have you been all this time? Tell us something, man!' Rael was very lively.

'I've been in the desert…' he said, he didn't know what to tell him.

'In the desert? Are you telling me that you have spent the last fourteen years in the desert?' Exclaimed Rael.

Fourteen years? Siro was surprised. *Has it been that long?*

'What have you done during this time? You don't seem to have married,' he said and winked. 'Did you join the Bindagi? Are you a desert dealer?'

'No, I…'

What do you want me to tell you? Siro thought.

'I survive… hunt…'

'Impressive,' Rael said. 'Living adventures, huh? From here to there. Ah, you make me so jealous! Sure you have met many girls who…' His wife gave him a disapproving look and he changed subject. 'Well, never mind. Tell me something else, have you ever returned to Merco?'

'No,' said Siro. He wasn't even sure if he could find its old location.

'Good, good. Do you know what happened this morning?'

'What?' Reni asked, though reluctantly, maybe she suspected that Rael would tell them something silly.

'It was unbelievable. The miners and farmers have passed the palisade, crossed the Undershell right to Adon's palace. They were hundreds, and it gets better…' Rael paused to make sure everyone listened. 'A Daughter of the Light was leading them.'

The two girls from the Palace didn't buy it and even his wife told him it was a lie. Eliria, however, enquired Siro with her eyes.

'I swear it's true. Ask anyone,' Rael insisted. 'You don't know the mess they've made. What a shitshow! As soon as the Daughter of the Light got into the palace, the Beasts have charged against the followers. The guildsmen have spent the afternoon complaining and making their claims. They don't know where they're going to get fresh slaves from…'

'Fuck the owners… Screw them and all the Beasts!' Said Reni.

'Adon will provide for them,' Vela said.

Siro was surprised by that comment.

'Is he a true Son of the Light?' he asked.

There was silence in the room. People's faces were full of shadows casted by the candle flame. The bowls were empty on the table, and Siro wondered if he had done well by bringing the subject up after such a pleasant dinner. Mirna got up and picked up the table. Ranzeh and the other children ran away as soon as the bowls were removed, free from the shackles of such an unfair conviction.

Eliria put her hand on Siro's shoulder and told him to follow him, but before he could move, Rael asked him a question:

'I don't know... Do *you* think he is a Son of Light?'

He thought the answer for a few moments. It was very rare that a Son of the Light could also be lord of the Beasts, but the way in which Matildet had entered the palace, without hesitation, had baffled him.

That was what she wanted from the beginning... He told himself. *She just wanted me to bring her here. I was just a tool.*

'I don't know,' he said in the end.

'Alright...' Rael exclaimed. 'I thought you were an expert on the matter. Weren't all your stepmother's stories about them?'

'Rael, leave him alone,' said Eliria. 'Siro, can you help me find Ranzeh? It is time for him to go to sleep.'

While Siro looked at the drawings on the wall that Ranzeh must have painted when he was younger, Eliria came in and locked the door.

'Why did Rael say that?' Asked Siro softly.

'Ignore him. He has always been an idiot, although he can't complain. He's done quite well, all things considered. Ranzeh, where are you?'

Eliria's room was just the right size to accommodate a double bed and a smaller one for Ranzeh. The grey walls were decorated with a vase of red petal flowers and children's drawings on the bottom. A curtain full of holes covered the only opening to the outside. There was a laugh from the closet in the back of the room. Eliria passed by the beds with difficulty, stood next to the closet and knocked on the door.

'Is there someone?' She asked. She smiled back at Siro.

'No...' Answered Ranzeh's voice from inside.

'Too bad. I was looking for my child, but if he is not there, I suppose he'll have to do without a good night's kiss.'

The boy shot out of the closet and threw himself into her mother's arms.

'Segis has told me that he has seen the Daughter of the Light when he was with his dad and mom in the market,' said the boy, excited by the novelty. 'He told me she is very pretty.'

'Oh, really?' Eliria asked. 'Prettier than I?'

'No, not prettier than you, mom,' the boy denied. 'It is impossible that the Daughter of the Light is prettier than you because you are very beautiful.'

Seeing them hugging reminded Siro of Liduvin and himself. She had also been affectionate to him and she was not even her mother. If Eliria was the same, Ranzeh should count himself a lucky child.

'I don't want to go to sleep!' Ranzeh shouted when she left him on his bed.

'You have to sleep. Come on, I'm too tired to repeat the same show every night,' Eliria said.

'I want to play with Segis! He says that his dad bought him a turtle shell to play marbles because he's well-behaved, and I am well-behaved too, but I don't have any shell because...'

Eliria and Ranzeh got into an endless discussion, which the mother had to stop by saying nothing more. The boy did not want to get under the sheets. Siro understood. He also didn't like Liduvin making him go to sleep soon.

'If you get into bed, I'll tell you a story,' Siro offered.

The hunter had said it without thinking, but when he saw Eliria's pleading face and the child's interest, he could not refuse. Ranzeh remained silent and wide-eyed. It was amazing how much he looked after his father.

'Do you know the origin of the Children of the Light?' Asked Siro.

The boy shook his head.

'I only know that Adon is a Son of the Light. I think he's the last one, because there is no more.'

'Ranzeh, let Siro tell his story...'

'I don't know Adon,' said Siro, although that was only half true. 'But I can tell you where they come from. Do you know Philippe Keerine, the Creator?'

The boy said no and got under the bedsheets. Siro told that the Creator had seen a black stone floating in the darkness and that he had felt so sorry for it, he had dropped a tear just above. To better illustrate it, he picked up a stone from the ground, wet his index finger with the water in the vase and let a drop fall on it. The stone darkened where it had been wetted, but no plant was born.

How did Liduvin make a plant grow? He wondered.

'Why was he sad for a stone? I don't understand, I don't feel sorry for the stones,' said the boy.

Siro thought about it for a few seconds. The truth was that part was not clear to him either, but then he remembered that Liduvin always told him that particular stone was what he had always looked for and that it reminded him of the two people he loved most... Now that he thought about it, her stories were always the most enigmatic.

'When the tear fell, it formed the city of Teradam, the home of the Children of the Light. They were...' Siro continued. 'They were good and... they knew how to do... well... many things, but not everything, because they also need help.'

'Help for what?' Ranzeh was interested. Eliria listened just as much.

'Well... They don't know how to hunt or where to find food... Even in the middle of the jungle. They are clueless! Besides, they don't fight too well, they get scared when they see blood, but... But deep down they are good and... They defend us,' said Siro.

The day he had fought with Ubald in the oasis, the yellow queen's poison had left him so weak that Guido and Junal would have killed him without much effort if Matildet had not scared them away.

She could have left with them, Siro remembered. *She would have arrived at Undershell much earlier. Why didn't she do it? Or did she not expect to meet Adon?*

'They protect people, so they are the Creator's favourites,' he continued. 'He handed them Teradam. He said: *To you, who were born of destruction and hatred, I give you this world. Forgive us and live.* I don't know what these words mean, but for the Children of the Light must be important.'

Ranzeh wanted Siro to tell him more and he needed the distraction. Eliria approved and the hunter kept telling his stories. When she looked at Siro and Ranzeh, a smile was drawn on her lips. The hunter told him about Teradam, about the wonders that were inside the city of miracles: no one was hungry in there, nor thirsty, nor hot; there were rivers and waterfalls, it was an idyllic place where neither war nor misery was known. He talked about the Nightborn, those who had fallen from the sky to end the Children of the Light. He told him about Lexandre, the Son of the Light who had locked the doors of Teradam to the inhabitants of the dark, and who had condemned mankind to live alone in the desert where they were.

'Was Lexandre bad?' Asked Ranzeh.

'I don't know,' said Siro. 'Liduvin... she said Lexandre was forced to take hard decision, but she also believed that the doors of Teradam would reopen one day.'

'I want to go to Teradam!' Said the boy.

'So do I...'

Ranzeh asked him to tell another story, but Eliria said it was too late.

'Tomorrow,' Eliria said, but bit her tongue right after. She had assumed that Siro would be there the following night.

'It's all right,' the hunter agreed. Explaining stories was not so difficult now that he was more fluent with words. A few weeks earlier he would have been unable to do so.

It's all thanks to Matildet, he thought. The Daughter of the Light had made him practice every day, correcting him every time he said something wrong. She had been a pain for a long time, but in the end it had been worth it. Being able to tell the tales of Liduvin to a kid was perhaps the best thing that had ever happened to him. He noticed that his eyes were wet, and he covered them with his hand so the boy did not see him. Eliria kissed Ranzeh good night, and then turned off the lights. He took Siro to the next bed and stretched a cloth screen to separate one bed from the other. It had a decoration reminiscent of the Palace of Dreams. The two got together under the bedsheets. They looked into each other's eyes. Eliria stroked his cheeks and kissed his lips. One kiss and then another, and another and another.

'Wait for him to fall asleep,' Eliria whispered in his ear. 'It won't take long.'

Undershell's light shone through the window. Siro would have liked to look outside and see what the city of his childhood had become, but he still noticed that the tears wanted to come out.

'What happened to Nazeh?' Murmured Siro.

'He...' Eliria didn't know where to start. Her fingers were between the hunter's hair. 'One night he went out. It was shortly after moving in here. I remember because at first I was worried about what other people would tell me if Ranzeh cried every night,' she said with a nostalgic smile on her lips. 'He was just one year old then'.

She turned her head to see if the boy was sleeping and they kissed again. That time with more with more intensity, more desire.

'That night Nazeh didn't come back,' she said, when her lips parted. 'The Beasts... Hung his body from one of the mills of the city. Since then that I always have the curtain closed, if not, I stay all night looking at the roof where they found him, wondering who did it.'

Siro swallowed. The mind picture of his friend hanging made him sick.

'Please, don't explain anything I say tonight to Ranzeh. He only knows that his father is dead, nothing more. He's too young to know.'

'This city has not changed,' Siro recalled. 'There have always been dead. Parents talked about it, in the morning, when they found bodies around the neighbourhood. You can't protect your child from that.'

'We're leaving,' she replied. 'I don't want him to live through the same things I did. I don't want him to grow up thinking he has to avenge his father.'

'It's not revenge,' Siro protested. 'It is justice. Beasts kill us. They killed Nazeh... He was incapable of harming anyone, he was...'

'I... I don't know, there are many things you don't know about Nazeh. It's been a long time.'

Siro fell silent. There was a trace of guilt in Eliria's muted eyes. Her red hair cascaded on the pillow, her dress highlighted her breasts under the cloth. He was dying to travel her body with his hands.

'Nazeh had a very difficult life,' she continued. Her hands caressed his neck. They went up and down over his robe. 'You know, it's been many years, but I still remember how much he cried that night when the Beasts captured us. Every day of travel from Merco to Undershell I heard him sob. I also cried... The Creator shall hear us, we all did! We were just children. We hid our fear so that the Beasts wouldn't harm us, but not Nazeh. He said nothing about his mother or brothers. He just said he didn't want the rings. He was holding his arms. He squeezed them so hard that he hurt himself.'

He already knew what she was talking about. The first time they had seen each other while they were in the caravan with exiles from Undershell, Nazeh was a sad boy wearing iron rings along his arms. Those things drained his will to live. It was not until Merco's blacksmith removed them, that he started going out and playing in the jungle with him.

'When we got to Undershell, they took us to see an Elector,' Eliria continued. 'I hugged him, I did it so he wouldn't shake. He told me that... he wanted me to promise him that they wouldn't put him the rings again... I...'

'You...? He shouldn't have asked you. He already knew that would happen.'

'We did... Electors keep a record with our names, a lock of hair and some even make a charcoal portrait of the person. And, above all, he and I already had the Brand. Our fate was sealed from the beginning.'

Eliria made a pause to look at her son again. Across the room, Ranzeh slept peacefully. He was breathing slowly, face up, and with one hand next to his face, looking worried even in dreams.

'He screamed as they took him away, called his father... I had never heard him say anything about his father. Not before that day, nor after. I was so scared...' Eliria grabbed her arms. Her hair had bristled and shone, whitish, under the starlight that slipped through the holes in the curtain.

'And then?' Siro insisted, eager to know what had happened to his friend.

'Seven years went by before we met again... I was at the market, shopping and, suddenly, I heard a voice calling me. I didn't recognize him at first, but he did. He was in the middle of a row of slaves and ran away to meet me. He had grown a lot. He wore huge rings on his arms and looked so thin the first thing I thought was that he didn't eat. He said: Eliria, it's me! I'm Nazeh, do you remember me? I swear it took me a few seconds to react, but in the end, I did and... Then, a rope or a whip, I no longer remember, came out of nowhere and he fell to the ground. The Beasts took him.'

Eliria's green eyes no longer looked at Siro, they wandered in the depths of her own past.

'He... Nazeh got up, although the Beasts pulled him. I was so scared! But he didn't give up. I don't know how he did it. I should have realized at that moment, and not after so long, that he was crazy about me. He was risking it all. They could have killed him, and he just wanted to know one thing.'

'What?' Said Siro.

'To know when I would return to the market. He just wanted to know when I 'd be back.' Eliria covered her mouth to suppress the attack of laughter that mixed with tears. Even the hunter was smiling. And worst of all, I couldn't answer him, I don't know what was wrong with me, but I was paralyzed. I didn't even understand what he said at the beginning! It was... By the Creator, it was nuts. Just before the Beasts took him, I said: every two weeks!'

'And he showed up.'

'Yes, but not after two weeks, but two months. During that time, every day I wondered if Nazeh would have heard me at all with all the noise. I felt so stupid. Why did I not insist?'

Siro was surprised by his friend's behaviour. When she was little, Eliria would not have remained still while someone hurt one of her best friends. Under her skin, something had changed. It wasn't just the Beasts and their abuses; but the lowered heads and the empty gazes of the others, who resigned themselves to live and die with the Brand. All that was enough to drain any desire to open one's mouth... and his friends had spent fourteen years in Undershell! What atrocities would they have lived through in all that time?

'And after two months,' Eliria said, 'there he was. You should have seen his smile. That night his mouth must have hurt of so much smiling. We chat for a while. We knew there was not much time, but it was like he had the questions prepared. Years later, he confessed to me that he had looked so much forward to that meeting, that he had rehearsed alone the conversation we would have.'

'That's so like Nazeh,' said Siro.

When they were little, Nazeh talked about Eliria all the time. Whenever they did something, he planned everything for her to come along... but in the end she chose Siro. He felt suddenly guilty. He had not been a good friend, he had failed him and Eliria, during the Night of Fire...

'He wanted to know where I lived, where I worked, when and where we could meet to talk, if I was okay... He asked me everything!'

'What did you tell him?'

'That day? Almost nothing… He told me that he worked for the Arradens guild, the rock cutters, and carried bags up and down the mine day in and day out. And well, he used his arms, you know, he got where others couldn't… We met every two weeks, when he got a permit. We spent the whole day together. Those moments were so good that for a moment I forgot about the Palace of Dreams, Undershell… We were back in Merco, it was like playing in the jungle.'

Siro stroked her hair and kissed her lips. The two closed their eyes, their faces caressing each other.

'We talked about you,' Eliria whispered. 'We always did.'

Chapter 30: Make him come back

His ears were hissing, his eyes stung like if they had been filled with salt. The air was thick with the sour smell of the Firespreader. The explosion had been blinding. Every time he blinked, a bright light followed with a shower of blood and splinters. Outside the hideout, soldiers moved like puppets unable to stand.

Siro had to ask Eliria three times if she was okay before he understood her.

'My eyes hurt... they hurt a lot,' he thought the girl was saying. 'What happened?'

'The Firespreader... Firla's plan has worked,' Siro said.

Merco's leader had been very sly, waiting for the Beasts to get close just to blow them up, but what would happen now that the barrier had been reduced to ashes? The north of the marketplace was a smoking crater. A wail rose from the shadows, splinters of wood fell from the sky, and mutilated bodies crawled on the ground, but most were nothing more than charred fragments of men and Beasts. Firla stood before the smoke and flames. Her red dress was full of the ravages of the Firespreader. Jahisel stood by her side, shouting orders left and right to make sure the soldiers kept the formation. Siro had the impression Jahisel had a splinter or a spear stuck in his shoulder... the smoke and the fires made it difficult to tell for sure. He rubbed his eyes with muddy hands, hoping that the nasty sting would go away at once.

We must flee, thought the boy. The northern barrier had volatilized, and the Beasts were nowhere to be found. If they took that chance, they could escape, go around the square and head to the river... or to Liduvin. *Is she waiting for me?* He wondered.

'Eliria, follow me,' he said. They wouldn't have any other chance like that. If the Beasts attacked them again, they would all end up dead.

'I can't...' the girl told him. She was clinging to one of the supports on the platform, pretending that no one could take her away if she held on tight enough.

'We must go to the river! We can't stay...'

'What about my mother?'

What am I supposed to tell her? Siro wondered. Even if the situation had been different, he didn't feel like going back to see what the Beasts had done with Debra.

'...Why don't you go to your house, grab a good knife and chop off Liduvin's head? It's all that whore's fault,' she had said, her tone so empty it gave him the chills.

She deserves whatever happens to her, he told himself, seized by a sudden rage, but he couldn't say that to Eliria, or she wouldn't follow him.

'Nazeh is waiting for us on the other side of the river,' he explained. 'When the Beasts are gone, we will go fetch your mother.'

'No...'

'The Beasts won't stay here forever. We will be back when they are gone.'

'What if they take my mother?'

'Eliria... We will go to Undershell if necessary. But now we must go. Please.'

The children ran hand in hand to not lose each other while traversing the midst of the crater left by the Firespreader. They jumped over the ruins and kept watch not to slip. Firla's soldiers had not seen them, and if they had, Siro doubted they'd go after them.

Where are the Beasts? Siro wondered as he gazed into the lifeless blackness of the crater. For a moment, he dared to imagine that they had learnt the lesson and that they would not return... until he saw the flames. They moved in the dark. Siro was slow to realize that they were Rapids set on fire. The bluish fur of these animals contrasted with the orange of the flames. The fire drew desperate screams from them, charging in all directions, with their narrow legs. They came in droves from the other side of the crater and ran in the direction of the marketplace.

'Back, let's go back!' Siro yelled, and just then a Rapid leapt through the two children.

Siro felt the heat of the flames before he hit the ground. He kicked one of the Rapids aside and stood up.

'Let's go, follow me!' He helped Eliria up and out of the

slippery crater.

Firla's soldiers also had trouble with the Rapids. The animals sneaked between their legs, and the gaps between one shield and the next and caused the soldiers to fall or their clothing to catch fire. Firla stood on first line, beheading all those animals which were stupid enough to run passed her. The blade of her sword was drenched in blood.

'The Beasts!' He heard some soldiers shout when they saw the two kids, 'They're coming!'

A spear flew out of the ranks of soldiers and struck at Siro's feet; a couple more went over his head.

'We are children' Eliria yelled. 'Stop! Don't shoot!'

They won't hear us, Siro thought. He grabbed Eliria and pulled her back into the crater once more, to realize that the Beasts had already arrived. They went up preceded by the Rapids that they themselves had set on fire. Siro and Eliria threw themselves to the ground. The Beasts passed by, focused on ending Merco's last stand. Eliria hugged Siro, but he couldn't hug her back. His eyes were set on the Beast coming up the crater towards them. It carried a rusty sickle in its hand and a stubble of human ears dangling from the belt. It moved unevenly, as if it didn't know exactly what was going on.

The Beast had a cloud of white powder under its nose, chin, and among the thick hairs on its naked chest. Its laugh was as sinister as the eye tic that accompanied it.

'You're not dead...' the Beast hummed. Its eyes alternated uneasy between Siro and Eliria. 'You look like it, but you aren't...'

A man jumped over the children. In his hands, a double-edged spear spun and whizzed. Before the Beast could react, its left leg and sickle-wielding hand fell off, with a trail of blood.

Siro recognized Grinat. Liduvin's silent guardian had just saved his life for the second time.

The Beast was dying on the ground crying. Two more came closer. Grinat separated the spear into two halves and cut both their throats in a matter of seconds, without Siro being able to understand how he managed to pull that move. Three more Beasts joined the fight and suffered the same fate. One after another, they all fell with screams, curses and pleas escaping their mouths. Grinat did not show any kind of emotion on his face. He didn't get angry, he just did what he did best. Every time his spear moved; blood was shed.

He's unbeatable, thought the boy. He had seen Grinat train with other men from the village. He taught them how to fight with the double-edged spear, what posture to adopt, what movements were correct. From time to time, he fought with them, sometimes against two opponents at once and, rarely, against three; but not even in his best moments, did he fight at the speed at which he did that night. Siro had never felt so much admiration for anyone as for Grinat. He had always thought that when he grew up, he would be a silent guardian like him and protect Liduvin. He wanted to be just like him… until he grabbed him by the throat and lifted him up.

What's going on? He wondered. His feet hung inches off the ground. Grinat drove his spear into the ground and pulled a piece of purple cloth from between the folds of his cloak. He shook it in front of the boy's face until he understood what he wanted.

'Zuria? Are you looking for Zuria?'

Grinat nodded. The Beasts rose from the crater smoke, but the silent guardian ignored them.

'The river… She's by the river with the twins,' Siro said, although he had no way of knowing, it was just what seemed most likely. It had been hours since he had seen Zuria, since he had crossed the marketplace looking for Eliria.

Grinat's eyes widened. If it hadn't been for his oath, he sure would have yelled at him. He put the child on the ground and immediately carried him on his shoulder.

'Siro, Siro!' Eliria followed them as Grinat headed toward Merco's frontline.

The soldier immediately recognized the imposing figure of the silent guardian. They raised their shields and let them pass. On Grinat's shoulder, Siro swayed with each step. He could see the gleaming tips of the spears shining against the fire, and the backs of the soldiers who held them. An ash cloud hid the Beasts, it was impossible to know if they were approaching or not. Every now and then, a flare would appear behind the lines of the soldiers, and Siro knew it was another Rapid that had sneaked between the shields. Eliria had disappeared. He wanted to jump and look for her, but Grinat was holding him tight.

'Charge!' Someone said suddenly, and the command was repeated like an echo.

A wave of men rushed at them. The line broke, the Beasts

attacked them with arrows, hooks and torches from all sides. Their attack followed an insane logic. They charged and retreated, leaping over shields and taking those they could every time a hook struck one of the soldiers and knocked the rest down. Firla's men were afraid. What had started as a brave charge to drive out the Beasts had turned into a general rout. It was all yelling and shoving. Soldiers dropped spears and shields and ran to escape the carnage that raged around them. They fled through the middle of the medic field in the centre of the square running over their wounded comrades in arms. The wounded moaned as they were trampled and the Beasts, who followed them, took the opportunity to finish them off. Tersian's assistants tried to get in the way, but the avalanche of soldiers and Beasts engulfed them just like the rest.

Siro felt every push Grinat received as in his own skin. He looked for Eliria, but the girl had disappeared into the human tide. A man lying on a bloody blanket grabbed the silent guardian by the ankle.

'Help me!' He begged. His head was bandaged and his other hand had been amputated.

Grinat plunged the blade of the spear into his chest and pressed on. The man grew smaller behind them as they fled the shadows of the Beasts.

A mountain of bodies piled up at the foot of the southern barrier. The men at the top had killed everyone who had tried to overcome them.

'Open the doors!' The soldiers demanded from below, but the only response they got were arrows and stones.

They will not let anyone escape, unless Firla says so, thought the boy. He wanted to cry. Nothing made sense. The men on the barrier were his neighbours and friends, how could they do this to them?

'Open the gates, I command you!' The boy heard Tersian's voice and twisted over the shoulder of the silent guardian to see what was happening.

The shaman had slipped past the soldiers and was now among the shields and men at the barrier, who were pointing flaming arrows at him. In his hand he held an amphora with the symbol of a flame painted on it. It was full of Firespreader.

'Open it, for the last time!' Tersian threatened.

'Shoot!' Someone ordered from the top of the barrier. 'Shoot the shaman! Kill him!'

An arrow struck Tersian's leg. The young man fell to his knees in an unnatural position. The tip might had split his bone, but he did not drop the amphora. With a cry of rage, he threw it against the wooden wall and it exploded with a brilliant glow. The defenders flew into the air engulfed in flames. The soldiers gathering near the barrier fell to the ground, including Grinat, and Siro seized the moment to sneak away.

'Eliria!' He screamed from side to side, until he saw a red head sticking out from under a hemp shield on the ground. Siro remembered for an instant the day they had gone to the forest of hollow trees in search of glass, when they had done the same so that the Mongooses Band would not see them. The gazes of the two children met amid the chaos. Eliria did not hesitate for a moment, she ran to Siro and the two fled from there holding hands.

The soldiers escaped from the Beasts through the hole that the Firespreader had just opened, running over Tersian's body, not caring whether he was still alive or not. The shaman had a pale face and eyes lost in the night sky. A stream of blood stained his lips, which were still murmuring words that no one would ever hear. People trampled it and buried it a little deeper in the mud one soldier at a time.

They are killing him, Siro thought. *He has saved our lives and now... why is no one stopping?* If he had been as big and strong as Grinat, or at least as any other man in Merco, he would not have left him there. He lost sight of Tersian in the crowd. Eliria's constant jerks reminded him that they hadn't still made it to the river.

The Beasts of Dugol awaited them. As they descended the southern path, a storm of arrows fell on them. The alleys and abandoned houses poured more Beasts into the main street. The laces of their ropes closed around the necks, hands and legs of Merco's soldiers, who were dragged to the swords of those creatures.

Siro and Eliria were too small for the Beasts to pay attention to and they managed to get out of the ambush. Only a dozen of the soldiers who had been in the marketplace made it to the river bank. They abandoned any weapon or piece of armour that bothered them to flee right there and crossed the river without looking back, hoping that the Beasts would forget about them.

The two children could not follow them.

The river was full of bodies that floated trapped between the rocks of the ford. Women, men, children… There were so many that Siro felt guilty to be alive.

They were waiting for us. They have killed them all…

'Siro, look, it's Nazeh!' Eliria pointed towards the shore.

His friend was next to the deceased body of his mother. Sailia had an arrow stuck in the middle of her face. Siro looked at the corpse without knowing what to say or think. He was too tired to feel anything. He put his hand on his friend's shoulder and he winced.

'Mohaki was washed away,' he said. 'I couldn't find him…'

Nazeh's cheeks were wet with tears. A smear of snot covered his upper lip. His eyes were red and puffy, the likes of which he had never seen before. How many hours had he been mourning the death of his relatives?

'We must go,' Siro said. That was all he could think of.

'I must find Wangari, mum told me to keep an eye on him…'

Wangari can't even walk, Siro thought. *If the Beasts have fallen upon him, your brother must be dead, Nazeh. We cannot waste the whole night looking for a corpse.*

He could have tried to explain him that, but instead he said: 'Forget it.'

'The Muhara tribe buries the dead, they don't let the water wash them away. My father told me…' Nazeh said, and stepped into the river, among the floating bodies.

'Do something, please... Make him come back!' Eliria said.

Siro snorted and reluctantly stepped into the water. It was as cold as he anticipated. The pebbles from the river were slimy and made him sway. He splashed among the corpses of people and tried not to look at their faces so as not to recognize them, but most of the time it was inevitable. A dead hand brushed his knee, but he kept his eyes up. Those who had fallen face down were easier to ignore, but the others, with open eyes and puffy faces, made him want to abandon his friend to his own luck.

'Nazeh, stop!' His voice shook like a leaf.

'I have to find Wangari,' he repeated, as he checked the faces floating in the river.

'No. We are leaving. Now! If the Beasts find us…' Siro grabbed his friend by the wrist, but he reacted violently.

Nazeh pushed him when he least expected it and he fell ass

first into the water. Siro leapt out, driven by anger and cold, and shoved him back. The two children fell on the pebbles, punching and screaming.

'I brought her to you!' Siro was shouting at him, carried away by animal fury. He slapped his friend over and over. 'I have gone looking for her! You can't do this to me!'

Nazeh's head sank under the water and came out to take hit after hit, until Siro had had enough. He was wet, cold, and standing in a river full of dead bodies. He no longer had the strength to fight. Nazeh came out of the water coughing. His cheek was bleeding.

'I must find my brother,' was all he said.

'You're an idiot! Your brother is dead, everyone is dead!'

'Shut up!' Nazeh clenched his fists.

Eliria splashed over to where the two children were.

'Beasts are here... They are killing people on the shore. I think they have seen us...' she said. But Nazeh paid no more attention to her than to his friend.

Siro had had enough. He went to the other side of the river, intending to leave them both behind. If Nazeh didn't come with them, he deserved whatever happened to him.

Merco burned in the background, like an animal caught in a fire. The next morning there would be nothing left of the village that they had worked so hard to build. A group of men had descended the street that led to the square. They fought each other with savage desperation. The sound of metal against metal reached up to Siro. Grinat was there, surrounded by a group of Beasts that grew by the minute. The boy didn't want to see how it ended.

He came out of the river. He was shaking from head to toe. The grass dried his toes, and the murmur of the wind made the tops of the sycamores shake. The vegetation and the night made him almost invisible, but that no longer mattered to him. He dropped behind a tree trunk and buried his head in his arms, while he was carried away by a silent cry.

Liduvin was waiting for me at home... and now I can't go.

She had told him to hurry up, to come back soon, but no, he had had to warn Nazeh and go find Eliria.

Idiot, I'm an idiot! He told himself as he covered his face with sooty hands.

'Siro, don't cry.' That was Eliria's voice. The girl hugged him when she saw him. He leaned his head against her shoulder and closed his eyes for an instant. When he opened them again, Nazeh was standing in front of him. The fury with which they had fought minutes before was gone.

'I'm sorry', his friend said.

Siro wiped away his tears. There were few things in the world that made him more ashamed than crying in front of his friends.

'You two won't do that again. Never! I don't want to see you fight anymore!' Eliria scolded them, although there was a gleam of happiness in her tone, perhaps for the mere fact of being with both.

The boy nodded, but before he got up, an axe flew over his head and got lost in the vegetation. The Beasts had crossed the river, screaming and yelling.

Chapter 31: The Shell

She told him not to make noise so as not to wake the child. He nodded and opened her dress. She stretched out his tunic and the two, naked, one on top of the other, gave each other all the kisses and caresses that the years had stolen from them; but now they were no longer children and their bodies burned.

Siro was guided by instinct and her sensual movements that barely let him breathe. When he was little, the only experience he had had with sex was when he had caught Grinat and Liduvin together one day when he returned too soon from playing with his friends. At that moment he did not understand what was happening. The silent guardian grabbed the woman's breasts and rammed her ass with such vigor that at first he thought that he wanted to hurt her. He never said anything about what he had seen that afternoon, he was too embarrassed to ask anyone, and since then he tried to get home at sunset and not earlier.

The warm contact of Eliria's tongue inside his own mouth made him fly until the day that Matildet had kissed him by the pond.

I don't want to think about her, he thought. He kissed down her neck and grabbed her hair as she caressed his member.

'Move…' she said in a broken voice. 'Move, don't stop. Don't stop…'

And Siro couldn't stop. He stroked her breasts and she bit his lip; he was tugging at her hair and she was swinged her hips back and forth. His body trembled. Just before he came, she pressed her lips against his to suppress a cry of pleasure.

Matildet, he thought as he finished. *Matildet…*

She woke up hours later feeling dizzy. For a moment, it was hard for him to remember that he was in Eliria's room, somewhere in the galleries of the Rock.

He felt knackered after the chase through the streets of Undershell, but he couldn't sleep. He got up, careful not to wake

Eliria or her son. He pulled back the curtain and the city lights poured in. The Cross was abuzz with activity, although it was already late. Shouts and laughter could be heard, drunken songs and the constant resounding of footsteps that came from other levels of The Mouth.

There were lights in the marketplace, at the centre of the Cross, and even more in the twisted towers of Adon's palace. The lighting did not favour it; it made it more sinister and worn than during the day.

Matildet is there, with him…

Adon's smile disturbed him. He did look like a Son of Light, but was he? Matildet had gone upstairs and he… he had run away because he had thought it was a trap. Had she betrayed him?

Did she had it all planned from the beginning? No. It can't be. Even she is wrong sometimes, instinct told him. He had fled because he knew he would not escape the palace of the Beasts alive, but what about Matildet? Why should it be a safe place for her?

What will you do, wildling? Ubald's metallic voice echoed in his head. *Surely you think one day she will notice you, poor idiot...*

'Shut up!' Said Siro. He didn't realize he had said it out loud until he noticed movement behind him. Eliria had woken up. She was naked from head to toe. Her brown skin gleamed under Undershell's lights. Siro looked over his shoulder at her pink nipples, which danced with each step.

'You have this gorgeous woman sleeping by your side and you are looking out the window…' she said with a smile. She hugged him from behind and he felt her breasts press against his back.

Siro took her hand in an affectionate gesture, but he was still absorbed with the palace and the Great Shell that loomed like a ghost behind it. Eliria caressed his cheek and kissed him.

'I knew you'd come back to find me,' she whispered in his ear. 'I feel terrible for saying this, but even when I was with Nazeh I was hoping that you would come and save me from the Beasts, just like you did that night.'

'I lost you in the end...' Siro said.

He had thought so many times of the moment they had parted while running through the jungle that he had come to wish the Beasts had caught him too so he wouldn't feel so alone.

Fourteen years in the desert, he thought and did not believe it.

He looked at Eliria. There was very little left in his face of the girl he had been. What should she see when she looked at him?

'We did part ways,' she admitted. 'But if you hadn't come looking for me and my mother when everyone abandoned us, today we wouldn't be talking.'

Eliria put her arms around him and he hugged her back. The two of them stood, embraced and naked in the darkness of that room carved in the rock.

She loves me, Siro told himself. *She loves me and I… I can't stop thinking about Matildet. What's wrong with me?*

'You weren't scared at all,' Eliria said, kissing his neck.

I was, he thought. *Specially from your mother.*

When the Beasts had entered the basement, he had been more concerned about Debra breaking his arm, than of what those monsters wanted. Still, he felt like he had to apologize to her, or at least say something, but he didn't know where to start.

What can I say? I'm sorry I left your mother with the Hyena and Irad, but she was crazy and she deserved it?

'I've waited for you,' she continued. 'But I'm not kidding myself. I know you didn't come for me. Why are you here?'

Siro looked at the distant palace.

'Please tell me, Siro. I need to know it.'

'I found the Sacred Valley a while ago. Teradam exists. And the Daughter of the Light is the only one who can open the doors for me.'

'So it was you. You were the Free Man walking with Daughter of the Light everybody talks about. But why? Why are you accompanying her? What do you expect…?'

Siro just had to nod for her to understand.

'Oh no…' Eliria said, grabbing the blanket from the bed and covering herself, suddenly remembering she was naked. 'Did you do it for Liduvin?'

Siro looked down and remained silent.

'Answer me! Did you do it for her?'

'She is in Teradam. She waits for me.'

'She's dead!' Eliria yelled. Ranzeh shifted on his little bed. The mother lowered her voice. 'She is dead, and you know it! When the Beasts attacked Merco, they cornered us at the marketplace'

'So what?' Siro protested, although he knew where she was going.

'She wasn't there. She is dead, Siro, just like everyone who was left behind, just like my mother! You must accept...'

'She's not dead. I know. I heard her voice. She is waiting for me in Teradam… she is not dead!'

'I wish she was!' Eliria burst out.

Siro didn't know what to do. She was sobbing, but he was too angry to comfort her.

'Why couldn't you come back for me? I have waited for you! I've waited a long time!'

He didn't want to hurt Ellria, but he couldn't bear to be talked to like that either. It made him feel too guilty. He couldn't stay another second in the room.

'Where are you going?' She asked him as he was leaving.

'To the palace.'

'What? That's non-sense,' she said as he wiped away his tears. 'They won't let you in. What if they catch you? What if they see that you do not have any Brand...?'

'I don't know, ok?' He screamed. 'I just want to find Matildet!'

Eliria released him.

'Is that her name? Matildet? You and her…?' She tried to say but didn't dare finishing the question. 'It's not just because of Liduvin that you do all this, right? Is there something else...? Tell me please!'

'Goodbye, Eliria,' was all he said, and he left the room with only one idea in his mind.

In the living room, a candlelight illuminated Meres' slim figure. The hostess at the Palace of Dreams was helping an older man walk to the latrine. The man trembled. He was old, much older than any other person Siro had ever seen. Meres looked up. Dressed in nightwear, she had lost all the sensuality that she had when she received people at the gates of the Palace, but her face was still just as sweet.

'Good night, prince,' she said. 'Be careful if you go out.'

Siro remembered that, when he was just a kid, he had sometimes climbed between the chimneys that populated the outer part of The Mouth trying to keep up with the older children. At the top of the mountain, the Beasts had a rope system to send scrolls from there to the palace. If he was lucky, it would still be running.

He had walked through the galleries until he had found a

natural terrace overlooking the Cross. The terrace was a semi-circular platform large enough to hold ten or twelve people, but at that time of the night, there was only one couple hiding from curious gazes. Siro paid no attention to them. He clambered onto the rough rock and climbed determined to reach the ropes that linked the mountain and the palace.

The exterior of The Mouth was full of natural chimneys that the inhabitants of Undershell used to evacuate the fumes produced layers below. Siro was guided by the lights of the city and the stars so as not to fall. Higher up, he saw the silver glow on the spikes of two Beast guards.

Siro lay on his stomach. He had left Nazeh's old tunic before leaving Eliria's house. It was not comfortable to move in it. Between the smoke from the chimneys and the darkness, he crawled up to the two Beasts unseen. He examined the pulleys that held the rope that crossed the sky of Undershell between The Mouth and the palace. It seemed fragile, designed to support only the weight of a scroll.

One of the Beasts, the one with a black cape draped over his shoulders and two swords hanging from his belt, gazed from the edge of the cliff at the city and pointed downward.

'What do you say? Do I make it or not?' Asked the Beast in the cloak to the other one.

'What? That woman? No way...' it replied. 'Why don't you do something useful and go find me some Ardent?'

'Do you see a slave Brand on me, huh?' The Beast replied. 'I thought so... You go, and bring me a girl... A pretty one, not the ones you like!'

The Beast patted the other one on the back and they both stared down the cliff. Siro took the opportunity to get even closer.

'If you hit the woman, I'll go,' said the other Beast. 'If not, you go.'

'Deal,' the Beast with the cloak replied, spitting a gargle down the cliff. 'Oh yeah! Bullseye! Look at her. She doesn't even know what happened,' he said cracking up.

The other Beast grunted. The two of them had their backs turned, mocking the poor woman they had spitted on. *Now!* Thought Siro. He drew his knife and readied to jump at them, but just as he rose, he felt a foot stepping on his back.

'Easy, tiger!' Said a voice that was vaguely familiar. A hand tugged at his hair. He felt the cold blade of a knife under the chin.

'You two, the hell are you doing? Keep your eye open!' Another Beast walked by him. 'Don't you see that this fucking slave was going to cut your throat open?'

The two guards stopped laughing and walked over to the newcomers. Siro could not move. They had caught him and now he would pay the consequences.

'Did you hit the woman?' Asked the Beast sitting on top of him.

'Oh, for fuck's sake, Irad! Do you really think that matters now? Really?' That was the other Beast, the one telling off the guards. 'And you two useless fuckwits. Guards? You should be ashamed! Come here! What do you think Adon will say when he knows about you two?'

'We…' began the Beast that had challenged the other one to spit.

'Shut your dirty mouth! You two don't speak to me, got that? Your spears. Give'em to me. Now. You are discharged!

'Now take a good look,' the Beast sitting on top Siro whispered.

When the guards had handed the spears to the Beast who was yelling at them, the latter raised them, stabbing one in the stomach, and the another one in the neck as it tried to draw. He pulled the sword from the cloaked Beast's belt and finished off the other as it crawled across the ground. The Beast stuck the bloodstained sword at Siro's side.

'You've grown, boy!' The hunter recognized the eye-patched Beast. It was the Hyena.

'Right?' said Irad, not letting Siro make a move.

'You shut up!' The Hyena replied. 'What was your name boy? I can't remember…'

'Siro…' he answered as best he could. It was not easy to speak with a knife pressing against his throat.

'Okay, it's him,' the Hyena told him and gestured for him to stand up.

When he got up, he realized that this time he was taller than the two Beasts. It was no surprise, after all, it had been more than ten years.

'Look at him. Already a man!' the Hyena said sarcastically.

'But he hasn't gotten any smarter.'

Siro reached for his scabbard but couldn't find the knife.

'It has a very nice blade. I think I'll keep it,' Irad said, showing his rotten teeth. Siro was sure he had lost quite a few since he had last seen him.

'What are you doing here?' He asked them. 'You have killed two of yours...'

'Wrong,' the Hyena replied, showing him his own Mark: a sort of horned eagle and six spears stuck on it covered his shoulder. 'But who cares? The fuck are you doing up here?'

'It's none of your business.'

'Wrong again. C'mon, boy. Tell me. You are planning on kicking Adon in the balls, aren't you? Well, it ain't happening. Irad, cut the rope. We don't want this idiot to do things that he may later regret.'

Irad obediently sawed the rope that linked The Mouth with the palace of Adon. Siro tried to stop him, but the Hyena cut him off with one of the dead guardians' spears.

'Don't even think about it. You come with us, in one piece or diced, I don't care. Shahrokh wants to see you.'

Shahrokh... thought Siro. The Beast's bronze boots on the wooden floor, that forceful noise that had scared Siro and Eliria while they were hiding in the basement with Debra came to his mind. The last time he had seen him, he was facing Taurus, who had come between them and the Beast so they could flee. He hoped he be already dead by then, that the Firespreader or the spears of Merco's warriors would had ended his life, but fortune always favoured those ruthless beings.

'How did you find me?' Siro looked for a way out, but now that the rope was cut, he didn't know what to do.

'Are you kidding?' Irad said. 'We've been tracking you all day. Since you've left the Palace of Dreams.'

'Damn, Irad!' The Hyena scolded him. 'I know that when you were born the shaman was drunk and you slipped from his hands, but do you have to make it *so* obvious?'

'Hey, I only slipped twice,' Irad replied, offended.

As the Beasts argued, Siro desperately searched for an escape. Seeing Shahrokh was the last thing he wanted to do. What could he expect from that Beast? Surely, he wanted to finish what he had left in half so many years ago.

At the edge of the cliff, a few feet below where they stood, there was a metal ringed chain. The rings were so big that a small child could sneak through. The chain was suspended in the void, just as the rope had been, but from what he could see, it did not extend to the palace, but to the Great Shell, like an anchor. He saw the light of Adon's palace in the distance. Matildet was there.

'C'mon, walk! I've got better things to do! You hear me?' The Hyena snapped.

'No,' said Siro.

I'm not a child anymore, he thought.

The Hyena's head tilted, puzzled. He asked Irad for a sword, but Siro broke into a run and, before the Beasts could react, leaped into the void. For a moment, he experienced weightlessness as his entire body rushed against the houses of Undershell.

The impact against the chain crushed his arms. He felt his hands slip and he lifted his legs to support himself. He hung upside down, not quite sure where he had gotten the courage to do what he had just done.

'You, boy, come back!' the Hyena scream.

'You have a spear, why don't you...?' Irad suggested.

'Because we want him alive, you piece of mindless animal!' The Hyena was beside himself.

Siro ignored them. As they argued about how angry Shahrokh was going to be for failing in their mission, he doubled over and clung to the chain as best he could.

The road to the Great Shell was as long as it was exhausting. Hanging upside down, dizziness was continuous, but it was also the easiest way to move. He needed to reserve energy if he wanted to get to the metal structure that protected the palace. The gusts of wind made him stop from time to time, as did the pain in his muscles. In those moments, he hugged the rings or hung only by the legs.

He got to the Great Shell just when he thought that chain had no end. He carefully reached down and clung to the inside of that relic from ancient times. The Great Shell had a metallic structure inside that held all the panels that formed it. Siro would never have imagined that he would be so close, much less that he would touch it with his bare hands. Would the Children of Light have imagined that one day a human would use it to rescue one of them?

The Great Shell was filled with half-finished structures, black tubes and beams cut in half, as if it contained other things inside it long ago. *Were there houses in here?* He wondered. The shapes that were etched into the bright interior of the Shell reminded him of the early days of the village of Merco, when people marked their territory on the ground and placed one stone on top of another to build their homes. The remnants of the structures of the Great Shell were the same, they delimited spaces, but they were difficult to identify when standing vertically.

The scaffolding that surrounded the southern tower of the palace served to swap from the Great Shell to one of the palace's roofs . A couple of night birds took flight as he leaped over the tiles. The Beasts patrolled the outer and inner courtyards of Adon's palace, but no one was paying attention to what was happening above their heads. Siro was jumping from roof to roof. When Siro was little, people said that Dugol's tower was the last of all, the tallest one. If he was right, Adon would inhabit the same rooms now.

The inner courtyard was still lit up. The ceiling was covered by rectangles made of coloured fabrics. Between cloth rectangles, one could see inside. There was a pool surrounded by white marble slabs with fountains around it and a row of trays with food scraps and jugs lying on the floor. It was obvious that there had been celebration. The Beasts that were left around were singing, drunk, while the slaves picked up what they threw to the ground without saying a word.

He pressed forward and arrived at old Dugol's old tower. It seemed the least dilapidated part of the palace. The tower had bronze sculptures of women next to the windowsill, flags of the clans serving Adon waving around it, and a huge Brand, the cross and the vertical line, painted in a glowing white.

He put his hands between the slits in the blocks and climbed up. He heard noises coming from inside the old tower. Someone had entered the room. He let himself fall from the roof to the windowsill. It was wide enough so that he could stay there without being seen from the inside. He got as close as he could to hear what they were saying.

'I hope you like my room,' said Adon's voice.

'Not bad… Oh, what's that?' Where did you get it?' It was Matildet who was speaking.

'It's a token,' he heard Adon say. 'An old memory… But

tonight is not for memories. Tonight is about changing the world... Take off your clothes.'

The hunter stood still, waiting for what might happen. The window was open. A thin silk curtain was the only thing standing between them.

'Not that I want to offend you, Lord of the Beasts,' Matildet replied. 'But why don't we spare it for another day? You know, it's a bit late, we've had a drink...'

'I said take your clothes off,' Adon insisted.

Siro heard the two Children of Light struggle. Matildet screamed and he could no longer restrain himself. Against common sense, he entered through the window. The Daughter of the Light was so startled that she nearly fell on her ass to the ground. Adon, scared, raised his hands, but before he could say anything, Siro punched him in the face. The boy tried to defend himself, but the hunter grabbed him by his golden hair and smashed his face against the mirror that hung on the wall. He punched him twice in the stomach, knocked him against the foot of the bed, and lifted him by the neck.

Adon's face was a mess of blood and tears. The fearsome Lord of the Beasts trembled from head to toe.

'Do you realize what you're doing?' He said between sobs. 'I am a Son of Light...'

'What you are is a son of a bitch!' Siro snapped, and kept hitting him until the guards came through the door.

Chapter 32: The person you admire

'How long do you plan to sleep for, Unbranded?' The jailer's voice was accompanied by a few knocks on the bars.

I'll sleep until everything stops hurting, he thought. He had a sick burn on his hands, a wound on his buttock from a sabre blade, and bruises on his ribs and all over his body.

It was the second time that he had come, but Siro saw no reason to get up from the ground where the Beasts had thrown him. The ceiling was covered with thick cobwebs, blackened by the smoke from the burning pots that hung from the ceiling. The floor was even worse, full of excrement and piss in the corners. Rats ran free down there, chattering their teeth ominously and interrupting his sleep.

The jailer threw a bucket of water on him. Siro jumped up. There was laughter in the background, subsided as soon as the jailer turned his head.

'Have I given you permission to laugh?' Exclaimed the Beast. 'Do you think you are better than the Unbranded, huh? None of you are worth a fuck, if you ask me. You are mine, you will laugh when I say so, you will breathe when I say so, and yes, you'll fucking die when I say so!'

He tapped the baton against the bars four times. The blows echoed throughout the vault. *Do you want me to have a headache too?* Wondered Siro.

'You, Unbranded, stay awake if you know what's good for you,' it threatened.

The jailer walked down the corridor, crowded with cells, lord of everything. Siro watched his broad back drift away and heard him cursing in the distance. The noise was followed by the squeak of a door opening and closing, and a bolt, and then he knew the Beast would not be back for a few hours, when the bottle of Ardent was empty. The dungeon was silent.

The only light there was came from the kettles that hung from the ceiling. The Beasts had made a fire inside, and the light was seeping through the holes they had made in the base, keeping the whole place always in shadows. It was difficult to see who was in the next cell, although Siro wasn't sure if he wanted to know.

He had been down there for three days. He had a nickname, Unbranded and he was very hungry and in continuous pain. Adon's guards had been cruel to him: punches, kicks… One of them had hit him with a bronze fist in the ribs, another had split his eyebrow, or at least it felt that way.

To make things worse, he thought about Matildet all time. He had not seen her since his irruption into Adon's room. *Please, be safe...*, he wished, but every time he thought about her he imagined the Lord of the Beasts putting his dirty hands on the Daughter of the Light, and a blind rage invaded him, making him hit the floor, the bars, the bed ... everything he found.

An old man murmured in the cell opposite his. He did the same thing all day. Ever since he got up from his straw bed, he walked around and talked to himself, so fast and so quietly that it was impossible to understand a word. He had a tousled white beard and, from what he had seen, his left ear was missing. The jailer ignored him when he saw him perform his ritual. The old man must have had a good share of pain for that Beast not to care. In the cell to his left there was a man who cried from time to time, especially when the lights turned off. Siro had no idea what his name was, he only knew that he owed two hundred golden suns to a certain Beos the Impatient. To his right, on the other side of the bars, there was also someone, although he could not see him well. The man was so quiet that he sometimes thought the cell was empty, but he knew it wasn't. Whoever he was, he kept his eye on him. Every time he moved, the shadow seemed to turn its head.

It was time to eat, the only time they had all day long, and this time Siro was surprised. A slave brought him a bowl full of roasted pheasant with plums and dates instead of the usual brown glob. He noticed how the envious glances of his dungeon mates. His mouth was watering too.

'Why?' He asked, but he got no answer.

The slave was just a scrawny teenager with the Brand of Servants etched on his neck. He left the cell and went to the next one with another bowl of roasted pheasant. He put the bowl on the floor and there it stayed. The man in the shadows did not move.

'You have little time left,' said the prisoner on his left, the one who owed money.

Siro gripped the bars that connected the two cells.

'What do you mean?'

The man was sitting on the floor, his tasteless plate on his lap.

'You'll have good food for a while, then they'll take you away and you won't come back. This is the fifth time I see it. The same thing will happen to your partner, it is always like that. Can you give me some? I am very hungry…'

'Why? Where are they taking us?' Asked Siro, now the food didn't seem so delicious.

'If you give me some, I'll tell you.'

'Fuck you,' he replied and devoured the contents of the bowl in front of the hungry gaze of his dungeon mate.

'You'll die soon… What's the point of eating?'

Hours later the jailer walked in followed by two other Beasts. They went straight to him. The jailer's underlings had neck-cutters hanging from their belts and the symbol of Adon, the cross and the vertical line, engraved on the chestplates.

'It's the Unbranded,' he told them. 'Do what you want with him but be careful. He is not yet very aware he is a dead man.'

The escorts threw themselves at him. The first slammed Siro against the bars. The hunter reacted quickly and struck him a punch; but before he could go on, the other Beast had hit him on the bruised ribs. He bended over, knees to the ground, while those creatures beat him up and tied a rope around his neck to carry him away. He saw the ceiling of the passageway and the burning kettles as they dragged him across the grimy floor.

They seized him between the two guards and took him to another room. It was very different from the rest of the dungeon. It didn't smell of terror and excrement, but of perfumes made with wildflowers and the embers of a burning fire. They had prepared a kind of throne with colourful cushions and exotic fabrics. Adon was there with his entourage of masked Beasts.

The Lord of the Beasts had a purplish bruise around his eye, purposely hidden between his hair and makeup, but it was still too recent to go unnoticed; his lower lip was split, and hopefully he would have lost a tooth or two. His blue eyes followed Siro with little interest, as if the incident three days ago had been insignificant.

'Begone,' Adon said to the Beasts that had brought Siro.

The Lord of the Beasts looked very young, like he had only left adolescence behind, but his subjects obeyed him without questioning. As soon as the Beasts were out, the wizards and soothsayers descended the steps of the makeshift throne and began examining him. They wore coloured masks with different painted faces: one with a smile, the other with a severe grimace, one crying, and the last one with a surprised face. They wore black robes and long gloves that concealed their hands and arms. One of them examined his teeth, the other pulled locks of hair; the third one examined his body, maybe hoping to find some Brand, and the fourth merely threw some wise stones on the table and shook his head in a troubled gesture.

'He's healthy,' said the Beast with the mask of the smile.

'He's not healthy,' contradicted the one with a surprised face. Two of the amber had fallen off the table and the only one left was too close to the onyx.

'He couldn't be healthier,' said the wizard who had pulled out a lock of his hair. 'But he is very dirty.'

The wizard with the stern expression mask fell silent. He shook his head left and right, struggling to get to a verdict.

'He could be healthier. Have you seen his teeth?' He said as he opened the hunter's mouth.

'For what I need him, teeth aren't important, wizard,' Adon told him.

The Son of the Light descended from his throne and the four masked Beasts stepped aside.

'Hello, wildling, how did you like my dungeon?' Adon asked.

The Lord of the Beasts wore loose white clothing, a red cloak, and a necklace made of colourful crystals around his neck. If it hadn't been for the shackles that had him tied to the table, Siro would have strangled him right there.

'These wise wizards you see around you have given me their opinions on what I should do with you. Do you want to hear them?' The Son of the Light told him with a grin.

'Gut him!' Said the first.

'Behead him!' The one with the surprised face yelled at him.

'Rip off his legs and arms!' Exclaimed the one with the crying face.

'Throw him into the Biters' pit!' Said the one with the stern face.

Adon lowered his hands and the wizards shut up again.

'How about it? Any preference?' Said the Son of the Light as he circled Siro. 'I suspect none of them are to your liking... I think likewise. They are outdated ideas, but I don't blame them, they have been in the palace since the time my father ruled... and back then attacking the Lord of the Beasts in his own room was... Well, it was the best way to lose your head. They have lived through the blood wars, they have seen the Beast clans fight for Undershell's control, they have chased... and they have been chased. They belong to another time, and they need to learn that under my light there is no place for these atrocities, do you understand?'

'Answer when the Son of the Light speaks to you!' Shouted the Beast with severe face mask.

'Yes...' Siro replied, wondering where he was going with his stupid speech.

Now that he saw him up close, he didn't think he looked too much like Matildet. They both had golden hair, yes, but the shade of their eyes was different. She had them navy blue and that boy had them sky blue. The nose was not the same, nor was the shape of the lips, or anything in general. If they were real siblings, they should look a bit alike... or so thought Siro. Of course, from what Matildet had told him, the Children of the Light weren't exactly siblings to each other.

'I see we understand each other, wildling. I believe that each of us plays an important role in the world that I want to build. Not all of us can rule, nor do we all have to fight or cultivate a field, but we need to be united, don't you think?'

'Yes...' Siro answered mechanically. It was easy to see that the wizards had swords under their robes and he didn't want to give them any excuse to unsheathe them.

'Based on what I know about you, which is that you like killing my Beasts, sneaking into my palace uninvited, chasing Daughters of the Light through the desert and... Oh, yes, eating pheasant, I've decided you'd be an excellent candidate for the fight tower. Do you know what it is? No, of course not, you are not from around here... who explains it?'

'The fight tower is one of the favourite entertainments of our beloved Lord and Master Adon, Son of the Light,' said smiling Beast. 'It's a wooden tower where battles to the death take place between prisoners, mercenaries and other expert fighters from beyond the Great Shell.'

So that's what he wants, for me to take part on one fight after another until someone finishes me, thought Siro.

'Thank you, wizard,' said Adon. 'You know, wildling, I want you to fight for me and my court's delight. There is only one problem…'

The Son of the Light went to the fireplace. Siro lost sight of him for a moment. Tied up as he was, he couldn't turn his head. He heard him stir the embers and saw him return with a red-hot iron bar. At the tip of the bar, engulfed in a white and orange glow, was the symbol of the cross and the vertical line that he had seen so many times. The Brand was huge, much larger than the usual ones. Siro gulped, sweat accumulated on his forehead.

'If you want to represent me in combat, you must have my Brand, just like all those who are loyal to me. The symbol represents our ancestral home where one day, if Keerine wants it, we shall all return. It represents the Great Light; do you recognize it or is it too abstract for you? Oh, well, what difference does it make…? Grab him'

The wizards surrounded him and grabbed him to keep him from moving. Siro shook and screamed, but the shackles kept him from leaving the table. Adon held the iron within a foot of his face. Siro could feel its heat.

'Listen to me, wildling because I will tell you once and only once,' said the Son of the Light, his tone no longer jovial, but that of the ruthless creature he really was. 'I will be merciful to you. I will let you choose where I will brand you if you answer the following question. Think carefully what you say, because if I put this iron in your eyeball you will never see again… and by Keerine, there is nothing I want more right now.'

He grabbed him by the hair and tipped his head back. The metal was burning inches away from his face.

'The girl… is she a Daughter of the Light? Answer me!'

'Yes!' Siro answered.

'Thank you, that was all I wanted to know,' Adon said with a smile. 'You told me you wanted it in your face, right?'

Before he could say a single word, the Lord of the Beasts

pressed the iron against his flesh. The scream was deafening. He only put the iron down for a couple of seconds, but Siro felt he was dying. His body spasmed. The shackles opened wounds on his wrists. He shook his head from side to side and hit the stone in an attempt not to feel the pain that was preventing him from breathing. Tears streamed down as he twisted around. He whimpered like a small child.

'You should have never come to Undershell, wildling,' Adon told him, sniffing the burned flesh stuck to the iron.

He regained consciousness when the guards threw him into the cell, but he did not move from there. He spent the next hours lying on the floor. He was breathing heavily, like a dying animal. His hands were shaking. His cheek, his neck, everything burned. He had the feeling that the iron was still there and that Adon was still holding it. He did not dare touch his cheek, afraid of being left with half his face in his hands.

I'm dying, he thought every time he noticed the slightest pull.

No one in the dungeon said anything. Everyone knew they could be next. A boy with a shaved head entered the cell followed by the jailer.

'Let him heal your wound, Unbranded,' ordered the Beast.

The boy put down a bucket and approached him with a cloth dipped in Ardent. He put it between his neck and cheek. Siro fought the urge to slap him. This was worse than the wound itself, but if it was left untreated, it would get infected. He didn't fancy spending its last days spitting pus.

'Wait... I think we'll have to change your name,' said the jailer, grinning at Siro's face. 'Now you are quite an adonite, we cannot treat you like a slave. What do you want your Beast name to be?'

'I... am no... Beast,' Siro replied.

'I think I'll call you Fireface, what do you think?' The jailer laughed with his hands on his belly. The air escaped him as if he had never heard anything so funny in his entire life.

Fireface, Beast ... what does it matter? Thought Siro. He had more serious problems than that. He looked for his reflection in the bucket of water the boy had brought, but it was hard to see anything in that damned dungeon. He saw the shape of the Brand: the cross engraved between the neck and the jaw, and the vertical line across his cheek, with the tip just below the eye. Now it was his property. Forever.

'You, rat meat, get out of here,' the Beast said to the poor boy who had healed his wound. 'Fireface, we need to talk. Get up!'

Siro's first instinct was to shoot him a defiant look, but he had understood that if he wanted to survive in that place, he would have to choose which battles were worth fighting and which were not. He got to his feet with difficulty. His legs were shaking.

'You have to choose a weapon,' said the jailer. 'We have everything, but I can't let you choose everything, understood? For you there are knives, neck-cutters, short axes...'

'Weapons?' Siro didn't understand anything.

'Our beloved master has already told you. Tower. Doubles fight. In three days. And don't embarrass me by shitting yourself in the pants, okay? Try to stay put. It won't be easy. I know your opponents. Those bastards are formidable: Yashar and Vahid... Do they ring a bell? No, of course not. Whatever. You ask your cellmates who they are while you bitches fuck your asses between the bars... Hey, Fireface, you hear me?'

Siro nodded by inertia. He didn't know what to do with all that information. In three days he would face some Beasts that would try to kill him, period.

'You said doubles fight. Who is... my partner?'

The jailer raised an eyebrow and smiled, surprised that his prisoner was able to articulate an entire sentence.

'This is where you got lucky, Fireface, very lucky. I've seen Yashar and Vahid fight dozens of times and believe me when I tell you, you don't stand a chance. They are unbeatable... unless *he* fights, then the outcome is not so clear. I can't believe how lucky you are. You have no idea.' The jailer turned his head to the next cell, the one that seemed empty, had it not been for that lurking presence, and screamed. 'You, Quiet! Move your ass here, Fireface wants to meet you.'

Siro stared into the shadows, but the man hiding there did not move or respond to the jailer.

'Old dog... He doesn't give a fuck. Beatings are worthless... Think what weapon you want, Fireface,' he added and left the cell, locking it.

When the jailer had left, the dungeon was as sad and silent as before. Siro curled up, one hand on his neck, feeling the Brand and the faint smell of his own burned flesh. He covered his face so that the other prisoners wouldn't see him cry. The salt of the tears stung him as they passed over the wound. It was a strange sensation. As a child, the fact of not having it was exactly what distinguished him from other children. 'Free Child', they called him. Although he had felt marginalized many times because of that, he had also carried that nickname with a secret pride, as if the fact of not being branded as a property made him better than the rest. And now he saw that it wasn't. He was insignificant. The same insignificant being that he had always been: Siro, a slave of Undershell, labour and cannon fodder… and soon, a dead man.

It took him a long time to regain his composure. If he continued like that, he wouldn't even get to the day of the fight. Adon hated him, and he was as insane as the Beasts who served him. In fact, there was only one difference. The boy was smarter than the rest, he could tell. He closed his eyes and tried to think of another time and place other than here and now. He wanted to see the faces of Eliria and Nazeh as they played hide and seek among the vegetation. But his mind had room only for Matildet. He could see her at the top of the water tank, pushing her down the dunes. He could hear her laughter, or see her climbing the stairs of the palace of the Lord of the Beasts, or sinking in the lagoon without any fear of the monster.

'I'll see her…' he repeated in a low voice, over and over again.

It took him a while to realize that the man in the shadows was watching him. He was standing, clinging to the bars of the cell. He had moved without making a sound. Siro leaped to his feet, pulse pounding under the Brand. By instinct, he reached for the handle of the knife, but it was gone.

The man in the cell stared at him with bright green eyes. He was tall and strong, bearing the Brand of the Silent Guardians across his chest. *It can't be*, Siro told himself.

'Grinat? Is that you?'

Chapter 33: It chases and traps us

He looked imposing, just like when he walked around Merco. He was still tall, perhaps his back had curved a little. His veins stood out, thick as ropes, on his biceps. He looked steady like a rock, but Siro noticed something different about him.

It had been fourteen years since the last time they had seen each other… And it had not been a placid encounter. Scattered memories of the Night of Fire flocked to his mind: a piece of Zuria's purple dress, the silent guardian facing the Beasts emerging from the crater left by the Firespreader, the double-edged spear spinning like a silver and crimson lightning above their heads, the fire looming above the rooftops of Merco and the sour smell that filled the air. Grinat had saved him, but he had also terrified him. The silent guardian hadn't cared about Eliria for a second. The poor girl had had to follow them between the warriors and the fight, while Grinat carried Siro on his shoulder. The two children could have died that night, and it hadn't seemed to worry him at all… but did it make sense to reproach him for all that now, after so long?

'I didn't expect to see you here…'said Siro. The words sounded silly to him. Deep down, he was glad to see him alive.

'That makes two of us,' Grinat replied.

Siro took a step back in his tiny cell. Was it possible that the silent guardian had spoken to him?

'Don't pull this face, Siro. You are surprised that I speak, but it surprises me even more to see how much you have grown,' Grinat showed his teeth in a smile. His broken tusk no longer attracted attention now that his teeth were all blackened.

Siro was speechless and the same applied to the entire dungeon. One could only hear the ravings of the old man moving up and down in the cell opposite.

'I wasn't sure it was you,' Grinat said. 'You don't even have the same voice. But it is you, this attitude is yours .. and your eyes, you have the same eyes, although you no longer look the same.'

'A lot has happened since,' Siro told him.

Grinat smiled again.

The silent guardian could hardly remember anything about all the time they had lived in Merco. Siro realised every time he told him an anecdote or a moment that they had shared. It was as if little by little he had forgotten everything and had become one of the ghosts that inhabited that dungeon. Only occasionally some of Siro's words seemed to wake something up within the guardian, but as soon as he changed topic it was like starting all over again. Still, Siro couldn't help but grin. How many times had he wanted this man to talk to him as a child? It was strange, but despite the pain in his neck and cheek and the situation he was in, he was happy. They spent hours chatting. They did it in whispers and with an eye set on the corridor to see who was approaching, lest the jailer and the rest of the Beasts that prowled around made them shut up with their blows.

'I'm locked up here until I die, Siro. Memories hurt me. I have long realized that remembering and having dreams only hurts... What is the use of remembering without hope? I've been down here too long... Men aren't made to live in the dark that long,' his gaze faded as he said that. The wrinkles accentuated, like scars, around his eyes. 'Sometimes I wonder if I still am... a man'.

'What else could you be?'

'I don't know anymore...'

Grinat had arrived in Undershell a few days after the attack on Merco, chained to a car and accompanied by a few survivors. The Beasts made them walk day and night, and those who could not bear it, were left to die under the desert sun. They protected the women and children, who went in the cars, but didn't care about the men. No water or food was given to them. The silent guardian was somewhat luckier than the rest, a woman from the village felt sorry for him and shared her food with him when the Beasts didn't look. Most of them died. They wobbled during the day and cried at night. Every time someone asked for water, they were beaten and abandoned.

'Only ten of us made it,' Grinat explained. 'We heard children screaming. There were queueing to get re-branded with a bloody iron. It was horrible. For the men... The Beasts put us in a circle and threw a knife in the middle. They told us there could only be one left.'

Siro gulped. It seemed that the silent guardian aged with each word he spoke.

'Cairu was in that circle. He was tall for his age, but he was only a boy. I didn't start it. Someone went for the knife and then...'

'You don't need to tell me...' Siro said. The last memory he had of Nazeh's brother was from the Night of Fire. Cairu had gone to ring the bell and warn the whole village. If anyone had survived, it was because of him. He ran a hand through the bars to put it on the guardian's shoulder, but the man jerked back.

'All I could think of was that Bartus and Axelai could be there, in that line of children... I wanted to find them, I didn't care about the others. But they weren't there... Maybe they had never been in that queue, I just wanted them to be. When the fight was all over, they chained me up and brought me here. That boy didn't deserve what I did to him, Siro, none... None of them... but I needed to live to find those kids. For weeks I saw the faces, every night... And the anger was so strong that ... I thought it would explode. Now I... I don't feel anything. I've been down here a lifetime...'

Fourteen years locked up, Siro thought. In comparison, all his sufferings and loneliness paled in comparison.

They spent a long time in silence, accompanied by the crackle of the fire from the kettles and the noise of the rats moving from one cell to the other with impunity, until the silent guardian opened his mouth again.

'I think of Zuria and the twins... I loved them, Siro, and now I find it difficult to put a face on them.'

The Beasts... Always the Beasts.

Siro wanted to hit the bars, but it wouldn't have done any good. He wanted to know more about Grinat, but every question he asked made him regret it. There was not the slightest trace of hope in his words, not even a crazy and unreal hope, and that made Siro feel intense vertigo. What awaited him, then? Rotting down there, day after day, until one morning he didn't wake up?

As they spoke, Grinat remembered. The colours returned to his face and even a smile illuminated his face. He spoke of happier days, when the twins were his greatest concern and joy.

'Those children... There was no stopping them... Bartus loved to run through the jungle. He said that he wanted to be as brave as you,' Grinat said. 'And look, he was a disaster, he fell every two steps, but he got up and pushed forward. The other, Axelai, was calmer. He followed his brother, but he had a very different character. Did you know he collected insects?'

'I did,' he remembered the box of larvae and butterflies with sycamore chips. Little Axelai was looking for any excuse to show his collection.

Grinat's tone changed after that. His head had continued to sink into his memories and, from the look on his face, he no longer wanted to continue. He knew that, after the happy memories, came the night when the lights of Merco and the happy faces of Zuria and the twins had disappeared to give way to the flames and screams.

'She was in the river…' said the man. 'Her face… I, I couldn't do anything. I was too late.'

During the Night of Fire, while Eliria, Nazeh, and himself were in the river, he had seen the silent guardian fighting the Beasts. After so many years, Siro finally understood what had happened. Grinat had followed them to the river, which had turned black and crimson with the blood of all the people who had tried to flee that night. Zuria had been one of them.

'It wasn't your fault,' Siro stammered.

'No, it wasn't. We all know whose fault it was.'

Siro raised an eyebrow, not understanding who he was referring to.

'Don't you know anything about that?' Said the silent guardian, in a suspicious tone.

'What do you mean?'

'About Liduvin. You know nothing.'

'I know that…'

'You know her stories. She told them to me too, a long time ago… But you didn't get to know her, not like me.'

'We have time,' Siro snapped. He didn't like the way he talked about Liduvin.

'Indeed,' Grinat nodded regretfully. The two of them were down there, trapped in a dismal, pestilential eternity. He told him what he wanted to know.

'Liduvin and I already knew each other before we fled Undershell. We served in this same palace,' he began.

The first thing that caught his attention was the way she behaved. She was not like the rest of the courtesans Grinat had seen in Dugol's palace. She wanted to look like them and that is why she put on makeup, wore the most daring dresses, the finest fabrics, and the brightest jewellery. She wore perfumes that made men notice her presence long before they saw her, but she couldn't hide it. Not to him. Liduvin was not like the others, she knew things.

All her stories about Teradam —the Children of Light, the Nightborn, the promise of a city where everything was possible— formed a dream in the heart of a being that should never have had any. Grinat was nobody, just a guardian who had taken a vow of silence, as had been the custom in his order for generations. Years later, he still blamed her. She shouldn't have made him dream of impossible things. A silent guardian had to know his place. It was not a bad job after all. He could enjoy the ostentatious decoration of the palace, eat three times a day and have a warm bed where to spend the nights.

'My mistake was choosing her,' Grinat said. He sat on the floor of the cell, and Siro did the same.

Grinat chose Liduvin as his soulmate. The Elector who witnessed his sacred oath as a silent guardian heard his words and thus wrote them down on the scroll of oaths. The order jealously kept that ancient scroll. They only took it out of its leather case for occasions like those. 'Tell me, who shall your soulmate be?' Asked the Elector.

'I still remember that Beast, with his fingernails stained with ink and the feather in his hand...' Grinat shook his head left and right. 'That solemn question… They were actually asking me who would be the only person I could talk to for the rest of my life.'

Soulmate choosing day was one of the most important moments in the life of a silent guardian. It was the step from initiate to bodyguard. From that day he would go on to protect someone and that would be until one of the two, protector or protégé, died. Dugol, then Lord of the Beasts, had personally chosen him, Grinat, as the guardian of Liduvin. At the time, the silent guardian took it as an insult. He was destined to work for a powerful merchant, for an aristocrat, for a warlord or for Dugol himself, not for a courtesan. Why she? He was the best guardian of his generation, and everyone knew it. He did not understand until one day he saw Dugol and Liduvin chatting together. The Lord of the Beasts' gawking expression was more than enough. He loved her. His eyes sparkled when he saw her. He wanted his favourite courtesan to be safe, and when the Dugol wanted one thing, it had to be done.

Grinat accepted to protect Liduvin with his life. 'Are you ready to do your duty?' Had been the first question the Elector had asked him on the day of the oath. He had nodded, without a second thought. 'Who is and will be your soulmate?' He had said, and then he had doubted. Many initiates, especially those who started younger, chose a member of their family as a soulmate, in that way, they maintained family ties and somehow communicated with all friends and acquaintances. It was the most cowardly option and the biggest mistake a future silent guardian could make. After two or three years, all the initiates would have lost contact with the families forever. The instructors had warned them, but not all listened. With the time they were left with no soulmate to talk to and they became taciturn and bitter creatures. Luckily Grinat did not have that option. His family had sold him to work in the mines when he was just a kid, but the foreman who bought him soon lost him in a bet with a fur trader. He had ended up in the palace stables after two exchanges, a murder and a kidnapping when he was only seven years old. He had never seen his family again.

Then there were the ambitious initiates. They always chose to speak to powerful people. There were those who chose Dugol himself or one of his wealthy witches or advisers. It was a good option to prosper and not lack anything.

And finally, there was the most honorable option, but also the hardest: choosing the protégé as a soulmate. Grinat whispered Liduvin's name in the Elector's ear, and those were the last words he would share with the world for many years to come. From that moment on, everything he heard and saw would only be for Liduvin.

'That woman had me fascinated,' the silent guardian murmured. 'And because of that Zuria is dead.'

'But what does Liduvin have to do with all of this?'

'You really don't know, do you?' Why do you think the Beasts went through the hassle to come looking for us, just after the kicked us out?'

'But... I thought they had changed their minds. That's why they closed Undershell gates, right?' Said Siro, remembering the day of the Exile. 'They didn't want us to escape.'

'They didn't want *her* to escape.'

Siro was thoughtful for a moment, starting to connect the dots. It had always seemed very strange to him what had happened that morning at the entrance to Undershell. All the chariots, the animals, the people prepared to face the desert and, suddenly, the slaughter, the chaos, the Beasts that fired their darts mercilessly... If they were really going after Liduvin, everything made more sense. But why did Dugol have to go to such trouble for a courtesan? Was it really because of her stories?

'Do you remember a merchant from the Jade Valley?' Said Grinat.

'Infidas?'

'Yes, he convinced her to do it. I shouldn't have left that night, but... I was worried about the twins and Zuria and I left them chatting after the Council meeting.'

That very night, Siro and Nazeh had climbed the hill of roots upon which the Council House stood and had peered through the skins that covered the tent. Liduvin tried to convince everyone that they should go to Teradam and Firla had scoffed at the idea. At that moment, Infidas intervened. The merchant knew how to make people listen, perhaps it was his voice, or his reputation as a rich man. Either way, he had prevented either of them from making a rash decision.

'He convinced her to do what?' Asked Siro. He needed to know.

'That night when the Beasts attacked us, I was on patrol. I was in the jungle with some men from the village. We saw the fire and then we went back to our houses, to look for our families. When I got to Zuria's house, she had already left with the twins. I went to find you and Liduvin. You weren't there, but she was, with Infidas and four Beasts...'

'What were the Beasts doing there?'

'They worked for Infidas. They were planning to go to Teradam.!

'That doesn't make sense,' Siro protested. 'Why would she do that? And why didn't you go with her?'

'I couldn't. Not without Zuria and the children... And she knew it. She didn't care about us, Siro, not you, not me, not anyone... She just wanted to go to the fucking city of the Children of the Light. That was all she wanted. She started the fire, did you know? She incited Dugol to attack us so she could escape.'

'It's not true!' Siro yelled.

The guards rushed in, followed by the jailer, hearing the commotion.

'Quiet!' It said, accompanying the order with a spit into Siro's cell. 'One more word, Fireface, and you'll jump in the arena with no balls.'

Siro went as far from the bars as he could. His head was boiling with rage. How dared Grinat tell those lies?

When he composed himself, he realized that he had not explained a tiny detail to the silent guardian. He had seen the merchant again on the steps of Adon's palace, when he had arrived at Undershell with Matildet. Infidas hadn't recognized him, but he did. He decided to keep that information to himself.

So, Infidas and Liduvin went to Teradam He thought. *But Infidas is here. And Liduvin... why did she leave without me? It doesn't make sense, Grinat is lying to me... or isn't he?*

His breathing accelerated, he needed rest, water, air, whatever. *But why...? Why did she leave without me?*

Chapter 34: Injustice

'I want you to put on a good show. You, Fireface, the spear!' The jailer finished the sentence with a spit on the ground.

A beam of light crept in from the ceiling and illuminated the fight circle. The reddish columns and statues of wild creatures were surrounded by an eerie gloom. Siro grabbed the double-edged spear from a statue depicting a hooded warrior on his knees. The statue had the weapons resting against its arms sculpted into an arc. The spear was not well balanced, one of the two blades weighed considerably more than the other, and that made it clumsy.

On the other side of the circle, with serene face and clenched muscles, Grinat awaited him. The spears of the two contestants whirled in the air with a hiss. The silent guardian held back. Siro could tell. He pounced on the man with all his strengths, bringing the full weight of the spear down on his adversary and throwing a backward thrust every time he wanted to regain his position —just as Grinat himself had taught him when he was little— but the man was faster and had much more experience. His blows were hard as stones and precise like arrows. It was easy for him to disarm Siro and leave him lying on the ground.

'You're lucky the Quiet is on your side, Fireface!' The jailer yelled at him, looking at everything as he rubbed the nose of the statue of a gigantic snake. 'You alone against Yashar and Vahid wouldn't stand a chance... With him, though... Shit, Quiet, how many years have you been killing legends of the arena?'

Grinat didn't reply.

'You did better this time,' he offered the spear to Siro to get back to his feet. 'Now with the split spears, okay?'

'For all the Nightborns, he talks!' said the jailer, who didn't even seem upset that he had ignored him.

Siro wiped his forehead. The Brand on his neck was burning and he was exhausted, but he had to prepare. He spun the spear and parted it in half. Now he had one of the blades in each hand.

Grinat had explained to him many times that the usefulness of this was to join and separate the spear at the right moment to surprise the adversary. The double spear was not intended to stop blows, but to counterattack, wait for the first attack, and then land an unexpected blow.

The spears clashed again. Siro avoided the first blows, but Grinat moved faster and faster, to until his spear became a blur before his eyes. Siro fell to the ground after a spin from the guardian. It was so spectacular that even the jailer clapped.

'Okay, Quiet, you've had enough fun already. Lay down your weapons,' the Beast ordered.

He shot each of them a look. Grinat was standing, calm. Siro was huffing and wiping his sweat.

'I'll say it once, so listen well. Morning. Combat. Two against two… To death. Fireface, maybe you've heard of something called mercy. If you expect the Lord of the Beasts to take pity on you, you must know that isn't a thing… Adon has been coming to the fights for the last four or five years, since Dugol kicked the bucket. Yashar and Vahid are killing machines. Really, Fireface, if you had seen them fight you would be crying in your cell… What a pair of Beasts… You are so lucky to team up with Quiet. This fucker is scarier with a spear in his hands than all the Nightborns put together. Mind you, don't expect him to cover your ass. He never minded going back down the tower alone, did he?'

Grinat was silent. The jailer put a wicked smile.

'How many fights have you been in? C'mon. You don't want me to believe you don't count them, you lying pig, I know you do…'

But the jailer gave up when he saw the silent guardian's lack of interest and faced Siro.

'How many do you think he killed?' He asked the young man.

'I don't know…' he replied as he looked at the scars that covered Grinat's body.

'More than you'll ever see, I tell you.'

He soaked his face in the water from the barrels in the training room. He touched the Brand on his neck and looked at his reflection in the water. It was horrible, it disfigured him up to his cheek. Even when he spoke it hurt. Every time he saw it, he remembered the Adon's cruel face driving the burning iron into his skin. He felt the urge to cry taking over and quickly threw as much water as he could at his face to hide it. 'Why couldn't you come back for me?' Eliria had told him, sobbing. 'I waited for you! I've waited a long time for you!'. Her words were needles in his head. He had left his friend's bed to go rescue the Daughter of the Light, who had decided to enter the palace leaving him behind.

Stupid, he told himself. *How can I be so stupid?*

As he bandaged his hands to avoid hurting himself with the spear, he wondered what his adversaries would be like. The jailer kept repeating that they were real butchers. All day with the same song. He had seen them fight larger groups, taller and stronger mercenaries, better armed and more famous, and they always came out victorious. They were an unbeatable team… and the same couldn't be said for him and Grinat. And the worst thing was knowing that he was the weak point.

The training session ended. They were chained and taken to the cells. The old prisoner rose from time to time and murmured his ravings. Siro found it quite annoying, but luckily, he soon got tired and went back to sleep. He, on the other hand, couldn't try harder. Grinat's words tortured him. He couldn't believe a word of what he had told him about Liduvin. He couldn't believe she had betrayed them. She was not like that.

'Grinat, are you awake? I need to talk to you… The fight is tomorrow.'

'Another day, another fight, you have nothing to worry about,' the answer came from the shadows. The man moved and approached the bars. 'Stay close and fight like we've been practicing. Keep your distance with the opponent and don't take risks. Wounds don't heal well down here, I promise you.'

'What's the point?' Siro asked. 'Why fight if we have no escape?'

'If you're looking for hope, mercenary companies sometimes buy warriors of the arena… But that's not an option for me.'

'Why?'

'Dugol himself decided so. Instead of killing me for helping Liduvin escape the palace, he preferred to lock me up here until I died,' the silent guardian laughed. 'Who would have thought I would survive that bastard? For a moment I thought that Adon would be different, that he would pardon me… But you see, I'm still here. Little

Adon... Like the father, like the son. How could it be otherwise?'

'Adon is a Beast,' Siro mused. 'He is not a Son of the Light, no matter what he says, he can't be... They are not like that. How can people believe him?'

'You have to know that this boy was born from a prophecy, and many still believe it,' Grinat replied.

'Which one?'

'They say that he will open the gates of Teradam for us.'

'That's impossible, isn't it?' Said Siro.

'Does it matter? After so many years... I don't believe that Teradam or the Children of the Light exist.'

If you only knew..., Siro thought, but held back from saying anything.

'In this world there are only men and beasts. And if I think about it... There are only Beasts,' Grinat said.

'That's not true. What about you and me? We are not Beasts.'

'And what is the difference?'

'I am not a Beast. I'm not.'

'I knew you were just like us, wildling,' Ubald's metallic voice echoed inside his head, followed by Matildet's: 'They were men, just like you.'

Siro lowered his head feeling tiny in that cell.

The jailer came, barked some orders, and Siro and Grinat came out of their cells. Side by side, they walked by the rest of the inmates, who beat the bars and shouted to encourage the two fighters. The silent guardian looked more energetic than ever. There was a grin under his thick beard.

'Paint them,' the jailer ordered two child slaves. 'Make them look like adonite soldiers, not the stinking scum they really are.'

Siro knelt so the children could do their work. They painted black lines across his face with soot-stained fingertips. Then they did the same with the chest, arms and back. The boy who painted him breathed heavily. His hands were shaking, especially when they ran over the wound the Biter had given him.

They were given the double-edged spears and two silica knives. No armour, slaves like them had no right to it. Siro would have gladly returned to the cell, but instead he went up with Grinat in the wooden elevator that would take them to the battle tower.

'Do you hear the audience, Fireface? They are up there expecting a good fight. They are the highest aristocracy in palace, so don't embarrass me!' The jailer warned him.

I couldn't care less, Siro thought. The elevator was a wooden box with just enough space for two people. The hunter stood beside Grinat inside that cage. The children closed the door and joined half a dozen other children to pull the giant crank. The elevator came off the ground with a creak. Siro grabbed where he could to avoid stumbling. *Please don't let it fall*, he thought. The murmur of the people grew as they went up. Little by little, they emerged from the dungeon's gloom. They climbed the side of a tower riddled with sharp stakes pointing upwards. In one of them, Siro saw an impaled skull, the stake protruding from its mouth. They climbed higher and higher until, suddenly, the elevator stopped dead. They were suspended in the air, a few meters above the arena. Through the cracks in the door, they could see the audience sitting in bleachers around the fighting tower.

The clamour of the public died down. A black-robed wizard moved through the fight ring, wearing a smiling mask. The wizard addressed the audience, but it was difficult for Siro to understand what it was saying. It pointed to the wooden cage they were locked in, then pointed to an identical one on the other side. *Yashar and Vahid must be there.*

'Do you think we can make it?' He asked his partner, imagining what their adversaries must be like.

Suddenly, Grinat grabbed him by the neck and slammed him against one of the cage walls. The memory of the Night of Fire came to mind, when the silent guardian grabbed him in the same way to show him a piece of Zuria's dress.

'Confess or only one of us will come down,' Grinat said. His arm muscles were tense. A vein stood out in the middle of his forehead.

'What…?' Siro couldn't breathe. 'Why…?'

'I could have saved Zuria…. I could have done it if it hadn't been for you and Liduvin. Confess what you did if you want to live another day. Else, when…'

Siro punched him before he finished speaking. Then he felt a blow to his jaw shook his whole body. The elevator destabilized. The wooden cage swayed with the two men's fight. Screams and blows mingled. Siro lost sight of the spear. There was no place in there to use it. He hit Grinat because the man did the same. His fists fell on him like an avalanche. The man grabbed his hair and slammed his head into the door.

'Confess!' He said between gasps. He had grabbed his arm and was twisting it behind his back.

'Grinat, what are you doing? You're crazy…' said Siro, feeling the blood running down his forehead.

'I've been waiting for this moment for fourteen years… Fourteen years!' He replied. 'Confess at once or I will break your arm and kill you in front of all Undershell!'

'I don't know what you're talking about…'

'Everything you did, your whole plan was useless, don't you see? She betrayed you, and now she must be dead in some hole in the desert. Liduvin is dead… and you will be next if you don't confess,' Grinat said, drew the silica knife and put it in his throat.

With his free hand, Siro felt for the door latch and tugged on it. The elevator door slammed open and the two men plunged into the void.

They fell on the ring with a thud. In pain, Siro crawled across the sandy ground. There was a wound on his neck, like a scratch. He caught a glimpse of the wizard, who was looking at them through the smiling mask, and grabbed on his robe to stand up again. The wizard resisted, until a knife blade sprouted from his neck and fell dead. Siro rolled on the ground. Behind him, Grinat rose like a giant.

The audience of Undershell burst in shouts and applause after a few seconds of initial bewilderment.

'Why…?' Siro said, wheezing.

Grinat ignored him, he was looking for something. Siro saw one of the double-edged spears on the ring. The saw each other's intentions and pounced on the weapon. The hunter was faster, but the silent guardian kicked him in the chest making him fall on his back. As the two men wrestled for the spear, drums thundered, and the second cage opened. Two masked Beasts leapt from within. One of them somersaulted to the ground and, as he stood up, a flame erupted from its mouth. Grinat and Siro rolled on the ground to dodge the flames. Between the fire and the sand, the other Beast launched its attack wielding two glowing swords. One of the blows grazed Siro's back. It felt like thousands of ants devouring him at the same time. Before the Beast could finish him, Grinat seized the spear and charged forward.

'He's mine, Beast!' Grinat snapped over the clamour of the crowd. He turned to Siro. 'You don't move. You will confess!'

The Beast recoiled, overwhelmed by the silent guardian's attack, but then, with a rehearsed move, the second Beast leapt over the first and spread another flare towards Grinat's face. The silent guardian threw himself to the ground in time to avoid the flames. But the Beasts did not relent in their attack.

If they kill him... I'm dead too, realised Siro and launched himself into the middle of the fight to face the flame-spitting Beast. Seeing that their adversaries fought like lions, the two mercenaries withdrew to the other end of the ring. They wore dark colours, boiled leather armour and protections with the effigy of terrifying beings on their arms. The two Beasts removed the masks they wore and revealed their youthful faces.

'If we leave them alone, they'll do the job for us,' said the two-swords Beast, amused by the situation.

'Vahid, give me more magic. I can't focus. Voices won't shut,' said the Flame-spitting Beast.

'Don't finish it,' said Vahid. He reached into his pocket and pulled out a handful of white powder.

The Flame-spitting Beast buried its face in the hand of its comrade-in-arms and raised it back up with a whitish nose. His eye pupils were dilated, and a crazy grin filled his face. He grabbed a skin from his belt and bit off the cork. The Beast wore a black tube threaded into its right arm. A small flame wavered on the metal tip of the tube. He spat out some of the liquid in his mouth through the flame, and a cloud of fire lit up the ring.

'Great Adon! Noble folk of Undershell!' Vahid proclaimed, one of his swords pointed skyward. 'We are Yashar and Vahid, champions of the eastern desert. These deaths will be in your honour!' The Lord of the Beasts sat in the audience, on a luxurious throne, surrounded by advisers and courtesans. The Daughter of the Light was at his side and watched the show, covering her mouth with her hands. Matildet seemed okay. The girl turned her head to speak to Adon, but the young Beastmaster didn't listen. He returned the mercenary's salute, and then the Beast lowered its sword.

'Grinat, we must fight together, or they'll kill us. I don't know what you think I've done, but now we must be united... They're dangerous,' Siro said. 'Whatever it is, leave it behind, or we won't get out of... Grinat, you hear me!?'

The silent guardian had dropped the spear to the ground. He was crying.

'Bartus, Axelai... is it you?' The silent guardian sobbed.

'What did you say, slave?' Vahid snapped, blades clashing as he approached.

'It's me, it's Grinat, don't you recognize me?' The man said as he pitifully crawled toward the Beasts.

I can't believe it... it's them, Siro thought. With the tension of the moment, he had not recognized them, but they had the same face as when they were little, they looked just like Zuria. *What were they doing here?*

'Shut up and die, slave,' was Vahid's reply.

The Beast approached Grinat with swords in cross position, ready to behead him. Siro picked up the spear and stepped in between the two. Vahid didn't push back. It lunged at him with all its might, swords drawing bright arcs that the hunter deflected as best he could. Yashar took a sip from the skin and again spit out a blinding bolt of flames.

'It's me, Siro!' He yelled at them, trying to get them to react. 'Axelai, Bartus, it's me!'

But the Beasts continued their attack. Yashar spat his fire on Vahid's swords. The flames engulfed the steel blades. The audience applauded the diabolical spectacle offered by the two mercenaries.

Siro fell back with each blow, until he realized that the ring was getting narrower. A fall into the stake pit awaited him behind him. He tried a daring manoeuvre, split the spear in two and counterattacked as he turned around. One of Vahid's blades span in the air and plunged into the void. The sword sounded in the background as it bounced off the tower stakes.

'My fingers! My fingers!' The Beast screamed.

He had severed two of the Beast's fingers. He was about to kick it off the tower, but he thought that Beast was Axelai, and that held him. Yashar intervened. A cloud of flames followed him everywhere. Siro moved quickly to avoid the tongues of fire. The Beast was cunning, and it knew how to keep him at bay, far enough that he couldn't reach him with the spear.

He is trying to make me fall the other way, realized Siro, who was seeing again how the ring was getting narrower.

Yashar raised the skin to his lips, and Siro saw his chance. He grabbed the silica knife and threw it into the face of his adversary, who protected himself with the first thing it found. Now the skin was leaking, no matter how hard the Beast tried to. Siro hit him it in its stomach. Yashar fell to its knees with a grunt. The hunter put one of the spear tips under its chin.

'Let my brother go, slave,' Vahid had the blade of the sword against Grinat's throat.

Yashar jerked to try to get away, but Siro wouldn't let it. He pressed the tip of the spear closer against the skin. *It's Bartus*, he thought. *This Beast is little Bartus*. The contenders shouted at each other and threatened to kill their respective teammates. The hunter wouldn't budge, but would he really be able to? Would he kill Bartus if Axelai killed Grinat?

I can't..., he thought. *Please let him go, please...*

Undershell's folk grew impatient. Their blood-thirsty screams echoed throughout the grandstand. 'Kill him!' They bellowed, 'Kill him!'

'Do it, Vahid,' said Bartus, though Siro's spear was drawing blood on its throat. 'We are the heroes of the arena... we don't negotiate, and we don't give up. Kill them for me.'

'Don't!' Siro shouted. 'He's your father! He took care of you when you were little! He took care of your mother! He loved you!'

'Slave, you make me sick...' Bartus told him, struggling to free himself from Siro's arm. 'If you don't do it, I will.'

The Beast showed him the flame coming out of its right-arm tube and lowered it to the ground, where the flammable liquid had spilled. Siro grabbed its arm, but all he did was break the tube causing a deflagration. He rolled on the ground until he felt it disappear under his body and grabbed just at the edge of the ring. His body swayed on the void. He could hear the clamour of the crowd, the applause, the desperate cries of Bartus and the approaching heat. He looked up and saw a curtain of flames. A black silhouette loomed before him. Flames engulfed it; the eyes seemed about to pop out of their sockets. It looked at him for a second, and then Bartus fell over him, surrounded by fire. A slimy noise followed the fall, like a piece of meat bursting.

Hang on, don't let go, Siro told himself, looking for the strength to return to the ring. He expected to see Grinat dead when he poked his head out but saw a bright light instead.

Matildet was at the centre of the ring. Her dress glowed and made her face dim. The audience was speechless. Axelai had dropped the swords to the ground. His face looked like that of a child under the glare of the Daughter of the Light. Grinat moved his mouth at his side, recited a prayer:

'To those who have been born from destruction and hatred, I give you this world. Forgive us and live.'

'Enough,' Matildet said. She looked at all of them. 'This is over.'

Chapter 35: Those who hate us

'I must look for Liduvin... Pathetic son of a bitch. You were too busy, weren't you? Our mother asked for your help and you left... Do you think I don't remember? What about you, Grinat? As quiet as ever... Did you also have to go find Liduvin? That bitch... I hope the Beasts had fun with her...'

Axelai paused to catch his breath. Siro knew the boy was only provoking him. It was the logical next step after the hours he had spent blaming him for his brother's death... and for his severed fingers. He would no longer brandish the sword as before, nor would people look at him the same way. He would no longer be the formidable warrior he had been until this morning, but one more cripple lost in Undershell.

I don't want to think about it anymore, I don't want to...

'She just wanted you to watch her children while she helped deliver supplies, was it so hard for you to help out?' Axelai scolded him. 'If you had, she would not have known that the women and children were fleeing down the river and we would not have been ambushed... They were waiting for us, Siro, the Beasts were waiting for us all. They beat her to death in front of us. We tried to get her out of the river afterwards, but you know, Yashar and I were little, how were we going to move her? Could you have gotten Liduvin out, huh? Tell me!'

Siro remained silent.

Nothing he said could improve the situation... or make it worse. All three —Grinat, Axelai, and Siro— were locked in a gloomy cell, each chained by the neck and hands to one of the walls. The shackles forced them to stand and wounded their wrists, but that did not matter to the hunter. Over and over he heard Bartus' body crashing into the bottom of the pit.

'You are like us, wildling,' Ubald's voice reminded him, accompanied by a metallic echo.

'You were in such a hurry that night...' Axelai insisted

and suddenly burst out in laughter. The chains shook with every movement. 'I'm sure you haven't thought of us in all these years. Surely not... What happened to those two twins I abandoned? No, we sure haven't taken a single night of sleep from you. Who knows where you've been... Because I'm sure you didn't find her, huh? You didn't find Liduvin, am I wrong? You went looking for her and she was already dead? Or was she kidnapped...? Or perhaps...'

Axelai smiled. Siro looked away, but it was too late. He knew.

'No... It was much worse. She left without you... Yes, that's right. You had to meet somewhere and she did not show up, that's it, right? I knew it! I knew it! She left without her little boy... And without her dear protector, huh, Grinat? Did she abandon you both? What a nasty bitch...'

'I'm sorry that Bartus died,' Siro interrupted him.

'Don't call him by his wildling name, have respect!' Axelai snapped. 'His name was Yashar, and my name is Vahid, so...'

'I'm sorry he died... and not you,' he finished. 'I had always liked him better, at least he didn't walk around Merco with a box of insects like a retard.'

Axelai screamed in rage and yanked on the chains. That only served to bump his head against the wall and get even angrier. He was back to threats and insults.

Siro knew he had been mean, but he was fed up. Axelai had become a true Beast and he did not think there was any other way to deal with these beings other than harshly. 'What have they done to make him like that?' He had wondered at first, but now he didn't care.

He was looking at the latticework of the ceiling and the shadows of the rats that paced the rafters, oblivious to everything. He was thinking of Matildet, how she had jumped into the middle of the battle ring to stop everything. She had done it to save him, once again, but now he was impatient to know what would happen. How long would they keep them locked up down there?

When the Daughter of the Light had jumped, the audience had gone silent. They all looked at her illuminated body. Even Siro, who had seen her before, was speechless. Adon had risen from his throne with his hand up. That solemn gesture had been enough for Axelai to drop his swords to the ground and kneel despite his desire to kill Siro and Grinat. The former silent guardian had also dropped to his knees, and Siro had played along, not very convinced.

Adon had taken advantage of the general confusion to introduce Matildet:

'People of Undershell...' the Lord of the Beasts had proclaimed. Behold Matildet, Daughter of the Light, the sister I have been waiting for so long,' then he had turned to the Daughter of the Light. 'Why do you interrupt the fight, sister? Is it not to your liking?'

Matildet had looked around her. She was afraid. Perhaps the rest of the Beasts did not know, but Siro saw it in the way she bit her lip.

Say something..., wished the hunter.

'I accept the deal!' Matildet had shouted. 'Pardon my protector... and the other warriors,' she added, pointing at Siro. 'Stop the fight and I'll fulfil what I have promised.'

Whispering spread among the audience. The nobles of Undershell were disgusted with the interruption.

They're just Beasts, after all, Siro thought. *It doesn't matter if they are rich or poor, they just want blood.*

Adon grinned. He muttered something in the ear of one of the wizards and then the fighting area was crowded with guards. They surrounded them and captured all three. Axelai protested, Grinat let them do and Siro looked at Matildet without understanding what she was trying to achieve. They had been taken away and locked in this grey cell. The hours had passed and the only visitors they had were rats.

Axelai was spitting death threats. Siro would have done the same in his place.

'Axleai, stop it,' Grinat said suddenly. He had been deep in thought for hours. 'It's not his fault.'

Now he defends me? Siro was surprised. He had tried to kill him while they were inside that damn wooden elevator. *So many years in this dungeon have dried up his brain*, he thought.

'And since when do you speak?' The mercenary snapped. 'Stay out of it. You have no right to say anything after how you left us...'

'I went looking for you and Bartus, but I didn't find you...' continued the silent guardian.

'Bullshit! You went looking for Liduvin. You didn't care about us,' Axelai scolded him. Siro noticed that the boy couldn't even look his stepfather in the eye.

'Liduvin made me fall into a trap… When I found Zuria, she…'

'Bullshit! You never care about us, never! We were not your children. We were the children of a Beast, the whole fucking world said so! Why would you care? You tell nothing but lies! Why are you alive, Grinat, why couldn't you die like everyone else? You are a pathetic and sad being. Look at you! Who are you? Nobody remembers the strongest man in Merco, you are but a walking corpse… How dare you mention my mother's name after having abandoned us? How?!'

'You don't know what you're talking about,' Siro intervened, not quite sure why he was doing it. 'Grinat tells the truth. He was looking for your mother. You were much more important to him than Liduvin… and me. In the battle tower he couldn't raise his spear against you. He'd rather die than…'

'You shut up!' Said the mercenary. His eyes had filled with tears. His neck was injured from the chains, and his face was flushed with rage.

I wanted Grinat to care about me, but he only had eyes for you two, Siro thought. But he swallowed those words, he would not give him the pleasure of hearing them. Axelai had stopped being a boy who collected insects to become a Beast. He didn't even deserve the air he breathed, and even so, the silent guardian would have died for him. Just thinking about it made him want to strangle him.

'Don't hold a grudge against him,' Grinat said. 'Bartus has died in combat. He knew it could happen. All of us who fight in the arena know what can happen when we get up there. Don't seek revenge because it will consume you, just as it has done to me.'

'Who do you think you are? Shut the fuck up!' Axelai burst out, sobbing. 'You are nothing but ghosts! You should be dead! Why are you here? You've killed Yashar! You killed him and he was all I had…'

Siro felt sorry for him. Beneath his aggressive appearance, the Brands and the dark clothes, there was only a nineteen-year-old man who had just lost his brother.

'Fireface, Silent… Do you always have to do whatever the fuck you want?' The jailer appeared on the other side of the bars.

The Beast was followed by six guards, all armed with swords and bearing the Brand of the Lord of the Beasts on their shoulders.

He took out a bunch of keys and unlocked the cell.

'Free the mercenary,' the jailer ordered. Then he turned to Siro and Grinat. 'You had one fucking job, to fight Yashar and Vahid, not each other! Are you stupid? By all the Nightborn, it doesn't matter anymore... You are free too. Orders from Master Adon. Get out of my dungeon.'

The guards removed Axelai's chains. The boy did not think twice and launched himself on Siro. He rammed his head against the wall and raised his fist to strike him, but before he could do anything else, he had two swords pointed at his neck.

'Not that I personally care, but the Daughter of the Light wants him alive. Get out,' the jailer told him, while the guards held the young man at bay.

'You're lucky, as always,' the mercenary told the hunter. His cheeks were red from tears.

Siro saw the world blurred because of the blow. He really wished not to see Axelai ever again.

The guards released them all and escorted them down the long corridor. The old man who was humming in his cell gave them a blank stare before continuing with his walks and nonsense words.

'I want to see Ahr right away,' Axelai demanded as he was led by two guards.

'Well, good luck,' the jailer replied as he searched for the key to exit the dungeon. 'The Bloodseekers have got the fuck out of Undershell.'

'They what? My company? You're wrong, they...'

'They left. To the east. As soon as the fight was over,' he replied.

'You lie! Ahr knows that I am the best warrior he has...'

'You may be, but there are lots of kick-ass swordsmen. Yashar gave more of a show with the flames and all, and now it is a piece of meat that we have to collect from the moat... My condolences, by the way,' the jailer replied. 'Blame Fireface. He knows how to put up a fight when he feels like it.'

Thanks for making it worse, Siro thought. Axelai glared at the hunter. He would never forgive him.

They were taken out of the dungeon and placed in a wide courtyard, inside the palace walls. Siro recognized the place; it was the same place from where they had entered with Matildet the day they had arrived at Undershell. It was late afternoon and the sun was about to disappear over the horizon, beyond the Cross and the windmills that jutted from the roofs of the houses.

The palace doors were wide open. Adon and Matildet watched the prisoners from the top of the stairs, accompanied by the usual entourage of wizards, advisers, and Beasts bodyguards. The Daughter of the Light had donned a grey robe made of vast cloth. Her golden hair was hidden by a wide hood. The girl ran down the steps.

'Siro, how nice to see you!' She said. 'Are you ok? What is this...?'

Matildet pointed to the horrible Brand that Adon had burned on his neck. The hunter didn't feel like talking about it, not while the Lord of the Beasts was watching.

'What happens now?' Siro asked to change subject.

Junal and Guido then appeared and headed towards them. The small Beast had been groomed further since the last time they had seen each other. Guido, by his side, looked at the Daughter of the Light and the hunter with arms crossed.

'Miss Daughter of the Light,' Junal said. 'First of all, thank you for your visit. I hope you have enjoyed your stay at the palace...'

'Enjoy?' Guido interrupted. 'She's had to jump in the middle of the arena to stop a fight, and endure Adon's long hands, do you really think that...?'

'Would you shut up?!' Junal raged. 'Do you always have to do the same? Can't you see that nobody cares what you have to say, you disgusting worm?'

Guido grunted, but then dropped the subject. Junal cleared his throat and regained the flattering tone he always used with Matildet.

'I just wanted to remind you that you have a sacred pact with your brother, Adon, Son of the Light and lord of Undershell. We hope you will do your part and will not be tempted to leave town early. Master Adon would hate to have to take action against you or the wildling who always accompanies you... of course, he is no longer a wildling, from what I see,' Junal said sarcastically, seeing the Siro's Brand.

'Obvious, always obvious,' Guido said quietly.

'Why do you say that, Guido?!' Junal snapped. 'Can't you shut up for a second?!'

'If you leave without doing your part, we will kill the wildling,' Guido explained. 'No need to beat around the bush, Junal... The Daughter of the Light already knows.'

'Duly noted,' said Matildet. 'And fear not. I have made a promise and I plan to keep it. Let's go, Siro.'

The hunter followed the Daughter of the Light through the wall. He noticed the Lord of the Beasts' gaze on the back of his neck as he walked through the courtyard. The Beasts patrolling the wall watched them as they left that place.

Once they were far enough from Adon's palace, Siro breathed easy. They were going in the direction of the houses, towards the Cross. He did not know what to say, he had mixed feelings inside. On the one hand, he did not know what Matildet and Adon were up to. Why did she not tell him she was coming to Undershell to see her brother? He felt used. Although, on the other hand, she had saved him from certain death in the arena.

'We're in deep shit, Siro,' Matildet said. With the costume she wore, she looked like a slave. 'I've made a deal with that psychopath.'

'Why?' Asked the hunter. 'What does he want?'

'He has left me no choice. It is the only way to show that I am a *Daughter of the Light*, as you say around here. Funny, don't you think?' She laughed and then rubbed her temples.

The two of them halted to speak calmly. Matildet put her hands to her head and tugged the hair that was sticking out of the hood. *What's the matter with her?* Siro asked himself. There were many things he wanted to know, although the first thing that crossed his mind had nothing to do with the deal she had made with Adon.

'Are you good?' Siro asked him.

'What?'

'Are you hurt? The Beasts... Did they...?'

Matildet relaxed for a moment and smiled again.

'Siro, you are amazing. You have spent four days in a dungeon, they have branded you and those lunatics almost killed you in the arena... And you ask me if I'm okay? What were you doing that night spying through Adon's window?'

'I...'

'You're going a bit too far to see Liduvin again, don't you think?'

Siro didn't know what to answer. They stared at each other. Matildet was biting her lip. She was so close that he couldn't help but remember that distant day when they had kissed, by the pond. A tingling in his stomach. He wanted to grab the Daughter of the Light, pull her against him, and show her how much he wanted her. She took a step forward. *She wants it too*, he thought, with a certainty he had rarely felt. *Does she want me to kiss you now?* He was about to, but he saw a figure approaching them.

The silent guardian examined Matildet from head to toe before opening his mouth.

'I don't know if you are a Daughter of the Light or not, but many in this city will think so,' Grinat said. 'You do well disguising yourself.'

'Thank you,' the girl replied. 'I've seen you in the arena before. Are you...?'

'My name is Grinat,' he introduced himself.

'Grinat?' Matildet said. 'Really? Siro, is he the same man who...?'

'Yes,' said the hunter. 'What do you want?'

'I'm going east,' said the silent guardian. 'Now that I am free, I can go wherever I want. I won't stay here, not in this city. I will go east and search for the Bindagi. I hope they accept me in their tribe.'

'I don't know who these Bindagi are, but you could come with us,' Matildet suggested, breaking the awkward silence between the two men. 'The more we are...'

'You could stay with us,' Siro repeated, but he knew that if the silent guardian had decided to leave, there was little to say.

'I have a promise to keep,' Grinat said. 'A promise I made to Zuria.'

'Does it have to do with Axelai?' Siro asked.

'I talked to him when we were in the parade ground. I've convinced him to forget the idea of taking revenge on you... deep down he knows that Bartus' death is not your fault... And I, I know it too...' There was a note of spite in every word he spoke. Grinat had loved Bartús, despite the Beast he had become.

'And where is he now?' Siro said, he was worried that Axelai would change his mind and come back to take revenge.

'He has gone east, in search of Ahr and the Bloodseekers. He will try to find them and have him reinstated... but I will not allow him to be a Beast again. He needs someone to take care of him.'

I needed someone too, thought Siro, lowering his head.

'Yeah…' he said. 'It will not be easy. He hates us.'

'I have a lifetime to make him change his mind,' Grinat told him. He smiled for a moment and a row of blackened teeth cut through his lips.

Before saying goodbye, Grinat wanted to speak privately with Siro. Matildet backed away a few steps. When he was far enough away, the guardian spoke again.

'If you want to follow the Daughter of the Light, I understand, but don't expect to find Liduvin. If that night she left with Infidas and not with us, it was for a reason. And perhaps it is better. I'm sorry about what happened before, in combat, I… I went crazy, but what you did that night was… I can't forgive you, but I have to, because, thanks to you, I'm still alive, and… I have a reason to live. I forgive you, Siro.'

What do you forgive me for? He did not understand. When Grinat had attacked him in the wooden elevator, he wanted him to confess something, but what?

'I don't know why you're mad at me. I don't know what you think I've done. A lot happened that night. The Beasts attacked us and I just wanted to go back to Liduvin…'

The silent guardian's green eyes became two narrow lines.

'Goodbye, Siro. Beware. Undershell is not safe,' he said as he left.

The man disappeared in the direction of the Great Shell, which glowed orange with the last lights of the day. The man's cloak billowed over his broad back. Siro watched him. Their reunion had been fleeting and intense, and now he didn't think he would ever see him again. The moment he turned his head away, the man he had always admired would once again disappear from his life.

'Siro, I can't believe he was Grinat. It's incredible that you have met…' Matildet said, when he walked by her.

The hunter didn't stop, he continued towards the Cross.

'Hey, what's the matter, are you okay?' The Daughter of the Light followed him.

Don't think about it, he told himself. *Don't.*

'Siro, wait!'

The streets were still busy at that time. Slaves carried sacks from side to side, mule drivers yelled at each other for the animals to listen to them, and some idle Beasts laughed and talked about going to see someone in The Mouth. Undershell, the white houses crowned by windmills and the mixture of bittersweet smells of people and animals surrounded Siro. He walked aimlessly, guided by the same thoughts that he wanted to escape from and could not.

'Hey, stop!' The Daughter of the Light grabbed him by the arm. 'What's wrong? Siro, don't... why are you crying?'

'What do you want me to confess...?' He stammered.

The Daughter of the Light raised his face, taking him by the cheeks.

'Siro, we have to get out of here. Everybody is looking at us.'

Chapter 36: Hunters

When he was little, Siro was not aware of how dangerous Undershell was. He played in the marketplace or in the alleys behind the white houses with boys and girls whose faces and names had already been erased by time. He knew he didn't have to disturb the Beasts, or the merchants, or take anything that was not his. And he knew that if he followed the rules everything would be fine.

With adult eyes, everything changed. It was hard not to see the things that were wrong. It was dusk in Undershell, but you could still hear the hammering of the artisans and the noise of the chains of the slaves who, tied to each other, paraded through the streets in a resigned silence. Very few people moved freely amid this tumult. Most were aristocrats or errand boys, or sturdy porters working for merchants who had just arrived in town. It was difficult to see women, most of them covered themselves and hid their figure, especially when they passed before the hungry eyes of the Beasts.

Matildet was by his side, covered with the cloak, hiding her blond hair and her shiny dress.

'Siro, I think there is someone in that alley who needs help,' said the Daughter of the Light.

But the hunter didn't even look. He knew it was a trap. No one in its right mind showed weakness in Undershell.

It was difficult for him to take his eyes off the Brands that the slaves had engraved on the napes, cheeks, arms... The Beasts' guilds were ingenious when it came to branding their workmanship. They didn't want anyone to take someone who belonged to them. *Now I am one of them*, Siro thought, aware of the symbol that went from neck to cheek. He tried not to think about it. Every time he did, he saw Adon smelling the branding iron.

'Are you better?' Asked the Daughter of the Light.

Not as long as we stay in this city, he thought. They had stopped in traffic. A cart had plunged one of the wheels into a puddle in the middle of the muddy street and all the goods on it had fallen to the ground. Some slaves collected what had fallen, others stole secretly, and the Beasts prowled around them, drinking, and laughing at the merchant's misfortune.

There are more and more, he thought. It was time to leave.

A flight of wooden stairs led to the first floor of a gallery which Siro remembered having seen when he was little. Up there were shops selling steaming dishes, pottery, and exotic dresses. The gallery was lined with narrow doors that led to tiny houses where slaves lived crammed together. Most shops had just lit torches in front of their doors with the intention of attracting the last customers of the day. From there, they had a magnificent view of Undershell. One could even see the marketplace, with all its bright colours and lights, in the middle of the Cross.

'Hey, Siro, really, stop, I need to breathe,' the Daughter of the Light told him.

They halted on a narrow terrace, overlooking one of the last wells along Undershell. A flag with the cross and the vertical line symbol fluttered above their heads.

'You lived here when you were little, then?' Matildet asked. She wanted to chat, but he didn't. 'What's gotten into you before? I need to know you are fine…'

Siro hesitated for a few seconds.

'Grinat thinks I did something terrible, but I don't remember,' he said, as he felt the wound on his neck.

'What?' She exclaimed. 'When I saw him outside the palace, I didn't know if he was friend or foe. I saw you when you jumped into the arena… He was going for you, didn't he?'

Siro nodded. He told him about the Night of Fire, when the Beasts had attacked Merco and he and Grinat had met.

'He was looking for Zuria and the twins… I was trying to get to Liduvin. The Beasts killed his wife. The twins… Just today, one of them died because of me.'

Matildet pieced things together at once. She put her hands to her lips. She asked him four more questions and then dropped the subject, disgusted.

'I should have stepped in earlier,' the girl added. 'But I was paralyzed, I couldn't believe that Adon had led me to see that…'

'What have you promised him?'

Matildet took a few steps up and down the terrace.

'Adon is having troublse supplying the city. The population doesn't stop growing and his explorers bring him groups of slaves from all over. The city prospers... in its own way, and it turns out that more and more merchants are coming. They are running out of space. They need to expand, to the east.'

'There's the Great Shell to the east.'

'I hadn't realized...' Matildet said sarcastically. It was hard not to see that relic. 'But the Great Shell has holes in it. They can go under it. The problem comes after.'

'What about it?'

'There is a gorge. Adon says the soil is good and there is enough shade so that crops don't dry out. Also, it would serve as a way to contact nomadic tribes and to go to the... Jade Valley, he said? I'm not sure, but it doesn't matter. The problem is that the gorge is uninhabitable because of Mother Snake.'

'The Mother Snake?' Siro repeated.

'Yes, it happens to run by the gorge. Every twelve moons, according to his wizards,' he said, remembering.

'And what does he want from us?'

'He wants us to hunt her down.'

Siro's eyes went wide. He shook his head. The Mother Snake? Hunt it? No way. Even from afar, when he saw her running beyond the ravines to the north, she looked giant. And that's not to say it was the work of the Nightborns!

'Why do you want to help him?' Siro got angry. He didn't understand why they got into that mess.

'Well, now you're going to laugh... It turns out that *I* have to prove to *him* that I am a true Daughter of the Light, and that I am not deceiving him.'

'But you are!'

'Look, Siro, Adon is a madman... But he is powerful, and it is in our best interest to have him on our side. Without his help, I can't bring all these people to Teradam.'

That was the last thing he needed to hear.

'All these people? Do you want to lead the Beasts to Teradam?'

'They deserve a better life, just like everyone... Just like you,' she said. She tried to take him by the hands, but he pulled away.

'They're not like us,' he told her, pointing to his Brand. 'They are Beasts!'

'And what do you expect them to be, if they haven't known another life, Siro? Your hands aren't clean, and neither are mine! Things can't go on like this. What awaits all these people if they are led by psychopaths like Adon? He's only seventeen and already a remorseless sadist! I don't want this future for anyone. If they come to Teradam...'

They will destroy it, the hunter thought, but decided to keep it to himself. Right now, they had bigger problems, like the Mother Snake.

'Do you think we can handle her?' He asked after a few moments of silence.

'I have an idea... But I'll tell you about it later,' replied the Daughter of the Light. 'Where are we going now? We can't spend the night on the street.'

'Follow me,' Siro said.

The atmosphere was very different from the one in the morning, much more decadent. A few musicians were playing extravagant brass instruments in the marketplace, watched over by a Beast with its arms filled with red tattoos. They were chained to each other by the neck, and the few aristocrats and merchants out there threw some copper coins at them. The Beasts lived it in a very different way, they danced with the slave girls, tore their clothes and put their hands on them, they ate, drank and laughed and, from time to time, they shot darts with blowguns to try to tear the instruments from the hands of the musicians. Siro wanted to avoid them at all costs.

The Mouth, dark at that hour, loomed in front of the two. Torchlight crept out of the natural windows in the rock. In there the Beasts didn't sleep, for them the fun had just begun again. The Mouth had a gloomy aspect, as if it were a living entity, feeding on all the depravity of which the beings that inhabited it were capable of. It got bigger and stronger with each person that entered. Matildet was looking at the entrance, with a worried expression; Siro, on the other hand, had his eyes lost in one of the alleys that led to the market. The last time he had passed through there fleeing from the Beasts he had not seen it, because it was covered by the auctions platform, with those giant amphoras full of stuffed olives, but now that they had taken it apart, he could see it perfectly. He recognized it, he had walked that alley many times... when his mother sent him to the market.

At the end of this street is my parents' house. What if they still live there? He wondered, but immediately answered himself: *What does it matter?*

'Siro, those drunkards won't take their eyes off me, can we move, please?' Matildet said. 'What are you looking at?'

'Nothing,' he replied. And the two of them got inside The Mouth.

Chapter 37: With the Beasts

The inside of The Mouth was as lively as ever. The Beasts drank Ardent next to the torches the slaves had lit up throughout the galleries. The bronze and iron of the columns gleamed. The shadows of the people casted sinister shapes against the stone ceilings and statues that witnessed the frenzy, the leering stares, the rush, the fights, and the raucous laughter.

Matildet didn't leave Siro's side for a moment. Both walked the cobbled paths that were familiar to him.

Undershell glowed lower down, through windows carved into the rock walls. One could still hear the murmur of the windmills turning, slowly, on top of the houses.

'Is it here? Did we arrive?' Matildet asked him.

Siro nodded. Before knocking on the door, the Daughter of the Light put a hand on his shoulder.

'Wait, Siro, before we go in,' the girl looked around uneasily. There was no one in that section of the gallery, but there were close echoes. 'I know you don't agree with all this. Maybe it wasn't what you expected from me… but collaborating with Adon is the only way to help these people. You understand it, right?'

'You decide who enters Teradam,' he said.

'Yeah… I guess, but I don't want you to think that I don't consider everything you've done for me. We have been through a lot together. Do you remember the days we spent in the oasis, or when we were in that lagoon? When I heard the noise of the drills I ran like the wind…' said the girl, with some nostalgia. 'Do you remember the storm, when we were in the desert?'

'I remember.'

'I was scared to death, and you took my hand and told me to close my eyes, that we still had a long way to go… And you were still talking like… Well, you were trying very hard,' Matildet joked. 'Sorry, what I wanted to say is that, at that moment, you know what I thought?'

'No,' Siro replied.

'Well, that we were going to die... And you were telling me all that so that I would stop crying, but that you cared enough to tell me. When I left Teradam, I did not know who I would meet. I was scared, you know. And now... I'm glad it was you, Siro.'

The two stared at each other's eyes. The hunter was speechless. She put her hand on his cheek, stroked his beard, and lowered her hand to the Brand that now disfigured him.

'When the storm was about to hit us, I also thought I wanted to kiss you, just at that moment, and I don't know why I didn't...' she said, with a shy note in her words, but getting closer and closer to the hunter.

He went to meet her lips, but the door was suddenly opened.

'Siro!' Eliria threw herself into his arms without giving him time to react. 'Where have you been? Are you ok? What happened to your face? I was very...'

'Eliria, this is Matildet,' Siro mouthed, her friend hugging him. 'She is...'

'The Daughter of the Light!' Said his friend.

Matildet didn't know which way to turn. Eliria stumbled over her own words. Siro was silent and watched, his cheeks flushed.

'So you are Siro's friend?' She said. 'You two used to play in the jungle together and stuff, right?'

'I am,' Eliria said. Her voice was choppy with the excitement of the moment. She did not know how to behave in front of a divinity.

'He has told me a lot about you... Well, not *a lot*. This man isn't that kind that talk your ears off, is he? I didn't know you were still in touch, how is that...? You and him... I don't know, it seems that you have seen each other recently, right?'

Siro and Eliria began to speak at the same time and it was impossible to understand anything. Many things had happened, and the hunter had been so careful to avoid the Beasts, that he had forgotten to say anything about Eliria or where they were going.

'We have met again by chance,' his friend summed up. 'Please come in so we can talk. It's not safe outside.'

The house was quiet. On the table were a lit candle, food stains, and carved wood animal figurines. Eliria invited them to sit and asked them if they wanted something to eat while she went to the kitchen, from which a delicious smell of broth came out.

'You haven't wasted your time…' Matildet snapped, shaking her head towards the kitchen.

'I was fleeing from the Beasts and we met…' Siro explained, although he didn't even know why he was doing that.

'She's pretty… and I don't know why, but I think she likes you.'

Siro looked down. Matildet had folded her arms and was looking inside the house with a sour face.

'Mommy!' Ranzeh entered the dining room. 'I'm hungry! I know this because my belly hurts, and my belly only hurts when I'm hungry… Oh, hi, Siro! And who are you?'

'My name is Matildet,' the girl said in an affable tone. Her expression had suddenly changed. 'Who are you, little one?'

'I'm Ranzeh, and I'm not small, I'm already a big boy,' the kid's eyes were fixed on Matildet's blond hair. 'Are you the Daughter of the Light?'

'So it seems,' she said, and winked at him.

'Siro told me a story about the Children of the Light, that's why I know that you are a Daughter of the Light. Will you tell me another story, Siro? Where have you been?'

'I… I had gone to find Matildet.'

'Was she lost?'

'I was worried…' he said.

Matildet smiled at the answer he had given the boy. Ranzeh started recounting everything he had done that day without anyone asking him. After accompanying Meres' father to the marketplace, he had had to go to the Palace of Dreams to bring all the goods that his mother's friends asked him to do: perfumes, cosmetics, something to eat… Until the afternoon he hadn't had time to go play, and then he hadn't found Segis anywhere.

'I've been looking for him until the third night's horn sounded and then I had to go back and I got really bored… I can only play with the figurines, and playing alone is a bummer,' the boy told him.

'Don't you have little siblings?' Matildet asked him.

The boy said no.

'Same as me,' she explained. 'I always had to play alone.'

Eliria appeared with two steaming bowls in her hands. Siro got up to help her bring whatever was needed. She wouldn't take her eyes off him.

'Thanks for coming back,' she whispered in his ear at one point when he followed her into the kitchen to bring a jug of water. 'We'll talk later.'

Siro felt a bit uncomfortable with Eliria's attention. When he returned, Ranzeh was sitting next to Matildet.

'Sometimes mommy plays with me, but she doesn't have much time. Did your mommy play with you when you were little?' He asked her.

'I don't remember. My mother left us a long time ago. And my father is not one to play with young children.'

'You mean she's dead?' Asked the boy, unashamedly. 'My father is also dead, but I don't remember him because I was very young. Did your mother die when you were little?'

'Ranzeh! These things are not to be asked!' Eliria said, and then apologized to the Daughter of the Light.

'It's okay,' she said.

The four of them dined together, by candlelight, surrounded by the stark, grey decoration that the home offered. As they ate from the steaming bowls, Matildet asked Eliria as much as she could. She shared her story. Siro already knew it or had lived it with her, so he concentrated on the broth. Eliria spoke of the last time they had seen each other, fourteen years ago, when they had separated, and the Beasts had trapped her and Nazeh. She praised Siro every time she opened her mouth: 'If it hadn't been for him...', 'Luckily he helped me...', 'I would have been lost without him...'. She spoke of him as if he were a hero, although Siro did not see himself that way. What the hunter remembered most from that night was the fear. They had hidden and fled. Many others had fallen along the way: Taurus, Firla's first husband, who had died so they could flee; the entire group of Eder's soldiers —Siro remembered the ropes of the Beasts dragging Laonice towards the crater and Asteria fighting by his side—Tersian and the old woman Quela, who had failed to get through the south gate to escape the Beasts; the same for Firla and Jahisel, Zuria...

'... And Debra, don't you forget,' he heard Ubald's voice say to him. He stared at the candle on the table, trying to remove the icy eyes of that woman from his memories. The nightmares of that night had been with him for years and he supposed, although he didn't think he would ever ask, it haunted Eliria too. He knew the nightmare was far from over. It was enough to look around to see it. That was not a home, not a dining room, or anything... it was just the hole in which the Beasts allowed them to live. A hole for the slaves, each with a Brand, a guild and a master.

Eliria kept talking about them. Her face brightened with each word, she rested her hand on the hunter's arm and tried to get him to participate in the conversation with each anecdote, but barely let out a few monosyllables. Matildet had her full attention. She was not at ease; he could see it.

'We became friends because Nazeh insisted on following you...' he heard himself say.

Luckily that was enough to change the subject. They spoke briefly about Ranzeh's father, the time they had spent together, and how lucky they had been to meet again. Eliria had cried every night since the Beasts killed him. Siro had no doubt that his friend had tried hard to make her happy every day. 'We talked about you, we always talked about you,' she had whispered in his ear when they were in bed together, and afterwards they had made love as if it were something that had always been pending between the two of them.

Had she really loved him or had she no other choice? Wondered the hunter, feeling guilty.

'I have much more left than her memories,' Eliria concluded. 'I also have a child who won't sit still!'

Ranzeh ran around the table, blowing up a toy elephant figurine. He was trying to get his new friend to listen to him, but the Daughter of the Light still wanted to know more.

'And how have you managed to meet again?' She asked.

'When you entered Adon's palace, the Beasts chased me,' said Siro. 'They wanted to kill me. I arrived at The Mouth and hid in the Palace of Dreams...'

'I work there...'

Matildet pouted when she saw the girl's hand on the hunter. The young man noticed, although the grimace did not last a second.

'The whole city talks about you two,' Eliria explained. 'Today in the Palace I heard several people talking about what had happened in the battle tower. How a girl had jumped on the arena during the duel. Instead of condemning her, the Lord of the Beasts has introduced her before the entire court as a Daughter of the Light.'

'Guilty...' Matildet said, raising a hand in the air.

'She saved my life,' Siro said, and told Eliria about the twins and Grinat.

'It must have been very hard... I'm surprised that Grinat wanted to leave. He loved you very much,' the woman said.

'Axelai needs him more,' Siro said, omitting that to Grinat he was just a bitter reminder of how Liduvin had betrayed them on the Night of Fire.

Everything Grinat had explained to him about the Night of Fire, the Beasts, and Infidas was hard to believe. Liduvin would not have abandoned him without good reason, she was not like that. She was good to everyone, and she wanted to take them to Teradam, that had always been her plan to be out of the reach of the Beasts. But the truth was that the woman who had rescued him on the day of the Exile and raised him as her son, had abandoned the two men who loved her. He no longer knew what to believe. Did it make sense to go to Teradam now? Or was it the inertia of a lifetime wanting to see Liduvin again that still pushed him forward?

Siro gazed at the two women talking by candlelight. Eliria had become a beautiful woman. There was nothing left of the girl she had been, except the jungle eyes and the reddish hair. She loved him. He knew it and saw it every time their gazes met. She loved him, perhaps because distance and time had made the memory of that boy she had met in Merco, that boy who had stolen her first kiss, someone important to her. It was like a single memory where all the good things of her childhood lived. He was not part of Undershell —despite his origins, despite the Brand that scarred his face— and perhaps that gave Eliria hope that there might be another life for her and little Ranzeh.

And on the other side sat Matildet. A Daughter of the Light, but also a friend. They had been through the desert, the oasis, the hostile gorges, and the underground galleries that humans had forgotten centuries ago. He had risked his life for her and she for him, without being too conscious or thinking about the consequences of their actions. Hadn't he sneaked into the Lord of the Beasts' palace in the middle of the night, hoping to rescue her?

'Matildet, I would never have imagined that I would share a table with a Daughter of the Light,' Eliria exclaimed. 'Sorry, I feel ridiculous...'

'Come on... Thanks for letting us stay.'

'It's just that… If I had to say a place where I didn't expect to meet a Daughter of the Light, it would be here.'

'I also feel out of place,' Matildet replied, glancing around the humble abode where they stood. Siro was sure it had nothing to do with the luxuries she was used to in Teradam.

'So… can I ask you what you are doing here?' Eliria alternated her gaze between the Daughter of the Light and Siro. She looked afraid that she would take it badly.

'I have come here to offer you a better life.'

Before continuing with the explanation, Matildet wanted to make sure that no one else was at home.

'No… Well, Meres' father sleeps in the next room, but don't worry. The man is very old,' Eliria explained.

'Fine. Do you mind checking the other rooms and the kitchen?' She asked.

Eliria got up from the table, almost looking happy to be of use to a Daughter of the Light. Matildet waited until the woman had disappeared into one of the rooms to open her mouth.

'Can we trust her?' She whispered to Siro.

'Yes,' he responded instinctively. The question had taken him by surprise. Why should he be suspicious of your friend?

'You sure?!'

'Yes!' he repeated with more conviction.

Matildet nodded, when Eliria returned, she received her with a smile from ear to ear.

'Sorry about that, but we have to be cautious,' she apologized. 'What I am going to explain to you has to remain between us.'

Matildet told them what she had been doing in Adon's palace during those four days. After having her usual welcome dinner, which included music, dance, fire-eating shows, monkey fights, and all the food and drink imaginable, the Lord of the Beasts had wanted to negotiate with her guest.

'He is not a Son of the Light,' Matildet clarified. 'He's never set foot in Teradam, trust me. But for some reason, it looks like he has everyone convinced that he is, and I guess that's why people have so much respect for him.'

'It's because of the prophecy. It is said that Adon is the Son of the Light we were waiting for…' Eliria explained. 'But he's also the only son of Dugol, and his father was the one who kicked our families out of Undershell when we were little. This is how we got to the oasis of Merco and we met.'

'The Beasts tried to kill us that day,' Siro reminded her. 'They wanted to close the doors before we left.'

'Well, the son isn't a saint either,' Matildet added. 'Be that as it may, he has managed to dominate this city, despite the guilds, clans and aspiring Beast lords that pop up from time to time. Undershell is a dangerous place, but there is peace. Adon is smart, he knows how to keep his enemies at bay… And although it pains me to admit it, people love him.'

'They love that monster…?'

'I know very well what he is like, but his wizards, his soldiers, everyone around him believes in him. Seriously, they worship him like he's a god… But right now, it serves us well.'

'How?' Eliria said.

'He wants to go to Teradam and so do we. If he says he is going, people will follow. He would like to go alone, I have no doubt, but I have convinced him to bring all the people of Undershell with him… There is only one condition.'

Matildet then explained the problem with the Mother Snake. To gain the trust of the Lord of the Beasts it was necessary for her to prove to him that she was a true Daughter of the Light and what better proof than hunting down another god?

'And is that possible?' Eliria asked.

'We've seen worse, haven't we, Siro?'

Siro didn't reply. He didn't think he'd done anything more difficult in his entire life.

The door of the house opened right at that moment. Reni, Meres and Vela came in chatting with each other, but turned speechless when they saw that there was a Daughter of the Light in their own living room. It wasn't until Matildet greeted them that they exploded into yelling and jumping. They all spoke at the same time, bowed, and when one introduced herself, the other whispered into the third's ear: 'Have you seen her?' 'She is the Daughter of the Light that everyone talks about!'. Matildet gestured for them to sit down. It was obvious that they were dying to talk to her. They didn't even look at Siro, who was sitting directly opposite.

'Your Excellency Daughter of the Light,' Reni said, more daring than anyone else. 'It makes us unbelievably happy to have you in our humble house.'

'I can tell,' Matildet replied. The girls laughed at the same time.

Siro got up to close the door of the house and make sure that no one else in the gallery would know about Matildet. Situation was bad enough without the onlookers.

Undershell shone through the window of Eliria's room. If one didn't think about the atrocities happening in the narrow alleys of the Cross, it had a certain charm. It was the largest city Siro had ever seen, although he didn't know if there would be others. He knew that the Bindagi lived further east, but they were nomads, and that there was a place called the Jade Valley, although he didn't know its exact whereabouts. A gentle breeze stirred the curtains and ruffled his hair. He heard Ranzeh stirring in his bed behind the cloth screen.

'That's all that's left...', he thought looking at the lights of the city, and for a moment he felt small. What if that really was it? Perhaps it was true that there were no other people in that desert. The Beasts hunted and enslaved everyone they encountered when they went on an expedition. Had they managed to leave no other town or city to live in?

If so, what hope could all those people who wandered up and down the dark alleys, always careful so as not to upset their masters, have?

He felt a hand on his shoulder. It was Eliria. The woman looked at him silently. He could see in those green eyes that she had missed him every second since he had left in the middle of the night.

'I'm worried,' she said.

'Matildet has a plan. No need to worry.'

A plan I haven't heard yet..., he thought.

'It's not that, it's Ranzeh.'

'What is it?'

'He's been asking about Segis all day. Rael and his wife have taken him to see the Elector. When they return, the child will have a Brand... and I know that, in ten days, my son will also have one.'

Siro put his arms around Eliria and kissed her hair. It smelled of sweat, the cheap perfumes of the Palace and the cinnamon of their kitchens.

'In ten days, everything may have changed,' Siro said.

'Are you really going to face Mother Snake?'

'I must.'

'Why? Who do you have to do it for?'

'What do you mean?'

'I'd like to think that at least you're doing it for Matildet... And not for Liduvin. I know you wouldn't do it for me.'

'I don't want anything to happen to you and Ranzeh.'

'Why?'

'What do you mean why? It's your son and Nazeh's! I don't want anything bad to happen to you... You will come to Teradam with me and...' he tried to say, but Eliria kissed his lips before he could finish.

'Siro... You left my bed to go and risk your life for her,' Eliria said, although her voice did not sound like a reproach. 'I have taken care of him for six years. I can do it, I don't want us to be a burden.'

'But...'

'You worry me. Have you ever stopped to think what will happen if one day you enter Teradam?'

'Many times.'

'What if she's not there?'

'She is. I know.'

'Okay...'

The girl left his side and headed for the door, but before she got out, Siro made her stop. There was something he had to tell her; he should have done it years ago.

'Eliria, the last night in Merco... Debra, I mean, your mother, she was not well. She... She wanted to hurt me. I'm sorry I left her with those Beasts. I didn't want... I wanted no harm for her, I swear, but if we hadn't left...'

...*She would have broken my arm*, he thought, but couldn't tell her.

Eliria stood in the doorway for a few moments and then closed it with the two still inside. Leaning against the wooden door, she looked up, as if tears were about to rise and she didn't want to allow it.

'She didn't... That night she wasn't her. You know, Siro, I haven't told you before, but when the Beasts captured us, when they took us through the desert here, not knowing if my mother was alive or if I would ever see someone I knew again... I hated you. I wished you had died or something horrible had happened to you and Liduvin... I was angry, I'm sorry, but then I ran into someone who opened my eyes. I never would have thought that we would become friends... but we did.'

'I don't understand...' Siro said.

'My mother was not herself. She had always been cold, but that night something else was going on. He told me; he'd seen *that* before. The wound on her leg, the things she said, the way she grabbed you and how she ignored me and the Beasts. He was the only one who realized that something was wrong... That's why he took us out of there, to protect us.'

'What are you talking about?'

Siro heard something move behind the screen. He thought it was Ranzeh, but the figure who came out from behind looked nothing like a little boy. The hunter jumped when he recognized the Beast that had chased them through Merco during the Night of Fire.

'You've grown up, Siro,' Shahrokh said.

Chapter 38: When I find him

The black hair of the Beast, the teether-shaped earring around his ear, and the bronze shields that covered his legs… Shahrokh looked the same as when he had chased Siro in his nightmares. It was the same Beast that lurked inside the burning Merco of his memories, a dark creature that was after him and Eliria and that, on the worst nights, managed to catch them. He looked older, with sharper traits. Life might had not gone as well as he expected.

'What are you doing here?' Asked the hunter. His hand went to the hilt of his knife instinctively, but then he remembered that he didn't have it. Irad had taken it when they had met at the top of The Mouth.

'There is someone who wants to speak with the Daughter of the Light… and with you,' Shahrokh replied.

'Adon?' Siro became uneasy.

'Adon may be lord of all Undershell, but he is not the only powerful Beast in this city.'

'Siro…' Eliria intervened, still at the door. 'Do as he says.'

The hunter couldn't believe it. What did it all mean? At what moment had Eliria sided with those beings?

'Beasts like him killed Nazeh…' Siro tried to sound as dry as he could. He still remembered how Shahrokh and his band of Beasts had taken out the blacksmith and his family. He didn't intend to obey.

'Shahrokh is different! He has taken care of me since I came to Undershell. If he hadn't bought me, I…'

'What? Is it your master?' Said Siro. 'Do you have their Brand?'

'She doesn't need a Brand,' Shahrokh replied.

'He doesn't want anyone to know that we know each other. He thinks it's safer for me and Ranzeh if we go unnoticed,' Eliria added. 'He is not like the other Beasts.'

Siro had had enough. He headed for the door and told the woman to step away. Eliria saw that the hunter was not kidding.

'I would wait to open this door,' Shahrokh said, his calm tone made the hunter even more nervous than he was. 'Irad and the Hyena are waiting for my sign. They are commanded to enter and do whatever it takes to capture the Daughter of the Light, dead or alive. And the same goes for you. Out of respect for Eliria, I would rather not hurt you. It would be a bit absurd to have saved your life once and then had to kill you, but I have orders. And I always fulfil my orders.'

'I'm not going to follow you.'

'Siro, please listen to him,' Eliria took him by the hand, trying to make him change his mind. 'Shahrokh won't harm neither of you, right, Shahrokh?'

'I will return them safe and sound.'

'You are nothing but a traitorous Beast,' said Siro.

'It must be fate, but until a moment ago you two were talking about the basement where we met. I think you haven't forgotten what happened that night, who saved whom.'

Even if it hurt, the Beast was right. Debra would have broken his arm if it hadn't been for him. If he closed his eyes, he could still hear the brass of its boots echoing on the wooden floor. He saw Debra's icy expression, that rigid stance that hadn't changed even when Shahrokh had stabbed her leg to free him.

'Say it,' Shahrokh demanded.

'You saved us. I don't know why you did it.'

'Being born a Beast does not mean living and dying as a Beast. I keep up appearances, but I never forget that I choose my path. And now it's your turn, Siro. You and your friend will come with me, it's time for you to decide how.'

Siro looked at Eliria's eyes for a few seconds, begging him to pay attention. He opened the door and went out to the dining room, where Meres, Reni and Vela listened to everything the Daughter of the Light told them. Matildet gave Siro a smile when she saw him enter, but when she saw his face, she knew something was wrong. Then Shahrokh came in and there was an awkward silence in the room. The girls at the Palace of Dreams were restless. Having Beasts in the Palace was one thing, having them at home was a very different one. Matildet also saw that something was wrong. She looked at Shahrokh suspiciously.

'We have to go,' said Siro.

'So it seems,' Matildet replied.

Irad and the Hyena were waiting for them outside the house, each to one side of the door. Irad saluted Siro and bowed to the Daughter of the Light.

'What did we tell you? He's grown a lot, hasn't he?' It said cheerfully.

'What have I told you about keeping your mouth shut?' The Hyena elbowed Irad in the stomach, making it cough.

'And these two?' Matildet asked. 'Your pets?'

'We are partners, not pets!' The Hyena protested.

'Watch your mouth, Hyena, you are in front of a Daughter of the Light!' Irad exclaimed, but all he did was get its comrade in arms to land another blow.

Siro had seen them both a few days ago, when he had climbed to the top of The Mouth to find a way to reach Adon's palace. He had narrowly escaped and Irad had kept his knife, which right now hanged from its belt.

'Raduc wants to see them immediately. Let's get on our way before daylight,' Shahrokh ordered.

The group set out through the descending galleries of The Mouth. There were few Beasts in sight, and most turned away when they saw the five of them pass. Matildet had pulled back her grey tunic and pulled her hood up to hide her golden hair.

'Where are you taking us?' Asked the Daughter of the Light.

'Raduc Mastema has wanted to see you for days. He would have liked you to talk to him before Adon, but things don't always go as planned...'

'Is he your master?' Asked Siro, who was following closely behind.

'Shahrokh has no masters, he bought his freedom long ago,' said Irad, who was closing the entourage beside the Hyena.

'We are partners,' the Beast explained. 'We've been for long.'

Siro noticed that Shahrokh was limping quite a bit. It was difficult for him to put the weight on his right leg, and in fact they were slow because of him. He felt the Beast had tricked him. If he hadn't pounced on the Beast inside Eliria's room, was because he remembered how deadly his kicks were. Firla's husband, Taurus, and his soldiers, had been killed by the strength of his blows.

And how does he defend himself now? He wondered. *I guess that's why he still needs these two...*

'For how long?' Siro inquired.

'If you are thinking of the night we met, I have to say yes, we were partners back then,' the Beast replied.

'I thought you worked for Dugol,' Siro said.

'I'm a bit lost here...' Matildet snapped. 'What is this all about?'

'You are wrong again,' Shahrokh said. 'Back then, the Mastemas already had a mission for me.'

'Firla...' Siro remembered Shahrokh having spoken of her during the Night of Fire. Those three Beasts were searching for her on the sidelines of Dugol's attack. 'But why?'

'Raduc had plans for the Bindagi,' the Beast replied. Although it doesn't matter anymore. 'Firla is dead.'

That statement fell on him like a jug of cold water. For years he had assumed that Firla had died during the Night of Fire, either at the hands of the Beasts or by her own Firespreader, but hearing it from Shahrokh made it real.

'How?' Siro asked.

'I ignore it. I found her dead in the middle of the square, surrounded by the wounded. A Rapid was chewing her foot,' Shahrokh explained dryly.

Siro was silent, taking in what he had just said.

'Can someone explain to me what this is all about, please?' Matildet said.

Irad approached her, hunched over. The Beast cleared its throat for the Daughter of the Light to listen and then gestured for her to come closer.

'We've known Siro for years, though it's been a long time since we've seen our little friend. We found him, Eliria and her mother in one of Merco's basements. We used Dugol's attack to sneak into the village without attracting too much attention and ran into each other by chance. How nice is it that we meet again after so many years?'

'I don't know why you're happy,' the Hyena snapped. 'This wildling only gives us headaches.'

The Beasts, Siro and Matildet went into a barrack in one of the wide galleries of The Mouth. A small Beast, with a filthy dog licking its hand, glanced at them. It greeted Shahrokh with a nod.

'Tomorrow you must use the Crab gate. The clans are restless. They're looking for you, Shahrokh, and the two morons who follow you,' he said, pointing to a worn tapestry on the far wall.

'For a change...' Shahrokh replied.

Who are you calling a moron?!' The Hyena raised its fist against the small Beast, but the dog bared its teeth in defence of its master. The Hyena thought it was just some friendly teasing. Irad didn't seem to even notice.

Behind the tapestry was a stone door. Shahrokh reached into one of the holes in the rock and the door swung open. On the other side, spiral staircases led down into the depths of The Mouth.

The place seemed older than the rest of the galleries. The ceilings were higher, and there were colourful lights —fluorescent blue, yellow, and green— shining in the distance. The architecture of the place was familiar to Siro. The black tubes that ran along the walls, the railings that marked the path, the metallic noise of their steps... That place was just like the cave that Siro and Matildet had found under the waters of the lagoon weeks ago. 'The Third,' the Daughter of the Light had called it, although they were too far away for it to be the same extracting plant... or maybe not?

'The floor is treacherous,' Shahrokh warned them.

On both sides of the walkway one could see the abyss. Below, against the rock walls, there were small fires and silhouettes of moving men. The peaks hitting the rock echoed all over.

'Are they slaves?' Matildet asked.

'They are looking for pure glass, metals, and relics,' the Hyena explained from behind her. 'They all are property of the master Mastema.'

'So he does that...' she murmured.

'Master Mastema dedicates himself to everything that is profitable,' said the Hyena.

'He has had more jobs than anyone else,' Irad added.

'Are they children?' Matildet wanted to know. She looked at the distant silhouettes apprehensively.

'Some, although most are adults. Children are too valuable to Master Mastema. He doesn't like to waste them like this,' said the Hyena, and with that, spat into the void.

They came to a two meters high stone gate guarded by six

Beasts. Siro noticed one whose lips were stitched with a black thread and stared back at him with wild eyes.

'We came to see Raduc,' Shahrokh announced.

The Beasts sprang into motion when they recognized it. The ropes were stretched, the wooden pulleys rolled, and the inner gears turned. The gates opened to reveal a bright garden that contrasted with the gloomy mine in which they stood.

'I'll say it once and only once,' The Hyena spoke now at Siro, now at Matildet, to make sure they were listening. 'Master Mastema never receives anyone. The Creator himself could come down from the sky and if he didn't feel like it, he would stay at the gates, okay? He does not like those who are too smart or slaves who are not his... So do yourself a favour and behave.

'Alright, alright... Can we get in already?' Said Matildet.

Behind the gates, four vine-covered columns supported the central section of the garden. The room was full of puddles. The garden seemed built over an underground lake. Dozens of split columns acted as sentinels in that sort of obscure sanctuary. A single beam of natural light came in, from a dizzying height, for what must have been an ancient access to the interior of the mine.

Raduc sat on a throne of black marble trimmed with white veins. A line of human skulls with grim smiles were set at the top. The Beastmaster held its head in a bored gesture as it watched three children fighting in the middle of the garden. It looked up at the sound of the stone gate opening and saw Siro and the Daughter of the Light walk in. It straightened in his seat and clicked his back. The leader of the Mastema clan had a curved scar that ran from the top of his head to below his ear, across the face. It tried to hide it with a white beard and long hair, but it was like hiding blood under ice. Two scars shone just below the eyes, as if someone had tried to remove them years ago. It had a dark Brand running from face to chest: a horned eagle pierced by six spears that sprouted in all directions. It was the same Brand worn by the Hyena, Irad, and Shahrokh, but much larger. Raduc smiled at the newcomers, and Siro sensed that there was something rotten within that being.

'The Daughter of the Light and her paladin...' Raduc greeted them. 'I guess you already know who I am.'

'Not really,' Matildet replied, watching as the three children punched and kicked each other. 'But you must be the master of these lost cubs we have found,' she added, pointing to Shahrokh and the others.

Siro wished the girl would save her insolence for another time. Raduc rose from the throne and hissed like a snake. The children stopped fighting and took their master's place. All three had bruises around their eyes and white powder under their noses and above their lips. One of them had a gash on his head, but didn't seem to mind it.

'They keep it warm,' said Raduc as the children leaped onto the throne.

The patriarch of the Mastema seemed in better shape than Shahrokh, although it was probably more than ten years older. It wore a stained green cape that hid a broad-bladed knife with the silver head of an eagle on top of the hilt. It approached the Daughter of the Light first with a haughty gesture.

'You have already met the Lord of the Beasts,' Raduc said. 'The time has come for you to meet he who makes sure there is only one. Our interests have already crossed path more than once, Daughter of the Light…. And also with you, man of the desert.'

Siro gulped. They were in their den and surrounded by all their henchmen. If Raduc decided they weren't useful, it wasn't hard to imagine who would be the first to fall down the abyss.

'What do you mean?' Asked the Daughter of the Light.

'You may not know the history of Undershell, Daughter of the Light, and the man of the desert has spent too many years away to know the latest developments. Yes, I know you used to live here,' Raduc added, when Siro shot him a questioning look. 'It hasn't been so long ago from the blood wars. Back then, Dugol ruled. It was at that moment when all the clans of the city reached an agreement… those which survived,' of course.

'What are these blood wars?' Matildet said.

'Wars for the control of Undershell… A time that you wouldn't have liked to live through. Dugol spent the last two years of his reign struggling between life and death, like an insect, unaware of the annoyance they represent,' Raduc said, shrugging. 'Undershell needed a Lord of the Beasts, and the son rose to the occasion. The Mastema clan fought to ensure that Adon would be the new Lord of Undershell. Since then there has been peace, and our clan has thrived.

Miseries are long gone, but I still remember the days we used to raid caravans and break into guild workshops to kill and steal... and I miss them sometimes. Now everything is different, more organized, more secure, but our young Lord is becoming too ambitious for his own good. I suppose you will agree on that,' added with the eyes set on Matildet.

'And what do you expect us to do?' she said.

'Don't play fool with me. I know very well that you have spent four days in the palace, and I know that brat well enough to know that he will have done everything to get you on his side, and if he hasn't succeeded yet, he's probably managed to, at least, make you agree to something... Like... hunting the Mother Snake, perhaps?'

The Daughter of the Light looked down at the ground. Siro knew that she too was intimidated by the leader of the Mastema.

'I don't know if you will be able to get rid of that monster, all I can tell you is that whatever you do, you are betting on the wrong horse. Adon is getting lonely on his throne.'

'I'm on no one's side,' Matildet said. 'I have a mission much more important than your pity power struggles.'

'And that's the way it has to be. I hope you remember it, because there will be a moment when you may have the opportunity to decide... to influence the future of Undershell. You would do well to distinguish between what is an issue for the gods and what is an issue of the mortals.'

'Why does everything you say sound like a threat?', said Matildet.

'Sometimes, Daughter of the Light, when I imagine the future, I think that there is only one path, bright and straight, that leads us to live one more day. The other roads, the wrong ones, are like broken bridges that lead to a dark abyss from which one cannot return. I've looked down those bridges so many times that I'm not afraid to take risks, but you are a Daughter of the Light, and of Beasts like me you know nothing.'

Raduc looked at Matildet from above. The girl held its gaze, clenching her fists.

'What does he expect to find inside Teradam?' Asked Raduc.

The girl glanced at Siro, doubting if she had to answer that question.

'Adon wants the power of the Children of the Light. He

hopes to find Keerine's secret within Teradam,' she explained.

'And what is this secret?' Raduc asked. His eyes glittered with greed.

'Keerine's secret is the origin of the power of the Children of the Light, he who knows it dominates reality. The distances, the time, the best kept secrets, the deepest thoughts… everything becomes a single thing, it is the ability to know everything.'

'And you want to give him this power?'

'If he is worthy… He is a Son of the Light.'

Raduc burst out in laughter, echoing through the garden. A flock of bats escaped through the opening at the top of the cave. It seemed to Siro that Irad and the Hyena laughed too.

'I understand that it may be difficult to say no to the Lord of the Beasts, but you would do well to remember my words. Stay out of the Undershell businesses and everything will be better. Shahrokh, walk the Daughter of the Light out, I have yet to speak to the man of the desert,' said Raduc.

Shahrokh took a step forward, but before it took another, Matildet's dress shone with an intense glow. The Beasts recoiled, frightened at the sight, then the glow faded.

'Siro and I leave together,' the girl exclaimed. No Beast dared to contradict her.

'As you wish,' Raduc agreed. Beasts, out of here. You, Shahrokh, stay. I think you will find the story interesting.'

'I think I already know it,' said the Beast, as the rest of its comrades left the place.

'Stay,' Raduc insisted.

The leader of the Mastema looked at the hunter's face and wrinkled its nose when it saw the Brand of Adon.

'Siro, Siro… You don't know how many years I've waited to meet you. It's a pity that you have arrived when it is already too late. You are not even aware of what you've done, are you? I'll tell you something that not many people in Under-Shell know. You've seen the slaves I have working in the mines and all the Beasts I have at my command, but this has not always been the case. When I was young, the Mastema clan were nothing more than a group of unscrupulous looters,' Raduc laughed wistfully, and sat on the throne, surrounded by the children. 'I remember that back, uh, how long has long has it been? Fifteen years, perhaps? Everything was very different,

Undershell was a truly dangerous place, neither the slaves, nor the merchants, not even the Beasts had any shred of hope. People fled, corpses piled up in the alleys every morning and we, well... We were more part of the problem than of the solution... We heard a rumour about a new band growing Dreamstealer plants. Unfortunately for them, that was our business too... and it continues to be,' Raduc ran a finger under the nose of one of the children and wiped a spot of white powder. 'The Dreamstealer is perfect to train the cubs. It hardens them and turns them into real Beasts. None of them will thank me, but I am saving their lives... My Beasts and I decided to pay the band a visit. We found them while they were drying the leaves to prepare the Dreamstealer, they weren't expecting us... The faces they made as we killed them! They always beg, and I hate it, I prefer it when they grow a pair and put up a fight. There were children, but they were broken, they didn't even know where they were. We did what we always do. We chained them to each other and took them to sell, but there was one...'

Matildet kept a tight face. She despised that Beast. Siro knew that if she could choose, they would leave that place immediately, but he wanted to hear what Rad had to say.

'The kid was so thin and so disgusting... No one would buy him as a slave, only the most perverted beings in Undershell would have found a job for him. I had my axe at hand, so I said to myself, do him a favour, but then he said a name: Siro. And who is this Siro? I asked him. He told me it was his brother'.

The hunter was stunned. What was that Beast talking about?

'I decided to play along so I asked him: who is Siro? Is he one of these bastards? The boy said no, that he had abandoned him. A shame,' Raduc had a grin on his lips. 'What would you do to your brother Siro if you saw him again? Or better yet, show me. I gave him this same knife that I have here and I pointed out one of the band members who was still alive. The poor bastard was crawling to escape, but that boy didn't give him a chance... I decided to take him to see a trusted Elector, and what better Elector than my own brother? I explained what that boy had done to Arnufis,' The Beast laughed again and brought the hand to its head, as if it were one of its best memories. 'Too bad my brother never appreciated this kind of thing... He told me what I already knew. They would give us pocket change, so I decided to take him in and raise him with the

White Orphans. The Orphans aren't exactly friendly. I honestly didn't think the boy made it through the week, but he did… and I know they didn't make it easy for him. These little bastards do things I've never seen any grown Beast do. I have seen them torture animals for weeks, push each other off a well and every night I have to send my guards to prevent the older ones from raping the little ones. If you train them well and get them young enough, when they still don't know what is right and what is wrong, you can achieve tremendous results. From what I found out; the boy was not all there, if you know what I mean. It had changed hands about twenty times in the last four years. They used it to clean floors, empty latrines, feed animals, rob the naivest merchants and test substances that even rats don't want to taste.'

'What was his name?' Siro asked. 'What was the boy's name?!'

'You already know the answer,' Raduc replied. 'You've known it since you left Undershell without looking back, you've known it every day you've spent alone in the desert and I think you knew it too when you stabbed him mercilessly in the pond. He just wanted someone to hold his hand, Siro, someone to help him… And he found me.'

'You're just like us,' the metallic voice told him over and over again.

The image came to his mind like a blaze: the sun over the heads of the inhabitants of Undershell, the open wooden palisade through which cars emerged. His father walked to his left, dragging a wooden cart, so small that it seemed ridiculous that they had so few possessions after a lifetime living in Undershell; to the right, his mother, complaining about the the heat and, between them two, a small boy, with short hair, brown eyes disturbed by the crowd, puffy cheeks and a forehead beaded with sweat. He held his hand. He was the boy holding his hand.

'Siro is bad,' the boy was saying. 'He squeezes my hand. Mom, please! Take me, it's hot! Where do we go?'

And when the boy turned to him, a rose-shaped metal mask covered his mouth.

Chapter 39: Straight to the heart

East of the Cross, the sky was clear and blue. The wind kicked up swirls of sand that crashed against the steep walls of the gorge. The whole valley was in shadow. It was a humid place, full of pot-bellied lizards that crawled calmly knowing that no inhabitant of Undershell dared to venture out there.

For those who had been born in the city of the Beasts, there was nothing east of the Great Shell apart from a whitish desert where the nomadic tribes of the Bindagi were said to hunt extraordinary creatures. When the inhabitants of the city looked at the clayey and humid gorge, so different from the rest of the Cross, they dreamed of growing their crops there. How easy it would be compared to the fields they were used to! Half the work would be done once they had sown, not like in the west, where crops would wither if they were not watered every day. All the slaves, all the landlord Beasts had thought so. And all of them had discarded the idea when they remembered that the place was neither the people's, the Beasts', or their lord's. The eastern pass belonged to Mother Snake.

The rock walls were drilled on the gorge side, close to the structure of the Shell. The entire wall was packed with people who had come to see how the Daughter of the Light stood up to the century-old creature. Between the hollow rocks and the inner galleries, the expectant faces of Beasts, slaves, mercenaries and merchants stared. They fought each other for a place among the natural terraces that overlooked the gorge and contemplated —amidst whispers, elbows, incredulous laughter, and furtive bets— at the Daughter of the Light and the wildling who accompanied her.

Siro seemed to look back at them, from the bottom of the gorge, but he was really looking for Eliria and Ranzeh. 'We'll come see you,' his friend had told him that morning. 'Promise me that if things get complicated, you'll run away. She is a Daughter of the Light, but you are not.' He well knew that, but Matildet didn't seem to have them all the aces up her sleeve either. She had been quiet all morning, and her face had paled since they had passed under the arches of the Shell. She peeked at the horizon and waited for a signal to tell her that Mother Snake was coming, but it was still early. According to the forecasts of the court wizards, the creature appeared there twice every lunar cycle, and that day was today.

'I hope Adon's soldiers are watching. If they warn us too late, we will turn to puree. Do you remember the plan?'

Siro was quietly beside her. His cloak moved in the wind; he felt the weight of the knife hanging from his waist. Of course, he had understood the plan, it was very simple, but from understanding to executing there was a stretch. The hunter had his mind elsewhere.

Where are they? He wondered. Eliria and Ranzeh were nowhere to be found. He searched the faces, but how could he expect to see them? There were thousands of people gathered there. All the masters, wizards, and aristocrats of Undershell had come, servants included. Those who weren't there out of curiosity had gone to sell street food or steal from the clueless. In the centre of this picture of men and women emerging from the rocks like mushrooms, there was the Lord of the Beasts and his pompous retinue. It was too far to be sure, but Siro felt that Adon was keeping an eye on them.

'Siro, you hear me?' Matildet repeated. 'I need you to be focused. Do you have the knife?'

'Yes,' he answered and touched the hilt.

He had recovered it when in the Mastema clan's hideout. Irad had it on him and he had taken it back without a second's hesitation. The Beast had moaned at first, but when it had seen the hunter's face, it decided that it was not worth losing its few remaining teeth over a stupid knife.

'Are you okay?' Matildet asked him.

How do you want me to be okay? Siro thought, but instead of saying it, he shook his head up and down.

'What that guy Raduc said… I don't want you to think about it. Ubald … He attacked you and you…'

'I killed him. I stabbed him and let his body sink into the pond,' the hunter drew his knife and stared at the gleaming blade. He had cleaned it that morning for a long time. He wanted to clean the blood no one but him could see.

'Siro…'

'I'm fine,' he said, but it didn't sound like he was. 'It was him or me.'

He stared blankly at the horizon. He didn't care about the wind, the dampness of the gorge, the smoke signals that had long risen on the horizon and that neither of them seemed to have noticed. He was back at the pond, he saw a metal rose chasing him through the vegetation, a large and strong Beast that suddenly became a small and defenceless child, with the same brown eyes as him, the same as his mothers'.

'Liduvin saved me. She didn't see Ubald,' he heard himself say. Everything sounded distant to him, as if he weren't the one speaking aloud. 'She could have taken him... But she took me ...And I've never known why.'

'Siro, what are you talking about? I don't understand you,' Matildet said.

'The day of the Exile. I would have lived his life, they would have taken me to the Elector, I would have entered the Mastema clan, I would have become a Beast...'

'You're not like them.'

I don't know that anymore, he thought. Free Child. Wildling. Slave. Beast. What was he?

'There's one thing I don't understand,' Siro's mind searched through the memories of his childhood.

'What?'

'I did not remember it. Even now I'm not sure I remember it at all,' he said, more to himself than to the Daughter of the Light. 'I wasn't even sure that he existed until Raduc told us about him... I don't understand...'

'Maybe it's a suppressed memory,' Matildet said after a while in silence. 'Do you know what they are? When we experience traumatic situations, especially when we are children, we do this. We suppress memories... Rather than suppress, we hide them well within us. I know because... Well, it doesn't matter. What I mean is that you know it's not your fault. Nothing that happened that day was your fault. You were only a child.'

Siro didn't answer. 'Yes, it is,' the metallic voice inside his head repeated. 'You stabbed me and let me sink into the pond.'

The ground began to shake slightly. Tiny stones bounced off the gorge walls. Matildet pointed to the three smoke columns already rising on the horizon.

'Alright, the time has come,' said the Daughter of the Light, a sudden cough shaking her. It seemed the sand carried by the wind had gotten into her throat. 'Siro, the Snake is coming and it's all up to you. I stop it and you kill it! This is the plan. You know how to do it. Siro... can you hear me?'

But the hunter's mind had fled elsewhere, he was still emerging from Raduc's garden, thinking of the Beast who had tried to poison, rape and murder him, and who in the end had been left a mass of blood in a lost pond.

He looked down. His hand was empty. The knife was stuck in the sand, right next to his foot. He bent down and picked it up right away, before Matildet realised what had just happened. Suddenly he was very aware of his surroundings again. The ground was shaking hard. Undershell folk watched them, among the rocks, with growing unease. A large cloud of sand had made its way through the gorge, covering the smoke trails that the Beasts had used to warn them of what was coming. Rocks fell and bounced against each other.

'Siro, we can do it,' Matildet exclaimed.

'Yes,' he replied. He hid his fear as best he could. Mother Snake would be here shortly.

'Get behind me...' she said. The Daughter of the Light raised her arms in a cross. 'And be ready. We won't have another chance.'

He put a hand on her shoulder.

'Easy, I'm not running away,' the girl told him.

'It's for me. If not, I'll be the one running away.'

'Seriously? You are making a joke, *now*?' She said, with all that noise she had to yell to be heard.

'What if it doesn't stop?' He asked her.

'It will.'

The sand cloud reached the last stretch of the gorge, where Matildet and Siro waited. The hunter looked over the Daughter of the Light's shoulder. He saw something strange moving inside the cloud and his stomach clenched. The silvery body of Mother Snake was barely visible through the sand around it. Siro caught a glimpse of its glowy eyes. He blinked and Mother Snake was already on them.

'Cas... Please don't fail me now,' Matildet murmured and the sand cloud engulfed them.

He heard an exhalation, a sharp noise like two rocks colliding and setting off sparks. He felt himself fall to the ground, beaten by a wave of sand, and for a second he thought he had died, that the monster had run him over them and he was torn in pieces, buried and scattered at the bottom of the gorge. But seeing that for some reason he was still breathing, he got up again. Disoriented, he spun around and saw Mother Snake's head, just two steps from Matildet. The girl was on her knees, her dress shining, her hand raised towards the creature's nose.

She has stopped it, thought Siro, not quite believing it. *Matildet has managed to stop it.*

'Siro, now!' The girl yelled.

The hunter circled the head of the snake, which even at ground level, was as tall as two adults standing one on top of the other. The creature's trunk was just as thick. It was the largest being he had ever seen.

He plunged the knife into the creature's scales and crawled up its side. The Mother Snake didn't move, it trembled weakly, eager to devour the Daughter of the Light, but some force prevented it. He got to the top of the monster and walked over its back. The scales burned under his bare feet.

Rip its heart out and it will be over, Matildet had told him last night, as they prepared the plan… But first he had to find it.

He walked above Mother Snake in the hope of finding what the Daughter of the Light had called the *third vertebral scale*, but the divisions between scales were so fine that it was difficult to distinguish where one began and where another ended. Some scales had sprung up and exposed the black interior of the being. Siro was afraid of what he was about to do. A part of him told him that the Nightborns would appear to exact revenge if he destroyed their creation.

'Siro, hurry up!' shouted Matildet.

The hunter drove the knife into the first slit he saw and, prying, tore off an entire scale. Mother Snake didn't make a sound, it just kept vibrating as if it were about to explode with rage. Beneath the scale, there was a string of black veins. Stiff, shiny veins that twisted around each other.

It doesn't look like any snake I've ever seen, he thought as he looked inside, until he found a dark core, the size of a human head, where the veins met.

This must be it, he told himself, and plunged the knife through the multitude of veins until the dark mass was torn away. Mother

Snake shook and started moving again.

'Siro, what have you done?' Matildet said as she stepped out of the way of the creature.

Mother Snake gained speed little by little. Gripping the scaly skin, Siro watched Matildet grow smaller behind him. A white and a black jet shot out of the cut the hunter had just made. Black fluid fell on the creature's scales. Thousands of dark cubes sprouted from the stain, all at the same time. The wind tore them away and hurled them at Siro, who hid behind his cloak. It was the same substance that he had found in the door of that basement, while fleeing from the Biter. Matildet had warned him not to touch it if he didn't want the cubes to eat him. That thought returned to his head immediately when he saw that the cloak was gradually piercing, as if an army of moths were devouring it. He slumped over the Snake's side and cleaved the knife between two scales. The black cubes flew past the hunter's head and disappeared into the sky. Siro, clutching the knife, passed from one scale to another, careful not to fall.

Mother Snake's body zigzagged through the middle of the gorge, brushing against one of the gorge walls with a hideous noise. Stones were ripped and shot in all directions over the gigantic body. It jerked away from the rock and Siro turned his head in time to watch the other wall of the gorge grow larger and larger.

Shit, shit, shit, was the last thing the hunter thought.

The crash was terrible. An avalanche of sand and rocks spread over the back of Mother Snake. The black and white jet whirled in the air, searching for each other, sparking as they landed on the scales. Siro had dodged getting crushed by a hair. He had climbed on top of the being and moved to the other side just in time to avoid the crash.

Why does it keep moving? He wondered as he fought not to fall. *I've done what she told me! Go up to the back, lift the third vertebral scale and tear out the heart.*

He had followed all Matildet's instructions, of course... Instead of 'heart', she had said another word at the beginning: 'control unit'; and instead of 'scale' she had said 'plate'. Then she had seen that Siro struggled understanding those concepts and had changed the vocabulary for a simpler one. He had been embarrassed to see her speak to him like a child, but why was it his fault? The Children of the Light spoke in a very strange way!

Mother Snake emerged from the gorge. It was moving in a

straight line through the desert, leaving a trail of yellow sand behind it. Siro felt stitches in his arms. The wind blew the holed cape as he crawled toward the head. Half blinded, he felt the shape of the scales and counted them, one by one, to arrive at the correct one. The back of Mother Snake burned. The scales looked like they were made of overheated metal, leaving his fingertips and forearms numb. He traced the scales with the tip of the knife to see where one ended and the other began. He stared at the blade and tried to ignore the fact that it was the same weapon that had taken his brother's life.

Don't think about it, now don't think about it..., he said to himself.

He pushed forward, afraid that the knife would slip from his hands and he would lose the only hope he had left. He heard Ubald's voice, this time speaking to him from under the pond: 'We are made for each other, wildling, why don't you come? Down here I am very alone, we could hold hands...', he would say and accompany each phrase with a metallic laugh. 'He needs someone to take care of him,' Grinat's voice told him as he followed the stepson he had raised and abandoned the boy who had always admired him. 'Forget about Liduvin,' he added. 'You and her...?' Eliria hinted inside his head, and the memory of his friend grabbing him by the wrist when they were alone in the room would assail him. 'It's not just because of Liduvin that you do all this, right?' 'Will we see the Children of the Light?', 'It has to be our secret'.

Move, don't listen to them and move..., he demanded of himself. *You are almost there.*

He felt the snake's head, he could picture it turning around and swallowing him whole, but the creature seemed obsessed with taking him to the other end of the desert. He reached out to drive the knife, but Mother Snake was going so fast that even that gesture could rip him from the back and send him flying. He took it slow. He explored the limits of the scale until he found a slit.

Siro was prying with the knife. He screamed with each attempt, as if each jerk had to rip his arm off. The scale shot out, the edge slitting his back. It felt like a whip. The scale had split his cloak in two, leaving a deep red line on his skin. He narrowed his eyes and gritted his teeth. The knife was gone from his hands. It had flown away.

Not now..., he thought. He looked into the entrails of Mother Snake. A core, large like a watermelon, surrounded by black veins, awaited him. Inside, a red light flickered, mocking the hunter's bad luck.

I will go to Teradam, He said to himself.

He reached into the black veins with both hands and tugged at the core.

Siro opened his eyes when he noticed a scorpion pacing over his bare belly. He slapped it away and got to his feet to fall back quickly. The legs couldn't hold him. He crawled through the desert on all fours. There was something sticky in his hair. He touched it and saw that blood had been drawn on his head, but that was not what frightened him the most. There was a black and white stain on the sand. He looked at his whole body from head to toe. When it had ripped out the core, a white and a black jet had shot out of the surrounding veins. He had turned away and fallen from Mother Snake, but that didn't mean the jets hadn't reached him. He was afraid of being eaten by those strange cubes Matildet had warned him about. He looked at the back and the palm of his hand, felt behind his ears, looked under the armpits, arms, belly, legs, under the feet and even inside his pants.

No stains.

How could I have been so lucky? He thought, relieved.

Mother Snake had stopped some dunes ahead. Its dead body was covered in sand and pierced by the same liquid that had failed to kill the hunter.

What a strange animal, Siro told himself, examining it from all sides. Mother Snake's eyes were two holes covered by a glass casing, and now that he looked at it, the scales were too straight to be natural.

They are bolted, he observed. *What is this supposed to be?*

The liquids that had come out of the veins had opened a hole in the belly of Mother Snake. It was big enough to fit a man. Out of curiosity, Siro stepped inside. What he saw inside he would never have expected.

It was supposed to be Ignea's mother, the woman who the Nightborns had turned into that monster, doomed to traverse the desert for all eternity searching for her daughter. That was what Liduvin had told him, but inside Mother Snake there no blood, bones or entrails but piles of white boxes, perfectly fitted lockers, panels with symbols, green, red, and blue lights.

This is not an animal, not a god... What is it? He wondered.

Someone had built that, and perhaps the answer to his questions had vanished with the two human skeletons that lied inside, in the part corresponding to the head of the Mother Snake. The skeletons had traces of clothing on them. One of them had a broken skull and the other had a hole in his forehead, as if a third eye had come out. The two had died chained to one of the bars inside. The floor was littered with junk Siro had never seen before, containers that had once held food and now only held dust.

He went outside. This was not right. It was too strange. Why had Liduvin told him a story about Mother Snake if it was very clear that...?

'It was a lie', Siro said. 'It was only a story... Liduvin only told stories... Then Teradam...?'

A cloud of dust had appeared in the distance. Someone was approaching from far away.

If the Beasts see this... they will think we have deceived them, he realised.

The riders arrived almost an hour later when the sun was already setting. The horses stopped abruptly and fanned out in a semicircle. Junal and Guido led the group. They both scowled as they saw Mother Snake's corpse being consumed by flames.

'What happened?' Junal asked as it dismounted.

'Fire burst when I cut out the heart. I barely escaped,' Siro lied.

He had used two of the flamestones he always carried with him. He had rubbed them, causing sparks to fall on the black liquid. The charred holes in the cloak had made him think that perhaps the black liquid in which those cubes grew would be flammable. After trying and seeing no effect, he had tried it with the white one, almost out of spite, and it had caught fire so quickly that he had had to run away. Now Mother Snake was a carcass that continued to burn and click from time to time.

'And you haven't done anything, huh?' Junal insisted, staring at him with suspicious eyes.

'Why are you asking obvious questions?' Guido intervened. 'He has a cut on his head...'

'Will you shut up?!' Junal wrinkled his face like a dog about to bite.

Siro let the Beasts examine the remnants until to their heart's content, but the truth was that there wasn't much to see. Junal looked at Mother Snake pretending to be unimpressed, but the way it walked, with trembling legs, gave it away. No one had seen anything like it.

Siro waited patiently for all the Beasts to finish turning to satisfy his curiosity. He was exhausted, and for the first time in his life, he missed Undershell. He wanted to go back and hoped they would do before dark. Junal approached him to give his own verdict:

'Not bad, for a wildling... I see that bearing the Brand of our beloved Adon has given you strength. The Lord of the Beasts told us to congratulate you if you managed to catch Mother Snake...'

'...And cut off your heads if you failed,' Guido added.

'Guido, why...?' Junal raised his hands strangling an imaginary neck. 'For all the Nightborns, forget about this idiot. Congratulations, wildling, you did well. Come on, let's go back.'

Siro followed them. He mounted one of the horses, behind one of the Beasts. He had never ridden and, despite his feelings for the Beasts, he was grateful that it was one of them that held the reins. Just then he realized that Matildet was not among them.

'Where is Matildet?' Siro asked.

There was a moment of silence. The two Beasts looked at each other and hopped on their horses. Siro repeated the question.

'When will you tell him?' Guido asked.

'Will you shut up, you piece of worm?' Junal scolded him.

'When will you tell me what?' Siro looked from one Beast to the other.

'Nothing!' Junal exclaimed. 'Come on!'

'The wildling is not stupid,' Guido replied. 'It's the Daughter of the Light. She's not okay.'

'What?' said Siro. 'What happened?'

'We don't know,' Junal explained in the end. 'But it doesn't seem right.'

Chapter 40: Teradam

It was about time. Siro clenched his teeth, preparing for what was to come. The grains of sand began to jump. The moon and stars shook, they knew they were about to be eclipsed. He heard the characteristic noise of the tower. A reddish spark ran through it from bottom to top and then the Great Light appeared riding the dunes. The sky turned white and Siro covered his eyes with his hand. He could see his own fingers bathed in a glow that caressed him, like the waves of a lake explore the land that surrounds them.

He had gone up to see the Great Light so many nights of his life that it was strange to see it again after so long. For years, the City-Tear and the surrounding dunes had been the backdrop to his frustrations and dreams, and now, after so many difficulties, after shedding his blood, being bitten by the creatures of the desert, stalked by the Beasts and branded for life by their Lord, the fact of being so close to the gates of Teradam aroused not excitement but a deep anguish.

We called it Teradam, the city of miracles... Matildet had told him one night like that. But that night was already very far away.

'My eyes hurt...' Ranzeh said childishly.

The boy sat next to him, he had insisted on seeing the Great Light when it appeared, and Siro had told him that he could join him.

'Come on,' said the hunter. He grabbed his hand and the two of them went down the outer slope.

Hundreds of lights crowded the foot of the mountains, between the shops, the carriages, the stalls, and everything the people of Undershell had been able to bring. They had spent two weeks traveling through the desert and it had not been easy. Sandstorms had followed them. There had been fights and killings between rival clans during the night, and the Beasts, as always, had abused their power. The caravan had left a trail of dead buried in the desert, but now that they had arrived, no one seemed to think of that. Teradam, the house of the Children of the Light, was the only thing that mattered.

Siro watched the twinkling lights. This used to be his little secret world, and now the Sacred Valley belonged to everyone. A group of onlookers glimpsed at the adult and the child going down the mountain. Siro paid them no attention. They spent the whole day doing the same, there was always some small group of idle slaves following him around since he had killed Mother Snake.

Ranzeh's mother was waiting for them, her arms folded.

'Mom, I've seen it!' Ranzeh said.

'Very good,' Eliria relaxed and kissed him on the forehead. 'But remember that you cannot go up alone. I don't care what the other kids do, okay?'

'But… What if Segis wants to go up?'

'Only if you go with me or with Siro. Not alone,' the mother insisted.

The boy didn't protest much more. Eliria told him to go to the tent, the adults had to talk. As soon as they were alone, Eliria approached him and put her hands on his chest. Eliria looked at him in a way that was already more than familiar to Siro. Their lips met in a passionate kiss.

'Did he behave?' Her friend asked.

'Yes,' said Siro. The truth was that for being so restless, Ranzeh was a good kid. He had so many things that reminded him of Nazeh, that he didn't mind spending time with him. It was like meeting an old friend, although the age difference made him see everything with different eyes. He knew it was a parody of a friendship that time would no longer return.

'You have to talk to her, Siro. She's getting worse.'

'I know.'

'What did Adon tell you?'

'He wants me to do something for him.'

'What?'

'You can imagine…'

Eliria's eyes saddened. The woman hugged him. A spark of desire ran through Siro. During the two weeks that they had spent travelling the desert towards the Sacred Valley, the two had not been able to suppress their attraction. They met at the backs of cars, kissed and touched, undressed each time the caravan stopped at an oasis, and they had slept together almost every night since the journey began. Siro felt bad every time he gave in to his instincts, but it was impossible for him to see Eliria and not imagine her naked, lying on the wooden floor of a car or arching against the palm tree of some lost oasis. All this time, Matildet had been ill. She had fallen into a kind of flu that had her coughing up all day. She could hardly move, the fever didn't go down and she looked thinner every day. After killing Mother Snake, Guido and Junal had taken him to see her. She already seemed feverish back then, her eyes opening and closing against her will. The Daughter of the Light's health deteriorated day after day… and he couldn't help but seek out his childhood friend every time anguish suffocated him.

She's dying, and I'm with Eliria.

'Talk to Matildet,' she repeated. 'She needs you by her side. We all need you.'

Siro nodded. He held Eliria in his arms and then said goodbye. He would have slept with her, closed his eyes and forgotten all about his troubles, but they would still be there the next morning, and he had a decision to make. Adon had left him no alternative.

The Lord of the Beasts had requested his presence, so had their soldiers told him when they had come to find him that same afternoon. Adon's tent was planted on top of one of the seven hill and it wasn't exactly small. The interior was of an elegance that Siro found of poor taste: wooden columns with inlaid fragments of marble, figures of goldsmiths, gleaming china, weapons stands, cushions and luxurious furs showing that when the Lord of the Beasts travelled, he couldn't do without his toys, just as he couldn't do without his entourage of wizards, bodyguards, and half-naked courtesans.

Sitting on his throne, Adon let one of the girls put grapes in his mouth. The so proclaimed Son of the Light caught them between his teeth, not caring whether the courtesan's fingers were caught in between or not. On one side of the tent, Junal watched him with its small eyes; Guido, on the other hand, was barely paying attention to him, distracted by a tray of roast chicken and a bowl of candied pears. Siro saw Infidas half hidden among the wizards. The man who had been Merco's most famous merchant stood out among the court for his shimmering dress and jade-adorned dreadlocks. Siro still didn't understand what he was doing there. How could he have gone from being an exile to being part of the court of the Lord of the Beasts? If Grinat had told him the truth, Infidas was one of the last people to see Liduvin alive during the Night of Fire. Siro wished he could exchange a few words with him, but the merchant was always by the Lord of the Beasts' side.

'Thanks for coming so quickly,' Adon said sarcastically. He knew perfectly well that his Beasts had given him no choice. 'Do you know why you are here?'

Siro didn't reply. He wanted to punch that arrogant grin out of him, but he would be dead before he laid a finger on him. Ten bodyguards Beasts stood in front of him, each with a sword, long as a man.

'Answer when our beloved master speaks to you!' Junal yelled.

'It won't be necessary, Junal,' Adon waved him off the impertinence, and addressed the hunter. 'Four days ago I sent a dozen of my best warriors into Teradam. None of them have returned. Either the Children of Light treat intruders so well that neither of them wants to return... which I doubt, because everyone knows how I detest traitors... or I can start looking for another dozen Beasts.'

Siro did not know the answer, but he sensed that they would never see those warriors again.

'My sister is getting worse every day,' Adon added, referring to Matildet. 'She can't move, and none of my shamans or wizards can do anything. Teradam's gates are open in front of our camp and it seems that I am left without many alternatives... What should I do?'

You could go in, thought Siro. *Aren't you a Son of the Light?*

'What do you want?' Said the hunter, although he already knew the answer.

'I have thought that my brand-new subject could enter Teradam in my behalf and bring me the secret of the Children of the Light'

Just what I was afraid of.

'What secret?' Siro asked.

'The secret of their powers, of course,' Adon sprang to his feet and descended the stairs until he stood in front of Siro. He clapped his hands twice and all the Beasts, courtesans, and wizards rose and left the room. Only Junal and Guido stayed. 'Don't you know the story?'

'I don't.'

Siro knew many stories of the Children of the Light, all those that Liduvin had taught him, but none about the secret of their powers.

'Have you heard of the Advectum?' Said the Lord of the Beasts. 'They say it's because of it that they are so powerful. The Advectum gives them this glow, links them to the most remote stars, and brings Keerine's grace and power. I want you to find it and bring it to me.'

A spark of greed appeared in Adon's azure eyes. If the Lord of the Beasts got Matildet's powers: the control he had over the structures of the Children of Light, the ability to dominate terrible beings like the Mother Snake and the rest of his secrets, people would follow him like a flock of sheep. Siro pouted. It was what that psychopath lacked, access to Teradam and the powers of the Children of Light.

'You don't seem to like the idea,' said Adon. 'I sincerely believe that if anyone can trick the Children of the Light into letting them get close to the Advectum, it is you. After all, you've been dealing with Matildet for quite some time. I'd even say she appreciates you, if it weren't because you're just a pet to her...'

Siro clenched his fists. Adon was crying out for a few teeth to snap out of him, but Guido had one hand ready on the axe in case the wildling didn't know how to behave in society.

'I guess I don't need to tell you that pretty Eliria and little Ranzeh will be very disappointed if you fail too,' Adon added. 'Don't pull that surprised face. I know everything that happens in Undershell... I am the Lord for a reason.'

That put Siro on alert. The fact he knew about the existence of Eliria and Ranzeh was bad in itself, but if it had also reached his ears that him and Matildet had met with Raduc Mastema and its clan, the trust Adon had in him, already fragile, could end up breaking.

'Leave them alone,' Siro told him.

'That's up to you,' the Beastmaster replied curtly. 'Bring me the Advectum and nothing will happen to them.'

'And then? What will happen if I bring it to you?'

'I promise to be magnanimous. I know how to reward those who serve me faithfully,' he added with a hypocritical smile. 'You will depart at dawn. You have three days.'

'What if I don't make it back?'

'In that case, we'll have to change our action plan. If the Children of the Light do not understand what diplomacy is, my

Beasts will do what they do best.'

Blood and fire, Siro thought.

'And how will I know what is the Advectum?' Asked Siro.

'I'll leave it to your judgment. Undershell trusts you.'

'Fuck off,' the hunter snapped. 'You are not a Son of the Light and you never will be, even if you get their powers.'

This was not amusing to the Lord of the Beasts. A shadow of rage crossed his face.

'I have a very special place for a promising kid like Ranzeh. He could be part of my personal guard one day… For his mother I have more immediate plans. You would do well to remember it.'

Siro had come out of the tent with more problems than he had when he entered.

I can't go to Teradam, he told himself. Adon would not be magnanimous and he knew it. Once he had the Advectum, whatever it was, he would be of no use to the Lord of the Beasts. He could run away, but what would happen to Eliria and Ranzeh then? And Matildet?

Distracted by his thoughts, his steps led him towards the cave where he had lived for years. The sun was setting, and the dunes shone varnished orange. Among the hills he saw the silhouettes of slaves moving and casting long shadows on the sand. It was strange to meet people in that corner of the world, but the truth was that the inhabitants of Undershell had not wasted their time. They continued their frenetic activity despite the distance from their homes. The slaves set up stalls and tents for the newcomers, unloaded the cars that arrived every day from the city, made sure that the animals didn't escape and generally survived as best they could in an inclement area such as the Sacred Valley. Siro grinned. It was like the early days of Merco. Everything was rushed to start over. Some ten thousand people had camped around the hills, all convinced by Adon's message that it was time to return to the City-Tear. 'Keerine has called us!' He had told them in his speech after the news of the death of the Mother Snake had spread throughout Undershell, from the Cross to the hideouts of The Mouth. 'The Daughter of the Light and his champion have been sent to tell us that the time has come for us to return. The days of the Split are over. The Children of the Light have heard our voice, Teradam's gates will open for us.' And thus families, slave guilds, merchants, peddlers, mercenary beasts, nomads, false prophets, and adventurers of all kinds had packed and set out on their way. They had arrived four days ago and the Sacred Valley was already a chaos.

People turned their heads and pointed at Siro when they saw him go by. It was a strange sensation for a man who had spent more than half of his life alone and in silence. They all murmured. The most daring came to speak to him, others gave him gifts: delicacies and amulets that would protect him or give him luck. A woman had tailored clothing for him, and now he was dressing in the Undershell style. He wore baggy pants and an open beige tunic. That made the feeling of the Free Child that he had had all his life vanish. He felt like a slave, but at least he didn't feel alone. All Undershell knew that it was he who had killed Mother Snake.

They had seen him descend into the Sacred Valley, accompanied by the Daughter of the Light, when she had opened the gates of Téradam. It had been an overwhelming moment. They all watched in silence from the top of the hills. Matildet spoke in his ear:

'Don't go in, Siro, even if the gate opens, don't go in,' the girl's voice sounded weak, like a branch about to break. 'Promise me.'

Siro had given her his word. Teradam was imposing, the tower was gigantic, it was the largest structure he had ever seen, twice the height of the Great Shell, at least. The circular base of the tower implied that an entire city was hidden within. 'See you soon,' he had heard Liduvin's voice say to him, but now he doubted... Had he really heard or had he imagined it?

'Cas, open the door, for heaven's sake...' Matildet had said. She had raised her hand to the sky and within a minute the massive gates of Teradam had risen with a deafening screech.

A chilly wind had come out of the dark interior. Nothing could be seen beyond the threshold.

'Don't go, Siro, stay,' Matildet had told him. 'If you go in alone...'

But she hadn't been able to finish the sentence. A coughing fit had seized her. The Beasts of Adon had been quick to arrive and stand guard in front of the entrance to Tear-City. Since then no one entered without authorization from the Lord of the Beasts himself. The people had camped on top of the hills and seen Adon's twelve warriors cross the threshold. None had returned yet, and people talked. 'Do the Children of the Light really want us here?' he heard the slaves say as he walked by, 'Maybe it would be better if we went back now', 'What if they don't let us all in?'

'What will Adon do if he doesn't get what he wants?' was the question for Siro. The Lord of the Beasts had also risked a great deal, leaving Undershell half abandoned. He didn't believe that the Children of the Light would cede their powers to the first stranger to walk through the gates. He wasn't fooling himself, there was something wrong with all that. The disappearance of the warriors, the words of Matildet… He had wanted to enter Teradam for so long that he had never considered the possibility that it could be *dangerous*.

'Hey, Siro! Look, it's Siro!' Said a familiar voice.

A group of children ran up to him. In the front were two girls who carried an ostrich tied with a rope. They were Maia and Cas, the girls he had met when he arrived in Undershell. The girls must have gotten into a car when they saw that everyone was leaving and they'd taken Queenie everywhere. Siro had never liked the animal. He still remembered the pecks on the head. The girls used the bird to carry packages and run errands, thus making a living. Somehow, that animal had tamed itself, perhaps it had gotten used to humans. The girls, however, didn't come alone, around them was a group of dirty children, with fewer teeth than they ought, that chased Siro around all day.

'Siro, the Orphan Sisters want you to lit these candles around the Daughter of the Light, they say they drive away evil spirits,' said the girl that Matildet had renamed Cas.

'They're old ladies who don't know anything… I'd throw them out,' Maia said. 'Do you want to come with us? We are going to explore the mountains to see if we can find lizards.'

'Another day,' Siro lied. The days of exploring and making mothers suffer were long over for him. 'But I know two boys who will want to play with you.' And that was how he had introduced Ranzeh and Segis, Rael's son, at the time. Ranzeh had been very happy to make new friends; Segis not so much, he was not seen in a good mood since he had returned from his visit to the Elector.

'Tonight I want to see the Great Light, but my mother says that I can't go alone because I am small and when you are small you can't go alone to places. Can you come with me so I'm not alone?'

Ranzeh had asked before rushing off with his new friends.

Siro had said yes, and he had waited, lost in thought on the top of the hills. He had watched the opening of the City-Tear until dusk and had remembered the days when he racked his brains on how to enter. He knew he would never have done it without Matildet. The Children of the Light only opened the door to other Children of the Light.

'You have to talk to her, Siro,' Eliria had told him. He already knew. He knew it all too well.

The interior of the cave looked the same as when he left, a couple of months ago. Perhaps there were more piles of sand, and a couple of clay bowls had fallen to the ground, as if some clumsy lizard had wandered the shelves. The water tank was leaky and useless at the bottom of the cave, but they didn't need it, the people from Undershell had brought enough water supplies, and if all went well, they would keep coming. The cherry tree trunk where the cloak hung looked withered now that nothing was hanging. The glass jars and cages had a layer of dust on top, and the scarce food left had already rotted. The cave had a musty smell, but it was a safe place for Matildet. The Daughter of the Light rested on the skins of hyenas and mongooses. She breathed weakly, as if getting the air to reach the lungs was already painful enough. Her face was pale, her cheeks sunken, and her golden hair was plastered to her forehead.

'This afternoon they brought me three sticks tied with the tendons of a new-born lamb,' Matildet said. 'They say it is an amulet and that it will heal me.'

'It is true?' Siro asked.

'If I could trade it for my meds, maybe…' Matildet replied.

The girl reached out hand for the white backpack with a shaking hand and took out the flask. It was empty. 'This is keeping me alive, Siro!' She had told him long ago. The hunter felt guilty. He had found one of the coloured nuts inside the bag that the Beasts had left in the pond. He had kept it the entire trip, only to end up giving it to a girl in the Palace of Dreams when he was fleeing from the Beasts. He had told her that if he took it, she would be as beautiful as the Daughter of the Light and she had let him in. 'Idiot', he told himself. 'I'm an idiot'.

'What is it? Perhaps the wizards can help you…' said Siro.

He hated to think that someone from Adon's court might have the solution, but couldn't see Matildet suffering like that.

'No, Siro. No one can help me. It's the air out here. It's not made for us... It kills us if we don't take medication. It's been days since I ran out of pills. When I left Teradam I knew that I couldn't be away for too long. It seems like forever, doesn't it?'

'Then you have to go back to Teradam! There will be medicines.'

'I wish it were that easy,' she replied, coughing. 'Teradam is not as you imagine. There are very few of us left and we live on the upper floors of the tower... or we did. The lower part is abandoned. It's a ghost town.'

'Are there medicines or not?'

The Daughter of the Light didn't answer. She was looking up at the ceiling of the cave. Her eyes were red. The tears were pooling and the girl made an effort to hold them back.

'Siro, listen to me well. I don't want you to enter Teradam... You must understand what is happening. You killed Mother Snake, didn't you?'

'Yes,' the hunter replied, although he didn't know what it had to do with it.

'And did you think... It really was a snake?'

'No,' he replied after a short silence.

'I see you're getting savvy,' Matildet smiled. 'Things are not as you think. Mother Snake was used to transport raw materials and people between stations. Do you remember the underground base, do you remember the Third, with those drilling machines? Everything is connected and controlled from the tower. Mother Snake too. They know that something has happened to it and that is why they have opened the gates. Someone has opened them for us, the problem is that I don't know who it was...'

'Do the Nightborns know?'

'Forget about the Nightborns and the Children of the Light!' Matildet exclaimed. 'That doesn't matter anymore. What matters is that *they* have opened the gate, not me. If it was Cas, there's still hope, but if it was Mark... I shouldn't have taken so long to come back.'

Matildet was sobbing. Tears trickled down her cheeks and splashed onto the blankets. Siro was sitting next to her, not knowing what to do.

'Adon wants me to go to Teradam. Tomorrow at dawn. I have three days to bring the Advectum back,' he said.

'What? How can he know about the Advectum? And how does he expect you to bring it to him? The Advectum is… You can't take it away!' Matildet stammered. 'Siro, listen to me, forget about Teradam. You can't go in alone, they will kill you. Mark is crazy and dangerous.'

'I'm going in.'

'You can't take the Advectum…'

'…And I won't.'

'Then why are you doing it? Is it to protect Eliria and Ranzeh? Run away with them. The time is now. You could convince other people to follow you too. I've seen how they look at you. They respect you, Siro. You could do it. You would be a better leader than that psychopath Adon. You could give them a different life. A better life…'

'Merco also had to be a better life for everyone and it ended up in flames,' he replied. 'The Beasts don't renounce to anything and this is their world. Wherever I go I'll find them… Always. I will enter Teradam.'

'Siro, no,' she said, her cough growing more violent, the words breaking up. 'Is it because of Liduvin? Is that it? She's not in Teradam! I swear! I know you think you heard her, but I swear she isn't… I don't know what happened to her, but you have to forget…'

'It's not about Liduvin!' Siro snapped. 'It's not for Eliria or Ranzeh! It's not because of any of the slaves or any of the Beasts you want to save! And it's not for me!' He grabbed the medicines flask and held it to her face.

His hand was shaking. Matildet exchanged her gaze between the object and the hunter's scars.

'It's not for any of them,' Siro insisted.

Matildet stretched out her arms and he hugged her. They were silent for a long time. The tears of the Daughter of the Light fell on him.

'Stay with me tonight,' she told him.

They laid down next to each other. They stared at the ceiling of the cave. It was a black, starless sky. They held hands without saying a word.

'How can I retrieve a repressed memory?' He asked her. The

Daughter of the Light had mentioned that concept, *repressed*, the day they had confronted Mother Snake, and Siro kept thinking about it.

The girl laughed and coughed.

'You're crazy, Siro... I don't know, it's very difficult,' Matildet replied. 'Are you saying it because of Ubald?'

'I need to get over it.'

'I needed time and help.'

'What had you forgotten?'

Matildet remained thoughtful for a long time.

'My mother,' she said at last. 'It's strange. I lived as if none of that had happened. I played with my dolls and looked for my mother around the house. When my father came in the evening, I asked him where she was. Where is mom? I said... I think at first, he told me, but one day he got tired. She didn't want to, but it hurt her. Every time I asked him... He sure wanted to slap me. He'd think I was teasing him, but I wasn't. I needed help to remember and now when I think about it I... I had forgotten that my own mother had died... One day a glass fell from the kitchen table. It broke into pieces and everything came to me suddenly. The windows shattering, the furniture, the explosion... I had seen it all and I had hidden it inside me because I didn't want to remember what had happened to my mother. I hid in the closet. I didn't want to go out. I didn't understand what I had seen and it scared me... I needed someone to explain it to me and a lot of time. That's what you need, time.'

But we don't have it, thought the hunter.

They kept talking and remembered the nights they had spent together in the desert by the bonfire. Matildet remembered the moment when he had offered her a snake to eat.

'I'd never done something like that...' she said. 'But I have done so many things since I left Teradam... things I never thought I could do. No matter how it ends, I don't regret anything...'

'You broke my water tank,' Siro reminded her.

'And you killed that poor little bird.'

'It was yummy.'

The girl shook her head and kissed him on the cheek. With her eyes already closed, added:

'I'm glad I met you.'

For the first time in days, Matildet's face was calm.

The next morning, the gates of Teradam awaited him. The black opening expelled and sucked air, as if the Tear-City needed to breathe after so many years of seclusion. Siro had prepared himself thoroughly before leaving the cave. He carried the double-spear dangling from his back, a satchel with provisions, and a pair of waterskins tied together. The people of Undershell had been waiting outside the cave from dawn. Secrets didn't last long in that place, and now everyone knew that the man who had hunted Mother Snake was the one chosen to meet the Children of the Light. Rael and his family were there, also Maia, little Cas, and the whole group of kids. They all looked at him with a mixture of respect and admiration. The girls from the Palace of Dreams had come too, wishing him luck, and attracting the glances of the male attendants. Ranzeh grabbed his leg and Eliria hugged him.

'You must come back,' she told him. 'Promise me.'

'I will,' Siro replied, trying to look confident.

'We will take care of Matildet. Don't worry about her… Just be careful.'

People watched him from the hills, both Beasts and slaves. Adon and his court had taken the best place in the crowd. Three days the Lord of the Beasts had given him… Siro knew that entering Teradam was no guarantee of anything, not even if he brought the accursed Advectum, but that was not what he was looking for. He felt the weight of Matildet's flask in his pocket. He didn't know what awaited him, or if he'd find this Mark or Cas. Nor could he trust Liduvin's stories, because now he knew that they were only tales for children.

She's not in there, he told himself. *You know she is not in there...*

'Do you think she will one day notice you, wildling?' Ubald's metallic voice spoke in his ear just when he was a few meters from the gigantic gates of Teradam.

'I don't care anymore,' he answered into the air.

He had stood up to a Biter, survived desert storms, hunger and thirst. His hands were stained with the blood of his forgotten brother and Bartus. He had lost friends like Nazeh along the way and had to say goodbye to Grinat, the only man he could have considered a father. He had seen his village burn as the Beasts slaughtered Tersian, Taurus, and so many others. He had felt the pain of fire and steel and loneliness, and for more nights that he could count, he had waited for this moment to come.

'To you who were born of...' He tried to recite the words Liduvin had taught him but left them mid-sentence.

And with a determined step, he crossed Teradam's threshold.

Printed in Great Britain
by Amazon